# SMOKING CIGARETTES

REGINALD L. HALL

WRITERSANDPOETS.COM, LLC
MOUNTAINSIDE, NEW JERSEY

Copyright © 2005 by Reginald L. Hall
Published by Writers and Poets.com, LLC
Cover Design by Marion Designs
Consulting provided by Earl Cox & Associates Worldwide
Edited by Audra Shivers

Printed in the United States of America

Publisher's Note:

Library of Congress Catalog Card No. 2005924213

ISBN Number 0-9762710-2-8

Writers and Poets.com
P.O. Box 1307
Mountainside, New Jersey 07092
http://www.writersandpoets.com
sales@writersandpoets.com

First Printing

Quantity discounts are available. Contact the publisher for
more information.

*In Loving Memory of*

*Henry Ford Christmas*
*&*
*Luke Blackwell Sr.*
*&*
*Willie Rutledge*

*You will never be forgotten because the love and the memories will always stay in our hearts.*

# Acknowledgments

First of all I need to thank my heavenly Father up above for allowing me to pursue my dreams and for helping me to reach my goals. I am so grateful to serve Him all day, every day.

My mother and best friend, thanks for the undying support and love you give me every day. I know that I am a piece of work, but through all these years you have steered me in the right direction and I thank you for that. I love you, Mom. A special thanks to my grandmom (Chicken) for her gracious wisdom. It's because of you that I am who I am today. I'm gonna give you some money, okay? Don't spend it all in Atlantic City because if you do there's no coming back for more.

To Grandma and Grandpa Hall, thanks for putting up with a grandson like me. To both of my brothers, Ricky and Ralpheal, I bet you never thought it would be this big, huh? Now since we all are grown, we'll have to take care of Mom together.

Sweet kisses to the one and only girl in my life, Kaniyah Macmillan. You are my heart and my soul—I could not imagine a day without you.

I gotz 2 give a shout out to my crazy azz familee. God has sent you all in my life for a reason, I clearly don't know what it is though, but I have to say, I wouldn't change you all for the world. My aunts Diane, Gloria, Connie, and Adrian; my uncle Junie is upstate, but he's still holding it down; bring ya ass home and stay home. My uncle Pop, I got you on your next bottle. So just keep tossing 'em back.

My super cousins Richard, Anthony, Mark, Nicole, Stanley, Camisha, Mona, Susan, Andre, baby Eric, Robbie, Shaneera, Jabriea, and Andrea here we gooooo.

To my uncle Frank and my aunt Diane, the most powerful two, there is no one that can understand me like y'all do and I'm here 2 tell you how I appreciate y'all every day.

You haven't had a cheese steak until it is made from Andre Macmillan at Jim's Steaks on South Street. Keep 'em comin'.

To my best friend in the entire world, Dele. The Africans haven't seen beauty until they have seen you. I cannot live this life by myself and neither can you so let's do this together. Hold on cuz it's gonna be a bumpy ride.

Miesha, a sophisticated lady! I can't even tell you how you got a spot on this page because you are never there when I need you. But one thing I can say is that you're always on time. And a ride or die BITCH at that and that's what a young man like me needs in his life.

To my gay mother and father; every gay man should have a pair of these—Daniel and John. Thanks for the love and support that you both show me every day. I can't stop loving y'all if I tried. And on that note, I can't 4get my gay brothers—Rantonio, Hueshaun, Sam and Stephan.

Yo, I gotta get these damn haters off my back, damn!
Anyway, sorry for the interruption, now where was I?

I see y'all peekin', thinking I forgot y'all, but I didn't. My extended family; my baby boy Rondell, damn. I can't even call you that no more cuz you a grown man dawg!

Ms. Debbie, Kaira (mother of the cutest set of twins on earth), Maishanna, Fatima, and Tyree.

A special shout out to Robin and Jeff. When I find my special someone, I want our relationship to be just like y'all. To all my nephews; stay in school. I can't name 'em all cuz it could be more than I know of.

R.I.P. to the man that inspired me to write and stay focused, Malcolm Starks. You will always be remembered.

To the Best Publicist that money <u>can't</u> buy,

Monique Ford. After I finish digging your foot from out my ass I would like to thank you for all your support and keeping me focused during the dark times of my life. God has sent you from heaven and we have grown to work together and I know that you will always be there even when everything else fails. Love you, girl!

A glorious thanks to my fairy godmother Carla for all the encouragement and willpower. You are truly someone that appears in a flash, thanks.

Roll out the red carpet for Mr. Earl Cox and his lovely associates. I thank God for the day when you walked through that lonely forest and tripped over that rock and found me. No one could have done it better. Thanks for believing in me and seeing my worth. Thanks to my famous editor Audra Shivers, cuz I know I have made a lot of mistakes.

I have 2 holla at my girl, the girl that could not have touched a piece of paper with a pen better; my big sister Brenda L. Thomas. I know I can be a pain in the ass with my many questions, but thanks for answering them even if it is 3 o' clock in the morning. You go, girl!

Speakin' of paper and pens—we're all in this 2gether. I come from a whole family of writers and there are a lot of us. What? You didn't know, well let me remind you: Shawna Grundy, Alyce Thompson—I see you girl; Zane, Kashamba Williams, Solomon Jones, Karen E. Quionnes Miller, Hickson, Tracy Brown, Daamiah Poole, Marlene Taylor, Asante Kahari, Treasure E. Blue, Elizabeth Gore, K'wan, Shamora Renee, Chandell Bey, Nikki Turner, Shannon Holmes, Lynnette Khalfani, O. Salik-Evans, T.N. Baker, Rikeem Wilburn, James Earl Hardy, Mark Anthony, and last but not least, my main man Brandon McCalla.

One Luv to my barber/stylist Niyru for keepin' me looking so fresh and so clean and the coolest probation officer in the game, Mary Ellen. Shout out to you for keeping my azz out of jail.

To all the bookstores that showed me love throughout my trying times—Ms. Betty and the entire staff at Liguorius Bookstore; thanks so much for your support.

Tara, at Border's Express at Liberty Place, you know I'll shut shop down for you girl.

A special shout out to Ms. Emelyn and her staff at Meja Books in the Tristate Mall in Delaware.

Shout out to Rita at Border's Express in the Gallery. And mad shouts to Cindy and the whole Staff at Walden Bookstore in Long Island, NY; Emperiam Books (Tiffany and Zahir).

The radio stations; thanks for all your support: The Dreamteam (Power99), Golden Girl and Qdeezy. Tarsha (Jonesy aka Ms. Jones), Todd Lynn, DJ Envy, Miss Info, and the whole Hot97 staff. WHAT radio, the Wendy Williams Experience, thanks to Art and the entire Experience staff, Power105, and Philly 103.9 The Beat.

To all the street vendors in NYC, thanks for pushing my books and helping to make my dreams come true—Che, Sidee, and Fatima.

Mad shout outs to Janyra, Thais, Cindy, the Hudson family, Darylisha, Jerome, Andre, Keith, Wayne, Grandpop, Mrs. Darlene, Robin, Pastor Ricky, Aunt Dar, Tony, Maxwell (crazy ass), Shon, Stevie (boo boo), Shauna, Tamika, Young Sir, Sharon, Pooh, Keyon (thank you for Prince), Donnie, Neisha, Kyron, Terrence, Chuck, Keisha, Jorell, Job, Peaches, Tyrea, Diana, Jay-Z, Queen Pen, After 7, Donnie Simpson, Kimora Lee Simmons, Charlie Mack and 215 Entertainment, Bow Wow, Dr. Al Mameniskis, Tracie, Gwen, Deon, Robert Datner, and to all my readers all over—I thank y'all for the support, letters, e-mails, and the constant reviews. This is the second time around so here we go again. God bless to all and to all good night.

# Prologue

*"Why, oh why, I gave you several years of my life and it just ain't right. What's your perception of love, now how many times did we say it was over and how many times did we not leave? There's no sense in this love hangover, please come back to me 'cause I can't forget your ways, I still remember our first kiss. I'm nervous and trembling...*

*Late in the midnight hour, I see the etch of your face, and it makes it hard for me to breathe. What can I do to change your decision, please work with me. Sometimes my eyes won't close from weeping and sometimes I can't wake up from sleeping, 'cause you keep calling me in my dreams, I can't forget your ways I still remember our first kiss. You got me nervous and trembling. It's not healthy to keep smoking these cigarettes, and only you can help me quit."*

-Tweet-

# Smoking Cigarettes

## The Jump Off
## October 2001

The room was dark when Paul threw me down on the bed and began kissing me nonstop. I grabbed the back of his head and forced his tongue into my mouth. I had wanted Paul for a very long time and nothing was going to stop me from having him at this very moment. He tongued me down as I felt his long rod pulsating through his sweats and banging up against my waistline as his weight buried me deeper into the bed.

"What's up, baby boy?" he asked.

"You," I said between kisses. I rose up to take off his fitted (a cap), and began rubbing my hands through his soft, jet black, wavy hair. I lay back as he slid on top of me and started grinding to the sounds of R. Kelly. After leaving two hickeys on both sides of his neck, I grabbed for his thermal shirt and pulled it over his head, exposing his hairy chest. I began sucking his nipples very hard as I flipped him over and he landed with his back pressed firmly on the bed with me grinding on top of him.

As I kissed and caressed his entire body, he kicked his Nikes off onto the floor. I worked my tongue from his chest to his belly while slowly approaching the top of his sweats. I loosened the string as I glanced up at his face to notice his eyes closed tight while he licked his lips back and forth.

I knew that he loved this moment, and unbeknownst to him I loved every minute of it as well. I unclipped his Walkman from his sweats and then tugged on the top of his waistband, sliding his sweat pants all the way down to his ankles. I grabbed at his ankle socks and pulled, until all three articles of clothing, including his Walkman, landed on the floor. I worked my way back up to where I could see his long dick throbbing, waiting to be released from his striped boxers. When I pulled his dick out, I began deep throating him slowly. He grabbed on to the sheets as I closed my eyes and slurped his magic stick, leaving my saliva dripping down onto his pubic hairs.

"Take your pants off," he said in a deep voice when I looked up at his face and saw him still licking his lips. I unbuckled my belt and unbuttoned my pants and then slid them off and threw them on the floor next to his socks.

"You ready for me?" he asked with his eyes halfway closed, high from the Dutch he had just smoked. I turned around and sat my anus directly on his face as I continued to go down on his dick. He munched my ass slowly as I licked every drop of his pre-cum from the head of his muscle. He penetrated me with his tongue until my cave was nice and wet for his grand entrance.

"Let me tap it," he said as he got up and I crawled to the head of the bed for him to bang me doggy style. I could feel his rod entering me from the back; it felt like he was ripping my insides. The head of his dick was all in the gut part of my stomach as he switched gears from slowly stroking to quickening the pace—he strengthened his muscle to go deep. I closed my eyes and took in all that he had to offer as I relaxed my butt muscles while he entered my domain.

I squatted over, smothering my face into the pillow, as he plowed my ass harder and harder. I felt his hairy balls touching my bare skin as I started to scream into the pillow. The air in my bedroom became limited as the sweat of lust poured from our bodies.

In my mind I knew that this wasn't the right thing to do since I was committed to Troy, but since he had gone out of town for the second weekend in a row, I knew that it would be a matter of time before my hormones would get out of control and I would need me some loving fast.

"Paul, fuck me harder," I said, lifting my face from

9

the pillow so he could hear me chant his name. The more I yelled his name and gasped for air, the deeper he went into my rectum. At this point, all I knew was Paul was the best dick I ever had and I wouldn't mind doing this again and again. I knew that cheating was the wrong thing to do, but how could something so wrong feel so right?

At that very moment he flipped me over and began fucking me missionary style. I held my knees toward my chest to give him better access. In and out…in and out…I counted every stroke in my head. I reached up and planted a very soft kiss on his pink lips and he started to kiss my neck as I grabbed his back, holding on for dear life.

"What's my name?" he said softly in my ear while R. Kelly sang through the stereo speakers that he didn't see anything wrong with a little bump and grind.

"Paul," I said while taking every inch of the dick that was given to me.

"No nigga, what's my motherfucking name!" he said louder.

"Daddy!" I screamed as he seemed to tear every tissue of my rectum.

"I'ma 'bout to bust, baby," he said, grabbing me tighter. "Yeah!" he yelled as he proceeded to bang my back out and jerk me off as I felt him reach his peak. I reached mine and busted my entire nut on my stomach.

I could feel all of his hot, steamy fluids leave his body and enter mine as he slowly licked my nipples. All that love juice dripped down my body onto my Versace bed sheets. He collapsed on top of me as I lay there wondering what I had gotten myself into. My mission was accomplished because I didn't have any real feelings for this man—I only wanted to fuck him. My true love was for Troy.

I continued to lie there pondering my thoughts and wondering how I could love a person the way I loved Troy and then turn around and cheat on him. Was I becoming the type of person I despised?  I hated cheaters; was I becoming one of them?  I looked up at Paul's face as he turned to me and smiled.  I smiled back at him knowing this would be the first, and last time, we would have sex.  I couldn't do anything to ruin the love that Troy and I shared.  I mean, maybe Troy and I didn't have the best life, but I admit that we shared something special.

"What are you smiling at?"  I asked him while staring into his eyes through the darkness.

"I'm not smiling.  I'm actually laughing at your dumb ass."

I looked at him with a puzzled expression.  "Why are you calling me dumb?"

"Because just like I thought, you're a faggot ass ho just like the rest of them.  I know that you and your boy Troy are still fucking around even though you told me you aren't in a relationship with anybody.  I just wanted to see if you was gonna suck my dick and you did.  As a matter of fact, Troy was the one that set this shit up with you and me."

I pushed him off me and stood up.  I knew he had to be telling the truth because I never told him about me and Troy and I never even mentioned his name.  "Paul, what the fuck are you talking about?"  I asked for reassurance.

"Bitch, shut the fuck up!  You know what the fuck I'm talking about.  You think we just met by coincidence.  No, baby, Troy set this up between us.  He wanted us to meet just to see if you would talk to me and to see if you had the balls to cheat on him.  Not only did you talk to me, you sucked my dick, and I fucked you.  So like I said, you're nothing but a faggot ass ho just like I thought."

I jumped out of the bed and ran over to the dresser to turn on the light.  Paul lay there holding his dick in his hand, laughing.

"Bring yah pretty ass over here and suck it some more," he said, waving his pale dick back and forth.

# Smoking Cigarettes

My heart began to pound inside of my chest. I needed something to be done fast. How could I bargain with him to keep this sexual escapade between us? I walked over to the bed and sat at the foot. "How do you and Troy know each other?"

"Suck my dick and I'll tell you," he responded, still grinning. He was cute, but my burning heart wanted him dead.

"Paul, I'm serious."

"Nigga, I'm serious too. I need some more head, that shit felt good. I knew that you were lying about being in a relationship, because the way you suck dick, I know someone had to have you to himself." I looked at him and then down at his hard rod. I smiled and realized that he had me eating out the palm of his hands. I leaned over, grabbed his dick, and stuck it so far into the back of my throat that I gagged. I went up and down on it with my tongue while thinking of a slick way for him not to tell Troy about our time together.

When he took my head and held his penis in my throat, an idea came into my mind. I lifted my head from his knob then got up and walked back over to the dresser to turn off the light. I commenced to suck his dick more and more until his burst of angel cream exploded into my mouth. He then rolled over and fell asleep.

He held me close as he lay with his dick pressed firmly against my ass. I slid his arm from around me then got up from the bed and grabbed the phone from the nightstand. I paged my brother Rafeek and put in the code 911. I paced the floor until Rafeek called me back.

I answered the phone on the first ring; I didn't want Paul to be awakened.

"Hello," I whispered into the phone while watching Paul flinch.

"Wassup, you paged me?" Rafeek yelled into the phone, which was normal for him.

"Yeah, I am in some deep shit."

"What do you mean you're in deep shit?"

"It's a long story and I'm sure you wouldn't want to hear it."

"Well, what the fuck do you want me to do?" he yelled into the phone.

"My boyfriend just beat me up," I said, trying to sound hysterical.

"Well, where the fuck is he?  What happened?"

"He just came in from work and started hitting me. I think he was drunk.  After he stopped, he laid there and went to sleep," I said sniffling.

"All right, man, I'll be there," Rafeek said before the line went dead.  I lightly sat on the side of the bed so I wouldn't awaken Paul.  I began to try and think of a fast plan before my brother would get here.  I already knew that whatever scam I had in my mind, my brother was with it. It was a good thing he had never met any of my boyfriends. He would never know if Paul was really my boyfriend or not.

After about twenty minutes, Rafeek was at my front door.  He didn't ring the doorbell; he just tapped lightly on the wooden door.  I walked down the hall and opened the door as he came right in wearing a long Woolrich coat with fur on the hood.  He stood there in the middle of the floor looking like a replica of me, standing five feet ten inches tall with a caramel complexion and curly hair.  People always said we looked alike.

"All right, what the fuck is the problem?  Where he at?" he asked, walking toward my bedroom without waiting for a response.  He walked into my bedroom while sexy ass Paul lay across the bed still snoring.  "Wake his punk ass up!"

"No, no, wait a minute," I said, softly.

"What the fuck you mean wait a minute?"

"What are you going to do to him?"

"I'ma kill this pussy."

I looked at him with amazement and terror. "What do you mean you're gonna kill him? I mean, how you gonna just come in here and kill somebody?"

"Like this," he said, as he pulled out a sharp 11-inch blade then pulled the sheets back, exposing Paul's naked body. "Wake the fuck up, pussy!" Rafeek yelled as Paul opened his eyes and turned over. Rafeek jumped on top of him, ramming the blade into his chest. I jumped back and covered my face as Paul yelled to the top of his lungs.

"Aww, shit!" Paul screamed in agony as Rafeek kept stabbing away into his chest and stomach until Paul couldn't move any longer. He gasped for air as Rafeek took the blade and cut him from the middle of his throat to his earlobe. The tears ran down my face because I could not believe what I saw.

"Now, I bet you won't hit no one else, faggot!" Rafeek said as he jumped up from the bed and spit on Paul's corpse.

Rafeek turned and looked at me. I had never felt so afraid in my life.

"Go wash this off," he said, handing me the knife that dripped with Paul's blood. I covered my face and took a deep breath before taking the blade and throwing it into the bathtub. I let the water run over it before I started to wipe it off with a washcloth. I walked back into the bedroom where Rafeek was wrapping Paul's body in my Versace sheets. I handed him back the stainless steel blade; my hands were still shaking. Before I knew it, he had uncovered my entire bed and threw the contents on the floor—pillows, covers, comforter, and of course Paul. His Walkman, clothes, and sneakers were wrapped separately in a pillowcase.

I could see Paul's foot hanging out from the bottom of the sheet as Rafeek began rolling him up a little more. I knew that no one deserved this type of treatment, but what was I to do? I mean Paul was out to get my ass and I had to think quickly before I would let a piece of dick come between me and Troy. As Rafeek dragged Paul's body down the hall, I began to think. Was I a murderer because I called my brother to come and handle a little bit of business for me? What would happen now? Was I going to jail? I knew my brother killed a couple of guys from around the way and even though he got caught, he somehow was never found guilty. What would make this time any different?

"Why the fuck are you just standing there? Help me with this shit!" Rafeek spat while taking off his Woolrich and throwing it on the couch. I couldn't believe what the fuck had just happened here. A minute ago this nigga was fucking my brains out, and now he was lying on my living room floor wrapped up in my sheets, dead. Now I really knew the meaning of the old saying, this was all good just a week ago. I reached down to help pick up Paul's body when I felt a great eruption in the pit of my stomach. I held my torso with one hand and held my mouth with the other as I ran down the hall into the bathroom to vomit.

Just the thought of touching a dead body made me sick. I flushed the toilet and stared into the hole as I watched the water spin and then go down the drain. What the fuck have I gotten myself into? I kept asking myself. I hoped God could forgive me for real this time. I couldn't imagine how Paul's family was gonna feel about this shit that I had just caused. Paul and I had only seen each other a few times on the stroll, there really wasn't much that I knew about him except that he lived at home with his father and stepmother, and had a brother three years younger who kind of resembled him. Knowing Paul was a junior, his father was sure to flip when he found out.

"Would you come the fuck on and help me with this shit and stop stalling? I have some other business to take care of!" Rafeek yelled from inside the other room.

"All right, here I come!" I yelled back, trying to

wash my face and get my mind right. I walked back down the hall to where Rafeek was standing over Paul.

"So, what are you gonna do with him?" I knew my brother was crazy. I always wanted to know how crazy niggas think, and where they hide their victims.

"Hold up, I'm thinking...shit," he said, rubbing his head. "Do you have a box? A big box?" he asked as he looked up at my terrified face.

"No, not that I know of. Oh, yes I do. I have the box that my Christmas tree came in," I said as I suddenly remembered.

"A'ight, where is it?"

"It's in my bedroom," I said, while turning around to walk toward my oversized walk-in closet. I grabbed the box and emptied it of all the Christmas tree branches then dragged it down the hallway.

"Open it and stop looking like a little bitch," he spat. "You're the one that called me the fuck over here to handle this so you knew what was up," he said, trying to lift Paul to throw him into the box. The first thump I heard I knew was Paul's head hitting the floor through the thin cardboard box. I kicked it over for Rafeek to fix his body inside of it the way that he wanted.

"Where's the masking tape?"

"The only thing I have is that thick gray tape."

"That's even better. Go grab that real quick," he demanded. I ran into the kitchen and got the tape from the drawer then ran back to give it to him. The cool air that came in from the window added more vibration to the way I was already shaking. I stood back and watched Rafeek as he taped the entire box, including all four sides.

"Come on and help me carry it downstairs and into the car," he said, grabbing his coat. I went into the closet and put on a thin sweat jacket, and then proceeded to help him with the remains.

By the time we got to the bottom of the steps and

outside I was already ready to throw up again. I still couldn't believe what had just happened. Together we walked the box outside. I didn't see Rafeek's car anywhere in sight. I saw my car still parked in its space with a yellow cab parked next to it.

"Where's your car?" I asked, searching around the parking lot with my eyes.

"I don't have my car, my boy let me borrow his cab."

"So we're gonna put this inside the cab?"

"Yeah, we're gonna put it in the trunk."

I sighed as I thought about the whole situation. One lift into the trunk and we shut the hood. I looked around the parking lot of my complex to see if anyone noticed us, but I knew it wouldn't be a big deal because it looked like I was just helping my brother get a Christmas tree into the car.

"You better not say shit to anyone about this," he said as he turned to face me.

"I'm not. Why would you even think I would say something? Who would I tell?"

"I don't know, but I know faggots like to run their mouths," he said, opening up the door on the driver's side.

"So, wait, you're calling me a faggot?"

"Nigga, I know you and I know that you have a big-ass mouth," he said, getting into the car.

"Where are you taking it?"

"I don't know. Don't worry about all that," he said while pulling his skully down on his head. He started the car and put it in gear as I stood there and watched him speed away out of the parking lot.

## Young Love
## December 2001

"This has been the worse fucking Christmas of my life. I lost my job, I don't have a man, no money, and my rent is due. My final check should have been here last week," I said, as I went on and on, rambling to my best friend Kevin on the telephone. He wasn't doing a thing about what I was saying, just sitting there letting air pass through the phone.

"No worries, no worries, it'll get betta, mon," Kevin said in his Jamaican accent.

I am still deeply in love with my ex-fiancé Troy. The thing I miss the most is the way his smile used to light up the room through his dark chocolately skin.

I took the phone and held it tight to my ear, just to hear Kevin say he would call me back because his mother had to use the phone.

Kevin and I have been best friends for seven years now. We met when we were working at McDonald's on Broad Street in downtown Philadelphia. I was sixteen and he was eighteen. I knew he was gay when I first laid eyes on him. He was taller than me at the time. His skin was darker than average and had a glow, thanks to Jamaica. He and his family moved to the States when he was fifteen, and he has been here ever since.

After hanging up the phone, I walked over to the dresser and squirted some lotion in my hands, then started to apply it to my face. I stood in front of the mirror and stared at my chunky body for about thirty seconds, and then sat on the side of the bed. I was thinking about how my life would have been if I were heterosexual.

I wondered if I would have had a couple of kids by now at twenty-three. I had made some accomplishments in life—I'd graduated from Cheyney University, got my own apartment, and a car. So what if I lost my job and drive a Plymouth Neon—it's mine. The phone rang. I turned around and glanced at it as it rang again. I grabbed the caller ID and saw the number. I let it ring again before the answering machine picked it up.

"Hi, this message is for Rashad Smith, this is PECO Energy calling and we just wanted to let you know that you are 72 days past due on your electric bill and we are scheduling for your service to be shut off by Friday if we don't receive a payment." I turned my head and smiled at the floor. Stand in line, I thought to myself.

It seems like the more I try, the harder things get. I wished Troy were here. I missed him so much, and being with him made me feel like I was somebody. I know he had been through a lot with his family, but that's why I was there to take care of him. I couldn't believe he would leave me to go have sex with someone that didn't even equal up to my standard. I felt a tear drop down the side of my cheek. I wiped it away swiftly as the phone rang again. It was Kevin.

"Sorry, mon, but meh mudder had to call her peoples. You OK?"

"Yeah, I'm fine," I replied. I told Kevin how badly I missed Troy and how I was gonna do whatever it took to get back with him.

"Now, you know dat whenever you try to get back with one of your exes, it doh work out."

I held the phone tightly to my ear and glanced at the floor. I noticed that I hadn't had a good pedicure in a while. Shit, I didn't have anyone special in my life so I really didn't need one. I tuned back in to Kevin's rambling.

"Well, you will do whatever you want, mon, but doh come back to me in the end. Doh say, I ain't tell you so."

I continued to listen to him talk as I sat there in

silence. Kevin has never had his heart broken. He has never been in love with anyone. He just takes a relationship for what it's worth and that's that. I finally told him that my Xanaxes were working and I was on my way to sleep. I hung the phone up and slid underneath my plush covers.

I lay there feeling so hopeless, wondering what I was gonna do for income. I closed my eyes thinking of the day when all this shit was gonna be over. I turned over as a chill came through my body with Paul's presence. Even though I had cleaned my apartment thoroughly, I could still smell him and the scent of his cologne. I had vowed to myself that I would never think about the events of that horrific night. After about ten minutes, I drifted off into a deep sleep.

The next day I awoke to snow falling outside my window. It was noon. I jumped out of the bed and ran into the bathroom. My dick was hard as hell. I released myself into the toilet thinking about what I was gonna do for the day. I popped a DVD into the machine and began to watch *Legally Blonde*. I lay on the couch, watching the movie from beginning to end. By the time it was over the snow was slowly coming to a halt. I got in the shower and then got dressed so I could drive over to West Philly to visit my goddaughter and maybe get some peace of mind.

I stayed there for most of the day until it started to get dark. I came back home where my depression was waiting for me. I didn't even get in the door good when the phone started ringing from bill collectors. I sat down on the living room floor and called my mother.

"Yes, Rashad," my mother said in her typically calm voice.

"Mom, what are you doing? I have to talk to you."

"I'm reading my newspaper as I always do. What's the problem?"

I held my head with my hands. "It seems as if things

aren't working out the way that I want them to," I said, dryly.

"Well, Rashad, everyone has his days when things don't seem to go right, but you can't let that stop you. Just keep speaking to the man upstairs and he'll provide a way."

I felt a lonely teardrop slide down my cheek. "But mom, it's these bills. They seem to be piling up and there's no way I can pay them. I need help bad. I didn't even pay my rent yet, and the electric company is threatening to turn off my service."

"How much is your rent?"

"Seven hundred and fifty-five dollars," I said with a sigh.

"Well, Rashad, I have some bills that I need to pay myself, but I'll see what I can do to help with your rent. You need to call the electric company and get on a payment plan. I know they got some kinda program for low-income customers...I don't know about no income, but give it a try. I'll try to help as much as I can but I can't make any promises. Did you go out today?"

"Yeah, I went over to grandma's house to see the baby," I said, smiling as I thought about my precious godchild.

"Oh, yeah! How is she?"

"She's fine. It seems like she's trying to talk."

"Well that's good. Let me get back to reading my paper. I'll talk to you a little later, OK, young man?" she said while ruffling her newspaper in the background.

"OK, bye-bye," I said.

As I continued to sit on the living room floor, I rested my back against the sofa, and then picked up the phone to dial Troy. His younger sister answered the phone.

"Troy is not here," she said in a preteen voice.

"Well, when he comes in, could you please tell him that Rashad called?" I knew she could tell that I was eaten up inside by the way she said that she would tell him that I called. I tried to call Kevin but that was not successful because his brother was always hogging up the phone. I figured I'd bust it up with a little PS2 before popping two Xanaxes.

Before I bounced into bed I sat down in front of the computer in my room and logged on to the Internet. Kevin called but he couldn't get through since my line was connected to the PC.

"Welcome," the AOL man called out to me in a loud tone. With no e-mail from people as usual, I immediately went into a chat room called "Philly Man for Man." I browsed through numerous screen names.

*Are there any cuties from Philly?* I typed in the send box. Not even fifteen minutes had passed before I got a response.

*Right here.*

*Where?* I typed in the box.

*Germantown.*

I sat there as my Xanaxes started to take effect. I asked him if he was cute, and of course, he said yes. *Well, let me see a picture of you then*, I typed. He quickly got out of the chat room. I started typing smart remarks into the send box when he came back and asked me if I was talking about him.

*You must be ugly*, I typed back into the box. Then, I was given instructions to look into his profile. I did and there it was, a picture of him. I was shocked because this boy looked sexy as hell.

I leaned over to look at the clock, it was a quarter past midnight and I hadn't eaten yet. I got up and ran into the kitchen to the refrigerator to take out a bowl containing some chicken wings I had the night before.

I placed the entire bowl into the microwave and then prepared a cup full of ice for my cherry Kool-Aid. I grabbed the bowl out of the microwave, charged back to my room, and then made a pilot on the floor in front of my bed. I sat in front of the TV to watch *Boyz 'N the Hood* when I heard a popping sound below my bedroom window. I got up and ran over to turn the light off before grabbing the phone to call my mother. The phone rung four times before she answered.

"Hello," she answered, sounding half asleep.

"Mom."

"What?" she said, sounding annoyed.

"I think someone just got shot below my bedroom window," I said in a whisper.

"What do you mean?"

"I just heard some popping sounds and they didn't sound like firecrackers either. Do you think I should call the police?"

"No, because you really don't know what it was that you heard, and if so, I think you should mind your business because you don't know what's going on." We sat on the phone in silence for about thirty seconds while I gazed out the window through the blinds.

"Is that all, Rashad?"

"Yeah, I just wanted to see if I should call the cops or not."

"OK, well I'm going back to sleep."

"All right, I'll keep you posted if something else happens."

"OK, bye."

I peeped through the window again and then backed away. I didn't think the sounds I heard were firecrackers—they were much too silent. About ten minutes later the parking lot was swamped with police cars. I continued to stand by the window to watch the action. I saw a white cop with a mask over his face help another guy put a heavyset man into a body bag and then place him in the back of the ambulance. I stopped for a second, then looked around my entire room. There was dead silence. I glanced down at the half-eaten bowl of chicken wings on the floor; I had lost my appetite. By the time I snapped out of my daze, the action that had taken place outside my window was gone.

I had never seen so many cops in that parking lot at one time before. I picked up the bowl of chicken wings and didn't even bother to wrap them in any foil; I just stuck them in the fridge. The phone rang. I peeked at the caller ID. It was Drew.

Drew was another friend of mine. We had known each other for about two years. I didn't answer because it was getting kind of late. My pills were kicking in and besides, he probably just called to tell me about someone he was fucking or about a ball that was coming up or something. Whatever he was trying to say I wasn't trying to hear. I went over to my desk and plopped down in the chair.

When I sat down I had ten unread messages on my computer—all from one screen name, Scooby-Doo. I read each message. This person was asking for my phone number and wanted to know my name. In my book, that was too damn personal. Nevertheless, like a naïve young boy that I portrayed to be, I typed my name and telephone number in the box and then immediately asked his name. He told me it was Calvin. I nudged my top lip to my nose then shrugged my shoulders before rudely shutting down my computer and walking over to my bed. About twenty minutes later, the phone rang.

"Hel-wo, can I speeck wit' Rashad?" a garbled voice asked as if he was eating three cheeseburgers.

"Who 'dis?" I asked rapidly.

"It's Calvin."

"Wassup? Lemmee call you right back," I said before he could get another word out. I hung up the phone. I wasn't really gonna call him back. He was cute in the photo, but it might've been old since he sounded like he was fat. I took my ass to sleep because I was tired—tired of all this bullshit that life was throwing at me.

The next day when I awoke, I turned over and grabbed my pillow then squeezed it tight. The sun was shining right through the seam of the mini blinds that dressed my bedroom window. I said a silent prayer asking the Lord to help me through my painful life.

I asked him to help me pay these bills and find me a job better than the one I had recently been fired from— working in customer service at the credit card company. I couldn't believe that job lasted less than two weeks. I recalled happier times when me and some of my friends weren't living legit. Man, did we get paid though. I think we worked every bank on the East Coast before I caught a charge and stopped. We wrote so many checks—I had my nigga Chad making the checks for me, I had my nigga Melvin and Dave opening up accounts, and I had Mia and April cashing checks. It was easy for me to get paid because I knew some bitch that worked at the bank. We were crafting our asses off. You couldn't tell me shit. I bought so much shit with my money and that's how I put myself through school. I stole from white people all over the world, and after all that massive spending and buying unnecessary things that I didn't need, I was broke.

The ringing phone interrupted my thoughts. It was my cousin Shay-Shay. I grabbed the phone anxiously.

"Wha'chu doin'?" she said in her 52$^{nd}$ Street ghetto girl voice. She was very upbeat for it to be so early in the morning. Her mother and my mother are sisters. Shay-Shay had recently given birth to a baby girl, my goddaughter, Kaniyah.

The whole time we were on the phone she laughed about me not having employment. After about ten minutes of just laying there with the phone to my ear, I told her I would call her back. I got up, grabbed my robe, and walked into the living room to sit on the couch and stare out the window. Someone slipped a white envelope under my door. It was from the management office of my complex. It stated that I was past due on my rent, and if I didn't pay soon, they would have to evict me. I placed the letter back into the envelope and placed it on top of my desk. I started up the computer in my bedroom and was glad to see more people in the chat room than usual. I started listening to Toni Braxton's CD. It seemed like the words to her song were just what I needed. I didn't have any idea how I was gonna pay these bills without a job. December was ending and there were only two days left before the New Year.

Calvin called wanting to know why I didn't call him back the night before. I had to quickly think of a lie so I wouldn't be known as a bullshitter. I told him I was gonna call him when I got back in the house. I really didn't have any plans for the day, but I decided to go to my grandmother's house to visit my goddaughter. As soon as I returned and walked in the door, the phone was ringing.

Damn, can't I get in the house and take my coat off before this damn boy starts calling me? I said to myself.

"Wassup?" Calvin asked.

"Nuffin." I rolled my eyes in the back of my head as I held the phone with one hand and shuffled my arm out of the sleeve of my coat with the other. I started to walk toward my room.

I turned on the lamp on the nightstand by my bed and began to unlace the shoestrings in my sneakers. We sat there silently on the phone for about five seconds before I started to ask him questions.

"Where do you work?"

"McDonald's."

Hmm, I thought. Well, at least he has more than me.

"How old are you?"

"Twenty."

OK, him being twenty to my twenty-three was not that big a deal, I thought. He also told me he has a son named Jon. I paused for a minute.

"How old is your son?"

"Nine months."

I sat toward the front of the bed, massaging my back on the pillows. As the questions about life started to go on and on I looked at the clock and saw that it was half past one. The conversation was getting better and better. I slipped on an old pair of shorts and a beat up T-shirt—my pajamas—before I changed my position by lying across the bed. I didn't realize that there was an incoming call waiting to be answered on my line. I clicked over, it was Kevin—at the moment I was finally getting my groove started. Kevin would have to call me back.

I immediately clicked back to the other line where Calvin was humming a tune to one of Aaliyah's songs. I didn't have a need for any Xanaxes tonight. All my focus was on what Calvin had to say. I rubbed my belly when he told me he weighs 155 pounds. I felt very fat at that moment. I leaned over to a streak of sun catching my eye. Morning had arrived and we were still on the phone talking as if it was noon. We finally came to a decision to hook up later that day. After all, it was New Year's Eve.

I walked over to my computer to see if he had sent any more pictures. He had sent five of him and his son on Christmas day. Two of the pictures were of him flexing his muscles. One of the pictures was of him sticking his tongue out and another of him acting very silly with his son, and the final picture was him just sitting there. I saw how strong and masculine his hands were in the pictures and at that point he had me hooked. I wanted to meet this guy. He was sexy.

From the conversation, he seemed very intelligent and I knew he had been through his share of ups and downs. He took charge of the conversation.

"Are we just meeting up or are we going to do something?" he asked.

# Smoking Cigarettes

"I don't know, what do you want to do?"

We agreed to go to the movies. There really wasn't anything out to see, but I did want to see the new Tom Cruise movie, *Vanilla Sky*. Therefore, it was a date. I immediately became excited. I looked at the pictures one more time and suddenly became rock hard. I couldn't wait to see this boy. He was still on the phone and he never knew how I pulsated from his pictures. I couldn't wait to feel on those strong hands.

His eyes were like deep dark tunnels that his eyelashes floated above. His facial structure seemed flawless. In one of his pictures he wore a black hat that sat on the back of his head. The waves throughout his hair flowed like the Caribbean Sea. During our conversation he confessed from being twenty, to nineteen, and then finally, eighteen. My first instinct was to completely back up. This boy was too young for me, but then I thought it wouldn't hurt to have a few friends even if they were younger or older. He told me that he attends Catholic school in the Center City part of Philadelphia, he's in the 11th grade because he got held back, and his parents are aware that he is gay. He stated that he had to work later that day but he would be off in time to catch our date. I continued to sit there looking at his pictures.

I got up and studied myself in the mirror. I didn't like the way my body looked. My stomach was enormous. I did not want to let the phone go, but I needed to get some sleep and so did he. He insisted on staying on the phone with me until we both fell asleep. I didn't wanna make myself or him feel uncomfortable so I let the conversation go on.

Before hanging up the phone, he said good night in a sweet voice. I sure did like the sound of that voice. I hung up the phone with a smile. The phone rang later that morning. It was my mother.

"Don't you have to go and get your glasses today?"

she asked. By this time it was after ten o'clock. I had forgotten all about having to go to the eye doctor to pick up my glasses. I hated wearing them. They made my face and my nose feel funny.

My mother insisted that she'd be here in less than thirty minutes to get me because although I had a car of my own, I didn't feel like driving, it was too early for me. I was extremely tired but I couldn't wait until it was time for me to see Calvin. I decided not to take a shower yet. I was just gonna throw on some clothes and save my bathing for later.

My mother beeped her horn twice. I grabbed my jacket and my cell phone then ran out the door and down the steps. I hopped in the passenger side of my mother's vehicle and she could see that my depression had been replaced by a smile.

"I have a date." I offered the information even though she didn't ask.

"With who?"

"Some boy I met on the computer." She continued driving as if she didn't hear me. I started laughing. She turned and smiled. My cell phone rang, it was Drew. He was always loud. My mother could hear him from her side of the car. I anxiously told him that I have a date.

"With who?" he asked.

I explained to him that I was in the chat room the night before and he laughed.

"Well, how old is he?"

I gulped my tongue to the back of my throat and looked at my mother to make sure she wasn't listening.

"Twenty," I whispered into the phone. I lied because I really didn't want anyone to know that I was going on a date with such a young boy. Drew giggled some more. I was glad to know that he was happy for me. I practically rushed to get my prescription glasses. They had a slight tint of yellow so people could just barely see my eyes. My mother liked the glasses, but somehow they seemed funny looking on my face. As bad as my mother wanted to spend the day with me, I had a date and I wasn't going to be late. She dropped me off at my loft and I went into my apartment.

Calvin called me from work. "Wassup?" he asked.

I smiled. "Nuffin, I'm about to get dressed." He giggled. I giggled. He told me his cell was shut off and if I had tried to call I would have gotten a disconnected greeting. I laughed.

"It's not funny," he protested.

"I'm sorry." Hell, I don't know what I was laughing for because mine was gonna be turned off soon as well. I told him that I couldn't get dressed and talk to him at the same time so I had to go.

"A'ight. Meet me at seven o' clock in Germantown."

I hung up the phone, then flopped down on the edge of the bed before deciding to call Kevin. He answered on the first ring.

"Wut you doin'?" I asked.

"Ah, cookin' dey." I told him that I have a date tonight just in case he wondered where I was.

"You have ah date on Old Year's night?"

"What's the problem with that?"

"It weird, daz all."

Kevin always thought that the New Year's celebration was a time to spend with family, but that's what Christmas was for. I suddenly became excited all over again and told Kevin that I met the guy through the Internet. He laughed.

"Some ah dem people dere crazy."

"Not all, and besides, it's a first time for everything. Well, gotta go," I said before placing the phone on its hook.

I stripped myself down to my underwear. How could I dare show off this fat ass body to anyone? I would kill to lose fifty or sixty pounds. I slipped my boxers down to my ankles, then looked at my dick and laughed. When it was time for me to have sex, I would have to find my dick by lifting my stomach first.

I threw the dirty clothes into the laundry and went into the bathroom. I lit the candles that surrounded my tub, then filled the tub with warm water. I stepped in, and laid back on the base. I closed my eyes and thought about Troy and how I missed him. I never really wanted to break up with him, but it seemed as if I wasn't a priority for him. He never really noticed what a good thing he had fucked up. I was very good to him and I tried like hell to make it work. I even went to the extent of sending him flowers to that shitty job of his over at UPS.

These niggas don't know when they have a good man even if the motherfucker is standing right in their face. Before I knew it, a half hour had passed, and I had to go. I got up and grabbed the clippers to give myself a quick shape-up; I was a little rough around the edges. I really didn't know what would be a good thing to wear on a first date. I went into my closet and grabbed a pair of faded Guess jeans and a gray Polo shirt. That should match with a pair of all white Pumas. I was set. I got dressed and dashed on some cologne that Shay-Shay bought me for Christmas.

I brushed my hair, put on my jacket, grabbed my cell phone and keys, and I was out the door. I jumped into my Neon with the tank on E and down the road I went. I really didn't need any directions because I called Calvin and he gave them to me as I was driving. Along the way I had to stop and get gas with the money I was using for the movies. Calvin and I made a deal that I would pay for the movies and he would pay for dinner.

I hated going on a new date in this lifestyle with someone. I never knew who was gonna pay.

I was slowly approaching Manheim Street, the

block that Calvin lives on. I double-parked right in front of his house—it was big. The light was on and the door was halfway open. A slim, short, dark-skinned man, smoking a cigarette, walked out onto the porch. He came to the edge of the porch and took one last long puff before plucking the cigarette into the grass. He started walking down the steps toward my car.

I lowered the music and rolled down the window as he came over to the driver's side.

"Hi, I'm Bob, Calvin's father." He extended his hand through the open window.

"I'm Rashad," I said as we shook hands. Calvin came out of the house and walked toward my car. He seemed thicker than he had appeared in his pictures. He was smiling from ear to ear, and had a really cute face. He flopped down on the passenger's side of the car. Calvin's hair was sharp. The front of his shape-up was nice, and it went into a sensual fade, I loved it. He had nice, fine hair above his lip. He wore a pair of Girbaud jeans, a white T-shirt, a blue Gap jacket, and a pair of black Nikes.

"What you looking at, faggot?!" he yelled.

Damn, this boy talks loud, I thought to myself. I put the car in gear and to the movies we went.

* * *

## The Answer Is You

We could not decide which theater we wanted to go to, but finally settled on the one in Neshaminy Mall.

"So, how have you been for the last couple of hours?" he asked, breaking the silence in the car.

"I've been cool, I am very excited about our date. So, your father seems real cool. I'm assuming that your parents are aware that you're gay and are OK with it?"

"Yeah, everyone knows, but he's not my real father, he's just my stepfather. And they're cool with it. My mother says that as long as I stay in school and continue to bring home good grades, then that's all she is concerned about. Does your family know about you?" he asked, while popping a piece of Starburst candy in his mouth.

"Yup, everyone knows about me. And they don't have a problem with it either. So where's your real father?" I asked, holding out my hand, motioning him for a piece of candy.

"He's around. I talk to him all the time. He owns a bar in Germantown."

"So, what does he say about you being gay?"

"He doesn't say anything because he doesn't know.

I turned to face him and started to laugh. "How come your mother and stepfather know about you and he doesn't?" I asked, turning back to face the road.

"I guess I never got the chance to tell. I think I'm a little scared to tell him."

"Why?"

"Because he pays for my school tuition and buys me clothes and things. I think if I tell him, he's gonna stop doing all that stuff for me and my mother can't afford to pay my tuition all by herself, and I don't want to go to a public school. I clowned too much on that free education, and that's how I got held back."

"I feel you. But do you think your dad would really do that to you?"

"I don't know what he would do, but at this point, I can't afford to find out."

We talked like we'd known one another for years. My cell phone rang. It was Mia.

Mia is one of my friends I've known since junior high school. She is brown-skinned and short with a DD cup and a wide ass.

"Yo," I hollered into the phone.

"Rashad, where are you?" she asked in a proper, yet sexy voice.

"I'm on a date, why?"

"Because I wanted to know were you going to church tonight with me and April?"

I turned to face Calvin.

"Hold on, let me ask my date first," I said, while putting the phone down in my lap. "This is my friend Mia and she wants me to go with her to church. Would you like to go to church with us tonight?" I was trying to talk to Calvin and focus on the road at the same time.

"Sure, I don't mind," he said. I picked the phone up from my lap.

"Yeah, we'll go. What time do you want us to meet you?"

"Meet us at 11:00 in Darby at the Methodist Baptist Church."

"All right, I'll see you at eleven." I responded.

"OK."

"Bye," I said, hanging up.

That would be nice for Calvin and me to go to church on our first date. Our night just got better. We were going to the movies, then to dinner, and then to church. What more could I ask for?

During the course of driving, we shared a

conversation that covered many subjects. He started to tell me stories about his school and his ex-girlfriend that was now his baby's mother.

When discussing their relationship he seemed a little edgy. Not paying attention to what he was saying I noticed a few burn marks when he raised his pant leg just as the street lights illuminated the inside of the car. I started listening again when he mentioned that during his ex-girlfriend's pregnancy he had made a few smart comments to her regarding oral sex. He had asked her to suck his dick and she had said no. He told her that he had a dude on the side that could do a better job, and she flew off the handle. While he was asleep, she boiled a pot of water and threw it on him. He suffered third degree burns.

She is serving time in the juvenile detention center for girls and her mother has custody of their son. He said he goes to see him and gets him from time to time. Upon approaching the mall I noticed a full parking lot. We drove around while chugging bottles of Smirnoff Ice until we found a space. I put the car in park as Calvin opened his door then jumped out to run to the other side of the car and open my door. I was extremely charmed by his manners. He took my hand and lifted me out the car. He shut the door behind me and then put his arm around my waist as he escorted me to the mall entrance.

"Oh shit, I left my phone in the car," I spat.

"Give me the keys," he said, as I placed them in the palm of his hand. He quickly ran back to the car and grabbed my phone as I stood there watching his sexy ass walk back. Shorty looked good walking with that bad boy stroll.

My dick suddenly got hard. I turned away as if I wasn't watching him. After buying two movie passes for *Vanilla Sky* we decided to walk around the mall since we were fifteen minutes early. As I stood in front of Modell's Sporting Goods, I glanced at every basketball jersey, wishing for the right body to fit into one. I turned to Calvin as he smiled.

"Let's go before the movie starts," he said.

I obliged. We walked into the semi-full theater and found a seat in the middle section in the second to the last row. The lights went dim as I sat down and sipped on my Coke. My adrenaline pumped through my veins like flowing water. I couldn't help but turn my head to look at this B-boy who sat next to me. Baby was looking good. He grabbed my hand and lay back in his chair as the opening credits of the movie began.

Tom Cruise did not satisfy me in this movie. I didn't understand shit and Calvin had to explain part of the movie to me. I couldn't wait until it was over. I squeezed his hand tighter.

The movie ended and I walked toward the exit then looked back to see if he followed. I wondered if anyone was gonna look at us funny since we were a couple of homosexual males holding hands in a predominantly heterosexual movie theater. I checked my watch and it was quarter after ten, only a couple of hours before the new year.

"Let me drive," he said anxiously, as I quickly hopped in the driver's seat.

I don't even know this boy so why would I let him drive my damn car? I thought to myself before we switched seats. At eighteen, Calvin was old enough to have a driver's license, but he hadn't bothered to get one. Although he knew the basics, he needed work on turning the corners. We drove back down Roosevelt Boulevard, passing different restaurants because we didn't know where we wanted to eat. The time was winding down and pretty soon it was going to be a new year. We decided on Crown Chicken on Broad Street.

I hopped out of the passenger seat looking nice in my new eyeglasses with the slight yellow tint. I went into the store and placed our order while Calvin parked the car. When I went back outside to tell Calvin the total of the bill, he went into his pocket and pulled out a load of twenties and gave me a ten. I ran back to pay for the food, and then we were on our way. We were in perfect time to meet Mia. We pulled up in front of the church the same time as she and her sister April. We got out of the car, leaving the hot food in the backseat. I walked up to Mia's car window as Calvin walked up to her passenger side window, giggling.

"We come to praise the Lord!" Mia said, imitating an old lady's voice as she got out of her car. The four of us laughed as I introduced Calvin to the girls. We walked up some steps that led into the church. The inside was packed with people of all ages. One of the ushers had to set up some chairs in the aisle because there were no seats remaining in the pews.

So, April sat in front of Mia, I sat behind Mia, and Calvin sat in back of me. I had my attention fully focused on the preacher. When the preacher called for everyone to stand, Calvin tapped me on my shoulder as we stood up to praise the Lord. I smiled. I had no doubt in my mind that this boy would be a great asset to my life. Midnight was slowly approaching. The pastor ordered everyone to get on his or her knees to pray.

I lifted my head up to see every head in the church down. There were people yelling and thanking the Lord for their blessings, there were people yelling to thank the Lord for forgiving their sins. I just bowed my head and thanked him for the lessons and the blessings he provided me throughout the year and asked him to please continue to show his presence in my life and continue to bless me in my future endeavors. I had never spent New Year's Eve in church before and it was a great experience. It was now five minutes after twelve. It was a new year—2002.

I hoped this would be a good year for me because I had been through some shit in 2001. But all my mistakes were in the past now and I was down on my knees praying for forgiveness of all the wrongs that I'd done.

After church was over we gave one another hugs then left. Calvin and I headed back to my apartment to eat. He seemed very impressed by the way my apartment was decorated. We walked to the kitchen as the phone began to ring.

"Hello," I greeted, cheerfully.

"How de date go?" Kevin asked.

"Well, I'm still on it, and Calvin is standing right here. Do you wanna speak to him?" I handed Calvin the phone.

"Hello?" Calvin said as he grabbed the phone.

"Hey, wha gwan?" Kevin said before introducing himself. I sat at the kitchen table admiring the black paintings I had on the wall that I had bought from the flea market a while back. I reached into the carryout bag to place the food in the microwave. I noticed Calvin smiling on the phone and answering a lot of questions as Kevin drilled him.

"I'm eighteen," was the next thing I heard him say. His eyes lit up as he gave me the cordless phone.

"Hello?" I said eagerly.

"That chile lying," Kevin accused.

"Why would you say that?"

"Because if that boy was eighteen, he would not be sitting there," he said, quite seriously. I paused. Kevin paused. "You serious?" he asked.

"Well, that's what he said."

"If him is eighteen, me nah approve, me nah approve dat."

"Well, we can talk about it later, I don't want to be rude to my guest. Goodbye."

I pressed the phone's off button then placed it down on the glass kitchen table. Calvin sat diagonally to me as we ate fried chicken; macaroni and cheese; and hot, soft buttered rolls. Without even clearing off the table I got up and went into the living room with Calvin following behind me. I went over to the stereo and popped in Phyllis Hyman's Greatest Hits CD. I sat on the couch and grooved to track number three, *The Answer is You.* Calvin lay next to me placing his legs over mine. I had the opportunity to check out how bad his legs were burned. I lifted his pant leg and all I saw was layers of skin that seemed to have been removed from elsewhere and placed on his leg.

He informed me that both of his legs were burned from his ankles to his buttocks. While looking at his burns and dead skin, I thought how disgusting it looked and wondered how I could be with him intimately. I love to look at people's legs and I have a foot fetish that is out of this world. This poor boy had it all when it came to looks, but underneath his clothes there was no use. I lowered his sock to see the burns that were sure to sink past his ankles.

I sat there in silence, but in my mind I was screaming to the top of my lungs. He acted as if his disfigurement didn't bother him at all. I leaned my head back and sighed. All I could imagine was how I could continue to look at him in the same light. It shouldn't matter if he had a lot of burns on his legs or not. But how were we gonna go to the beach? Then I thought, hold up, this boy is only eighteen. I'm not doing anything with him. He's not even on my level. He hasn't lived yet. He doesn't know how it feels to live on his own and pay bills. He lives at home with his mother. What the hell can he offer me? He seems smart, but that can be deceiving as well.

Calvin noticed the daze in my eyes and I had to snap myself back into the reality of sitting on my sofa in my living room with an eighteen-year-old boy listening to Phyllis Hyman.

"What are you thinking about?" he asked.

I looked him in his eyes. "Just thinking. I'm going through a lot right now." I began to elaborate about everything going on in my life—from my job, to breaking up with Troy, to being alone in this cold, cold world.

"Well, you're not alone," he interrupted. "I know how it feels. Even though I only work at McDonald's, my job gets on my nerves, and I have bills too."

"What do you mean?" I asked him.

"I have a cell phone bill and I have to buy my own clothes and shoes sometimes plus take care of my son."

I looked at him and told him how I wish I was in his shoes. Shit, if I still lived with my mom I would have no worries and no bills. I wouldn't have to worry about anything at all.

I am a mama's boy all the way. I love my mom and at times I wish I had never moved out. I have been living on my own since I graduated college.

"Man, listen, you don't have anything to worry about, your mother takes care of you," I schooled him. "By the way, what does she do?" I asked, still letting the sweet sounds of Phyllis vibrate through my ears.

"She does hair. She has her own salon set up in our house."

"Oh, OK, that sounds cool."

"Yeah, but she doesn't make that much because she doesn't have a license so she can't promote the business the way she wants to," he said as his eyes met the floor.

"Well, Calvin, like I said, you're still young and you still have some growing up to do so live your life and take things slowly."

We talked until about three in the morning. I knew I couldn't keep him out any longer; he was still under his mother's roof and needed to respect the household. I wished he could spend the night because I hadn't been held in so long. I needed a man to comfort me, even if it was only for one night. We gathered our coats from the closet. I raised the dim lights in the living room as we proceeded out the door.

While waiting for the car to heat up, I switched the radio to Power 99. Calvin was staring out the window at the other cars that filled the parking lot, then he turned to me.

"What do you think about me?" he abruptly asked.

I hadn't even thought of that yet. "I think you are a very nice person, very young at heart, and also smart for your age."

"Well, would you want to be in a relationship with me?"

"Well, personally I think you are too young for me." I really didn't want to let him down, but I had to think about the situation. He is sexy, but just too young for me. I pulled off, listening to him talk about his past relationships with several people. A lot was beginning to go through my mind. I felt a rumbling noise on the front right wheel of my car. Maybe it was just the excess snow on the ground.

"A'ight, let me ask you the same question. What do you think about me so far?" I said as we approached Interstate 76.

"Well, I think you're extremely handsome, sexy, and not to mention intelligent. Also, I think we would make a dynamic couple."

I smiled as I continued to focus on the road ahead. Knowing that he thinks I'm sexy, I will never let him see my fat-ass body naked.

While driving back to his parent's house in Mt. Airy, all I could think about was how I was gonna get my bills paid without any money. I rolled the window down, letting the wind hit my face while doing 80 m.p.h. on the expressway. Calvin's head was bobbing to the music. I glanced at the clock, which read 3:27 a.m. I slowly approached his block and pulled in front of his house.

"I had a nice evening," he said, smiling.

"So did I."

# Smoking Cigarettes

He got out of the car and let me know that he would call me tomorrow. I sat and watched him walk toward his house. Suddenly, he turned around and started coming back toward the car.

"Would you like a kiss?" he asked.

My mind froze. Sure, hell, why not? I thought to myself as I positioned my lips for a kiss. His lips slightly touched mine. The kiss was cordial—it was the first kiss on our first date. I smiled at him as he smiled at me. I watched him walk back toward the house before I pressed my foot on the gas pedal.

As I drove home letting the gusty night air hit my face, I summed up the whole evening's events. I wondered if he really liked me. He's too young. He probably won't call me anyway. Tonight was a nice night and he was such a gentleman.

I can say that he's more of a man than all the maniacs that I'm used to dealing with. I'm tired of boys who want to be faggots all their lives, running up and down 13th Street—a stroll in the Center City part of Philadelphia where there are a lot of gay clubs and what not. That is the street where I met Sean, Mike, Dwayne and Troy. Sean was a cutie. I always had a crush on him. He stood about 5'11" and 165 pounds, with a pretty caramel complexion. I loved to kiss his lips. He made me feel special. We met while Kevin and I were walking to the pizza store. Sean had asked his sister to ask me what my name was because he wanted to holla.

Yes, I do regret even giving that nigga the time of day. About two weeks into dating he decided he wanted to have a threesome with me and another boy. Now, that shit I was not having. Then, there was Mike. He was sexy but dumb as hell. Mike was brown-skinned with a low haircut and about 5'11" and 175 pounds. He had a lazy eye, but obviously his eye wasn't that lazy because he had it on everyone except me. I had to beg him to take me out, and when he finally did, all hell broke loose. I asked this nigga to take me to Six Flags. He finally took me after about twelve times of me asking him. I also had to pay for it. Once we arrived, he decided to dump me, and then had a nerve to want to ride back in the same car with me. Now, if I was a shitty individual I would have let his ass walk or let him get home the best way he knew how.

Dwayne was my cup of tea. He was a true THUG. I love me some roughnecks.

Dwayne had brown skin, and just looking at his braids made my dick hard. He had the juiciest lips. I just knew that it would not be an easy task for me to win him. He had all the cunt boys on his dick. I couldn't even imagine how it would be if we ever hooked up. I came to realize that this chocolate cutie was too rough for me. He had two children and beat up his mother and his lovers on the regular. I could not even be in a ring with him. Whenever I saw him out, no matter how many times, I'd smile at him. He'd look at me one second then turn his head the next.

I have known Dwayne for about a year now, but last November one of my friends called me from his house. I saved the number to my caller ID, then had Drew call him for me. The next day Drew spoke with him over the phone. He told Dwayne that I had a crush on him and then Dwayne wanted to know who I was. Once we exchanged numbers I could not believe what was happening. What would I do with a nigga like him? He was extremely sexy and a true thug. I wanted to be down with him in every way. He invited me to his house to see who I was. I knew I should have worn a shirt that didn't reveal the true size of my stomach. I guess he didn't like what he saw. We had a conversation that lasted about two hours; I thought we were hitting it off.

Maybe I was asking him too many questions. He probably thought I was Wendy Williams the way I was drilling him. After our conversation I went home and he told me he would call later. Well, to make a long story short, I haven't heard from him since. I was mad as hell because I really needed a man like him in my life, a man to hold me, embrace me, and protect me.

Last, but not least, Troy. I fell in love when I first laid eyes on him. We met on 13th Street in July 2001. It was the day before his 21st birthday, and a mutual friend of ours invited us to go to Six Flags with him and his friends. All I needed to know was that Troy was going and I was there. He was the sweetest thing and had the most precious smile I'd ever seen.

At the park I had the time of my life. There was me, Kevin, Troy, Chris, Demetrius, and Jamal. Even though Troy was shorter than me, his personality was taller than the both of us. After we left the park I called him the following evening. We talked all night long, and after we got off the phone at eight in the morning, he came to my apartment so we could hold each other and sleep. I just laid on his chest, hoping that he could make things better. When I met him, I had just quit my bullshit data entry job.

I inhaled as he exhaled and I could smell the scent of cigarettes on his breath. I hated that scent but I opened my eyes and looked up at his dark face and smiled as I held him tighter. I wanted that man. I had chosen him.

Throughout the time Troy and I dated, we started to realize that our viewpoints on life were completely different.

Plus, although I never felt insecure about him, I wondered why he spent so much time out of town. I started to question him after he went to Atlanta two weekends in a row and never stopped to think that I would want some of his weekend time. Even when he asked me if I minded him going, and I told him yes, he went anyway. I had called his house numerous times thinking that he was running errands or something, but the whole time I was calling, he was in

Atlanta. I waited patiently for his return.

It was Labor Day weekend so that made the weekend even longer. By Monday he still wasn't back. By Tuesday he called to let me know that he was back and was very tired from his long train ride from Atlanta. He said he would call me later. He made it seem like everything was OK even though he had defied my wishes and had also lied. I let him have his rest but we damn sure were gonna talk about it later.

As I lay there that evening in bed, I realized it was eleven o' clock and Troy hadn't called back yet. My adrenaline began pumping faster and faster through my veins. Blood was beginning to rush to my head. I jumped up and threw on any piece of clothing in my path and then ran out the door to my car. My heart pounded and words came out my mouth like a madman on crack. *I'm gonna fuck him up!* I repeated to myself as I drove to his house in South Philly.

The air was dark and all I could think of was this nigga was trying to play me. I had enough brains to park my car around the corner and not on his block, just in case he tried to mess up my car. I stepped out the car, then called him from my cell phone and told him to meet me at the door. Once inside, I sat on his sofa. He sat across from me staring into my eyes, asking me what was wrong. When I didn't say a word he ran upstairs to his room then closed the door. In less than ten seconds I was standing on the opposite side of the door telling him to open it. He declined.

I really wasn't feeling this moment at all and from the sound of his voice, neither was he. "Go home and calm down, then we can talk," he had said.

"I'm not going anywhere until you open the fucking door!" I said in a rage. I had my fist balled up tight. I continued to yell as I heard him light a cigarette from the other side of the door. Within a matter of seconds we both got quiet.

"Are you calm now?" he asked, while inhaling the smoke from the cigarette.

"Yes, Troy, I'm calm. You know if I really wanted to I could just break the door down and get you," I said right before he exhaled the smoke. I led him to believe that I was calm.

"I know because it's not that hard to do," he said, opening the door as I swung my right fist into his eye. The cigarette he had been holding flew, his body dropped to the floor. I could not believe what I had just done. I turned around and walked back to my car, hoping that Troy would follow behind me. I turned around and no one was there. I got in my car then called Drew on his cell phone. I cried all the way home. Drew tried to calm me down but it wasn't any use.

He couldn't believe what I had done either. Troy was my baby, so how could I have put my hands on him? I had asked myself that over and over again.

As I approached my apartment complex, I thought about my night with Calvin and I had a sudden joyfulness in my heart. I skipped all the way to my apartment and ran inside to call Kevin, but since it was so late I decided I'd just talk to him tomorrow.

A little after 7:30, the phone rang. Who in the hell could be calling so early in the morning? I thought to myself as I rolled over in the bed. I grabbed the phone off the base.

"Hey," someone said. I realized it was Calvin. I leaned back on a pillow and grabbed the remote control to turn on the TV. "I don't feel too well," he said.

"What's wrong?"

"My stomach hurts real bad and I've been spitting up all morning."

I smiled. Out of all people, he called to tell me that he was sick so I could go to his house and take care of him.

"Do you need me to bring you anything?" I asked, hoping he'd say yes.

"Yeah, can you bring me some ginger ale?"

"Yeah, but I have to run some errands first, then I'll be there, OK?"

"OK."

I had to visit a few of my family members before I could see Calvin. I still hadn't gotten my Christmas presents from my grandparents so I decided to go visit them and see how much money they had to offer.

Ever since I was a child my grandmother always gave me a card with money in it for Christmas. Now that I am an adult nothing has changed. I needed all the help I could get for my rent. I thought about what I was going to wear for the day. I decided on my tan Dickies. I knew that outfit would complement my tinted glasses. I went to my aunt's house first, then to the store to buy a small sandwich before going to grandma's. I sat in her kitchen and ate my sandwich. I could not get Calvin off my mind. All I could think of was his sexy persona. I thought I'd give him a call. He was not feeling any better. *My baby is sick*, I said under my breath. I knew I had to take him some ginger ale. My grandfather was talking on the phone and my grandmother was asleep when I left. I walked out the door and into the cold air. After visiting my grandparents I had collected a total of $10.

I was glad I was going to see Calvin. I was getting away from my problems for a while. I got in my car and turned on Ja Rule. I wondered if Calvin would be in bed. Did he know how to fuck? All those thoughts raced through my mind. I approached his house and he met me at the door in a pair of Scooby-Doo pajama pants, plush terry-cloth robe, and slippers. I was happy to see him.

"Are you OK?" I asked.

"Naw, my stomach still hurts a little, but it should be OK now that you're here." It was time to make my entrance and meet his family. I walked through the double doors and to the right of me was a wall full of pictures—Calvin when he was younger, pictures of him and his mother, and a sharp picture of him and some girl on a prom. I walked into the living room where there was a black piano and more pictures. I immediately knew that whoever had decorated the house had very good taste. I started walking toward the dining area where his entire family was sitting at a huge table.

"Hello," everyone said as a big happy fucking family. I looked at each one of them with a smile. In the room were his mother, his grandmother, his aunt, and two of his younger male cousins. Over in the corner I saw a little playpen with a baby's tiny head coming through the end of a blanket. That must be Little Jon, I thought. Calvin motioned for me to have a seat. As I sat at the end of the table a dog jumped up from around my feet and ran into the kitchen with a small kitten following behind him.

"Cute dog," I said.

"His name is Shane," Calvin said.

"And, the cat's name?" I eyeballed him.

"His name is Patches." I shook my head obliging. His mother sparked up a conversation with me.

I really was not in the mood to be answering a lot of questions. Calvin's stepfather was walking around and seemed to make sure that he kept an eye on me. Calvin's mother asked me how old I was and I rebutted with a lie saying that I was twenty; twenty with my own apartment, a car, a college degree, and that make-believe good paying job I'd told her son about. Now, if she believed those lies, then she deserved all the dumb shit coming to her. Calvin ran upstairs to tell another one of his cousins to come down and meet me. When he returned, a tall skinny fellow followed behind.

"Ron, this is Rashad, and Rashad, this is Ron," Calvin said, introducing us.

Ron waved his hand in a shady hello. I watched him as he sat down in the chair across from me at the table. He was quite tall and dark-skinned. He also had long black hair with a streak of blond. He couldn't be any more than eighteen. Once he sat down, he just sat there with his arms folded.

"Y'all wanna play a game?" Calvin said in an outburst of energy. His grandmother smiled.

"I'm ready, what game are we going to play?" she asked with excitement. Calvin looked my way, asking me if I knew how to play *Greed*. I sat there totally confused. I never played that game before nor had I ever heard of it.

Throughout the rest of the evening we all shared a good time playing Monopoly. That was something I knew, and I was winning at it since I was cheating. Calvin's stomach was feeling much better until the baby woke up. His mother rushed over to the playpen as Little Jon started to squirm.

She picked him up and I could see his cute little face struggling to keep his eyes shut. I got up from the table and walked over to her, holding out my arms as I asked to hold the baby. I cuddled him in my arms as if he was my own. I looked down at his face wishing he was my child. I glanced over at Calvin to see if he was looking, he was. He smiled as if he knew what I was thinking.

I gave Jon back to Calvin's mother as he started to whine, and she stuck a bottle in his mouth then looked at me and winked. She was a light-skinned, pretty lady for her size. She was a little overweight but it wasn't anything that a little Slim Fast and a couple trips around the track couldn't cure.

It started to get late. Calvin's grandmother and aunt were getting ready to go home. Neither one of them had cars so they had to wait for a cab. After his mother took the baby up to her room the crowd that was in full effect when I first arrived was now dying down to the last people—Calvin, Ron, and me. After everyone left, Ron decided to go back upstairs to Calvin's room to use the computer.

"Would you like to come upstairs?" Calvin asked me. I didn't have anything else better to do.

"Sure," I responded. He led the way. I walked up the first flight of steps where his mother's room was. The hallway was very dark so I couldn't see that much. We passed by a bathroom and an extra room that was used as a storage place for clothes. We walked up a second flight of stairs that led to a guest room and a small space for the dog cage. He then led me to his room.

His room was no more than the average teenager's room. He had pictures of Lil' Kim on the wall, pictures of Angelina Jolie when she starred in *Tomb Raider*, and a whole lot of pictures and accessories of Scooby-Doo. I stood there for a while just looking around. Ron sat at the computer chatting with people in the chat room. I walked over and stood behind him, recognizing the screen names of the people he was chatting with. Ron was slightly feminine, but no more feminine than Calvin. I backed up and sat down on the bed watching Calvin teach Ron how to get in and out of the different chat rooms. When Calvin removed his robe and went to turn on the TV, I noticed that his back was skinned. He turned around and asked me what I was looking at. He explained that he had had a skin graft operation where the doctor had removed his skin from his back to put it on his burned areas. I shook my head from right to left, recalling his girlfriend's abuse, and wondering how someone could do such a thing to another human being.

Calvin came and sat next to me. I leaned back on the bed while unbuttoning the top button of my Dickie's shirt because it started to get warm. Ron turned around and looked then turned back around. Calvin slid off his slippers, and then lay back beside me.

"Come here," he demanded. I smiled at him as he grabbed me and leaned me over so that I could lie on his chest.

I moved over a little closer as I glanced up at the TV, which sat on top of his dresser, and noticed Jenny Jones. Before we got too comfortable he got up and turned off the light before lying next to me. I kicked my timbs off and began watching the first segment of the show. It was about ladies with big breasts, a show I didn't particularly want to see. By the end of the first segment and before the Sprite commercial came on, Calvin's tongue was in my mouth. He grabbed the back of my head like he wanted to eat my entire face. But hell, I sure wanted to eat his. By the time the commercial ended, we were under the covers, laughing. Ron turned around when the Scooby-Doo phone started ringing.

"Hey, Scooby, what's that noise?" Shaggy called out. That was the cutest thing. Calvin jumped up to answer it.

Ron got up to stretch, then gave a brief yawn.

"I'ma 'bout to go to bed," he said, looking at me and smiling. He walked past Calvin who was still on the phone and then proceeded down the hall to the guest bedroom. Calvin hung up the phone.

"Damn, he didn't even shut my computer off," he said in disgust. I pulled the covers up to my chest while looking at Calvin as he walked over to the computer. He shut the system down and came to bed.

"Do you think your moms gonna say sumthin' about me stayin'?"

"If she didn't say anything yet, then she must have forgotten that you were here, so let's just go to sleep," he responded with a sense of wisdom. I like that in him. He got under the covers and I laid my head on the top part of his chest then closed my eyes. Before I knew it, he was snoring, and so was I.

# Smoking Cigarettes

The sun awakened me on this bright Sunday morning. I was still lying on Calvin's chest. This was the beginning of a new month and rent was due immediately. I didn't know where I was gonna get the money.

I needed to stay calm. I was in the arms of a guy who I admired, so I should just make the best of it. I rubbed his chest, but it seemed like the more I rubbed the louder his snores got. I rubbed, and rubbed, and rubbed. I could see a bulge in the genitalia area of his pajama pants. I lifted the top of his pants and the elastic of his boxer briefs. I saw his dick just lying on top of his fresh pubic hair. The head looked like a ripe mushroom and I couldn't wait to have that inside of me.

My mouth started to water, I wanted to taste him bad but I didn't want him to wake up. I let go of the elastic and it snapped back to his skin. I sat up as his eyes opened.

"Wake up, sleepy head," I said, as he rolled over to face the window just as the phone rang. He jumped up and ran over to answer it as I swung my legs out the bed. It was his mother calling from church. I didn't think she realized I was still there until Calvin told me she said it was OK since his cousin was there also. Calvin went into the other room to feed the dog. Ron came into the room and sat down on the bed.

"Did you have a nice sleep?" he asked with a sarcastic smirk on his face.

"It was cool." I smiled back at him. He began going through Calvin's dresser drawers looking for something to wear. He pulled out a pair of tan pants from the Gap. Calvin hurried back into the room, grabbing the pants from him.

"You didn't bring back the last pair of pants that you borrowed," Calvin said. The both of them stood there debating back and forth about a pair of pants. I looked over at the clock on the VCR and decided it was time for me to go. I stood up and walked over to the dresser. I looked at myself in the mirror and noticed a picture stuck in the mirror's frame of Calvin and his friends. I pulled the picture off and stood there staring at it. It was Calvin, his cousin Dontae, and a petite, slim girl. Calvin came up behind me looking over my shoulder.

"That's Little Jon's mother, Camisha," he said. I carefully studied the picture of their smiling faces standing next to a tree. Calvin wore a pair of blue jeans and a white sleeveless shirt with his cell phone clipped on his belt. He was holding a shopping bag. Dontae was a much chubbier, light-skinned brother, and he had a curly Afro. He wore a white T-shirt and was carrying a gray backpack. The girl seemed bigger than both of them. She had a chocolate complexion and wore a black blouse with the top buttons undone, showing her mere cleavage. She sported dark sunglasses.

"Can I have this?" I asked. Calvin looked down at the picture, then at me.

"Go 'head, you can keep it." I pushed the picture into my back pocket.

"Well, I gotta go," I said, reaching for my coat.

"Yeah, before my mom gets back from church."

"I thought she didn't mind that I spent the night."

"Yeah, but if you're gone when she gets back then it won't be such a big deal. Besides, it won't seem like you're wearing out your welcome." We both laughed. I started walking down the two flights of steps with Calvin following behind. I got to the door, then turned around.

"It was fun," I said, looking into his young eyes.

"Thank you for bringing me the soda, playing the games with us, and spending the night...that was unexpected," he replied, as he stared back into my eyes. We smothered one another with wet kisses then I turned and walked out the door.

I warmed up my car then turned onto I-76 east, proceeding home. By the time I reached my apartment a load of depression came upon me. I walked in and threw off my coat. I noticed that the red light on the caller ID was not blinking. I picked up the cordless phone and dialed *69 and got no response. That's how I knew that my non-basic service had been suspended. How could I live without my caller ID, three-way calling, and my call waiting? I hadn't paid my bill in months.

I knew that it would be just a matter of time before the basic service would be cut off too. I hated having a welfare line! If people called and got a busy signal, they would really know I was having financial problems, and I have an image to uphold. I picked up the phone to call my grandmother. I needed money to pay my phone bill the quickest way I knew how, but to my luck no one answered. I sat at the foot of the bed and remembered the picture that was in my back pocket. I pulled it out and looked at it with a smile. I walked over to the mirror on top of my dresser and immediately found a place for it.

"I love you, Calvin," I said aloud with no one to hear but me, the furniture, and the walls in my apartment. Fuck that phone bill, I thought. I have a new friend now and I won't let anything steal my joy.

I stripped myself of my clothing, put Phyllis Hyman's CD into the disc tray, ran a hot bubble bath, and then sat in the tub letting the sweet sounds of *Betcha by Golly, Wow,* take me away. I had mixed feelings about the night I had before and how I was still so much in love with Troy. All the emotions that I was starting to feel for Calvin were all the feelings that were left over from Troy. I love Troy with all my heart and I didn't want us to be apart for anything in the world. I'm tired of living my life between men.

I just want to find a stable man to settle down with. Although Calvin is only eighteen, he has the mentality and the wisdom of someone my age and I don't want to let that go, but I think I have to because he's still too young. No matter what, I have to tell him that we can only be friends because I love Troy too much to let him go.

It wasn't meant to be this way. I had my whole life planned out—I was supposed to finish college, then go to medical school, and get my Ph.D.

Where the fuck did I go wrong? All my life it seems like I keep meeting these fucked up men that don't have anything going for themselves. I pray to the Lord every day for him to guide me; I need guidance in the worst possible way. I spent so much money on LA Weight Loss it's not even funny. I want my motherfuckin' money back. I didn't lose a pound; OK, maybe four pounds, but what the fuck. Am I supposed to lose a pound for every one hundred dollars I spend? I picked up the phone to call my mom, but before I had the chance to press the button the phone rang. It was Calvin.

"Wassup, sexy?" he said in a muffled voice. I smiled immediately. I was glad that he called while he was on his lunch break. He told me that he was thinking about me but he couldn't talk long. It was sad that the conversation was cut short because he was needed at the front register. I clicked him off the line and dialed Troy's number. He answered.

"What are you doing?" I asked as I listened to him let out a big sigh. My guilt got the best of me and I suddenly wondered if he would mention anything about Paul. If he didn't say anything about him, then neither would I.

"What do you want, Rashad?" he asked, sounding frustrated.

"I'm just calling to talk to you." I felt hopeless and didn't want him to hate me any longer so I ended the call.

I needed to think about my bills anyway. My mother was doing all that she could to help me with my rent. I came up with five hundred dollars—I borrowed three hundred from Kevin, and two from Shay-Shay.

# Smoking Cigarettes

I knew Calvin didn't want to see me down in the dumps and would love to lend me a helping hand, but being the person that I am, I couldn't take that boy's money. But when Calvin came to my house straight from school and looked into my eyes before placing his entire unendorsed check in my hand, I was undoubtedly grateful.

My eyes lit up with disbelief. Calvin was the man.

* * *

## Can't Knock The Hustle

"Well, that was nice of him to help you out," my mom said on her cell phone while driving to her doctor's appointment.

"I am so amazed by that," I continued.

"Well, how old is he?"

"I think he's twenty-two," there I go lying again. But whatever it took for me to be happy, my mom was all for it. Troy had never done this for me. Hell, he barely bought me dinner. But I thought we had something deeper. With Troy it was more than just the money and it was more than just the physical thing. We had a bond because we knew how it was to be broke.

But he really didn't treat me the way that I wanted to be treated. I hate men like that. I wasn't gonna give myself up to him although he wanted me to. I had my eyes on someone else and I still do. His name is Basil. Basil is sexy, and he's bowlegged. I wanted him for a while. I used to fuck with one of his friends back in the day, and now I want him. That's the whore inside of me that's just dying to come out. How do I know what love is? How do I know what it feels like to love or be loved? I realized that I'm not in love with Troy, I never was. I just lusted over his chocolate body and I refused to be by myself. I must don't know what love is because if I did I wouldn't be thinking anything about love for an eighteen-year-old boy. How could I love him and I haven't known him for a week?

I paid my rent, and the end of the week came quicker than I thought. Calvin called me early Friday morning wanting to see me this weekend. Fuck, he took the words right out of my mouth because as bad as he wanted to see me, I wanted to see him. I wasn't going to seem too obvious so I made him wait a couple of hours.

# Smoking Cigarettes

Now that I had paid my rent I needed some money in the worst way. I didn't have any materials to start my craft. That's a term that gay folks use to denote a form of hustle, or writing bad checks for that matter. It's an easy way for us to get money to live the high-maintenance life some of us exhibit. I wrote so many bad checks in my day that it wasn't funny. But now what?

What the fuck am I supposed to do for money? I had to think quickly.

It was early Saturday morning and Kevin and I were on a serious mission. I found a couple of spare checks lying around my apartment, so the plan was that we were gonna go to the check cashing place to see if we could cash them. They were all personal checks—I wrote one out for $800 and another one for $600. The first check-cashing place we arrived at was on Girade Avenue. Whatever it was I called myself doing, it wasn't working. My game was all wrong and that place was not having it. The next place we decided to go to was on Broad and Olney. We had to fill out these little blue cards so we could get on file with the company, but that didn't do anything but take up time. I wasted more gas and more money than making money. I was drained. We hopped in the car and I looked over at Kevin and he looked at me.

"Wha you looking at?" he asked, a smirk on his face. I looked at him in dismay.

"What are we gonna do now? I don't have any money and I still have other bills that I have to pay." I put the car in gear, turned up the radio and headed toward his house. Once in front of his door, he jumped out.

"Ah'll check you out later," he said, motioning to me. He slammed the door and I pressed my foot on the gas pedal and floored down Walnut Street. The sun was beginning to set. The drive to Calvin's house was slow and steady.

I approached his block then pulled into a parking

space behind his mother's van. Before getting out, I pulled down the visor from overhead to fix myself in the mirror, and then stepped out of the car. I wore a pair of gray sweatpants, a tan thermal shirt, and a pair of gray Pumas. I tried my best to suck in my stomach. I rang the doorbell then waited patiently for Calvin to open the door.

"Hello," he said, grinning from ear to ear. I smiled as I walked past him toward the dining area where I saw a lot of older ladies waiting to get their hair done. I waved at them as Calvin and I walked toward the kitchen where his mother was. I greeted her and she asked me if I was hungry. I answered no. I sat down at the kitchen table as his mother left to tend to her clients. Calvin poured a glass of cherry Kool-Aid, then came over to the table and sat across from me.

"Wassup?" I asked. He looked a little tense. I got up and walked around the table to massage his shoulders.

"That feels good, baby," he said, closing his eyes. I could tell that something was bothering him. I found out he had the same problem as me, money problems.

"Nigga, you live at home with your mom, what kind of money problems are you having?"

"My mom doesn't give me money for everything, that's why I have a job. She pays the bills and helps me take care of Little Jon, so I can't be asking her for any money, I buy my own clothes." I sat back in my seat and asked him for some of his Kool-Aid. I took off my jacket and he hung it up in the living room. When he cane back in the kitchen I had already drank half of his juice. He came and stood in back of me. I leaned back on his stomach.

"Let's go upstairs," he said.

I got up and before I could make a complete turn to face him, he grabbed me and pulled me close. I grabbed the back of his head and planted the biggest kiss on his full lips. He then turned around and walked toward the hall and I followed behind him, holding his hand. We walked up the two flights of stairs to his dark room. I walked over to the bed then turned around just as he threw me down and jumped on top of me. He was kissing and caressing my entire body. The scent of his cologne smelled so good. I tongued him down the same way he tongued me. He pulled off my shirt and started licking my hard nipples nonstop. I grabbed his head, motioning him to stay on beat as he reached for my pants. I tried to stop, but reality said go for it. He kissed my neck and ran his tongue up and down my earlobe. I had never been to ecstasy but I think I was on my way. After yanking my pants down to my ankles and sliding them off, he yanked the top of my boxers then slid them off too. My dick stood brick hard as he commenced to removing his shirt. I kissed his sweet neck and licked all over his chest as his body maneuvered on top of mine. I wondered where this eighteen-year-old learned these moves. He continued to suck my nipple while fingering the other. He then stuck his tongue so far in the back of my throat that I started to gag. He kissed my lips and my neck and worked his way down to my stomach. Laying flat on my back made my stomach look flat and I loved it.

He licked past my pubic hairs and stuck my dick in between his soft lips then tickled the head with his tongue. I arched my back while grabbing his head and jamming my dick into his mouth. After about five minutes, he began licking my inner thighs.

"Turn over," he said in a sexy voice. I was so glad that the lights were out because I didn't want him to see my body just yet. I turned over and grabbed the pillow and held it tight as he lay on my back and massaged my butt cheeks. I felt his tongue start at the top of my neck as he made circular motions to the bottom of my back. I gasped, I had never been so relaxed in my life. My mind was yelling, More! More! I turned over and grabbed my dick and jerked it as he licked my nipple. He then went back to massaging my dick with his ever so warm tongue. He started to deep throat me until I nutted all over his face, leaving my white mesh of cream hanging from his lips.

\* \* \*

"What are you doing next weekend, bitch?" Drew asked. He had called after I had gotten back home from Calvin's.

"I don't really know why? What do you have in mind?"

"Well, there is a ball at Paradise Island on Saturday, are you goin'?"

"I have to see what Calvin is doing."

"You still talkin' to that little boy?"

"Yeah, but I don't think that I'll get into a relationship with him because he is kind of young."

I let Drew know that my heart was still on Troy. It didn't seem to matter to Drew. As long as I was happy.

"I need to borrow forty dollars," I said to him in the midst of our conversation.

"Well, how are you going to get it?"

"I'll stop by and get it later on." It was never a problem to get money from Drew as long as I paid it back in a timely matter.

"Well, just call me when you're on your way."

"OK," I said, then hung up the phone. I had a job interview later that day at the credit union. I jumped in the shower then went into my room where my green Tommy Hilfiger khakis, green striped button-down shirt, and money-green tie laid stretched out on my bed. I walked over to my dresser and lotioned my body down. I looked into the mirror and noticed a pimple that was starting to grow on my forehead. I knew I had to make the best of the interview no matter what. The rain was coming down hard, but that was not gonna stop me from attending this open house. I always liked attending job fairs because it seemed like I always got a job through them.

After finding the place in the Greater Northeast area, I searched the parking lot for a space. I got out of the car as the rain poured over my face like my bathroom shower. I ran into the vestibule area of the building where four white men in suits were standing. I immediately saw a sign that read, "Job Fair This Way," with a black arrow pointing the way. I walked down the hall and into a room where about six people sat watching a video. I was greeted by an old, medium-sized white lady who had on a pair of cheap reading glasses. She pulled a clipboard with an application stuck to it from under the television stand and handed it to me. I sat down at the wooden table and began filling it out. It asked for more information than I was willing to give. But I needed a job so I had to go through the process. Once finished, the lady told me that someone was gonna be with me momentarily. As I waited I watched the stupid video repeat itself about how the credit unions were established back in 1960.

"Rashad Smith," a petite lady called my name in a professional tone. I stood up and grabbed my wet leather jacket to follow her as we walked down the hall to a small office. I sat down smiling from ear to ear as if I was enjoying her company as she glanced over my résumé. She looked and smiled.

"So, tell me about yourself," she said. I started talking about how articulate I am and so forth. I had to make it known that I was a very friendly person. I was applying for the teller's position so I had to appear like I was a people person. The interview lasted for about 25 minutes. She told me that she would call me within the next two days. I didn't want to get excited just yet because I still didn't have a job and her words were just that, words. I got into the car and turned on the radio. The rain seemed to have let up a little bit. I called Kevin.

"Hello," his mother answered.

# Reginald L. Hall

"Can I speak to Kevin?"

"He's not here, call him back later," she spoke as if she wanted to rush me off the phone. I threw my cell phone down on the seat and floored the car onto I-95. I was beat. Going to interviews always took a lot out of me. I rushed into the bedroom, took off my clothes, and hopped into bed. It was about three-thirty when Calvin awakened me with his phone call.

"Why are you not at work?" he asked. I forgot all about that stupid lie that I told him about having a job at one of my former places of employment, Bankruptcies Express.

"I got off early today because I didn't feel well."

"Aww, poor baby. Are you OK?" He flattered me with love.

"I'm OK, I'm just tired."

"Well, get some rest and I'll call you later, OK?" I put the phone down, turned over and then fell back to sleep.

* * *

"If this phone don't stop ringing!" I yelled out while grabbing it off the base.

"Hey, Rashad, it's Monica."

"Wassup, girl, wutz the deal?"

"I got a credit card number for you."

"Hol' up," I said as I scrambled around looking for a pen. "OK, read off the numbers." I jotted them down carefully.

"I'm still at work. I'll call you back later if I get some more," she said before hanging up the phone. Monica is a girl that I used to work with at the credit card company. She would call me from time to time with credit card information so I could process it to have a new card sent to a dummy address. I guess you can say she was my partner in crime. The same company that fired me was now gonna get a taste of what I can do. Little did they know that what goes around, comes around, and I didn't give a fuck any longer. I got up and went to 7-Eleven. I bought a bag of Doritos; a Snapple iced-tea; and a sausage, egg, and cheese biscuit. Later that night before I fell asleep, Calvin called.

"Hey, sexy," he said.

"Hey, boy," I said excitedly.

"I just called to say good night."

I thought that was rather thoughtful of him. "Yeah, I'm tired and I'm about to go to bed."

"OK, I'll just call you in the morning."

I hung up with a hard dick just from hearing his voice. I rolled over and turned off the light that sat on the nightstand and once again fell sleep. About 2 ½ hours later a sharp pain in my stomach awakened me. I felt dizzy. I held my stomach and ran into the bathroom where I sat down on the toilet holding my stomach until some action occurred, but nothing happened. I got up and went into the bedroom to call Calvin. Luckily he heard the phone through his hard sleep.

"Calvin, I don't feel well," I said gasping for air.

"What's wrong?"

"I don't know, my stomach hurts very bad." I looked down at my stomach and it seemed larger than usual.

"Well, did you go to the bathroom?"

"Yeah, but nothing came out."

"Well, just stay calm, do you need to go to the hospital?" he asked as I dropped the phone and ran back into the bathroom throwing up everything in my stomach. I sat on the side of the toilet trying to catch my breath. I picked up the phone where Calvin was holding patiently.

"Are you OK? What did you eat?"

"I bought some stuff from 7-Eleven earlier."

"Well, don't eat from that place anymore."

"Thank you for staying on the phone with me, Calvin," I said as I got my senses together.

"Don't worry about it, as long as you're OK. Let me get some sleep because I have school tomorrow," he said, before hanging up the phone. I placed the phone down on the sink and grabbed for the mop to clean up the mess that had missed the toilet.

I lay in the bed all day rubbing my stomach. Drew came over to cook me something to eat.

"Bitch, you should sue," he said.

"I knew you was gonna say something of that sort as a way for me to make money."

"That sandwich that you ate could have expired. Did you read the package before eating it?"

"No, but I should have. Man, I never felt that much pain before," I said, sipping the tea that Drew made for me. We sat at the kitchen table eating baked chicken with rice and gravy. One thing about Drew was that he always made it his business to make sure I was OK, no matter what. I enjoyed his company as we sat at the table and talked for hours. My throat was still sore from throwing up all that food.

"Well, are you going to the ball next Saturday or what?" he asked.

"Well, yeah, I'll go if I'm feeling better. How much does it cost?"

"It's free."

"OK then, I'm definitely going." I got up from the table and walked toward the living room just as the phone rang. "Drew can you get that for me please?"

He answered then told me it was the credit union. I went into the bedroom and picked up the phone.

"I have it!" I yelled to Drew.

"Hi, this is Mr. Moss calling from Sun Credit Union, and I would like for you to come in for a second interview."

# Smoking Cigarettes

"I would love to," I said, trying to sound chipper.

"Well, when is a good time for you?"

"Anytime that's good for you."

"Well, how about Monday at three?"

"Sure, I'll be there, and thank you so much." I hung up the phone and ran into the living room to share the good news with Drew.

"Biiittcchhh, you better get those coins, girl!" he said, giving me a high five. We both began to laugh as I sashayed back into the bedroom sporting a long, couture, Ralph Lauren robe.

The phone rang again and it was Calvin. I was happy to speak with him, but I would have been happier if it was Troy. Even though it was nice to have someone like Calvin in my life, Troy was the man I wanted. I sat back down on the bed as Calvin asked me if I was OK. He told me about his day at school and made sure he told me that he wanted to see me next weekend. I obliged, but Saturday I was booked because I had already given Drew my word that I would go to the ball with him. Drew left quietly after washing the dishes and cleaning the entire kitchen.

The rest of the night I made it my business to prepare my attire for the interview because I was destined to get this job. I couldn't imagine how life would be if I had to move back home with my mother. The house is very small and I don't even want to think about living there with my stepfather who I can't stand along with his bad-ass twin daughters. They are 12 years old and three minutes apart. I always said that when they get older they are going to be dykes. One day I caught them kissing another girl who lives on our street. They think they are ready to have sex, but the funny thing is, they don't wanna have sex with boys. They wouldn't know what a dick looked like if it fucked them. If I could help it, I would never move back to that hell hole my family calls a house. I have my peace here where no one can bother me, and thank the Lord I have my freedom.

* * *

"Mr. Smith, Mr. Moss will see you now," a gray-haired lady said in a sweet voice. I could tell she smokes cigarettes and drinks coffee—the brownness around her teeth looked disgusting. I grabbed my book bag and my jacket and followed her into this big room where I was asked to have a seat at a big wooden table that could seat twelve. After about five minutes a middle-aged white man came into the room bearing a great smile.

"Hi, Mr. Smith, I'm Mr. Moss," he said, shaking my hand with a masculine grip. Where were my manners? I didn't even give this man the grace of my standing to shake his hand when he entered the room. He sat in a chair directly across from me.

"Well, Well, Mr. Smith, I have heard a lot of great things about you," he began the conversation in the best way possible and then got down to business. He informed me that the starting pay would be $10.00 an hour upon completion of a background check. I sat very attentive to what he had to say. I had changed the last four digits of my social security number around on my application so hopefully I could get past the credit card fraud charge I caught last year while out shopping with my friend Tasha. By the time the interview was over I had him eating out the palm of my hands. I walked myself out the front door, all smiles. He said he would be getting back with me in a couple of days.

I waited by the phone for three days and the guy from the credit union hadn't called yet, so I called him, but of course I got the voice mail. I left a message and about one hour later he called me back. I was taking a nap so I didn't get the message until I woke up.

"Unfortunately, Mr. Smith, while running your

background we found some disturbing information that will deter us from hiring you. I do apologize, and good luck." I picked up the phone and dialed my mother just to get a busy signal. What was I gonna do for money now? The depression made me sick.

The phone began to ring.

"Hey, it's me. I was just calling to say good night." Calvin sounded sweet and serene. I mumbled the words good night as my head hit the pillow and I pressed the off button to fall back into my trance.

Later the next day the doorbell rang. It rang again. I opened the door to see my mother standing there, soaking wet.

"Why are you still sleep? It's after twelve o'clock," she said, rushing into the kitchen as she took off her wet coat.

"I don't have a job, and no way to pay my bills. It seems like the only fun and cheap thing to do nowadays is sleep." She placed her coat on the back of the kitchen chair, poured herself a glass of water, then sat down.

"I'm on my way to my doctor's appointment. I just stopped by to see what you were doing."

After drinking her water and placing her glass in the sink, she grabbed her coat.

"I don't have any money," I said to her as she went into her pocket and pulled out a twenty-dollar bill then placed it in my hand.

"You need a job," she said, while walking out of the door.

"Rashad Smith!" a stern voice hollered out from below. It was a FedEx carrier. He walked up the second flight of steps.

"Are you Rashad Smith?" he asked.

"Yes," I said as he handed me a pen to sign on the dotted line. It was an envelope from the credit card company I used to work for. I opened it as I walked back into my apartment and closed the door behind me. It was my final check in the amount of $175. My frown suddenly turned upside down as I rushed into the bedroom to find something to slip into so I could run to the bank. I remembered that Drew said that the ball was tomorrow. Now that I had some money I was definitely going. I jumped in my car, ignoring the drizzling rain, and sped off to Kevin's house first. I beeped the horn three times before he appeared in the doorway carrying his black vest.

"Hey, mon," he said cheerfully, as he got into the car. I drove down Walnut Street toward the bank, and then to the barbershop to get a haircut because I wanted to look like new money. I decided to try out a new barber since the one I would normally go to was closed. Monica called my cell phone to tell me that she had received the credit card and it was time to head to the mall. My face lit up with joy. I told her that I would see her later this afternoon, as a tall brown-skinned man motioned for me to get in his chair.

I walked over, leaving Kevin still sitting in his seat as I sat in the barber's chair. I imagined being in the bedroom with this guy as he began shaping me up with the clippers. As the music began to play we both chuckled to the lyrics of the new song, *My Neck, My Back.* I sat there watching him shape me up as he licked his top lip, leaving his pink bottom lip free to my imagination. Before I knew it, he was done. He waved the mirror in front of my face so I could check out my new do. I stepped down and handed him a ten and a five as I turned around and reached for my coat. I motioned for Kevin to come on as we walked past the Jamaican barbers snickering at how cunt we were. I dropped off Kevin at his house so I could go home to take a shower.

I spent ten minutes in the shower letting the extra hot water tap my body. I put on some lotion very quickly just so I could be on time to meet Monica at the Gallery. I hopped in my car then drove down to Center City where I parked in the mall garage.  I noticed Monica standing there with her brother and her girlfriend.  I walked over to her and gave her a hug while she introduced me to her little entourage.  She went into her pocket and pulled out a Platinum Visa card that was issued to Mary Stevens.  I smiled, snapped my fingers and said let's go.

The first stop was Total Sport on the second level of the Gallery, we racked up on all the fitted hats.  Then we walked over to Strawbridge's, where we each bought two Rocawear sweat suits and an unlimited supply of jeans and sweaters 'til our hearts were content.  We walked over to Footlocker where I was gratefully gifted with two pairs of Air Force Ones and a pair of all-white Air Force 2s.  Monica engaged in a pair of Dolce & Gabbana boots and shoes and her girlfriend splurged on Ralph Lauren Polo jeans.  We all walked over to Dr. Denim, where she treated her brother to a pair of Timberland boots and you know I couldn't leave that store without getting a pair too.  We all walked back to the garage to drop off the bags.  My cell phone rang, it was Calvin.  I cheerfully answered the phone.

"Guess what, I'm in the Gallery.  Do you want anything?" I asked him.

"Just get me what you think I should have," he said as I hung up the phone.  We began walking toward Kmart where I racked up on underwear, T-shirts, and socks.  I also bought my mother a camera since her birthday was coming up.  My feet were starting to get tired but that didn't stop my show.  We walked down to the Net shop where I purchased a pair of Girbaud jeans for Calvin and me.  And, to my surprise, while I was getting on the elevator, Shay-Shay was getting off.

"What are you doing here?" she asked excitedly.  She knew exactly what was up.  "Well make sure you get me a pair of Timberlands, a size nine."

She made it known what she wanted and walked me

to Lady Star shoes to get it. It started to get late and the stores were beginning to close. My feet were aching and my hands were tired from carrying so many bags. We decided to call it a night and start back up in the morning at the Cherry Hill Mall. I threw all my bags into the trunk and sat down behind the steering wheel as I threw a Destiny's Child CD into the player. I drove through the night listening to *Survivor* and thinking about Calvin. Within about a half an hour I found myself pulling up in front of his door. From his doorway, he watched me get out the car. I walked toward him and placed a soft kiss upon his juicy lips.

I walked past him and sat down in the living room. I noticed that there wasn't any noise.

"Where's your mother?" I asked.

"She works part-time at night cleaning the bank. Come upstairs," he said, taking my jacket and placing it on a hanger. I walked up the two flights of steps to his bedroom. When I turned around he was shoving his tongue down my throat. I grabbed his hard dick and started stroking it through his school uniform pants. I started kissing his neck then moved down to his chest. I licked over his belly button and began to unbuckle his belt. The musk from that area and the smell of his cologne signified heaven to me. I pulled his dick out through the hole of his Scooby-Doo boxers and began licking it up and down as I seductively kissed the head. His dick was long and fat and it graced my mouth lovely as I was being fed my meal of the day.

He then lifted his dick over the elastic part of his boxers as I began tasting him some more. He grabbed the back of my head and began pumping his dick into my mouth. His round knob tapped my tonsils as I gasped for breath between pumps. His balls hung just right as they tapped against my chin and wiggled with every stroke. He began forcing himself into my mouth harder and harder.

# Smoking Cigarettes

"You gonna let me nut in your mouth?" he asked, as I shook my head obliging. He pumped his long dick repeatedly into my warm mouth and after about five more strokes he let out a great deal of teenage cum into my mouth as I grabbed his butt and pulled him in closer while he ran his fingers through my hair. He backed up with semen dripping off his dick looking like he could have taken a picture for a porno flick.

I got up off my knees and began staring into his eyes. He kissed my lips one last time before going to the bathroom to clean himself off. I sat down on the bed and gazed at the pictures that hung around his room. I then thought about the bag of clothes that I had for him in my trunk.

"I'll be right back, I have to go get a bag out of my car," I said to him as I ran down the steps. By the time I got to the door his mother was pulling up in the van. I walked out to my car waving at his mother and getting the bag from the trunk.

"How are you, Miss Linda?" I sang cheerfully, as I helped her out of the van.

"I'm fine. Is Calvin in the house?"

"Yeah, he's upstairs changing his clothes because we're about to go to the movies." We walked in the house and I went back upstairs to check on Calvin.

"I bought you a pair of jeans," I said, entering the room to see Calvin in his boxers. The burns on his legs looked awful and I couldn't believe I was actually falling for him. "What movie are we gonna go see?"

"Well, we should go see *Orange County*, I heard it was funny," he suggested. Just then the phone rang. "Can you get that please."

I picked up the phone, and it was his cousin Ron.

"What are ya'll doing?" he asked.

"Calvin and I are about to go to the movies."

"To see what?"

"*Orange County*, why, wassup?"

"Because I'm bored and I don't want to stay in this house tonight. You don't have any friends that I could double date with?"

"Well, let me call around and then we'll call you back, OK?" I hung up the phone. The first person that came to mind was Kevin, but I knew he didn't have any money, so the second person that came to mind was Drew. I dialed his number.

"What are you doing?" I asked as I watched Calvin get dressed. I was horny enough to go a second round. "Would you like to double date with me and Calvin with his cousin Ron?" Drew said yes. I immediately called Ron back and told him to meet us at City Hall in an hour. After I stood there looking at the fine dick that this boy had on his body, I had no other choice but to meet Drew and Ron after Calvin and I went a second round.

## Oops

I don't know why I was spending money like I have a job. There was barely any gas in my car and now I was going to the movies knowing that would cost about $15 for the both of us plus popcorn, soda, candy, and all that shit. First, we all went to a party given by one of my former coworkers.

Calvin could not contain himself with the liquor. He might have only been eighteen but he had a lot of age with him. After he had more than his share, he told me that he and his family would be moving out of their house because they couldn't afford to keep it. I could very well relate because my family had to move into a much smaller house after they couldn't afford to make the payments either. We left the party and arrived at the movie theater where I paid for the tickets for Calvin and me, and Drew paid for the tickets for himself and Ron.

"It's about time you paid for sumthin," Calvin said sarcastically.

"Shut up," I told him as I grabbed his hand. We walked into the semi-full theater. Once the lights went dim, Calvin and I went at it. Our lips met once again as we tongued each other down not paying attention to the opening credits. We held hands through the entire movie. I felt very close to him. Close enough to think I was falling in love.

\* \* \*

"That movie was funny as hell," I said to Kevin the next day on the phone while getting myself ready for the ball. I began telling him about my session with Calvin. "And I would like to know how did his dick get so big?"

"Well, I ain't know," Kevin said, doubting.

"Well, I don't know if I can be with him for long anyway."

"Why is that?"

"Because I think I'm still in love with Troy, and besides, his legs are burned and that scares me."

"What you mean, it scare you?" he said, chuckling.

"I mean that I love to look at guy's legs. Now how can I look at his legs in the summertime?"

"Well, you gonna have to get ova it. You get used to it as time passes. Just when you hah the chance to start touching it more, then you get used to it."

"Well, I don't think that is sumthin' that I can overlook."

"You be fine."

"OK, well let me finish getting myself together so I can be ready when Damien gets here," I said before hanging up the phone. I slid my legs into the pants of my velour Rocawear sweat suit that I bought from the Gallery yesterday and slipped on an oversize gray shirt. I also wore a pair of high-top Air Force Ones. I looked at myself in the mirror and blew a kiss as I heard Damien's horn beep downstairs.

Damien and I met four years ago in college. He moved to Philly after graduation and he loved to go to balls, never missing any of them. I darted out into the parking lot and into the jeep that Damien purchased off my back when I was crafting very heavy. We drove all the way to North Philly to the L & J Hall where the ball was being held. I saw Troy looking very sexy. He was there and ready to be judged for one of the face categories.

"Wassup, Rashad?" he said walking toward me with a pair of Christian Dior sunglasses on looking like an ebony male escort. I licked my lips completely. I stood there smiling in his face wanting and wishing badly that I could give him a kiss.

# Smoking Cigarettes

I leaned over and whispered in his ear, "Meet me tomorrow at Penns Landing on the top pier at three o'clock." He looked deeply into my eyes and said OK. My heart pounded with suspense. I really wanted to know if he was gonna meet me there or was he just saying that so I would get out of his face. I'm tired of living in this world by myself. If Troy meets me tomorrow I will flip the script and propose to him this time, even though I don't have any money or a ring, and no matter how much my feelings grow for Calvin, my heart will always beat for Troy.

By the time we walked into the hall, the ball was starting and the whole House of Prestige was taking center floor for the runway. I was not amazed to see many members of the house wearing black, but what I was amazed to see were the naked bodies that were displayed. I mean these boys were showing it all—their chests, six-pack bellies, and of course their dicks. That just had the crowd of faggots watering from the mouth and I must say I was one of them.

I walked around and stood on the side as Damien went to the front and posted his video camera, hoping not to miss one shot. It seemed like all the boys were wearing the same thing: cowboy boots, tight jeans, big buckle belts, and sunglasses. I stood there with my hands in my pockets watching the boys walk down the runway. People I met down 13<sup>th</sup> Street were now starting to come over and greet me with hugs and handshakes. I stood there for about thirty minutes watching members from different houses vogue down the runway. I was still thinking about what I was gonna say to Troy when Drew approached me.

"Bitch, did you see how good Dwayne looks tonight?"

"Where?" I asked anxiously.

"Ova' there, look dummy."

I moved my eyes to focus in on him and there he was standing there with a white T-shirt looking fine as hell.

His braids were done just right to catch my attention and others. Before I knew it he was coming toward me. The closer he got the faster my heart beat. I started to smile and before I knew it he turned to his left and gave someone a hug, then sat down.

Damn, I thought to myself. My legs were starting to hurt, and after standing in the same position all night, it was time for me to sit down. Some guy named Irvin was more than happy to offer me his seat and I sat down like the real cunt that I am.

The ball was just about over and I made it my business to be the first one out the door before the fight started between the House of Rodeo and the House of Karon. I dashed to the jeep with Damien and Drew following right behind me. The whole ride home I wondered if the plan that I had all wrapped up for tomorrow was actually gonna work. I sat silently while Damien and Drew laughed and recapped tonight's events. By the time I got home I found that Calvin had left numerous messages on the answering machine, which I ignored while I pulled out a pen and paper to write Troy a letter.

I thought of Troy, Calvin, and a little of Dwayne. I really need to have someone like Dwayne in my life, but I knew deep down this was not the time for him to be settling down with a wholesome person like me. I pulled off my shirt and pants then stood there in my navy blue boxers as I began rubbing my cool hands across my warm stomach. I exposed my dick through the slit of my boxers and began to stroke it back and forth before I went into the bathroom to get some Vaseline.

My blood felt like hot lava as it ran through the inside of my body. I walked back into my room and lay on the bed imagining what would it be like to have my dick in Dwayne's warm ass or what it would be like to have his dick in mine.

# Smoking Cigarettes

I licked my lips thoroughly while smoothly stroking my muscle. I put some more Vaseline on the head just to keep it slippery. Thoughts began to enter my mind about the boys I saw tonight at the ball. I began thinking of their rock hard bodies being in the same room with me or better yet the same bed. I'd put my tongue on every inch of their bodies to make sure I kept them wet. I started to stroke harder as I closed my eyes and thought about the times I could have had sex with Dwayne in his apartment. I knew if I had, he would have put it on me so hard that my body would have quivered.

My mind switched gears and I thought about Calvin kissing my neck and licking on my nipples. I squeezed my dick tighter and rubbed my balls. I took my hand and began fondling my nipples as all my blood rushed to the head of my dick and I exploded all of my tenseness onto my stomach. I laid my head back on the pillows while still staring at the cream dripping from my dick down to my balls. I rested myself on the bed for about five minutes before getting up and washing myself off. I walked back into the room and began my letter to Troy.

*Dear Troy,*

*I have missed you so much, and these past couple of months have been hell without you. I hope that...*

Before I knew it, I had fallen fast asleep.

* * *

I almost slept the entire day away. I jumped up and grabbed my cell phone from the charger and called Monica. I was surprised she hadn't called to wake me up.

"Wassup, who is this?" I said rudely into the cell phone.

"This is Cynthia. Wassup, Rashad."

"Is Monica there?"

"Sure, hold on," Cynthia said before putting the phone down.

I sat on the phone still wiping the sleep out of my eyes and stabilizing my balance.

"Yeah, wassup?" Monica asked excitedly as she got on the phone.

"Why didn't you call me so we could go to the mall?"

"Because I had to do something for my mom today. Did you go to the gas station to check the card to see if it works?"

"No, I'm gonna try it later on and then I'll give you a call back." I hit the end button on the phone. If I could fill up my tank with the credit card with no problem then I was home free, the card still worked. I should have been on top of my game and woke up a little earlier.

I looked over at the alarm clock and it was already twelve-thirty. While doing my morning routine the thought of Troy popped into my mind. I broke into a cold sweat as the phone began to ring.

"Wassup, shawty?" Calvin said in one of his sexy yet masculine voices. I rolled my eyes in the back of my head and mumbled hello into the phone. "I called you last night to say good night but you weren't home, so I left you a message."

"Yeah, I got it but I didn't call you back because when I came in from the ball it was too late. What are you doing today?"

"Well I'm supposed to be helping my mother pack today and my aunt is coming over to help. I really want to see you today. Do you want to meet up when I'm done?"

"I have something to do but after that I can call you and we can take it from there."

"All right, so call me later on."

"OK."

I ended the call and threw the cordless phone on the bed. I thought about all those cute-ass boys I saw at the ball last night. It had me in a frenzy. I went through my closet to lay out the clothes I was going to wear for the day. I decided on a blue-and-white jersey and a pair of light-blue Girbaud jeans that I bought two days before.

What if I ask Troy to consider being back in a relationship with me and he says yes? What am I gonna do with Calvin? Well, he is too young for me anyway so we can always be friends.

After I got dressed, my mother called.

"Rashad, I need you to go get Brian for me." Brian was my two-year-old nephew. I breathed heavily because I just knew that I was cutting it close when it came to the time.

"OK," I said, looking at the alarm clock.

I ended the call, grabbed my sneakers, and then rushed into the living room while stumbling to put them on. I grabbed my coat from the closet and began racing out the door. It was already a half past one and I still hadn't gone to the gas station to see if the credit card was still active or not. I jumped into my car and without letting it warm up I sped off in the direction of North Philly. I hoped that Brian's mother had him dressed and ready to go.

The day was so clear. I approached the house and saw Brian's head trying to see over the glass in the storm door. He opened the door smiling at me and while I didn't have any time to smile back, his mother grabbed him from behind and carried him to the car.

"You're a big boy now, you get to sit in the front seat," I said to him while assisting her with putting the seatbelt on.

"Thank you for coming to get him," she said, while running back to the doorway out of the cold.

"No problem," I said as Brian and I said our

goodbyes. I had to make it from North Philly back to Sharon Hill in less than thirty minutes. Now I knew that would take a miracle because I didn't know where I was going and I was already starting to get lost. I found my way to the expressway and hit it. My mother was waiting in the doorway to greet Brian because she knew that I was pressed for time. After dropping off Brian I continued down the street heading back to the expressway to meet Troy. The clock on my dashboard read 2:51. I reached into my coat pocket and pulled out two love letters that he had written me. I was gonna use them as bait to have him thinking of the times when we were both in love with one another to see if he remembered telling me that he loved me and it was me that really made him happy. I thought, he's probably not even gonna show and I'm wasting my time and gas that I don't have to drive all the way down to Penn's Landing. I stopped and waited at a traffic light.

I looked at the dash. The clock read 3:06. I pressed my foot on the gas when my cell phone began to play a Mickey Mouse tune. I answered it after noticing a strange number appear.

"Hello?" I answered.

"Where are you? I have been waiting out here in the cold for over ten minutes." I began to smile. It was Troy and he was waiting.

"I'm about five minutes away. Sit tight, I'm on my way."

Once I finally reached Delaware Avenue I had to search for a parking space. I ended up parking on a small street that was not too far from where I was meeting Troy. I walked down the cold street and up the steps to a bridge where there were three huge statues of children holding hands. For it to be as cold as it was, there were a lot of couples, mainly white, kissing and holding one another.

I walked and walked and there was no sign of Troy at all until I walked around to an area where he was sitting off to the side on a stone bench wearing a black vest with a long-sleeve shirt underneath, holding on to a book bag.

He sat there shivering while looking at me like he wanted to ask why I had asked him to come down here today. I nervously walked over and sat down beside him. I stared straight ahead not knowing what to say.

"It's cold out here," he said before I could spark up a conversation.

I looked at him then went into my pocket and pulled out the envelopes that contained the letters. I unfolded the letters and passed them to him.

"Do you remember when you wrote these to me?" He reached for the papers and let out a big sigh. Even though it was cold my underarms were beginning to sweat. He read a section of the letter and answered yes. I wondered why he looked sad. I prayed that he had not actually set me up with Paul that night and hoped he wouldn't bring it up.

"Well, do you still feel that way about me?" I asked to break the ice. "Do you still love me?" He sighed again. I nervously wondered what he was thinking.

"Rashad, I will always love you. Things have happened in my life and different events have occurred as to where I don't feel the same way I did when this letter was written."

"So you don't feel this way about me any longer?" I asked, hoping to get a different response. But before I gave him a chance to speak I began my spill. "I realize that I have done wrong and I am sorry for what I did. I love you and I want us to be together again." My hands were starting to get chilly. My cell phone rang and I didn't even bother to answer it. "I mean I wouldn't have asked you to come all the way down here today in the cold if I didn't mean any of it." It seemed like he wasn't going to say anything about that bitch-ass nigga Paul after all, and what he had set out to do. Since he hadn't heard from him, Troy should have known that I wouldn't cheat on him even though I did.

He looked ahead watching the birds fly down in front of him and huddle around a piece of bread.

"I'm cold, do you wanna go get some coffee or something, because it's too cold to be talking out here," he said after handing me both of the letters. We got up and began walking.

We walked two blocks toward South Street and found a small coffee shop called Xando's. A slender white hostess who greeted us led us to our table. I sat back in my chair as he ordered two chocolate Espressos for us.

"Thank you," I said, nodding my head toward him.

"No problem."

"So what was the real reason why you asked me to meet you down here today?" he asked while lighting a Newport.

"Well I really didn't know how to express myself to you but I have fallen in love with you and I don't want to let you go." I didn't know if I sounded sincere enough because the look on his face said he was not buying it. The waitress returned with our drinks. I took the straw out and began licking the coffee from the bottom. He sipped his drink slowly.

"Well, like I told you, there are so many things going on in my life right now that I really don't have time for a relationship and the issues that come along with them. I'm in school now and I just started working so I have to concentrate on those things. Now, I'm not saying that we will never get back together but I just can't be in a relationship right now." I sat there and watched his lips move but I felt there was nothing coming out.

"So, you've started school already?" I said, changing the subject.

"Yeah, I started taking classes to be a paramedic. I have a lot of homework that has to be done."

# Smoking Cigarettes

"I understand." In my mind I really didn't understand. I thought this boy was gonna come running back to me just like I thought I would him, but my plan was not working. It began to get late and I did tell Calvin that I was coming to his house later on, and I still had to go to the gas station to see if the credit card still worked. After a long and drawn out conversation we said we would be just friends. I wasn't satisfied, but at this point I didn't have a choice. We walked out the door into the cold. He reached over and gave me a hug.

"I'll talk to you later, I have to see what time the bus comes," he said, while zipping up his vest.

"Why are you catching the bus?"

"Well, how else am I supposed to get home?"

"I'ma take you, stupid."

"Why are you calling me stupid, that's your car and I can't just assume that you're gonna take me home." I laughed at him as we walked to the car. I was happy to be inside of a warm car. I threw a Phyllis Hyman CD in as I warmed up the car. My cell phone rang.

"Hello, are you still comin' ova?" Calvin asked.

"Yeah, I'll be there later. Just give me about an hour." I said, speaking directly into the phone hoping that Troy was not paying attention.

"OK," Calvin said. I ended the call.

"Who's that, one of your dates?" Troy asked while gazing out of the window. I laughed.

"No, that wasn't. That was my young bull, Calvin. He likes me but he's too young," I said, trying to change the subject.

The ride to Troy's house was silent. In South Philly it didn't matter if it was cold or hot, the niggas were still out. I dropped him off and we shook hands as a farewell, although I was awaiting a kiss. I drove straight to the gas station. The card was still active. I filled my tank up and began my journey to Calvin's. I pulled up in front of his house and saw the porch light on and empty boxes galore on the porch. The door was already open so I rang the doorbell twice, then walked in.

"Hi," Calvin said with a gigantic smile on his face. I gave him a hug then he grabbed his jacket.

"This fuckin' place is getting on my nerves," he blurted while grabbing my hand and pulling me out the door.

"Let's go to your house, 'cause my mother is stressing me the fuck out." I didn't even know what was going on but I followed him outside and into the car anyway. "I will be glad when I go to college or sumthin' cuz that bitch is ruining my fuckin' life." I proceeded to put the car in gear and drive down the street onto the expressway. The ride was in total silence. He had things on his mind about his mother and I had things on my mind about Troy. As I pulled into the parking space Calvin's attitude suddenly became freer.

He turned up the radio and began shouting out the words to DMX's *Party up.* I turned it down because with my depression starting to kick in and the noise, I was beginning to get a headache. He followed me up the stairs into my apartment. I had clothes thrown everywhere because I had recently washed them and still needed to fold them and put them away. I walked back into my room and threw my sneakers off into a corner.

Calvin stood in the hallway staring at me, waiting for me to say something. I guess the silent treatment was killing him. I walked past him to go back into the living room and began folding clothes. I started with the socks. I grabbed one then he grabbed one.

"I don't need any help, thank you."

"What's wrong with you?" he asked, trying to make eye contact.

Why the fuck should he ask? I thought to myself. I didn't answer him. I just continued to fold my clothes.

# Smoking Cigarettes

"Did I do something wrong?"

"No."

"If it's money, don't worry about it. I'll help you."

I looked him in his eyes and shook my head. By that time I was now folding my shirts. He snatched my Polo shirt out of my hand and threw it on the couch.

"Rashad, what the fuck is wrong with you?" I lifted my head from my chest as he moved in closer to my face.

"You wanna know what the fuck is wrong with me?" I said, staring back into his eyes. "Do you really want to know?" He took a deep breath, all the while not taking his eyes off me. "I'm still in love with my ex and he doesn't want me. Now, I said it, are you happy?" He looked down at the floor. "I don't know what to do, Calvin. You're a nice person, but you're just too young for me. I need a man. A man that can help me out and give me the strength and the courage that I need. I wish you could be that man but you can't. You still live at home with your mother. What can you possibly have to offer me?" His eyes were still pointed toward the floor. "I don't mean to be harsh, but it's the truth. I have so many problems and you can't fix them." I tapped his chin as he slightly looked up into my eyes. I squatted down on the floor and he did the same. The radio played Rick James's *Ebony Eyes*.

"Take me home, Rashad," he said, looking at the carpet.

"Why do you want to go home?"

"Because I don't feel comfortable here."

"How are you gonna be my nigga if I can't tell you how I feel at times? I'm going through a tough time right now and all I'm asking is that you be there for me."

"I am here for you but you're making me feel uncomfortable," he said, gazing into my eyes. The radio began playing *The Closer I Get to You* by Roberta Flack. I looked up at the rest of the clothes laying on the couch.

"Can you spend the night with me?"

"No, I don't feel comfortable."

I got up and proceeded into the room to put on my shoes. He stood by the door waiting patiently to leave. I grabbed my keys and ruffled my arms into the sleeves of my coat as we walked out the door.

"I'm not going home, I'm going to my grandmother's house."

"Where is that?"

"Southwest Philly, on 58th and Kingsessing Avenue." I was so grateful that I didn't have to drive all the way to Germantown. The whole ride was in total silence. I kept looking at him through the corner of my eye and he continued to look straight ahead. Fuck it, I said in my mind. If this nigga don't understand me and don't want to be with me then fuck it. I reached into my inside pocket and pulled out the picture he had given me. I had grabbed it from my mirror before putting on my shoes. I handed it to him. He took the picture without saying a word and began rolling down the window. He flung the picture into the midnight air while still staring forward. I pressed my foot on the gas until I pulled in front of his grandmother's door. "Right here," he said as I almost went past it. He got out, then slammed the door without giving me so much as a goodbye.

Before he even got to the steps I sped off. I turned up the radio and began to blast Usher's, *You got it bad.* I retraced my driving back down Chester Avenue so I could find the picture that he threw out of the window. It was laying there in the street untouched. I hopped out the car to retrieve it, then hopped back in. This boy could really like me and I was acting stupid. Your blessings may come in all shapes and sizes, I said to myself. And maybe he just might be one of them. I looked up at the dash and it read 1:50 a.m. About fifteen minutes later, I was back in the house folding the rest of the clothes and putting them away.

# Smoking Cigarettes

I was beginning to get sleepy, as today had been a long day.

\* \* \*

"Another credit union is having an open house on Tuesday," my mom said while reading the newspaper as she sat on the couch waiting for her chicken to finish frying. Today was Monday and I didn't have anything else to do with my life so I sat at my mother's house all day and watched videos.

"Your ass need a job," my mother said. She threw the paper into my lap. I picked it up and began skimming through it. I took a pair of scissors and began cutting the ad out and placed it on the arm of the couch. My mind wasn't focused that much on finding a job because I hadn't spoken to Calvin in two days. My mom looked at me and saw all the depression on my face. She turned her head toward the TV.

Just a year prior, I was sitting on top of the world. I had so much money from crafting it wasn't even funny. It's true how fast a person can go from sugar to shit. And right now I was definitely shit. Even Kevin found a job working at Capitol Blue Cross. And I was still sitting here feeling sorry for myself. After the chicken finished cooking I wrapped a couple of pieces in aluminum foil and headed home. I needed to save all the gas I had for the open house I was attending tomorrow. I walked into the house to prepare for the next day. Calvin hadn't even attempted to call me, so I called him. I let the phone ring three times.

"Hello?" he answered.

"Are you mad at me?" I asked, quivering with guilt.

"No, I was gonna call you later."

"How was school?" I asked just to keep the conversation flowing.

"It was cool. I have to study for a big test that's coming up. And, we have to be out of this house by Friday." I took a deep breath because I knew moving was not an easy thing.

"Well, if she needs some help I'll help pack but I ain't lifting no damn boxes." We both chuckled.

"I miss you," he said with sincerity.

"I miss you too." I felt since Troy didn't want me any longer I might as well start something new with the young buck.

Throughout the entire week things had been crazy. I went to the open house and that stupid ass credit union made me take a hard-ass test I knew I wasn't gonna pass. It rained all week and today was only Thursday. Calvin wants to take me to dinner. He said he would be at my house as soon as he got out of school. At about 4:25 p.m., my baby was walking across the parking lot from the bus stop. He had on a puffy yellow coat that was soakin' wet. The look on his face wasn't pleasant at all. The rain just poured over his face like a shower.

"This shit ain't funny," he said as he walked past me and straight upstairs to my apartment. Just to make me stop laughing, he walked into my bedroom and fell right onto my bed, coat and all. This was not funny because I just changed those damn sheets and now I would have to do the laundry all over again. Not only did he fall on the bed, but he twirled within the covers as well. I became furious as he seemed to be having the time of his life. He then jumped up and pulled me down on the bed onto him.

"This is fun," he said, laughing.

"I have to clean this shit up," I spat.

"It will dry!"

"So what, I don't want this dirty-ass rainwater on my sheets."

"Well, it's dirty now and you don't have a choice but to wash it." We began tonguing each other down.

# Smoking Cigarettes

"Let's hurry up and leave before it gets too late," I suggested. We somehow made our way to Olive Garden on City Avenue after having quick sex. I just loved the way that boy lays pipe. Although we didn't have actual intercourse yet, he sucked my dick good enough to make me feel like I was in heaven and I gripped his long pipe just the same.

We walked inside the restaurant and were greeted by a short older lady. She passed us two menus, then guided us to a nice corner booth. After about five minutes the waiter walked over to us.

"Hey, Rashad. How have you been?" I knew Ramon from when I used to work here. He was gay as well, with brown skin and a bush of dreadlocks flowing down his back. His black tie complemented his white shirt very well. He smiled as he pulled out his pad and pen to write down our order. "So what's been goin' on?" he asked. I pointed over to Calvin without saying a word so he would get my point. Calvin sat there with his hat tilted to the side as he lay back in the chair. Ramon cheerfully bloated.

"How old are you?" he asked Calvin without hesitation. It's bad enough that Calvin is young, but he has the nerve to have a baby face, too. Calvin looked at me and I looked at Ramon.

"Oh," he said, after neither of us answered.

"What do y'all want?" he said, changing the subject. Calvin and I giggled and began to order. I ordered the lasagna and Calvin ordered the chicken and noodles.

Throughout our meal I felt my energy being sniped into him. Calvin was everything that I needed and wanted at this very moment. We discussed each other's goals and how we were going to focus on our relationship. Ramon kept coming to our table, checking to see if we needed anything. Then, the restaurant started to get crowded. A huge family sat across from us making a whole lot of noise and I just couldn't take it any longer. Calvin asked for the check.

"You're paying?" I asked, because I knew my funds were limited.

"Yeah, I got it. I'll just have to ask my mom for some money so I can get a bus pass for this week." I loved the way he took charge of the evening. After paying the check he walked around and helped me with my jacket. We held hands all the way to the car, not caring who was around or who was watching. I tongued him down inside the car as we held hands the entire ride home.

Days and days went by and Calvin didn't realize all the stress that I was going through. He thought that everything was fine with me when they really weren't. He finally moved in with his grandmother where he would only have a spot on the couch. His mother moved to New Jersey to be with his grandfather. She and Calvin's stepfather had broken up because of the financial stress. The only reason Calvin stayed in Philly was because he went to school here and he wanted to finish out the rest of his years 'til graduation.

I sat on the couch at his grandmother's house with my head leaned back. I needed all the peace that I could get.

"What's wrong?" Calvin asked. I continued to lay there giving him no answer at all. Without saying another word he grabbed me and pulled me toward him. He embraced me tightly as I rubbed his head in deep thought. Little Jon began to cry and Calvin went over to pick him up from the crib. He came and sat next to me while rocking the baby back and forth. I smiled at them when I took the baby and began rocking him myself. I felt like this was my family.

I did all I could for Little Jon even though he wasn't mine. I crafted him a lot of clothes when I had that credit card, and bought him a lot of Pampers. I was so proud of

# Smoking Cigarettes

Calvin. He took care of his son, he made sure I was OK, and he was making it to school every day, trying to make something of himself. Calvin had big dreams. He wanted to be the next big name in Hollywood. He wanted to become an actor. He made it known that nothing would stand in his way.

I looked down at the baby's face and cuddled him in my arms until he fell asleep. Calvin had already stretched out on the couch and had fallen asleep himself.

Later that night he woke up and called Dontae.

"I can't get no peace man!" Calvin shouted to Dontae on the phone. I just sat there on the couch listening.

"What happened!?" I heard Dontae yell.

"My mom wants me to go to Jersey with her to help her clean up my grandfather's house this weekend," Calvin said, sounding frustrated.

"So, what's wrong with that?"

"I wanted to chill with Rashad this weekend. That's why I can't wait till I turn twenty-one so I can do whatever the fuck I wanna do." I had to interject in this conversation just so Calvin could see things from his mother's point of view.

"Let's think about it, Calvin," I said as he turned around to face me while holding the phone to his ear. "Your mother basically lost everything, the house and her business. So this is a very crucial time for her and she needs you now more than ever. You don't know the pain she's going through." I started to get emotional because I started feeling the pain my mother had when she lost her house a few years back. "It's OK if we don't see each other for one weekend. You need to go be with your mother and help her." Dontae must have agreed. Calvin smiled at me before charging at my lips with his.

"Now I see why I'm falling in love with you," he said under his breath, but I heard him loud and clear. I sat back and continued to watch cartoons.

"I'm hungry as hell," I said, squeezing Calvin's back passionately.

"What do you want to eat?" he asked. "I'm gonna cook. Do you want some breakfast food?" I looked at the clock and it was quarter to eleven at night, but a little breakfast at the end of the day never hurt anyone.

"Yeah." Calvin walked back into the kitchen and put it down. He made scrambled eggs, pork sausage, home fries, and pancakes. He sat a gigantic plate in front of me and my mouth began to drool. Other than at a restaurant, I had never tasted scrambled eggs that fluffy before. And I never had pancakes that melted in my mouth that way. I cleaned my plate. Calvin looked at me then down at my plate. I laughed and he laughed too. It was kind of funny.

## If Push Comes To Shove


I have to keep myself busy while Calvin goes to school. I can't remember my life ever being so empty. I mean it seems as if I don't have a life at all. I can't seem to find a job to save my soul, and rent for the next month is about to be due. I need to take my black ass back to church and learn a thing or two about where I came from and learn more about the Lord. I need to ask the Lord to forgive me for all my sins. If only I can just stop sleeping with these damn boys and find me a nice young girl to settle down with. I always wanted to have kids some day.

Mia and I always said that if neither one of us was married by the time we reached thirty-four, we would marry each other. That sounded like a plan, but what were we supposed to do about kids? I was not getting on top of her to stick my dick in her pussy. Besides, she was not gonna suck my dick. I hated the thought of the whole thing. I don't like girls. I never have. And to have sex with one of my best friends would be disgusting.

What I needed to do was think about the situation at hand. I was too busy keeping Troy on my mind with his stubborn ass while I tried to figure out how I could make things better between us. I had to realize that there was no us. I just needed him in my life to fill a void. I have Calvin to think about, and anything I need I'm sure Calvin will provide.

As I lay in the bed I wondered what would become of my life. I leaned over and picked up the phone when it rang.

"Hello," I said with my eyes half closed.

"Hey, wassup?" Calvin said in a soft tone on the other end.

"Nuffin, I actually just woke up, what are you

doin'?"

"I'ma 'bout to go with my friends, Eric and Tyree, to Delaware real quick. I'm not gonna be that long."

"Why do you have to go with them to Delaware?"

"Because I'm bored and I don't wanna sit in the house all day. They are getting upset because I spend so much time with you. They're saying I forgot about them."

"OK," I finally said, feeling like I had to give my seal of approval.

"Oh, and my mom got me a new cell phone so get a pen so I can give you the number." I jumped out of the bed to search for a pen and take down the number.

After we said our goodbyes I couldn't wait until I had a chance to speak with him later. I began to think about his friends that he was about to take this ride with. I knew these friends of his 'cause they were always in the chat room. Now, Eric tried to holla at me while I was with Troy. I had met him on the Internet. He was kind of cute to be a big boy.

He was light-skinned with long braids. I loved his look and he knew a lot about cars. He said that his father owned a fleet of cars. Anyway, I wondered when he and Calvin became such good friends? I remembered Calvin telling me that Eric had tried to suck his dick one night in the backseat of Eric's car, but he said that he had turned him down. If that were the case, then why was he with him now? The thoughts began to run through my mind as if I were somebody's baby's mama. Now, to another story— Tyree. He told me straight up that he had a crush on me and always had.

He was light-skinned like Eric, except he was skinny and cute. He kind of resembled someone that I knew, but I couldn't put my finger on it. I just knew that he looked very familiar. I soon realized that Tyree had a boyfriend and he would call to talk to me while his boyfriend was asleep. Now that was some shiesty shit, but that's how the faggots played. Also I had a problem giving him play if he didn't have a job. It wouldn't make sense if we both didn't have jobs now, would it? Besides, he dresses in drag and that's one thing I don't do, drag queens. Now, since both of these boys have crushes on me, and I am now messing with Calvin, my man should not be going anywhere with those fools without me. So, I did what any bitch would do, I called his phone. The phone rang three times before he answered.

"Hello?" he said.

"What took you so long to answer your phone?" I asked, cutting to the chase.

"It was in my pocket and at first I didn't hear it ring because the music was up loud." Nothing led me to believe that there was any funny business going on so I had to act as mellow as possible.

"What y'all doin' now?"

"We're still driving," he said with minimum noise in the background.

"Well, just call me later when you get a chance," I told him before hanging up. I put the phone down on the base and continued on with my day while my man was out and about. I did a lot of cleaning up around my apartment. The one thing that I hated about cleaning was mopping the kitchen floor.

I blasted my music very loudly while I went to work on the floor. I needed it to shine for when my man came home. I'd rest later, I told myself. About an hour and a half later I called Calvin's phone again, and this time, I got no answer.

I tried not to think devilish thoughts. I decided to relax and light some aromatherapy candles and wait for his arrival. I soaked in the tub for about an hour while thinking of his long magic stick and how I yearned for it. While leaning my head back on the base of the tub, the phone rang.

"Hello," I answered, just knowing it was Calvin. I felt a glow on my face instantly when I heard his voice on the other end.

"What are you doing?" he asked.

"I'm chillin' in the tub, waiting for you to call."

He began chuckling. "After I'm done with my boys I'll be over, all right? Where do you wanna go tonight? Or do you want to stay home and chill and watch a movie because I really don't have much money."

I thought to myself that this nigga had already done enough for me so it was OK if he lacked funds right now. "That sounds good to me," I told him.

"Well, I'ma call you when my friends drop me off and then I'll be there, OK?"

"OK." I hung up the phone and smiled. I continued to lay my head back on the base of the tub and let my mind drift away. I couldn't wait until Calvin graced my doorway with his presence. The things I yearned for in a man, I just knew Calvin had them.

The man I could chill with, laugh with, cry with, and share all my dreams with. His mother sure had a winning child, and I would be there for him through his ups and his downs, through thick and through thin.

I didn't mind spending my Sunday with Calvin eating pizza on the living room floor while watching *I Love Lucy* reruns, or simply playing around and throwing kisses to one another.

"You are all that," he said, without warning. I turned to him and smiled.

"Where did that come from?"

"I don't know. I just thought I'd say it just so you'll know." I smiled at him and continued to watch Ricky Ricardo yell at Lucy for spending the bill money at the mall on a dress that she wanted to wear to a party she was supposed to attend with Ethel.

"Eric is mad at me," he said, tilting his head toward

the floor.

I turned and looked into his eyes as he started to look up.

"What for?"

"You know, he still likes me, and I told him that I was with you.   Not that we were in a relationship or anything but that we were dating and I'm hoping to get in a relationship with you in the future.  He got mad."  I muted the TV because I wanted to know more.  I kind of had a feeling that some shit was gonna start because Calvin and I started hanging around each other more, and those lifeless faggots were gonna get jealous.  I listened for more.

"He also said that you weren't good enough for me and I could do better.  He doesn't want me to call him anymore, nor does he want to hang with me."

Calvin had a sad look on his face.  My blood was boiling.  I had grown to like Calvin a lot and I would do anything to keep him happy.  I couldn't stand around and let some stupid-ass faggot make my baby feel this way.

"I told you he tried to talk to me, right?" I reminded him.

"I already knew that, and the thing about it is that we have been friends for about five years, and now he wants to act like this.  He's mad that we are together; it's either he has a crush on me or he has a crush on you."  I could tell Calvin was angry.  Eric must have meant a great deal to him for him to act this way.

"Well, if you truly feel as though he's a true friend and you want to remain friends with him, I think that you should call him and speak with him about the situation."  I didn't know if the advice I was giving him was good or not because deep down inside I could care less about Eric and I sure didn't need my man hanging around him anyway.

"No, if he don't want to talk to me then I won't fucking talk to him then," he spat.

"Now, are you sure that's what you want to do?" I

asked, although that was music to my ears; however, I needed to know how he really felt about this. I also didn't need him hanging around people who weren't gonna be true.

I could tell by the look on his face that this had saddened him greatly. I embraced him with a hug as tight as I could and planted a soft kiss on his forehead and told him that I would always be his friend no matter what happened to us. He looked at me and shook his head obliging. I couldn't wait until I saw Eric out at the clubs. I was gonna give him a piece of my mind.

Valentine's Day was slowly approaching and I couldn't wait to find out what my treat from Calvin was going to be. Troy was not out of my life totally. I spoke with him on and off through the week letting him know that I was looking forward to spending my Valentine's Day with him. It seemed that no matter how many times I had sex with Calvin, or how many times I looked into his face, my heart still beat for one man. It was something about Troy that I just couldn't let go.

I know how much Calvin cares for me and I know if I were to turn my back on him now he would be so hurt. I never made it my business to hurt people's feelings so I wasn't about to start. And, in all honesty since I've been dealing with men he seems to be the only one who looks out for me in my time of need.

I have no choice but to look past his burned legs and some of his feminine tendencies, and the rest of his flaws, to get to know the real him.

"You know I don't celebrate Valentine's Day. Valentine's Day is for pussies." I had to listen to Troy's negative ramble on the phone. I wanted to do what all lovers do on that day. I wanted to go out or stay in. I wanted someone to buy me a bunch of roses and chocolates. I never had that done for me before. I never understood why I was always excluded from the lovey-dovey bunch. Why the fuck couldn't I find somebody that was gonna treat me like the queen that I am, dammit!

"So, can I come over on Valentine's Day?" I asked Troy in the middle of his talking.

"I might be busy that day, but if I'm not, I'll let you know." Of course I hated the rejection—all queens hate rejection.

"At least we should go out and have a good time," I said, trying my best to break him, but he wasn't budging.

Three weeks had passed and I hadn't heard from the credit union yet, so I guess that meant I didn't past the test. Calvin's ex-girlfriend was released from detention on house arrest, and yes, she was becoming a pain.

"Hi, I'm Camisha," she said as she stuck out her hand to give me a handshake while holding Jon with the other.

I shook her hand with the enthusiasm of being introduced to an ex. I really didn't know if she knew that I was fucking Calvin, or if she knew that I knew everything that had happened between them.

"Why is she here anyway?" I asked Calvin, while walking up the steps and into the house.

"My mother wanted to see my son so she called her to bring him over here." I turned my nose up after noticing her show off her Louis Vuitton skirt while exposing her county administered ankle bracelet.

"I ain't got nuffin' to say to that bitch, I hate her ass," Calvin continued. I went to the door while Calvin went into the kitchen to talk to his grandmother. Before I got to the door, Camisha and Calvin's cousin Shauna were coming in because it was starting to get cold. Camisha quickly passed the baby to me as she lost her balance while coming in the house. I grabbed the baby right before Camisha hit the floor.

"Are you OK?" I asked, while moving toward the couch and holding Jon close.

"I'm cool," she said, getting up. I admired her toned body that Calvin never spoke about. Jon's mother was about three cents short of a dime; in other words, she was hot. Her titties were nice and perky and her shoulder-length hair looked magnificent in those curls. She wore Louis Vuitton as if she had it like that. I saw why Calvin chose her to bear his child. She was pretty, very pretty. But it must have been something for Calvin to leave her and choose to start messing with dudes. But who was I to judge? Calvin came out of the kitchen and walked straight past her and over to me.

"Let's go," he demanded. I walked over to Camisha and gave the baby back to her. I then started to follow him out the door while saying my goodbyes in a hurry.

"That was rude," I scolded him once we got outside.

"I told you I hate that bitch."

"Yeah, but you don't have to be so rude in front of your family." He just looked at me as he stood by the passenger-side door of the car waiting for me to disarm the alarm so he could get in. We jumped in the car, then I put the car in gear and sped off with an attitude.

"Where are we going anyway?" I asked him with a rush of anger.

"Wherever the fuck you wanna go, I don't care."

"Well, can we go to the movies?" I was about to take that route to the theater.

"Yeah, what do you wanna see?"

"Well, I want to see *Super Troopers*. I think that movie is gonna be funny." All of a sudden I wasn't angry with him anymore. He extended his hand for me to hold while we were driving. I held it affectionately as we drove to the movies.

On this lonely Tuesday night the movie theater was empty. We sat in the middle section so the screen would be directly in front of us. I was always a sucker for comical movies, and watching one about some crooked-ass cops pulling people over on the highway for dumb shit was right up my alley. I hate it when cops do that, just so they can make their quota.

The movie began and it seemed like I started laughing before the opening credits started. I snuggled up against Calvin so tight.

"My dick is hard," Calvin said abruptly. I looked at him then down at his sweats and his dick was hard as a rock.

"How can a movie like this make your dick hard?"

"I don't know," he said, shrugging his shoulders. I thought real hard about what I was about to do, and honestly, it was wrong and I don't engage in these types of activities because I always said that I was going to be the one and only faggot who was brought up right, and no matter what, I would always be the one who carried himself with class.

I looked around the theater and there was no one there but us. He was looking good with his fitted tilted to the side. He stared straight ahead as if he didn't know what I was about to do. I glanced down at the hammer and tapped it. It jumped like it was ready to be swallowed. I pulled the hammer out from his sweats and his boxers and went to work. I slopped his dick down like this was the first time I ever tasted it. I closed my eyes and felt like I was in heaven. I carefully looked up at the movie screen to make sure I wasn't missing anything, I wasn't. I continued going up and down on his dick like I owned it, because I did. I sucked his rod like it was a Charms cherry blow-pop.

I yanked his boxers and his sweats down some more so I could have more room to maneuver. He laid back in the chair and grabbed the back of my head and forced himself into my mouth until I choked. My spit slid down the side of his dick while he paused for a bit, leaving the head of his dick rubbing my tonsils. I tried to lift my head, but the force from his hands wouldn't let me. He let loose just to jam himself into my mouth again. He let out a big sigh and uttered, "I'ma 'bout to nut," as he exploded his ice cream into my mouth. Man, if my mouth were a pussy I would have gotten pregnant for sure.

I held his load of cum in my mouth for about three seconds before spitting it out on the floor. We began tonguing each other down while his dick started to get soft. I rubbed it as he jumped because the after effects were still taking a toll on his body. His dick got real soft and limp. I tucked it away in his boxers and we continued watching the movie. The usher opened the door behind us, waving his flashlight. We both looked straight ahead and giggled.

* * *

"I had a good time tonight," I told him as we walked to the car. We held hands in the car again. It seemed like we couldn't get enough of each other.

"I have a taste for some ice cream," I told him.

"Hmm, I wonder why?" he said, laughing. I pulled into the McDonald's drive-thru. I really couldn't hear what the cashier was saying because Calvin turned the music up so loud that I had to scream in the speaker for a damn ice cream cone.

We continued our journey back to my apartment to finish what we had started. The lingering taste of my ice cream made me focus on the treat I was going to get once we arrived at my place. I peeped in the rearview mirror and saw lights flashing from a cop car that was pulling me over.

I turned the new Ludacris song down to focus on why I was being stopped by these stupid-ass cops in Darby Township. And, to think we had just finished seeing a movie about this. Talk about jinx. I let go of Calvin's hand as we sat there wondering what was about to happen.

# Smoking Cigarettes

I rolled down my window when I noticed through my side-view mirror the cop getting out of his patrol car. From what I could see, he was a young, African-American guy; he looked like a rookie.

"May I see your license, registration, and insurance please?"

I had to ask out of curiosity, "Why did you pull me over, sir?" I looked up at his brown-skinned face.

"Because you ran through a stop sign," he spat.

"No I didn't."

"Yes, you did. You slowed down but you didn't come to a complete stop."

Calvin began looking through the glove compartment for the items that the police requested. In about six seconds flat, police cars surrounded us. I looked over at Calvin and he tilted his fitted a little lower. I looked up at the cop and passed him a phony driver's license, and an expired registration and insurance card.

"May I have your car keys please?" he asked.

"What do you need those for?" Instead of giving me an answer, he grabbed for his flashlight and began to shine it in Calvin's face.

"What's your name?" he asked with a snap of bass in his voice.

"My name is Calvin."

"Lift up your hat so I can see your face," he demanded.

Calvin slowly lifted his fitted. I looked back at the cop.

"Do you have identification on you?" the officer asked.

"I have my school I.D.," Calvin responded.

"Can I have your keys?" the officer spat for the second time.

By then another officer was already on Calvin's side waiting for him or me to make a false move. I passed the officer my keys after shutting the engine off. He grabbed them and threw them on the hood of the car.

"Sit tight," he said before walking back to his vehicle. Calvin and I looked at each other. He cracked a smile that let me know that everything would be OK. My heart raced because I knew that all the things I passed him weren't kosher.

My license had been suspended for some time now, and I was behind in paying my car insurance so that had been canceled. I can't remember the last time I renewed my registration, so anyway you look at it, I was fucked. Calvin turned the radio up to listen to some tunes while we were waiting. I couldn't stand the suspense so I turned it down and grabbed his hand. I held it tight as I looked around to notice about five police cars surrounding my car making sure I didn't go anywhere. There was no other choice but to wait patiently for the officer to come back to the car. I was so embarrassed to have Calvin find out about my irresponsibleness this way. After about five minutes the officer approached my door, and I let go Calvin's hand to roll down the window.

"Did you know that your insurance is expired?" the officer asked.

"No, I didn't officer."

"Yeah, well it is, and whose license plate is this on the car?"

"It's mine, sir." Obviously, at a time like this I had to respect him.

"The plate is coming back registered to a 1985 Chevy Lumina. Who owns a Chevy?" I didn't have an answer to give him since my brother had stolen it from someone else's car.

"Step out the car," he commanded while backing up and pulling his nightstick from his side. I looked at Calvin as the other officer tapped on the passenger side window ordering him to get out the car too. We stepped out.

# Smoking Cigarettes

"What did I do, officer?" I asked, turning around and putting my hands on top of my head as I was told. Calvin was just as confused as I was. All the other officers exited their cars and came over to find out what the officer was going to do with us.

"Where are we going, sir?" I asked in a frenzy.

"I'm taking you in." That wasn't the answer I was looking for.

"How old are you?" The one cop asked me while the other cop questioned Calvin.

"I'm twenty-three." Calvin looked at me and I looked at him. One officer took off Calvin's fitted and threw it in the back seat.

"How old are you?" the officer asked him.

"I'm eighteen," he answered, not letting the cop see him sweat. That's one of the things I loved about my bad boy. He never backed down from anything. One officer placed the handcuffs on me as the other officer placed handcuffs on Calvin and we were both placed in separate cars. Through the little bit of light that shined in the streets I could see the glittering from Calvin's eyes. I watched him the whole time making sure they didn't harm him. No matter what I'd done, he didn't have anything to do with it. The police commenced to search my car to find nothing but a few pieces of toilet paper and a couple of pieces of used condom wrappers. I looked up to a tow truck heading our way, coming to get my vehicle.

As I sat in the back of the police car I thought about what would have happened if we had never been pulled over. I'm sure Calvin would have made love to me tonight like no other. My dick was getting hard just thinking about it. I could feel my pre-cum ejecting from my dick as I imagined the setting of us making love in my bedroom. I stared out of the window into his lonely eyes and thought about how he was feeling right now.

I hoped he wasn't mad at me for this. I started to

think of all sorts of crazy things. What if they found a warrant on me that they wanted to take me in for? What if someone had been murdered and I fit the description of the killer? Damn, I left my cell phone in the armrest. I should have used it to call my mom, damn.

I watched my car get lifted by the tow truck as the cops stood around, laughing. An officer jumped in the front seat of the car where Calvin sat and pulled off. I wonder where they are taking him? I asked myself. Then, the young officer hopped in the front seat of the car where I sat.

"Where are we going?" I asked, still handcuffed in the backseat.

"We're going to the station," he said in a stern voice.

"What did I do?" I asked again.

"You lied about the license plate, you lied about your insurance, and your driver's license is suspended so you shouldn't be driving anyway."

"What are you going to do with my friend?"

"He's going back to the station too," he said while looking at me through the rearview. "Tell me something, what were y'all two doing together anyway?" he asked as if it was any of his fucking business.

"We were coming from the movies." I shouldn't have said anything because who the hell was he to question me about my affairs? It only took us about three minutes to get to the Darby station. When we got there, Calvin was standing on the steps with his hands in his pockets. The least he could do was help me out of the car while I had on these tight-ass handcuffs.

"Wait here and I'ma call my mom to come pick us up," I told him, as I was led inside the station. The officer finally took the cuffs off me and let me sit down.

"Can I use your phone?" I asked the officer. He stared at me up and down as if I was speaking another language. He nodded his head for me to use the phone on the wooden desk. I turned it around and began dialing my mother's number.

"Yes," she answered the phone sounding half-asleep.

"Mom, I got stopped by the cops," I told her feeling ashamed of myself.

"Where are you?"

"I'm sitting in the Darby police station. Calvin and I went to the movies."

"Well, where is Calvin?"

"He's outside in the cold waiting for me."

"You're at the Darby police station around the corner?"

"Yes. All right," I said before I put the black phone back on the base and began looking around the precinct at all the mug shots of people who were wanted for some type of crime. I watched the officer write out about nine traffic violation tickets—it seemed like it was taking him forever. My mom and Calvin entered the station followed by three more policemen. My mother had a startled look on her face when one of the officers revealed Calvin's true age.

"They were supposed to be going to the movies," I heard my mother telling one of the officers.

For the life of me I never knew why that cop was so interested in our ages. My mother told him again that we were friends. She and Calvin sat outside in the car while the officer continued to write out all the traffic violations. All this paperwork he was doing just for me to throw every ticket in the trash. I was wondering what Calvin and my mom were discussing in the car. I hope she didn't con him into telling her everything.

The officer finally completed all of the citations and stood up to give me his spill. He asked me to sign at the X.

"Signing on the X does not show that you are guilty, it just shows that you received this citation and you have to appear in court within ten days…" and blah, blah, blah. I held my head up with my hand and looked him dead in his eyes as he talked.

"Where can I pick up my car?" I asked, gathering the yellow slips he had given me. I shoved them into my pocket.

"At Sam's impound yard on Chestnut Street."

I nodded my head and walked out the door to find my mom sitting patiently in her car with Calvin stretched out across the backseat.

"So, what did they say?" she asked as Calvin's head popped up.

"He said that I had to respond to the citation within the next ten days, the usual," I said. I turned around and looked at Calvin. He sat in the backseat with a smirk on his face. I turned around knowing that my baby wasn't mad. We drove to Calvin's house listening to the grooves of Jaheim.

It was a drag not having a car or the money to get it out. I needed $185.00—$70 for the towing and $35 a day for storage fees—it had been two days. I had no other choice but to call my deadbeat-ass dad for the money, or at least half of it, and get the rest from Calvin.

"I'm glad the police didn't call my mom," Calvin said during our brief conversation on the phone after he got home from school.

"I'm glad they didn't either. She'd never let us hang together again. I need to know how the hell I'm gonna get my car back?" I was hinting to see if he was gonna help, but he told me he didn't even have money for a bus pass, so that was a no go.

The next day my mother got off work early to help me get my car out. She loaned me the money and told me that as soon as I get a job I'd better pay her back. I needed to get a release from the police station before I could retrieve my vehicle. Going back and forth from the station to the impound with different papers was starting to irk my nerves.

I finally got my car back with no license plate and no inspection stickers. The stickers that I had on the windshield were counterfeit so I knew they would be scraping them off. I didn't know what I needed to do to get a new license plate or new stickers. I was just happy to have my ride back. I'd consult with my brother to get me what I needed.

\* \* \*

Ron and Calvin were acting funny all week. Valentine's Day was tomorrow and I couldn't figure out what they were up to. Ron was dating a white guy named Joseph. I had never seen Joseph in person, but I had talked to him online quite a few times. All I knew was he was a white dude with braids, and from what I could tell, Ron was in love with him. I had tried to play matchmaker a while back with Ron and Drew, then with Ron and Kevin, but my skills never worked. After all that, Ron ended up with a white guy. More power to him.

"So, what you gwan to do for Valentine's Day, mon?" Kevin asked me as we chit chatted over lunch at the Italian Bistro in downtown Philly.

"I don't know. I wish I could have made plans with Troy, but he's actin' so stupid. I'll just say this, call me tomorrow at ten and ask me who I am with. The person's name I tell you will be my Valentine." He laughed at me while scarfing down free dinner rolls. I knew he wouldn't have a Valentine.

The day of waiting finally came. I always wanted to be in love on Valentine's Day. Unfortunately, this day was not the day for that. I cannot find true love to save my damn soul. At least Damien gave me a $250.00 payment for the jeep I sold to him a while ago when I was rolling in the money. After I had spent it all I didn't have a source of income, so I sold my assets, and the jeep was one of them. It was one of those Geo Trackers. I hated it anyway.

I needed to use the money from Damien to make my Valentine's Day with Calvin special. He planned to come to my house after he left school. I had to make sure that I had everything in place. I bought balloons, flowers, cards, teddy bears, a Ralph Lauren Polo sweater, and to top it off, I cooked him a wonderful meal—fried chicken, macaroni and cheese, dinner rolls, and string beans. I let the balloons float through my apartment, and the flowers were cut just right. I dimmed the lights and turned the music on low. I wanted us to savor every moment. I jumped in the shower so I could smell fruit fresh when he entered. I looked in the mirror one last time to fix my hair and to make sure that my clothes fit my body to the T. I sat in the living room until about three thirty. I knew that was the time he would be ringing my bell.

I heard the doorbell ring once. I remained on the couch. It rang again. I walked over to the door and checked around the room to make sure everything was in place. I opened the door to his smiling face as he held a single red rose. I took it and gave him a kiss.

"This rose is for the first month that we've spent together," he said, as he kissed me again. He pulled out a pink rose, knowing it is my favorite color.

"This rose is for the second month we've spent together," he said, before kissing me again. I backed up for him to enter. He placed his book bag on the floor and started to tongue me down like never before. I kissed him back, wondering where was my box of chocolates, my teddy bears, my big red box with the bow?

He released me and looked at the teddy bears I had bought for him. I watched him walk over to the gift bag and pull out the sweater without reading the card first. He turned around and hugged me. I hugged him back wondering if he was waiting to surprise me with something other than two single roses.

"How was your day?" he asked. I told him everything was fine. He walked into the kitchen admiring the lovely meal I prepared for us. His cell phone started to ring in his book bag, and he ran into the living room to answer it. I sat down on the couch tossing the teddy bear in the air. At least he did get me something, and it is the thought that counts, right? It didn't matter if I didn't get a box of chocolates or teddy bears or diamonds or anything like that, at least he is here with me.

"I have to go," he said, hanging up the phone.

"Who was that?"

"That was my grandmother. She wants to take me, Shauna, and the baby out for dinner." He saw the fire in my eyes. "Baby, I just can't tell her no. She asked me to come home. Are you gonna take me?"

I was at a loss for words as I sat back down on the love seat trying to gather my thoughts.

"Doesn't she know it's Valentine's Day, and I wanna be with you?" I spat.

He kneeled down in front of me. "I know, Rashad, and I wanted to spend this whole day with you too, but I can't tell my grandmother no." I looked into his eyes as our lips met passionately. I tried to understand. I mean, he should do what his grandmother asked. "Now, are you gonna take me?"

"All right," I said, as I walked into my room to get my shoes.

For the whole ride to his grandmother's house, I didn't say one word. How could this be happening? We drove in front of his house and saw his cousin Shauna, waiting on the steps.

"See, she's waiting for me," he said, holding his Valentine's Day goodies in his hand. "I'll call you later," he said as he slammed the door shut. I don't even remember him saying thank you.

I quickly dialed Shay-Shay's number on my cell phone.

"Hello," my other cousin, Tamika, answered.

"Where's Shay?"

"She's on the porch talking to Pookie."

"All right," I said, hanging up the phone. Pookie was Shay's baby's father. She had been having problems with him lately with paying child support and of course, cheating. After this episode with Calvin I was not going to go back home and sit by my lonesome.

I pulled up in front of my grandmother's house to see Shay and Pookie still on the porch talking. I hopped out to a corner full of boys. Some of them were cute and some weren't, but they all had one thing in common, the hustle of selling drugs. It was nice outside for February, but somehow I wasn't feeling this day at all. I walked past Shay and Pookie and into the house where Tamika was adding the finishing touches to her man's gift. Tamika is older than me, and is the daughter of my mother's other sister. I used to live with Tamika a while back when my stepfather and I weren't getting along. She has her own house, and even though she has struggles in life, she always makes sure she comes out on top.

"Whose flowers are those?" I asked Tamika, pointing at the freshly cut roses dipped inside the antique-looking vase on the dining room table.

"Those are Shay's; Pookie just brought those for her." My depression began to return. I walked into the kitchen to say hello to my grandma who was putting something good inside the oven. She turned around and looked up at me then continued her business. I was feeling lonely. I could not worry about Shay on the porch arguing with her boyfriend, and I could not worry about Tamika in the dining room wrapping her man's gift. I needed to be loved very hard at a moment like this. The only person I could love, hold, and cherish was my goddaughter, and she was asleep on the sofa. So I did the next best thing and went to sleep right beside her.

I only slept for about thirty minutes or so. I felt even more miserable when I awoke. Shay was sitting at the dining room table rocking Kaniyah back and forth. Tamika and her boyfriend were sitting at the table as well.

"What's wrong with you?" I asked Shay because of the grizzly look on her face.

"I hate him!"

"Who?"

"Pookie, I can't stand him!" I looked at the pretty flowers he had given her.

"What happened? How can you be upset on Valentine's Day? He brought you some beautiful flowers," I said as my grandmother interrupted, looking at the vase.

"They are beautiful," she said, walking back into the kitchen.

"I should take 'em and throw them in the middle of Race Street," Shay spat while still rocking the baby back and forth. Tamika and I began to chuckle.

"Well, what happened?" I felt it was my duty to ask again.

"I just hate him. I wish I never met him."

My grandmother came back into the dining room then sat down and lit a cigarette.

"Well if you don't like him then why did you have a baby by him?" she asked.

"I don't know," Shay replied.

"That's because you was being stupid. You know you didn't like the man. I don't know why you even went as far as to have a baby," my grandmother continued as Tamika felt it was time to give her man his gift. I envied them all. I watched as he opened the box to find cologne and a sweat suit. I watched as their lips met.

"Thank you," he said to her. Man, I was through. I

played around with my cell phone until I got up enough courage to call Troy.  To my surprise, he answered the phone.

"Hey, Troy. Happy Valentine's Day," I said with great excitement.

"Yeah, yeah, whatever.  Wassup, Rashad?"

"What are you doing?" I asked, hoping I could swing by to see him.

"Nothing but sitting here on the steps with my little sister."

"Well, I'm coming over," I said, without giving him a chance to turn me down.

"OK."

I left my grandmother's house hoping that my Valentine's Day could be saved before the clock struck midnight.  By the time I reached his house it was already dark and he was no longer sitting on the steps.  No one was outside anywhere.  I parked my car and began to knock on the door.  His stepfather opened it.

"Is Troy in?" I politely asked.  He didn't say anything.  He just turned around and hollered up the steps for Troy to come to the door.  Troy came wearing a red-hooded sweatshirt, shorts, and black dress socks.

"Damn, nigga, are you comfortable or what?" I asked as I laughed and walked into the house.  No matter how Troy dressed, he was still my baby.

"Come upstairs," he said, while racing back into his room to avoid his little sister from following us.  I walked into his dark room where I had to turn on the light to see what was going on.  Troy sat in the back room watching TV while eating a tuna sandwich and string beans.

"Man what kind of meal is that?"  I asked, turning my nose up at the sight of it.

"When you don't have much, you have to work with what you got."

I sat next to him while he watched reruns of *Beverly*

# Smoking Cigarettes

*Hills, 90210.*

"So how was your day?" I asked, breaking the silence.

"It was OK. I hate Valentine's Day." I grabbed for his feet and began to rub his legs.

"What are you doing?" he asked.

"I'm rubbing your legs." I loved his legs. They were slim, dark, and hairy, and I loved to run my fingers up and down them.

"That tickles, stop," he said in a soft tone. I continued. "Stop!" he spat as he moved his legs away from me. I leaned over to kiss him, and he turned around and blew cigarette smoke in my face. He giggled.

"Can I have a kiss?" I asked. He turned his head around again and blew a whirlwind of smoke, then uttered no. I never understood how a perfect relationship could go bad. My heart and soul had gone into this man, and now he was sitting on the end of the bed like we were just friends, and always had been. I didn't like that at all.

"So, since we are here together, do you wanna be my Valentine?" I asked, hoping he would have second thoughts.

"No," he responded with no remorse. I sat there in his room as we continued to watch the show. My cell phone rang, it was Kevin.

"Yo," I greeted.

"It's 10 o'clock, bitch, who you wit'?"

Now I could tell he didn't have a life or anything else better to do but to call me at ten on the dot. "I'm over Troy's," I said, lowering my voice into the phone.

"Oh," he said, with a hint of delight.

"No, it's not what you think. Troy and I aren't even doing anything. He really doesn't want to be with me." Kevin got quiet.

"I'll call you when I get home," I said, ending the call.

116

It really made no sense for me to stick around, besides, I was getting hungry. I gave Troy a kiss on his cheek and he walked me to the door.

I decided I'd go home and lay in bed by myself. Hell, it's Valentine's Day and I know I love myself, so I might as well make love to myself.

# Smoking Cigarettes

## My Place

I was awakened by terrible thunderstorms early in the morning. To my surprise the electric didn't go out. It seemed like every time it stormed that would happen—one of the downsides of suburban living. I called Calvin to see if he had already awakened for school but I got no answer.

I was determined to lose weight and find a good job and keep it this time. I had to turn over a new leaf, so I started pounding the pavement. I got every newspaper there was—from the *Daily News* to the *Sunday Enquirer*. The thought of calling my old job where I worked in data entry was wrecking my brain too much, and I knew if I were to call them, I would be known as a failure. The whole point of me leaving that damn job was to further my career, build myself up, and go on to do bigger and better things. I never liked doing data entry anyway.

I sat in my car and waited for Calvin to get off the bus in front of his grandmother's house. He walked toward the house not even noticing that I had been waiting for him.

I was surprised to see him wearing the sweater I'd bought him. He also had on the sneakers he had gotten from my house. It was amazing that we wore the same shoe size. I rolled down the window and hollered his name. He turned and smiled as he walked toward the car. I got out to embrace him.

I never took my eyes off him once we entered the house and found no one home. I instantly became erect. He knew exactly what it was hittin' for. He came closer to me after taking off his jacket and placing it on the back of a chair. He kissed me while playing with my nipples. My dick stood straight ahead, stretching my sweat pants, and he felt every inch of it. I couldn't imagine us ever doing this kind of act in his grandmother's home, but it was happening.

He took me by the hand and led me upstairs into the back room, his aunt's room.  I walked up the steps holding on to his strong hands as he led me to the bed.  He licked all around my neck and up and down my chest.  I grabbed his head and pulled his lips closer to mine.  I opened my eyes to see his sexy eyes looking at me.

"Wassup?" he asked.  My body quivered once again.

"You." I grabbed his long dick and pulled it out of his uniform pants and inserted him inside my mouth.  I moved my head back and forth as he moved his hips the same.  His pants fell straight to his ankles.  He maneuvered toward the bed to move his aunt's clothes out of the way before lifting me up and tossing me on the bed.  He pulled off my sweat pants and yanked my boxers off as well.  He licked my dick up and down like a pro.

I knew exactly what I wanted to say but I just didn't know how to say it.  What would he do if I said it?  How would he take it?

"I love you, Calvin," I said between a breath while rotating my hips with my manhood in his mouth.

Did he hear what I had said?  He didn't say anything, but in that split second he lifted his head up.

"I love you, too."

Bingo!  I yelled in my mind.  I had this young boy sprung, and getting head from him wasn't bad either.  He began licking the opening of my muscle with his forceful tongue. He climbed on top of me, lifting my legs into the air.

"I think someone is coming," I said to startle him. He stopped, then continued to handle his business.

"My aunt doesn't get off till seven and my grandmother went to Baltimore, so we have plenty of time," he said at ease.  I knew where he was headed by putting my legs in the air.  It's not that I didn't want the turbo dick, I did. It's just that we didn't have a condom, and I wasn't ready to take his dick just yet. He played with my anus by rubbing the head of his dick up and down my crack. I then felt every inch of him enter me like a thief going into a jewelry store from a back street.

I gasped for my breath as he stared straight into my eyes while slowly moving himself in and out of my body. I gripped the sheets as my eyes filled with tears from the pain.

"Take it out," I begged.

"Hold up," he said, continuing to pump inside me. I dug my fingernails deep into his flesh.

"Calvin, it hurts," I said, begging for him to stop. He suddenly pulled his rod out from inside of me and began jerking it as I rubbed my hands up and down his biceps. I changed my position and began sucking all his fluids out of him. He collapsed his body on top of mine.

* * *

"So you mean to tell me you didn't have a job all this time?" my former boss asked me. I called her to ask for my old job back even though I told myself I wouldn't; however, desperate times call for desperate measures.

"No, I just got fired two weeks ago," I lied so she wouldn't think I had been unemployed. We had always been cool so there was no doubt in my mind that she would hire me back without asking a lot of questions.

"Well, you should have called us back two weeks ago. We are your family here and we will always look out for you." I smiled. "The data entry department is full right now, but I think they have positions open in correspondence."

"What the hell is that?"

"It's where they analyze bankruptcies."

"Well, what type of experience do I need for that?"

120

"I guess you would need to have basic computer experience. Just come here and fill out the application and I'll recommend you for re-hire."

"And, how much is the starting salary?"

"I don't know because I'm not too familiar with that department, but I'll let the supervisor know that you are coming. When would you be able to come in?"

"I guess I can make it tomorrow."

"Well, call me back in fifteen minutes. I'll walk over to her office and see what she says."

"OK," I said, hanging up the phone and praying to God that He would help me get a job. My mother always told me that your life is what you make of it and I was sure trying to do the best with what I had.

It would seem funny beginning a new position at the same company I'd worked before, but at this point I had no choice. I thought in my head over and over again— handling bankruptcies. I don't know a thing about that, but I am sure I'll be trained. I let at least twenty minutes pass before calling back. I didn't want to seem like I was pressed for the job even though I was. To let the time pass I straightened up my apartment and did a little dusting.

"Damn! I got her voice mail," I said aloud when I finally called. "Hey, Pat, this is Rashad. I was just calling you back to see what the outcome was. You can give me a call at 215-555-9683. OK, thanks bye-bye." I began to head to my bedroom to get dressed for the day. All I needed to do was come up with a hell of a plan to take care of my bills for now and worry about getting a job later.

As I drove to my grandmother's house I thought hard about what my next move would be. Suddenly a thought came to my mind. I remember Calvin telling me that his mother had opened a bank account for him in her name. He always carried his MAC card around in his wallet.

I didn't have to worry about Calvin thinking twice

about my idea because he was just learning about life and he wanted to learn how to craft but there was no one around to teach him. I would be honored to be the perfect teacher and show him that crafting is a beautiful thing. The only requirement is a drive to learn how to get free money and spend it without a conscience. Teaching Calvin the ropes of crafting would be a nice experience for us, and it would bring us closer—we could have a happier and stronger relationship.

No sooner had I reached my grandmother's house, it was almost four o'clock. I knew Calvin would be just walking through the door. I grabbed the phone off the wall and started dialing his number. I didn't have time to tell Shay-Shay about my plan because I had to tell Calvin while it was still fresh in my mind.

"Hello," he answered in a sexy voice.

"Hey, Calvin," I said, blushing like I always do when talking to him. I bypassed all of the sexy talk for at least a while so I could get down to business. He asked me to hold so he could answer the other line. I made small talk with Shay while on hold. She was changing the baby's diapers.

"I'm back," he said cheerfully. "Now, what do you want to talk about?"

"Well, you know how you always said that you wanted to know how to craft, right?" He sat silently on the phone as I continued. "I have an idea that will benefit both of us. How would you like to learn how to craft using your ATM card?"

"Rashad, there is only one problem."

"And what is that?"

"There's no money in my account. I think there is only about four dollars left in there."

"That's perfect. All you need to do is give me your ATM card and I'll do the rest."

"What are you going to do?"

"I'm gonna put some money in it for us."

"How are you gonna do that?" This boy had more and more questions for me to answer. "What am I gonna tell my mother when she asks me what happened to the card?"

"You can just tell her that you lost it or it was stolen but don't do that until I tell you to." I knew I needed to go into more detail with Calvin regarding what I was gonna do with his ATM card.

After working at a couple of banks I knew the ins and the outs of how their systems were set up. Calvin banked with Sunshine Savings and Loans in North Philly. I used to work there a while back. Using Calvin's ATM card, I would deposit checks that were drawn from another bank. Usually within two business days a check would clear without the issuing bank clearing it first. At that time, I could remove all the funds from the account using the ATM machine. I was all set for my plan to work.

The following Tuesday I had on my green shirt and tie, dressed to kill again, but this time I had an interview in the correspondence department of Bankruptcies Express. I was so happy when Pat had called me back to schedule an interview. It took me some time to get used to driving all the way out to Horsham, Pennsylvania, because I hadn't gone this way in so long. I had used the directions I printed from MapQuest to help me find my way. I sped down the expressway banging the latest tunes from KeKe Wyatt. I was falling in love with that CD. The sun was shining brightly and I had a good feeling about today since I had already worked for this company before. I rolled down the window letting the air hit my face as I watched Calvin's picture swing back and forth while hanging from my rearview. I approached the brown building where I had to be buzzed in.

"Hey, Rashad!" someone yelled from behind. It was Stacy. She ran up and gave me a hug like we were cool like that. I hugged her anyway. She smiled and asked how I've been and so on, like she really cared. All she wanted to know was if I was really gay or not. When I worked here before it seemed like that was the talk of the whole office. *That fucking faggot*; I knew that's what was in her head as she began checking me out from head to toe. I smiled. How could I be so fake? She then took my hand and guided me though the doors to the rest of the office where everyone stood up to admire my outfit. I walked around the entire room parading as if I owned the company or something. The truth was, these bitches were giving me my life and I was working it. Even though I didn't have a job, a bitch still knew how to throw on some clothes for an interview, even if it was only for a $10-an-hour job. I talked to Pat for about five minutes before a middle-aged white lady named Ellen greeted me.

"You must be Rashad Smith," she said, walking over to me and smiling.

I put my hand out to shake hers.

"Seems like you have quite a fan club around here," she said jokingly. I parted a smile as she guided me into a small room and asked me to have a seat at the table. I sat there as she walked out of the room, shutting the door behind her after letting me know she'd be right with me. I cuffed my hands and said a little prayer asking God to please bless me with this job. I didn't know how long I could keep asking my mother to support me. Ellen returned with another woman following behind her.

"Rashad, this is Lisa," she said, moving out of the way so that I could shake Lisa's hand.

"Nice to meet you," I said, wearing my million-dollar smile. I pulled out my résumé and laid it on the table as Ellen began speaking.

"So Pam tells me a lot of nice things about you," Ellen said, starting the conversation. "So tell me about yourself." I knew that was coming. I also knew that for this interview to go well I would have to speak like I had some education because my résumé wasn't selling me. I had no prior experience working with bankruptcies. After I talked for about fifteen minutes they smiled at one another, took my résumé, and told me they would call within a couple of days. I smiled then excused myself from the room. I walked out puzzled. Not because I thought I didn't get the job but because I wondered why they didn't let me know at the time if I had gotten it or not. Only time would tell. When I got to the parking lot, Stacy was there smoking a cigarette.

"So, Rashad, how did it go?" she asked. I knew she didn't care whether or not I got the job, she was just being nosy. She probably thought I was going to take her position away, but I knew she would keep it—she and Pat were cousins.

"It went fine, thanks for asking."

"Good luck, and I'll be seeing you," she said. I walked straight to my car without responding; not even a goodbye. I unraveled the knot in my tie and back home I went. My cell phone rang.

"Hello?" I answered.

"Wassup, shawty?" It was Calvin. As soon as I heard his voice the tip of my dick got wet.

"Hey," I said in a sweet voice.

"So, how did it go?"

"I think it went fine." I had told him that I took off today to go to this interview—I wouldn't dare let him know that I wasn't working. It was bad enough that his mother now knew my real age. I respected his mother for allowing me to stay in her son's life. She knew that I would do anything for him and the baby.

"Am I gonna see you later?" I asked.

"Naw, not today because I am supposed to go look at some cars with Joseph."

"Oh, OK, cool." I knew that even though Joseph

was Ron's boyfriend, he and Calvin were always cool. "So I guess I'll see you tomorrow then?" I asked, speeding down the expressway.

"We'll see," he said. I giggled. "Call me when you get home, all right?"

"I'll do just that," I told him before hanging up.

It's been two days and I haven't heard from that lady yet. I stared at the number on her business card that she had given me. I decided to call.

"Thank you for calling Bankruptcies Express, this is Ellen." It was her voice mail. I was not gonna hang up. I wanted her to know that I was still interested so I left a nice follow-up message along with my number. Now this is the part that I hated the most; waiting. While I waited I ran into the kitchen to check on the steamed broccoli I made to go with the baked chicken and rice I made for Calvin. This was the night for us to have a candlelit dinner. He said he'd be here in a half an hour. I knew it shouldn't even be that long since he said Joseph was dropping him off.

I heard the car tires screech as Joseph pulled off. I opened the door and our lips met for the first time in a week.

"It smells good in here, let me find out you cooked," Calvin said while palming my ass. He was looking extremely good this day rocking a silver Adidas sweat suit with a white T-shirt underneath. He sat down on the couch in the living room to watch *Madea's Family Reunion* as I lit the candles in the kitchen. Kevin called. I took the phone and walked into the bedroom.

"Wha you up to, mon?" he asked.

"I'm trying to get my groove on and you are interrupting me," I spat. "I've cooked dinner for Calvin and tonight is gonna be the night I tell him I want to be with him."

"Well, you not wit 'im, now?"

"No, we are just friends right now, but tonight I am

gonna tell him that I'm ready to be in a relationship with him." I tried to speak quietly so Calvin would not hear me. "I have to go. I'll tell you how everything went later, OK?"

"All right, more time."

I walked back into the kitchen and placed the phone back on the base. Calvin continued to watch the show while I made his plate in the kitchen. I started making small talk, asking how his day was at school and how are his mother and the baby. He told me that Jon has a cold and his mother is going to get him this weekend. As I began preparing our plates, he snuck up behind me and kissed me on my neck. He slid his ATM card into my pocket then turned to sit down at the table.

"This food is delicious," he said, chewing the meat from a chicken bone. After eating the last little bit of rice from my plate, I slid it over and rested my elbows on the table. I was ready to talk.

"What's wrong?" he asked.

"Nothing, I'm just looking at you eat." He smiled at me and I surely returned it back to him. "I want to talk to you about something important." He looked at me with curiosity.

"Did something happen?"

"No, it's not anything bad at all. I just wanted to talk about us."

"What wrong with us?" he said, confused. I took a deep breath and went straight for it.

"I'm ready," I blurted out.

"Ready for what?" he asked as he looked into my eyes like he didn't know what I meant.

"To be in a relationship with you," I said as he continued to eat his food. "Calvin, did you hear what I just said?"

"Yeah, I heard you," he said, not lifting his head from his plate. I took another long breath and then began clearing the table.

# Smoking Cigarettes

"So, what do you think?" I asked, putting my plate in the sink. He stopped and wiped his hands on a piece of napkin. He looked straight ahead, and I could see he was gathering his thoughts before responding. I knew I had caught him off guard. He had asked me over and over again would I be in a relationship with him, and all I could do at the time was tell him that he was too young. He showed me so much love and support, I decided I could not let him down by saying that I didn't want to be with him. Calvin had shown me he could take on the role of a man and take care of what's his. I will always love him for that.

"Rashad, I think we should remain friends," he said, looking into my eyes as I gazed back into his.

"What are you talking about, Calvin? I thought you wanted to be my boyfriend?" I replied, as my eyes filled with tears.

"Yeah, that's when I thought I wanted to be in a relationship, but now, I feel as though I need to be focused on school and my son."

I just couldn't understand where he was coming from. I sat in the chair that faced him at the table. "Are you sure this is what you want?" I asked, hoping he would change his mind or admit he was playing some type of trick. I moved in closer to him and grabbed his hand.

"I think I'm falling in love with you, Calvin, and the other day you said you love me too, right?"

"Yeah, I did say that I love you, but at this time I don't want to be in a relationship," he said, lifting his glass to drink his Kool-Aid.

I tried so hard to find reason in all this but it seemed like I couldn't. "So where do we go from here?"

"We can still be friends," he said, thinking that he'd make me feel better. I walked into my bedroom. After about two minutes, he followed.

"Are you OK?" He stood behind me, rubbing my shoulders.

"No, I'm not OK, Calvin. I thought we were gonna be together and now you're telling me that you don't want to be with me."

"No, I didn't say that I didn't want to be with you, I just don't want to be in a relationship right now. Look, Rashad, I have a lot of things on my plate right now. I have to think about school, college, and my son," he said while looking at our reflections in the mirror. I turned around and kissed him on the lips. He stuck his tongue deep into my mouth as I grabbed him closer.

"I need you, Calvin," I said as I stopped kissing him. He pulled back and sat on the edge of the bed. I sat down beside him. I leaned over to kiss him on the cheek, and he smiled. "So will you be mine?" He sighed again.

"I told you, I want to be with you but I just can't be with you right now."

"So, what the hell is that supposed to mean? You want me to wait until you are ready? How selfish is that?"

He got up and walked into the living room and then sat on the couch. I turned on some soft music to help ease my mind. All I could do was think about him, and although he sat in the other room it seemed like he was so, so far. I took off my shirt, leaving nothing on but my undershirt. I walked back into the living room and sat across from him on the sofa.

"I'm gonna wait for you," I said in a sleek tone. He shook his head up and down obliging and then stood up, indicating he was ready to leave. I walked him to the door and then planted a gigantic kiss on his lips before he walked out. I turned around and picked up the phone to call Kevin to tell him how my dinner went. I opened up my heart to Kevin the same way I would have opened up to Calvin if he had let me.

\* \* \*

# Smoking Cigarettes

On my way home after depositing the checks into Calvin's account, I stopped at the Chinese store around the corner to get three chicken wings and some fries. I loved chicken wings. They always seemed to help me when I was depressed. I walked in the house to see the red light blinking on the answering machine. I pressed the button to hear my messages while pulling out a plate.

"Hello, Rashad, this is Ellen from Bankruptcies Express. I'm calling to tell you that we would like to offer a position to you, if you are still interested. Please give me a call at 215-555-3697, thank you." I dropped the plate and the bag of wings on the counter and ran into my bedroom to call her back. Still remembering the numbers she said, I dialed immediately. After about two rings she answered.

"Hello, Ellen? This is Rashad," I said, smiling.

"Yes, Rashad, I'm glad you called me back. I would like to offer you a position starting at $10.00 an hour, is that OK?" There was no reason for her to even ask, I accepted the position. After hanging up the phone I fell onto the bed, relieved from all the stress of not having a job. I couldn't wait to call my mom and tell her. I would tell Calvin I received a promotion.

I began to believe that Camisha was affecting his decision not to pursue a relationship with me because she would always call his cell phone and ask him why he was hanging around with me. I knew that all these things were starting to affect Calvin; I hated to see him going through all this hurt.

The week was coming to an end and Drew was having a dinner for our friend Taz's birthday. I knew I needed to attend if only to show my face then leave. I really wasn't feeling it because Calvin was stressing over Camisha. She wanted to take him to court for child support after she learned that we were fucking. Contrary to what was going on between them, my crafting plan was working. I had to wait 'til midnight before I could see any available funds in the account. I told Calvin the basics of how it worked, and then I told him to watch the time so we could go to the ATM together.

We showed up at Drew's house sporting the same outfit. We were looking good. Drew cooked a great meal for Taz: fried chicken, baked mac and cheese, cornbread, and spinach. I also bought Taz a sweater from Strawbridge's with the money that I had left over from the last craft. The dinner party consisted of three couples: Drew and his friend Sam; Taz and his friend Monte; and of course, Calvin and me. We closed the evening with a run down 13th Street where we ran into sexy-ass Dwayne. I didn't want to make it seem like I had a crush on him because Calvin was there, and even though he didn't want to be in a relationship with me right now I knew I still had to be on my P's and Q's. I gave Dwayne a simple handshake and kept it moving. The night was fun and Calvin and I watched the clock as it ticked past midnight. I went to check the account at the machine and the funds were not available.

"It's not working," Calvin said sarcastically. I knew that it was just a matter of time. Since this was his first time he didn't know much about patience. We stood on 13th Street until about two in the morning. Everything was still the same; I wasn't missing much. Faggots, faggots, faggots; they all were downtown tonight. I saw a lot of old friends as well as old dates. I even saw some boys I used to fuck back in the day. Troy and Basil were down there too. Everyone was coming from a free ball being held around the corner at the William Way Center.

Calvin had already made prior plans to spend the night at my apartment, so after taking Drew home we decided to head in ourselves. Once I got home I removed every article of clothing on my body while Calvin lay across the bed. I lay next to him and kissed him on the forehead.

# Smoking Cigarettes

"I love you," I said to Calvin.

"I love you, too," he said, grabbing and kissing the back of my hand. Our lips met and I held him close to me and close to my heart. We fell asleep just past 3 a.m.

The next morning I was awakened by Calvin turning pages in *The Source* magazine that laid beside my bed.

"What's wrong with you?" he asked as I grabbed my pillow and held it tighter.

"Nothing," I said, getting up and walking into the bathroom. He continued to lie on the bed and flip through the pages. I walked back in the room and laid on top of the cover. I clicked the television's remote button on and off, realizing that the cable company had disconnected it. I didn't want to be embarrassed so I just turned it off before he noticed the fuzzy picture on the screen. I hadn't paid the bill in months so it wasn't a surprise that my services had been terminated. I turned around and grabbed him by his waist, fully embracing him. I pulled the covers back and looked at his dick swollen from not taking his morning piss. I started to throb.

He put the magazine down as I removed his penis from his boxers and tasted him for breakfast. He put his hand on the back of my head as I motioned up and down on his stick. When the phone rang I didn't stop. I kept going until it rang again. I reached over to answer it, leaving his large pole wet from his pre-cum and my saliva.

"Hello," I answered, while stroking Calvin's manhood up and down so he wouldn't get soft. I heard a faint cry on the other end of the phone.

"Who is this?" I spat. It was Drew.

"Rashad, I don't know how to tell you this, but—" I stood up off the bed, turning my back to Calvin as he put himself back in his boxers.

"What's wrong?"

"Dwayne was shot last night!"

"He was shot? Well, is he OK?" I said a quick and silent prayer to myself, hoping everything would be OK before Drew could answer.

"No, he's dead," Drew said, still sobbing.

"Oh my God!" I placed the phone beside me as I sat back down on the bed. Calvin grabbed the phone to talk to Drew. I grabbed the phone back from Calvin and began to ask questions in disbelief. "Who shot him, Drew?"

With his voice clearing up he began to speak.

"Marvin called me this morning and told me that after we seen Dwayne last night down 13th Street, him and his supposed-to-be boyfriend went back to Dwayne's house," he said, as I struggled to keep my balance and hear the rest of the story while Calvin watched every move I made. "Once they got home, Marvin said that him and the boy got into an argument. Then, Dwayne went to take a shower, and the boy shot him in the back of the head, leaving him to die in the shower."

"So, now what?" I asked Drew as I held the phone and stared straight ahead, forgetting that Calvin was still there with me.

"I'll try to find out some more details then I'll call you back."

"OK," I replied as I hit the end button.

"Are you OK?" Calvin asked, as I sat lost in space. All I could think of was Dwayne's pretty face and his luscious lips. I had a crush on him since the beginning of time. I loved his B-boy style and his braids. The tears began to flow. Calvin grabbed me and softly hugged me as I squeezed him back. I leaned back and looked into Calvin's eyes.

"What happened?" he asked.

"One of my friends was killed last night. Do you remember the dude with the braids that wore the white shirt last night?"

"The guy that was standing against the wall?"

# Smoking Cigarettes

"Yeah."

"With the braids?"

"Yup," I said, moving my head up and down and then covering my face with my hands. I couldn't believe that Dwayne was dead. Just two months ago I sat and had a long talk with him in his apartment. Damn, I said to myself, getting up and walking into the bathroom with Calvin following behind.

"Are you gonna be OK?" he asked, looking at my face in the mirror's reflection.

"Yes." I turned on the shower and let the steam fill the bathroom until I couldn't see myself in the mirror. Calvin returned to the bedroom and I began removing my boxers and my shirt before slipping into the shower. I scrubbed every inch of my body, thinking of all the torment that Dwayne must have gone through. I asked myself a bunch of questions: Did he suffer or did he die on the spot? Did he think the boy would shoot him? I was confused. I let the water run on top of my head while I collected my thoughts.

I heard a tap on the door.

"Drew is on the phone for you!" Calvin yelled, trying to be heard over the running water.

"Tell him I'll call him back once I get out the shower." I looked as the water ran down the drain. That's how I felt about my life, everything was going down the drain. I had just gotten a job, which made me know that there was a God and he was watching over me, but I still didn't have any money. It dawned on me that I needed to check the account to see if any funds had become available. I began washing myself up using a soap that Kevin had brought back from Jamaica, which he visited a few months ago. I hopped out the shower, then started to get dressed before calling Drew back for details.

"Yeah," said Drew, answering the phone on the first ring.

"This shit don't make no sense," I said.

"I know, just think if y'all would have gotten together, then this would have never happened." I turned around to Calvin who was already dressed and waiting for me.

"I'm about to take Calvin home so I'll call you later." I led Calvin to the car with the ATM card in my back pocket. We drove to a bank with a drive-thru ATM. I inserted the card then punched in the pin code. I heard the machine count out $400 in twenties. Calvin's eyes lit up bigger than two fifty-cent pieces.

The machine ejected the money into my hand as I sat in the car across from Calvin's smiling face. I counted out two hundred a piece for us, then drove off.

"I'm going shopping," Calvin said, counting his money.

"Damn, nigga. You should put that money to good use and spend it on your son," I spat.

"That's what I'm talking about. I'm gonna get him some new clothes and sneakers." In a split second I realized that although I now had some money, Dwayne was still dead. I got silent for a minute.

You thinking about Dwayne?"

"Yeah."

"Are you going to the funeral?" I had to think about it. Dwayne knew a lot of people and he was very popular. "A funeral slash fashion show," Calvin uttered under his breath as we approached his grandmother's house.

I kissed him on the lips, letting him know that I'd call him later, then I sped off with thoughts of Dwayne wailing through my mind. I didn't have a destination, but I knew I needed to go somewhere to be comforted. I decided to spend the day with Shay-Shay and the baby. We took a trip to the Gallery where we walked around all day and shopped. I spent the money I was supposed to use to pay bills. I figured that since I now have a job, I could spend the money and re-up later. I already had in my mind that I would tell Calvin that crafting didn't work any longer. I would then get more money out of the ATM and keep it without him knowing.

Shay and I walked the entire mall and eventually met up with a couple of people we knew from around the way, and had dinner with them. I bought a couple of pairs of pants, a shirt, and a pair of sneakers. Since I was starting my new job I knew that my wardrobe should be tight.

Later that evening I tried to get Calvin to come over and watch a movie with me but he had already made plans to go to a party with Joseph. I went to my apartment and unloaded my bags before trying on different clothes I had bought.

I got comfortable and watched Tyler Perry's play, *Diary of a Mad Black Woman*, seeing all the terrible things this black woman was going through with her husband, which made me think of Calvin and our relationship. One day we would be together like that, but we would never fight nor argue. Plus, cheating is not a word in our vocabulary.

I continued to watch the sad play until I fell asleep.

The phone rang four times before I was able to reach over and pick it up while trying to focus to see the time.

"Hello," I said in a grumpy voice. It was Calvin. I finally focused on the clock, it read 3:20 a.m.

"Wassup?" he said. "I was just calling you to say good night."

I tried not to disturb my sleep. "Good night," I told him before placing the phone in its base.

\* \* \*

Monday morning was the start of a brand new day

as I awakened with a smile because I now had a job and someone I could call my own. I sat up in the bed thinking about how much of a good time I had with Calvin just the day before. We went down South Street to shop, and he bought me a pair of the new Air Force 2s and a pair of Girbaud jeans. We purchased gay pride iron-on patches that we would wear together and we ate at Uno's. We had so much fun with one another, with the exception of Dwayne's death still on my mind.

After taking a shower I decided to wear my brand new khaki colored Girbaud pants with a matching Polo shirt and a new pair of Timberland boots. With my fly haircut and all, I looked like I was dressed for my first day of school. I jumped into my car and headed to Horsham, PA. To make it on time I took a shortcut through Broad Street. Once I arrived at work I had to go through orientation for about an hour where our benefits and what not were discussed. One of my club buddies named Kya was there. She is a fine, young, light-skinned girl that all the girls down on 13th Street want to be with. Her weave flows down her back like it's her real hair.

"Hey, Rashad!" she yelled to me from across the room.

"Girl, you gonna be working here too? What department?"

"I'm gonna be working in billing," she said, sounding happy to see me.

"That's what's up. At least I will have someone to go to lunch with now, someone who I can relate to." We laughed.

The room got silent as the instructor Mrs. Owens took the floor, explaining the rules and regulations of the company. I took notice of her Louis Vuitton blazer. Mrs. Owens is an older lady, like in her mid- or late forties, and the rumor around the office is that she has money and lives in a big house. She supposedly sent all three of her daughters to college without taking out a loan at all.

After orientation I proceeded to my department for further instructions. I walked through the office looking around to see where I would fit in, when a fat white lady named Annie greeted me.

"Hello," she said, as she grabbed my hand without me extending it to her. She walked me over to my new desk where I placed my jacket on the back of the chair and my book bag on the floor. She turned on the computer for me as I sat down. Then, she pulled up a chair next to mine.

"I will be your trainer," she said. I continued to look around at everyone as they looked at their computers and typed like they were zombies. I didn't even choose to make small talk with Annie just yet. I sat back and followed her lead as I watched her boot up my computer then go in and out of different programs. By the time lunch hour came around I was tired. I was ready to go home and it seemed like I had been here forever. I treated all the people from data entry to lunch with the money I got from crafting. I had a salad, figuring that this was a new beginning to my life, and it was time that I lose some weight. Although I ordered a salad I made sure I piled on extra dressing. The whole time I sat talking to my coworkers I eyed every male that walked through the cafeteria. I had my eyes on this one guy named Koz; he was sexy, and a shorty too. He was light-skinned with long braids that flowed past his shoulders. I loved his smile, but he had eyes on one of the girls sitting at our table.

"Did y'all hear about that young boy that was found in the dumpster behind the Sears in the parking lot?" Tina said. She had been my boss when I worked in her department. I immediately lost my appetite but didn't make it obvious as I continued to listen more while stirring my lunch around with my fork.

"For real! What happened?" asked Tye who sat next to me, eating a cheese steak.

"You didn't see the news this morning? And it was in today's paper. Some young boy, I think they said he was about 21 years old. It happened in Upper Darby." Everyone got quiet so Tina could tell the story as she went into a bag that sat on the floor next to her chair and pulled out the *Philadelphia Daily News*. "Here it is right here, 'Young Man Slain in Upper Darby.'" She proceeded to read the passage. I sipped my soda and sat quietly while she read through the entire article. I placed the lid back on my salad container because I knew I wasn't gonna finish it.

I learned that when Paul's body was found, he was without sneakers or clothes and all he had on his person was his Walkman. What would Rafeek do with his clothes? I wondered.

"Also, it says that he had a few teeth missing and his skin was sliced from both of his cheeks to his ears. The police have yet to find the killer and the motive behind the slaying but they are still looking. Funeral services will be held at Terry's Funeral Home in West Philly tomorrow at 11 a.m.," she continued.

As I sat at the table the story of that night replayed in my head and I wondered why Rafeek pulled out some of his teeth and cut the other side of his face. I shook my head back and forth as if I was disgusted like everyone else. My eyes started to water as I thought about the night Paul and I made passionate love and how I could feel his large dick sliding in and out of me. Just thinking about it made the tip of my dick wet from the pre-cum. By the time I snapped out of my trance I noticed that my lunch break was over.

The week was slowly coming to an end and I procrastinated about what I was going to wear to Dwayne's funeral. I knew I had to think of something quick because it was only two days away. I had already begun to have nightmares about him anyway, so Kevin and Drew came to keep me company throughout the week so I wouldn't be scared to go to sleep. I had enough money to get something new because I had paid my rent with the money left over from the craft. After getting about a thousand dollars from Calvin's account, it was closed.

Friday finally came and I was ready for the weekend with the exception of the funeral. I was very tired from working through the week. I went home and lay on the living room floor without even taking off my shoes and then I went to sleep. The phone rang, rang, and rang. I finally crawled into the kitchen and picked it up.

"Hello," I answered.

"Wassup?" said Calvin.

"Nuffin, I was asleep." I held the phone to my ear while listening to him sigh.

"What's wrong?" I asked, trying to wake up and get myself together. He sighed again. "What's wrong?"

"Rashad."

"What?"

"I don't want to be in a relationship right now," he said, as if the world was being lifted from his shoulders. I caught an instant headache.

"Well, you don't have to be in a relationship with me," I spat. At this point I was tired of fighting with him over the same thing. I crawled back into the living room and rested my head down on my arms as I listened to him tell me all the reasons he didn't want to be with me.

"So, can we be just friends?" he asked between sighs.

"Yes, Calvin, we can be friends. Now, can I go back to sleep?" The phone got silent like he was shocked at the answer he had just received.

"All right, I'll call you later," he said, breaking the silence.

"OK," I said, and then the line went dead.

I lay there on the floor for about ten minutes while gathering my thoughts. I tried to put all the negative bullshit that Calvin was giving me out of my mind. It had been a long week for me because I had to work and that took some getting used to, and one of my friends had gotten killed; now here he comes with this bullshit. I couldn't stand it any longer. I dialed Kevin's phone but he hadn't gotten home from work yet so I decided to get my haircut.

After leaving the barbershop, I admired my hair in my bathroom mirror. I was looking so fresh and so clean. I didn't want to waste my precious time on the likeness of Calvin, so I decided to call Basil's sexy ass.

The phone rang three times before he answered.

"Yo," Basil answered in his deep sexy voice.

"Wassup, Basil, it's Rashad."

"Wassup, Rashad, how you been?" he asked, sounding surprised by my call.

"I'm fine and yourself?" The other line beeped and I asked him to hold.

"Hello," I answered.

"Yeah, what you doing?" Calvin asked.

"I'm on the other line, I'ma call you back," I said without giving him a chance to respond.

"I'm back," I told Basil, who was patiently waiting. I heard him exhale the smoke from a cigarette.

"So, what's up with you?" he asked.

"I'm good. I have been trying to decide whether or not I'm gonna attend Dwayne's funeral. Are you going?"

"Yeah, I'm going, but man that shit was fucked up, and you know that they are looking for Shannon."

"Why would they be looking for Shannon?"

"Because everyone seems to think that Dwayne was set up and Shannon had something to do with him being murdered."

"Damn," I said, letting my eyes hit the floor.

"So, Shannon is wanted by a lot of people," he continued.

"Well, I just hope that they find all the evidence to

convict who they need to convict. Did they ever catch the boy who shot him?"

"Yeah, they say that he was dealing with some Muslim dude. He was trade. (A straight guy who has sex with dudes on the side—your basic down low nigga.) But he's in jail now."

"So what are you doing tonight?" I asked, changing the subject.

"Nothing, I'm just sitting back and chillin'."

"Would you like to do something tonight? Maybe we could go to dinner or watch a movie or something?"

"Yeah, that's cool."

"All right, that's wassup, you know where I live, right?"

"Yeah, I know where you live. Just let me take a shower and get myself together and I should be over in like an hour."

"OK," I said, gazing out of the window at the sunset as we said our goodbyes.

My mind felt at ease because I had had it in for Basil for a long time. I wanted him so bad but it seemed like every time I tried to talk to him his boyfriend was around. He assured me that they weren't together any longer. We never did do anything sexual, I just loved the way we laid in my bed and held one another. He was all man and just the man that I needed to keep my bed warm.

I decided to take a nice hot bath myself before I got my evening started. By the time I put lotion on myself and put on my underwear, Basil was at my door. I opened it just wearing my Polo robe and a pair of fuzzy slippers. He embraced me totally before having a seat on the couch while I went back into my room to finish preparing for our dinner at LaRose Café. I loved their food.

After about fifteen minutes of preparing I was done. I grabbed my keys and walked out the door, not even giving it a second thought that I hadn't returned Calvin's phone call. We drove all the way to North Philly so we could chow down on some soul food at the café. Since it seemed as if we both were watching our figures, we didn't eat much. I watched him as he excused himself from the table and walked to the restroom. His sexy bowlegged walk just turned me on. But at the table I started wondering what Calvin was doing. It seemed as if I thought him up because then my cell phone started to ring.

"What?" I answered quickly, sounding annoyed by Calvin's phone call.

"What are you doing?" he asked as if it was any of his business.

"I'm out," I spat.

"With who?"

"I'm on a date. Why are you asking so many questions?" I asked, trying to make him jealous.

"I was just wondering where you were, that's all."

"Well, I'll call you when I get home," I said, disconnecting the call.

Basil came back to the table; I smiled at him as he sat down. We decided to go back to my apartment for drinks and a movie. We paid our halves of the check since I knew he wasn't working and I didn't want to make it seem like I couldn't take care of my own. At my apartment we made ourselves comfortable on the couch. The phone began ringing; I answered on the second ring.

"How is your date?" asked Calvin.

"It's going OK. What can I do for you?"

"Is he still there?"

"Yes, I'll call you back," I said as I reached over Basil to hang up the phone. We positioned ourselves carefully so that we could cuddle under one another while watching *Misery*. I began to fall asleep while rubbing my hands over his hairy chest. I looked up at his face to notice that he was already asleep. I led him into the bedroom so that we could get comfortable. After settling under my nice warm sheets we fell asleep in each other's arms.

I dreamed about how my life would end up in five or ten years. It wasn't that long before the sun peered through the blinds. I began to smile when I noticed Basil awakening and fondling me under the covers as he lifted up my shirt.

He started at the top of my neck and kissed me all the way down my back. I grabbed my pillow but could not seem to relax. This was what I had been waiting for from Basil for a long time and I was finally getting the opportunity to get what I wanted. I felt his sweet lips tickle themselves down my spine to the crack of my love tunnel, but he didn't stop there. I didn't make a move, so he wouldn't think that I was awake. He removed my boxer briefs, then parted my ass like God parted the Red Sea. He entered my shack with his tongue, licking up and down my crack and sticking his tongue in and out my dark hole making me wet from the front and back. As I felt his wet tongue maneuver in and out my ass, I moved my backside up and down as he kissed and licked his meal. The sun was still shining brightly, and I turned over and opened my eyes just halfway as he put his muscular body on top of mine. I began licking on his neck and his chest; he tasted like salt. I kissed him and tasted cigarette smoke. He placed his long dick on my stomach and began moving up and down and grinding very hard. I grabbed his back.

"Do you have any condoms?" he asked. I pointed over to the drawer. My mind was racing. I had waited so long for this moment with him and I figured since I couldn't get it from Dwayne because of his death then Basil would be the next best thing. He reached over and stuck his hand inside the top dresser drawer and pulled out a latex condom. I laid back on the bed and thought about Calvin and how I wished that Basil was him. He removed the condom from the wrapper.

"Basil, I don't think I'm ready." He stopped in mid

air and looked me up and down.

"OK, so what do you want to do then?" He placed a soft kiss on my lips as he laid his hairy body on top of mine. I kissed his neck and tasted salt again. As we laid in my bed, I thought about what I wouldn't give to have Calvin lying in my bed right now. I wanted every inch of Calvin and not Basil. What was I thinking to even allow another man to come in and take his place? I held Basil in my arms and felt his dick touch up against my thighs as it was starting to get soft. In another life maybe Basil would have been right for me, and although I was horny as hell he would not get any sex from me. I tried to do everything I could to take my mind off Calvin, but I couldn't.

I made up a lie that I needed to take my mother somewhere, just to get Basil to leave. He got up and stood directly where my eyes could see him. His dick swung from side to side as he walked over to get his boxers and clothes that were hanging over the chair. He was very hairy. I wondered if maybe that was where that salty taste was coming from. He lit a cigarette as he began to put on his sneakers then gave me a hug as I walked him to the door.

"I'll call you later," I said to him, with Calvin fresh in my mind. He smiled as he walked down the steps.

I ran into my bedroom and picked up the phone to call Calvin. I looked up at the clock; it was 8:55 a.m. I dialed his number in a hurry for him to come over and relieve my tension.

"Hello," he answered. It was a good thing he answered because I didn't feel like asking for him. It would feel weird being on the phone with his grandmother with my hard dick.

"What you doing?" I asked excitedly.

"Just woke up, why?"

"Cuz I want you to come ova," I said, wishing he'd stop asking questions.

"Fa' what?"

"Because, I'm waiting for you."

"Rashad, I have to get dressed."

"You can get dressed when you get here."

"Man, I'm tired, this fucking baby kept me up all night."

"Please, Calvin can you hurry up and come over here?"

"All right, man," he said, before hanging up the phone.

While I waited I started to get my clothes together for the day. I really was beginning to hate getting dressed because of my weight. After about fifteen minutes I decided to call Calvin back to see if he'd left yet.

"Hello," he answered.

"Dang, you ain't leave yet?"

"I had to wash up."

"Calvin, you don't have to wash up, just come over here and bring your clothes and you can take a shower here."

"OK, I'm leaving out now," he said before the line went dead. I smiled, thinking of how things would be once he arrived.

I called back after twenty minutes and the phone just rang. His grandmother must have taken the baby and gone somewhere. Calvin was for sure on his way to my apartment. I laid out my blue shirt and denim jeans across the bed so everything would be ready once we got out of the shower. I ran to the window and saw Calvin walking up the street carrying his bag of clothes. I smiled, letting out a sigh and wondering how he'd gotten here so fast.

I opened the door and embraced him before kissing him gently while sucking on his tongue.

"What was the rush for?" he asked with a confused look in his eyes.

"Nothing, I just wanted you to be here with me." I

dropped to my knees and unzipped his pants. He placed his bag of clothes down beside the love seat. I pulled out his long, fat, love stick and slurped him like a 7-Eleven slurpee on a hot day. He laid back on the love seat and closed his eyes as I licked all over his stomach. I was beginning to like his distinctive smell and taste. I didn't taste the salt any longer nor did I smell the funk of cigarettes. I was with the man that I loved and cared about. I grabbed his big hands while my mouth did all the work on his dick. I didn't need to undress him fully, as long as I had access to the dick I was fine. He plunged himself deeper into my mouth as his liquid flushed my throat. He sank deeper into the love seat as I drank his babies. I left him lying there as he fell asleep. His dick was starting to get soft as it hung out of his Scooby-Doo boxers while I went into the bathroom for a hot bath.

# Smoking Cigarettes

## It Is What It Is

As we got ourselves together for Dwayne's funeral I became discouraged because I still could not believe that he was gone. I couldn't come to grips that one of my peers had passed on. The same guy who had 13th Street on lock was now gone. He was the cutest of them all. Man what a waste. How could anyone be so cruel to shoot someone dead in the head? It doesn't matter how many times a person cheats on somebody, they don't deserve to die. I had to deal with this funeral as well as plan my mother's 50th surprise birthday party. I knew that this would not be easy.

"Hello," Drew said into his cell phone.

"Are you ready?" I asked him as I exited the expressway to his house.

"Yeah, we all are ready—me, Taz, and Sam."

"OK, I'll be there in five minutes."

\* \* \*

We pulled up in front of the packed church in North Philly where there were two limousines parked out front and a hearse. I double-parked my car as one of the ushers came over to place a funeral sticker on the window. We walked up the steps to the crowded church and saw some familiar faces from 13th Street. We stood in the back of the line to have one last look at Dwayne before the casket would close. The closer we got to the casket my tears started to fall. Drew looked over at me with red eyes as well. A few steps away from the love that shoulda, woulda, coulda, was now laying there at peace. Drew and I approached the casket with deep sorrow in our eyes. I walked up to the sexy boy and felt his hands, they were cold as ice. His braids were neatly done as always and his lips were still plump.

The tears began to fall harder as I imagined us walking down the aisle together. Oh, I wish it could have been different. We stood in front of the beige casket where Dwayne was dressed in a black Dickie set and timbs, just like he would look if he was standing next to me. I missed him so much and wanted badly to be with him. I hated this day.

Drew wrapped his arm around me as I continued to stand and gaze at Dwayne's body. Dwayne had a frown on his face as if he was scared to be wherever he was. I leaned down and whispered in his ear, "Don't be scared because the Father is always watching over you and He'll be with you at all times so just hold on."

I didn't realize that I was holding up the line. I turned around and there wasn't a dry eye in the entire church. I stepped away so that others could get a chance to view.

On the ride back home I felt warmth in my heart to know that everything would be OK with Dwayne's family. My prayers went out to his family and the people that were dearest to him. After dropping Drew and Taz off, I went home. I didn't know how long it would be before I received a phone call from Calvin so I sat at my desk and began to make the arrangements for my mother's birthday party. I chose to have the party at the Brave New World nightclub on Sunday because 105.3 WDAS would do a live broadcast—it was oldies night. I would need to give the owner a $100.00 deposit and start mailing out the invitations.

Before the clock struck midnight, the phone rang.

"I was just calling to say good night," Calvin said, in a low tone.

"How come you haven't called me all day?"

"I went with Joseph to get his car fixed, and then

we got stopped by the cops on the way home."

"All right," I said, sounding sleepy. He wasn't calling from jail so I didn't inquire further. "I'll just talk to you tomorrow."

"Good night," he said once again.

"Good night."

* * *

"I hate having to ask my brothers for money to help with our mother's birthday party. If I had all the money myself I would not even bother to wait for them," I said to Kevin, while having an early breakfast with him at Denny's.

"Dey would probably help. Ah ain't see why not," he said, sipping his Lipton tea.

"I just hate asking people for stuff."

"Well, yo' mudda is dere mudda, too."

"But, they don't act like it."

"Ah feel you," Kevin said, then bit into a piece of his bagel. "Oh, ah tell you yet ah meet a fella?"

"Who?" I asked, in shock because Kevin never met anyone new.

"His name Jeremy and he work at Acme, ya know the one on City Ave?"

"Yeah," I responded, sounding very interested.

"He approached me first when ah was waiting for de late bus. Him bounce up to ask if ah know where to get good weed from."

"And, what did you say?"

"Cha, 'cause I Ja'can, I bound to know where to get ganja? Ah ain't tell 'im nutten, but he still ask meh my name."

"Well, was he cute?"

"He a'ight. Him wearing braids and he piping a lot."

"Smokes what? Weed or cigarettes?" I asked, while cutting up my sausage.

"Boat ah dem."

"Do you think that's something that you can handle?"

"Daz he. I'm not messin' in dat. He the one ruining him body," he said in a high-pitch tone. We began to laugh as I devoured my eggs, sausage, and home fries. I could see that Kevin was really falling head over heels for this guy; he had a glow in his eyes.

"Well, when am I going to meet him?"

"Jah know. We checkin' out the movies later."

"All right, I guess I'll meet him soon." We left the restaurant and I dropped him off at home, then went to my apartment to crash. I called Calvin numerous times and he didn't answer his phone. I also left him messages and waited for him to call me back. Still, no call from Calvin; I decided to take a ride over to his grandmother's house.

I didn't want him to know I was there so I eased my car up a little and parked in the space up the street. I grabbed my jacket then walked down the street to his door.

Tap, tap, tap.

I got no answer. I suddenly heard Calvin's voice talking on the phone as if he was arguing with someone. Without being invited in, I opened the unlocked door and entered. Calvin was standing in the dining room with the cordless phone up to his ear arguing about who should have sole custody of his son. I peeked over in the bassinet to find baby Jon still asleep.

Calvin turned around noticing me as I walked into the living room like a prowler. He looked at me as if he had been expecting me.

"Who are you talking to?" I mumbled the words through my hand so the person on the phone could not hear what I was saying.

"Camisha," he said in a stern voice. I could tell he

was upset by the way he was yelling at her. My nerves began to calm after I found out what was going on and why he wasn't answering his phone. I sat down at the dining room table, watching him walk back and forth in a white tank top and a pair of gray sweat pants. His dick dangled with rhythm as he paced the floor.

He looked at me as he fumed after hanging the phone up on her.

"What's her problem?" I asked, still sitting at the table. He walked over to me then grabbed the back of my head and tongued me down like he hadn't seen me in years. I grabbed his back and returned the favor. I felt his long muscle starting to become erect. I followed him upstairs to his aunt's bedroom.

About fifteen minutes into some hot, steamy lovemaking, Calvin and I heard a noise from downstairs.

I asked him what it was as he continued to pump harder inside me. This was the first time I let him inside of me without flinching or asking him to stop. I loved daddy's dick and I regretted the times I had passed it up. I heard the noise again. It sounded like the screen door opening and closing.

"Don't worry, that's my cousin coming in," he said while fully in the heat of the moment. I didn't think any more of it.

As I lay on my back getting pumped hard in my ass by the man of my dreams I closed my eyes and held him tight. I grabbed his back tighter before opening my eyes to see a shadow grace the light walls of the hallway. I assumed it was his cousin. As Calvin began to reach his climax I grabbed his back and squeezed him again as he began slobbering me down with his tongue. He pulled out of my anus and squirted his fluids onto my stomach.

"I love you, baby," he said as he collapsed on top of me with his sperm sandwiched between our bodies.

"I love you too, Calvin," I said before he walked

into the bathroom to clean himself off. I sat there for awhile to get myself together and aid my rectum, which was hurting like hell.

I wiped myself off with a towel that was next to the bed then pulled my pants up. I walked past the bathroom and slowly down the steps. I didn't see any sign of Calvin's cousin, but I saw Camisha. She didn't see me as I took quiet steps toward the bottom of the staircase. I saw her carrying an automatic handgun as she crept around the room.

How did she get in here? I wondered, and then I thought about how I hadn't locked the door after I crept in. Little Jon was still in the bassinet asleep as she walked over to him and placed her hand on his back. My hands began to shake when I realized that Calvin was finished washing himself. I thought he was coming down the steps, but he didn't. He walked back toward his aunt's room to see if I was there. I continued to watch every move that Camisha made. As she patted Little Jon on the back she took the semi from around her back and pointed it toward the baby's head. Before I could gasp, the baby made a startling noise before his death as Camisha pulled the trigger. I heard the loud pop as a bullet flew into his head.

All the food I had in me was thrown up on the floor, causing Camisha to turn around and see me. I ran up the stairs.

"Calvin!" I was terrified to see what she would do next. Calvin ran out of the back room to the top of the staircase where I was in the middle and Camisha was at the bottom. I turned around, holding my mouth, hoping that I could make it out of the house alive. Camisha stood there in tears.

"What the fuck are you doing here!?" Calvin shouted. "And what the fuck was that noise!?" I didn't want to say what the bang was. I was in shock, trying to hold my balance on the staircase so I wouldn't fall. Not saying a word to Calvin, Camisha turned around and ran out of the house.

My tears began to flow from my eyes like a raging waterfall as Calvin ran to grab me, asking if I was OK. I gasped for air.

"She shot the baby!" I yelled as Calvin's eyes got wider then he ran past me down the steps and over to the bassinet. I ran behind him, still catching my breath and holding my stomach. I ran up to see Little Jon in the bassinet lying on his stomach as if he was asleep, but through his pretty hair I could see a dark hole with blood oozing out and the smell of gunsmoke.

Calvin quickly picked up the baby and I stumbled to the phone to dial 911. Little Jon's eyes were slightly closed and his head was starting to turn blue. Calvin fell back on the couch while rocking his son back and forth telling himself that everything would be OK. I leaned over and gagged some more as the operator finally answered the phone.

"Police, fire, and ambulance," said the female operator.

"A baby has been shot!" I screamed into the phone.

"Is it your baby, sir?" the lady sounded calm.

"No, it's not my baby!"

"Well, whose baby is it, sir?"

"Does it fuckin' matter!?" Tears flowed from my eyes.

"How old is the baby, sir?"

"He's eleven months old." Calvin still rocked back and forth while holding his son's lifeless body in his arms.

"What happened, who shot the baby?"

"He was shot by his mother."

"What time did the shooting happen?"

"Bitch, you're asking too many motherfuckin' questions, just send an ambulance!" I hung up the phone and ran over to aid Calvin, who was now breaking down himself. I grabbed him and the baby and held them as tight as I could. I could hear Calvin whining, tears falling from his eyes. My heart fell. I didn't want this to be happening. I looked around the room to a blur, thinking how this was all a dream, but I realized it wasn't, and the blur was because my eyes were filled with tears.

Bang, bang, bang.

"Did someone call for an ambulance?" a tall white man said through the screen door.

"Yes, I did!" The paramedics rushed in and took Little Jon from Calvin's arms. His entire face was now dark blue. They laid him on the rust colored carpet and tried to revive him. The female officer standing behind them shook her head from right to left, stating it was no use. Little Jon was gone.

"Where's the baby's mother?" asked the female officer. She looked like the wife from the hit TV show *Roc*.

"She was the one that shot him," I interjected.

"I'm his father," said Calvin, as he wiped the tears from his red eyes.

"Did you actually see the mother do this to her child?" the female officer asked, looking me directly in my eyes.

"Yes, I did," I said nervously.

"Why would someone do this to their own child?" she said under her breath while looking down at the paramedics examining the baby and taking off all his clothes.

"So where is the mother now?" the male officer asked. He stood six feet tall and looked like Ben Affleck.

"She ran out after she shot him," Calvin said, wiping the snot from his nose and shaking.

"We are going to need the both of you to come down to the station," the female officer said. Calvin and I stood up and walked toward the door, leaving Little Jon laying on the floor to be examined.

"What happens to the baby?" I asked as the male officer looked at me.

"He has to stay here until the coroner comes," he said.

"Is there anyone else in the house?" he asked.

"No, it's just us," said Calvin.

"Well, you guys are gonna have to wait for the coroner with us," the male officer said while pulling out a pen and pad from his jacket.

I noticed more police officers walking up the steps in a pack—58th and Kingsessing Avenue was packed with police cars and ambulances. I turned around and started to walk toward the dining room past the crime scene. I sat at the table with the male officer.

"Now, tell me exactly what you saw." He passed me a few pieces of napkins so I could get myself together. While I was answering questions in the dining room Calvin was answering the female officer's questions in the living room. Calvin could not stop crying.

"Calvin and Camisha had just got finished arguing when I got to the house." That's how I started my statement. I really didn't know what to say. I felt nauseated and couldn't breathe. The only thing I could do at this moment was cry. Seeing the baby lying on the floor on top of the blanket wasn't helping at all.

It took more than an hour for the coroner to arrive and pronounce Jon dead. Shortly after that, Calvin's mother arrived. She screamed to the top of her lungs when she saw her grandchild lying on the floor not breathing. I gasped for air four times before the tears began to fall again.

"Who did this!?" Miss Linda yelled at the top of her lungs. Calvin ran to her with his arms out, tears rolling down his face as she started swinging her arms to fight whomever came her way. Calvin was caught by a punch to his head as he tried to grab her, when he succeeded, they fell to the floor in a crying heap. Miss Linda reached out her arms to grab Little Jon who wasn't responding. I laid my head down on the table and cried to myself. I had no one but the male officer who was waiting until I was done so he could ask me more questions. I reached into my jacket pocket, which was on the back of the chair and pulled out my cell phone to call my mother.

"She killed the baby," I tried to tell her through all my crying and the noise.

"What? Who killed the baby?"

"Camisha."

"Who?"

"Camisha."

"Who is Camisha?" she yelled, not understanding me.

"The baby's mother." I wiped my eyes as the male officer looked at me.

"Where are you?"

"I'm over Calvin's."

"Take your ass home now," she spat.

"Mom, I can't. I have to go down to the station with Calvin to give the report," I said while wiping my eyes with the back of my sleeve.

"Well, did you see anything?"

"Yes, I saw the whole thing."

"Well, go with him to the station and then bring your ass home and calm yourself down. Call me when you're done at the station."

"OK," I responded.

I got up from the table and walked into the living room where Miss Linda and Calvin were on their knees. The coroner was done doing what he had to do so now they were ready to take the baby with them. Calvin kept his mother restrained as they wrapped Little Jon up in his blue baby blanket and placed him on the stretcher then carried him out the door. I could still smell the gunsmoke and it was making me sick to my stomach.

"What happened, Calvin?" His mother asked as she got up and made her way over to the sofa. The female officer interjected.

"Excuse me, sir, but I'm going to need you two to come with me down to the station now." I went to the door to see a mass crowd standing out front as the sun was beginning to set. Action News, KYW-TV 3, and Fox29 were approaching the scene and starting to set up their equipment to do their broadcast. Calvin was kneeling on the floor with his head down.

"Come on, Calvin, we have to go with the lady," I said, hoping he would move, but he didn't. I walked over to him and grabbed his hand.

"I don't want to go nowhere," he said, still looking down at the floor.

"Calvin, we have to go, she's waiting for us."

"Didn't I say I'm not going," he said, looking up at me with red eyes. I turned and looked at the officer as she walked over to where Calvin was kneeling.

"Sir, I understand your pain and your frustration about what just happened but I have a job to do, and you, me, and Mr. Smith need to go down to 55th and Pine to discuss this matter because if we don't, I am going to start to make some arrests."

"And, what if I don't go?" Calvin asked, still looking down at the floor.

"If you don't go, then I will arrest you and you will be held on a murder one charge, and homicide, so I think it is in your best interest to go with me to the station."

Calvin then lifted up to grab my hand. I put my arm around him as his mother sat sobbing in a world of her own. We walked outside to flashing cameras and microphones being shoved in our faces, people asking what happened. We dashed into the police car and rode to 55th and Pine. We entered the station through the back and were led through some steel doors into the interrogation room. I looked around at the white walls as they put Calvin and me in separate rooms.

A male officer named Minderflack entered my room. He was African-American, in his late fifties, and had tons of gray hair. He pulled up a wooden chair and sat directly in front of me while sipping on a 7-Eleven coffee.

"So, what happened today?" he asked. I sighed before I began my horrific story. He listened to everything I said word for word, and watched my hand movement. He stared me in the eyes as he continued sipping his coffee. I wondered what Calvin was talking about in the other room. I know that the cops wanted to see if our stories were matching up. He paused for a minute, wondering why Calvin and I were upstairs for so long. Unfortunately, I had to tell it. Calvin could not deny that he was fucking me. Although Camisha's heart was still with him, he wasn't feeling her. He now liked dudes and I was the dude he chose, or was I?

After I finished giving my statement I was free to leave. I walked down the hall to wait for Calvin. I could hear the yelling going on from the room where he was sitting. I couldn't take what was going on around me. My tears started to fall as the door opened and Calvin walked out. I ran behind him as he was leaving toward the exit.

"What happened? What did she say to you?" I asked Calvin as I grabbed his arm. He didn't say anything, he just kept walking. I hurried alongside him to keep up. "Calvin, what did she say?"

"She talkin' 'bout if it wasn't for me arguing with Camisha, my son would still be alive." I took a deep breath.

"So, what do they plan to do now?"

"They're about to go to Camisha's house and get her. Call your mom and ask her to come get us, please."

# Smoking Cigarettes

He looked at me with red eyes.

"Calvin, my cell phone is in my jacket pocket and my jacket is at your house on the chair."

"Well, what the hell are we gonna do, Rashad!?" I ran back into the police station as Calvin began walking up the street. I tried to get the female officer's attention while she sipped her coffee.

Tap, tap, tap. I lightly knocked on the window. She looked at me, then walked over.

"Can someone please take us back home?" She looked me up and down.

"Sure, I'll take you back." She returned to the table where she had been sitting and grabbed her nightstick.

Once inside the police car we swung around the corner to where Calvin stood waiting for the bus. She slowly pulled in front of him then stopped. He looked at me through the window with his hands in his pockets. I opened the door and signaled for him to get in. I slid over, giving him room to get in before we peeled off.

Everyone was still crowding the streets once we arrived back at Kingsessing Avenue. Channel 6 and Channel 3 were just wrapping up when we stepped out of the patrol car. I grabbed Calvin's arm and led him inside the house where his mother and aunt were talking to the other police officers. Miss Linda looked at Calvin in disgust as he walked past her toward the kitchen. His aunt grabbed him and they embraced one another as tightly as they could.

I sat down in the chair to gather my thoughts while listening to Miss Linda and her sister discuss the funeral arrangements for Little Jon. My eyes began to water again. I got up and walked into the dining room to call my mother to let her know that I was done and I was about to go home. I didn't want to leave Calvin. When I walked into the kitchen he was on the phone talking to Dontae. He looked at me and motioned with his finger for me to come to him.

I walked over and he placed a kiss on my lips, then hugged me as I wrapped my arms around him.

"Tell Dontae I said hey," I said, while resting my head on his chest. I could hear Dontae's voice through the phone greeting me back. I walked back into the living room to where his mother and aunt were standing. I could tell that Miss Linda could still smell the gunsmoke by the way she kept sniffling. I walked over to her and gave her a hug. The police were just about finished doing their work with all sorts of white powder and yellow tape blocking off the bassinet area.

"My mother is on her way home," Miss Linda said to me after releasing me from her arms. "Where is Calvin?" she asked as she stood up and walked into the kitchen where he was. I sat down on the couch and talked to his aunt and cousin.

The streets were clearing and I was tired. My eyes were burning from all that crying I had done earlier. Calvin's grandmother had just walked through the door by the time we got word that Camisha had been arrested. Although Camisha had killed Little Jon in a jealous rage to get back at Calvin, she also took a piece of our lives away. It was her intent. She figured that by killing the baby, neither she nor Calvin would have custody of him.

I always thought that her mind frame wasn't set right.

\* \* \*

I tossed and turned the entire night, waking up in the middle of the night in a cold sweat from what I had witnessed earlier. How could the people in this world be so cruel? Little Jon didn't deserve to die over the bullshit that Camisha and Calvin were having. That baby had a chance at life and she took it. I hope she burns in hell for that. I understand that God doesn't like ugly and you can repent for your sins, but there has to be a point where God draws the line. Tears began to run down my face as I covered my head with the comforter before grabbing onto the pillow and letting the tears flow. Little Jon had only been dead for a little more than eight hours and I already was starting to miss his crying. I got up and popped some Xanaxes to try to relieve my stress. With all this going on, I damn sure would be calling out from work tomorrow. The pills began to take affect and I was more than happy to get some sleep, only to wish that Calvin were here by my side.

*  *  *

The phone was ringing off tha' damn hook. I grabbed it while trying to catch my balance from my hard sleep.

"Hello," I said in my morning voice. It was the female officer from the 17th district calling to ask questions again. I really don't need this shit early in the fucking morning, I told myself.

"How can I help you today?" I asked to prod her along as she beat around the bush about how my day was going. I wanted her to get straight to the damn point.

"Would it be possible if you could come down to the station and give a full statement to my sergeant?"

"Well, I'm not feeling good right now." I was still mourning over Jon's death.

"Well, I would like you to come down and give a statement to my supervisor because I really didn't want to bother the baby's immediate family at a time like this."

She had a nerve. What the hell was I, chopped fucking liver? That baby was damn near my stepson and I treated him as such.

"I don't think I'll have the strength to do it today," I said.

"Well we have a statement from the baby's mother,

and it's not good on your part, sir."

"What do you mean?"

"She states that you and her had a tussle and that you were threatening to take her son's life because Calvin told you that he didn't want to be in a relationship with you, and you became envious of her, Calvin, and the baby."

I pulled the cover from off of me and jumped out the bed.

"No, she didn't say that, ma'am," I spat.

"Yes, she did say that in a full statement that she gave me, my sergeant, and the commander, so I think it would benefit you if you were to come to the station immediately, sir." She rudely disconnected the call. My heart fell completely to the floor. I clicked the cordless phone on again to call my mom at work. I couldn't reach her so I called Calvin.

"Hello," his grandmother answered in a sweet voice.

"Hello, can I speak to Calvin, please?"

"He's asleep right now, may I ask who's calling?"

"Yes, this is Rashad and it's kind of an emergency."

"Well, I see if I can wake him, hold on." She put the phone down. "Calvin!...Calvin!"

I could hear sounds from other voices in the background when Calvin finally picked up the phone and the other phone disconnected.

"Hello?" he said.

"Calvin?"

"Yeah."

"Guess what?"

"What?"

"Camisha told the cops that I tried to fight her in the house yesterday and I threatened to kill the baby because I was jealous of you and her."

"I know."

"What do you mean, you know?"

"The cops called here this morning and said the same thing to me. They also asked were we in a relationship and I told them no."

"So, now what?"

"I don't know, but I know that all this shit between you and her is getting on my nerves, and now my son is dead because of it."

"What are you talking about Calvin? I never said anything to her about trying to kill your son and I am not jealous of her unless you were still fucking her," I spat. "Were you fucking her, Calvin?"

"No, why are you asking me some dumb shit like that?"

"Because this shit is getting too out of hand and I'm not going to jail for a crime that I didn't commit nor am I gonna be an accessory to the crime either!"

"Man, I didn't say you did anything, so calm down. Like my mom said, she's going to jail for a long time for murder and I am going to testify against her when the time comes."

"So, what are you going to do today?" I asked, changing the subject because I wanted to see him.

"I'm going with my mom to the funeral home and we are gonna go pick out the casket and stuff," he said, clearing his throat.

"Do you need me to go?"

"No, I think it's best that you stay away for now until all this is over with."

The sadness started to overcome my body once again. All the sadness that I felt at the beginning of the year was starting to resurface. I had made up my mind when I started working that I had everything that I wanted and now I was upset again.

"Calvin, what do you mean you need me to stay away until all this is over with? I am your friend and you need me just like I need you."

"Rashad, it's too much stuff going on in my life right now. I feel like an old man. My grades are slipping in school, my son was just killed, and I don't think I can take this any longer," he said, his voice cracking.

"I know, Calvin, but you need to know that it's not gonna always be this way. I know that this is an unexpected time for you and your family right now, but you have to believe in the Lord and have faith and know that He will pull you and your family through this." I listened to Calvin sob on the phone. I said a silent prayer, wishing that this all would come to an end.

"Calvin, are you there?" I asked, making sure I still had him on the line.

"Yeah, I'm here."

"Are you listening to what I am saying to you?"

"Yeah, I'm listening," he said, sniffling.

"I have to go to speak with the sergeant today down at the 17th district, are you coming with me?"

"Yeah, I'll go with you after I go with my mom and grandmother to the funeral home, OK?"

"OK." I hung up the phone. I sat on the side of the bed crying out to the Lord asking him to make things better in my life and in Calvin's life. How could things turn around so quickly?

# Smoking Cigarettes

## Always Will

Only Superman could pull off all the things that I just did. I attended Little Jon's funeral, which was nice. Calvin took it well, and so did everyone else, even me. Miss Linda really laid her grandson to rest in style. There were flowers everywhere and the preacher gave a good sermon, especially if it kept my attention. The baby lay in the casket with his eyes closed looking like a doll still in its package.

My mother's 50$^{th}$ birthday party was a bang, she was so surprised. She thought we were going to a concert to see the Whispers at the Kimmel Center on Broad Street. I had Mia's mother make up some fake concert tickets on her computer, and my mother fell for it. When we ended up at Brave New World we partied until two in the morning. I know she'll never forget that night as long as she lives.

The police found out the truth about Camisha, and I have to be ready to testify once her trial begins. I had to take all that I had been through in the past few weeks and put it all aside to head back to work on Monday. Mondays are always a drag—from waking up early in the damn morning to washing my ass and getting on Interstate 476 just to be stuck in traffic. Calvin and I were going through our ups and downs so I needed to find a way to make him feel special. Since my funds were limited I decided to write him a letter and enclose it with a rose.

*Dear Calvin,*

*I am sitting here at work thinking of you. I know the past few weeks have been very rocky for you and me, but I just want to let you know that we will make it together. I have fallen madly in love with you and no matter what happens between us, my love for you will never die. I do apologize if it seems like I'm smothering you because by all means I'm not. I love the way you treat me and I have never had someone in my life that treats me the way you do. I can't wait until we have sex again so I can feel you deep inside me and that's all I want to do is please you. You are my king and I can't see myself living without you and I want you to remember that I will always be here for you. We will make a difference together. I love you, Calvin!*

*Love Always,*
*Rashad*

I sealed the letter in an envelope and sprayed some cologne on it then graced it with a flower. I had decided to leave work early so I could surprise him at his school. Once I got there on this raining Monday I waited in my car for him where he could notice me—he did.

Walking up to the car, he smiled as the rain hit his face. I rolled down the window.

"What are you doing here?" he asked.

"I came to get you because it was raining and I didn't want you to catch the bus," I said as I unlocked the doors so he could get in.

As I pulled off I slid him the envelope that contained the letter, a 5x7 picture of me, and the rose attached on top. He smelled the envelope then began to open it.

"No, wait until later to read it," I said, reaching my arm over to stop him. "I want you to read it later when I'm not around."

He looked at me, smiled, and then placed the envelope into his book bag. We rode straight to his house because he said he needed to do something for his grandmother. I dropped him off, then went home, hoping to catch up on some sleep.

Later that evening Calvin called around 8:30 and

woke me up out of my sleep.

"That was nice," he said. I could tell he was smiling from the way he sounded over the phone.

"It was just a little something that I thought you needed to keep you focused and to make sure that you knew that I was going to be here for you no matter what happens."

We continued our conversation into the wee hours of the morning. I knew I had a long week ahead of me from writing reports, to analyzing bankruptcies, to filing them. I needed all the sleep I could get. I also had to consult with a lawyer to cover my ass in case Camisha and the system tried to fuck me while smiling in my face telling me one thing, and then another thing happens. Calvin felt that he was out of the picture; they told him that he was clear of everything. I was gonna make sure that they weren't gonna leave me holding the bag.

By the time Friday came I hadn't seen or heard from Calvin all week. His birthday was on Sunday, the same day as Easter, and I didn't have any money to get him anything. I was only making about $700.00 biweekly. That alone just about covered my rent. I also had other bills—my car note, cell phone, house phone, and electric. Not to mention feeding and clothing myself. By this time Calvin had gotten fired from McDonald's and was living off the money that he got weekly from his father.

"Hello," I finally reached him on the phone as I pulled into the parking lot of the building at work. "And, where were you all week?"

"I had to study for a test and I was tired all week. It took a lot out of me."

"Oh, OK. So how have you been? I miss you."

"I have been cool, just a little tired. Am I going to see you tonight?" It was Friday night and I really didn't have any plans. Kevin was now dating his new dude so I knew that he would be busy.

"Yeah, you can see me tonight. What we gonna do?"

"We can chill at your place and watch a movie if you want," he said.

"That sounds good. Do you need me to come get you?"

"Yeah, be at my house around eight, all right, shawty?" he asked, sounding sexy.

"I'll be there."

The weather was starting to break and the sun was shining and it seemed to be shining even more now that I spoke to Calvin. It's been three and a half months since we have been together and we have been through some shit. I sat in the car and reminisced about the good times that we had throughout the winter months like walking through the snow and getting stuck during a blizzard at the Checkers restaurant on Broad Street. I really missed him living in the old house that used to be his mother's. It seemed like we had more fun in that house, like I could come over anytime I wanted. His grandmother always has something to say about what's going on in her house. She got worse after Little Jon died. She doesn't want anyone in her house if she's not home, not even Calvin. But Calvin knew he could come to my house at anytime and he would always be welcomed.

At work the next morning, I stepped out of my car and walked toward the door where the ladies were standing having their early morning cigarette.

"Hello, ladies," I said as I walked past them. I walked down the long hallway to my desk and threw my bag down. There was a note on my desk stating that the supervisor needed to see me. I walked around to her office and saw her sitting at her desk while speaking with two white men. I knocked on the open door, letting her know that I had seen her note.

"Hi, Rashad. Would you please come in and shut

the door," she said, waving her hand inward. I had heard a lot of things about Ms. Marucci, my supervisor, but she never came off like the bitch everyone talked about. An older white woman, she could be in her late thirties or early forties. She sat at her desk sporting her long, black, shoulder-length hair and suavely done makeup that suited her face. She was dressed in a black pants suit.

"Have a seat," she said, pointing to the brown leather chair in front of her desk. She began to write on her tablet. I looked around the room glancing at the plain white paint that seemed freshly done. I planted my eyes on one of the men, he was smiling at me.

"Hi, I'm Detective Burkes," one of the men said as he extended his hand for me to shake.

"I'm Rashad," I said as I shook his hand.

"And, I'm Detective Adams," the other white man said, extending his hand as well.

"Well, Rashad. I am going to step out and let the detectives speak with you, OK?" Ms. Marucci said as she left the room, closing the door behind her.

"What can I do for you?" I asked the better-looking detective that sat across from me.

"Rashad, we work for the Philadelphia Attorney General's office and we are aware that Camisha Trowley is going to trial and we would like an audiotaped statement from you," said one of the men as he moved closer toward me.

"For what now?" I asked, getting agitated. "I'm tired of this whole thing. I gave the police report over and over again. I thought this was over and now the police are coming to my job. This is embarrassing."

"I understand," said Detective Adams as he moved his head up and down, "but all we would need from you is one last statement for the trial and then we would be done."

"See, this girl did a horrible thing to her son," Detective Burkes stated, "and we want to make sure that she stays in jail for the rest of her life." I took a couple of deep breaths and began to speak the same story I'd told a million times.

By the time I was done with the detectives, it was already past lunch time and I was damn hungry. I knew all the girls in the office would look at me once I stepped out the room. Two girls were huddled, pointing at me as I made my way to the cafeteria. All these people saw me and Calvin on the news in front of his house and all they could do was stare. I sat at the table drinking a vanilla Slim Fast shake as I watched everyone eat. I went to call Calvin because I knew that he'd skipped school and spent the day with Dontae. I guess whatever he was doing he could not hear his cell phone because he didn't answer.

Back at my place I tried to relax and read the directions on the bottle of some Xenadrine pills that I had purchased to lose weight. The bottle said that I should start off by taking one pill twice a day but I figured I would take two pills twice a day to get a jumpstart on losing my weight. After taking my pills I hopped in the shower to get myself ready to see Calvin. I was more excited to see him today because I hadn't seen him in more than a week. My baby would be nineteen years old coming this Sunday so I knew that I had to give him some special kind of loving this evening.

I pulled up in front of his grandmother's house blasting *Feels so good* by Mase. I was feeling like a little Mase tonight just to bring the feeling back to how things used to be. I waited for Calvin for about fifteen minutes before he walked out of the house and got in the car.

"You smell good boy, what are you wearing?" I asked him as I started to pull off.

"You like it? My grandmother bought it for me for my birthday," he said, smiling before planting a kiss on my lips.

"Yeah, it smells good. You should smell like this

more often," I said as we started to laugh while driving back to my place.

"Do you want to stop and get something to eat?" I asked.

"Yeah, let's go to KFC."

Once inside my place we had dinner at the kitchen table just as we did on our first date. I looked into his eyes, telling him how much I loved him and how I wanted to be with only him. The mood was right, but then he got quiet and looked down at his food.

"What's wrong now, Calvin?" I didn't want to ruin our night together.

"It's seems like you're pressuring me to be in a relationship with you and I don't want to be."

"Calvin, I know you said that you don't want to be in a relationship right now, but I need to know will we ever get into one? I love you Calvin, and I don't want to be with no one else but you."

"Rashad, I love you too, but it's like I have a lot of things on my plate right now and I don't want to be settled down with you at this point."

"Well, will we ever get into a relationship, Calvin?" I asked while nibbling on a biscuit.

"Yes, but just not right now." I got up from the table and walked into the living room and turned on the TV as I grabbed a DVD from the entertainment center. Calvin followed, placing his dick upon my butt. I turned around as we began kissing. He embraced me tight as I thrust my tongue to the back of his throat.

I couldn't wait for us to have this moment again. I dropped to my knees to taste my long-awaited meal. I unbuckled his belt and began to undo the two buttons on his Girbaud jeans. I felt my long friend just waiting inside his boxers for me. I pulled out his monster from his boxer shorts and noticed a few cuts and sores. I moved my head back to make sure I was really seeing what I saw.

"What happened to you?" I asked, still examining his rod.

"I was washing up real hard and some skin rubbed off."

"Well, have you been to the doctor?" I asked, still curious about what was going on.

"Yes, and he said that it was healing fine, no biggie," he said, tucking his love muscle back into his boxers.

I got up from my knees. That was the nastiest thing I ever saw. "Well, does it hurt?" I asked as we sat on the couch for the movie to begin.

"No, it doesn't hurt." His soft dick was still swinging.

"Wow, you were washing up that hard, huh?" I asked, sounding sarcastic.

"Yeah, I always scrub hard when I'm in the shower." I shook my head as we cuddled on the couch to watch *Nightmare on Elm Street 3*.

Calvin and I spent the entire night together laughing and joking about different events that happened in our lives. We kissed and touched, but there wasn't much that we could do with his dick still healing from the cuts. He was excited to be turning nineteen and having a party where he would invite all his friends and family to a club that his father owned in Germantown.

* * *

Easter wasn't the same for me now that I had gotten older. I used to remember the days when we were younger and we would make Easter Sunday a big event where we needed to buy new clothes and sneakers. I awoke to a dreary day still hung over from the night before. I lay in the bed thinking of the day before when Kevin and I went to the movies to see *Panic Room*. We ended up on 13th

# Smoking Cigarettes

Street where a party was going on. I had my first taste of the E drink. It was a mixture of different juices and Cognac with a twist of Ecstasy. I must have had about two of those because I can't even begin to tell you how I got home.

My head now pounded as I walked to my bathroom. I sat on the toilet to relieve my stress as I rested my head on the towel rack. When the phone rang I jumped up without wiping myself and ran into my room to answer it. It was Shay-Shay.

"Wassup?" I said, running back into the bathroom to sit back on the toilet.

"Nothing, are you going to church today?"

"Damn, girl, why the hell you up so early?" I was still holding my head to take away the pounding.

"Because I have to get me and my daughter ready for church. Are you going?"

"What church are you going to?"

"My mom and grandma is going to Monumental, but I'm going to the Salvation Army church."

"Why are you going there and not Monumental?" I asked, still trying to get myself together.

"Because I don't want to go there since everyone is going there and I don't want to be around them."

"Well, yeah. I'll be ready. What time do you want to leave?"

"Be here at 11:00."

"All right," I said, before pressing the end button. After getting myself situated I started to get myself together for church. Since it was the Salvation Army church I decided not to get all dressed up so I wore my cream Rocawear sweat suit. I was looking sharp. After going to church with Shay I would pick up Kevin and we would shoot over to Calvin's birthday party. I stopped by the store to purchase a card for him so at least I could show up with something.

By the time I got to my grandmother's house Shay had already had the baby dressed and was ready to go. Kaniyah was dressed in a red Rocawear sweat suit and a pair of red and white Nike sneakers. Shay was dressed in a pair of stretch linen pants, a pink shirt, and a pair of Chanel sunglasses. I carried the car seat to the car and fastened the baby in tight as we rode to the church. Once there I saw a few familiar faces I'd known since I was a shorty hanging around the projects. We walked toward the front and sat in the third row. I sat next to Shay who sat the baby on her lap as the preacher began to speak. I listened to the sermon as long as I could without getting bored. Before I could grace my eyes with sleep the preacher called on me.

"You," he said, pointing his finger at me, signaling me to step forward to the front. I looked around at the other people in the church and wondered why he was calling on me. Embarrassed, I walked up to the altar and stood there in front of the preacher who now had sweat dripping from his forehead. He seemed to be in his late fifties, and by the way he wore his robe I could tell that he was from the old school. He grabbed my shoulders and faced my back to the congregation.

"Put your arms above your head," he said, touching me with one hand while holding the microphone in the other. I put my arms in the air as told then closed my eyes and listened to the words that I was to repeat after him.

"Today will be the day that I throw all the demons that lie in my soul away," he said.

I stood there with my eyes closed wondering how in the world was this preacher going to take all the demons out of me? I balled my fist in the air as the preacher whispered in my ear.

"No matter how hard the road gets, or how long it seems you have to travel, everything will work out fine. You have to let God lead the way and just follow Him," he assured me. I shook my head up and down letting him know that he told the truth. He patted me on my back, letting me know I could have a seat.

Throughout my time in the service I wondered exactly what the preacher was talking about. Was he talking about Calvin? Or my job? What was he talking about? As church let out the preacher stood by the door while he shook everyone's hand and smiled. I didn't feel any need to ask him any questions as I shook his hand and darted out the door. I figured if I followed God and let Him lead the way as I was told then I shouldn't have any problems.

After I dropped Shay and the baby off at my grandmother's house I went over Kevin's so we could go to Calvin's birthday party. The streets were starting to get damp from the rain as we made our way onto the expressway to Germantown. It seemed like every Easter, no matter what, it would rain. We arrived at the club on 5th Street. I parked my car in front of the building where a lot of teenagers stood. I noticed Dontae standing out front talking to his friends. It was obvious that Kevin and I were the only older people that attended this party, not counting Calvin's family. I walked through the door where Calvin sat at the bar drinking a Sprite. He smiled at me as he walked toward me with his arms out, giving me a hug.

"Hey, Kevin," Calvin said cheerfully as he embraced him as well. I sat at the bar where Calvin introduced me to his father. I didn't have a chance to meet him at Little Jon's funeral because he was there for only a split second before he had to leave. He stood about five foot nine inches at 200 pounds, and his complexion was much darker than Calvin's. We shook hands. I could see that he was curious as to whom Calvin was dating. Out of all the boys that were there he would be doing a lot of wondering. I made my way through the crowd to the back where Calvin's mother, grandmother, and aunt were sitting. There was a Scooby-Doo cake on the decorated table that read, Happy 19<sup>th</sup> Birthday Calvin. I walked back toward the front where Kevin was sitting and joined him at the bar where Calvin and his friends started to take pictures.

"Oh, I forgot I left his birthday card in the car," I told Kevin so that he would walk with me outside to get it.

"Ah real out a place here," Kevin said. "We is the only two not in high school."

"Well, we don't have to stay here long. Just let me give him this card and then we can leave," I said, as we walked back into the club. Calvin wanted to take a few pictures with me before I left, and then Kevin and I were back on the road to my grandmother's house where there was a party going on.

My grandmother had cooked a turkey, ham, baked macaroni and cheese, candied yams, collard greens, rice and gravy, and some corn bread. We were ready to chow down. All of my family was there and then some. We had music, food, and fun. We really celebrated this Easter Sunday and I ate and danced the night away. I had to leave the party kind of early because I had to be at work bright and early.

\* \* \*

"Who in the hell could be calling me this time of the fuckin' night?" I said, looking over at the clock as I answered the phone.

"I was just calling to say good night," said Calvin.

"Why are you calling so late?"

"Because Ron is having trouble at home and after the party I needed to help him find somewhere to spend the night. He doesn't have anywhere to go."

"Damn, what happened?"

"He and his mom had an argument and he left."

"Well, I'll talk to you tomorrow," I said to him before hanging up the phone.

An hour later the phone rang again.

"What the fuck?" I said, leaning over to pick up the cordless.

"Hello?" I answered.

"Open the door," the deep voice on the other end of the phone said.

"What?" I spat.

"Open the door." It was Rafeek.

"What do you want at three o' clock in the morning?" I asked as I tried to open my eyes to focus.

"Open the door, I need you to hold something for me." I hung up the phone then walked into the living room to let him in.

"Now, what the hell do you want?" I asked as I sat on the couch, still stretching and yawning from my sleep. He walked toward me then reached into his pocket and pulled out two sandwich bags filled with green leaves in one hand, and went into the other pocket and pulled out three sandwich bags full of a white powder substance. He laid all five bags on the coffee table. He went toward his back pocket and pulled out a black handgun from his waist area then laid it down on the table.

Focusing my eyes on the table, I said, "What is all this shit?"

"I need you to hold this for me."

"Nigga I can't be holding no fuckin' drugs in my apartment!"

"Look, I did a favor for you, now the least you could do is hold a few grams for me. Put it in a safe place and I'll be back to get it later." He began walking toward the door.

"I'm not putting my hands on this shit. What if something happens?"

"Man ain't nuffin' gonna happen. Just put it away in a closet or somewhere, where no one can get to it."

"Well, here, I'll find a spot for you to put it because

I'm not putting my fingerprints on shit." I found a spot in one of the walk-in closets in my room. I moved my sweaters over and he stuck everything in the back then tucked it away nicely. I walked him to the front door.

"Nigga, how long do you need me to hold this?"

"Man, just hold it. I'll be back for it." He walked out the door, then down the steps.

I needed to go back to sleep but I couldn't, I was up now. I got on the computer to check my e-mail. After drinking a cup of hot tea I finally became relaxed and fell asleep.

At daybreak the damn phone ringing off the hook like crazy awakened me. The sun was shining and I had to get ready for work.

"Hello?" I answered.

"Rashad, where is your mother!?" Shay yelled into the phone.

"Why? What's wrong?"

"Your brother gets on my damn nerves. I had my daughter in here sleeping and the cops woke her up banging on the door looking for him at six o' clock in the morning. He doesn't live here so why were they coming here looking for him?" She asked as if she really was expecting an answer.

"Well, what did they say?" I asked, still trying to gain my composure as I stumbled into the bathroom.

"They said that they had a warrant for his arrest and they searched the whole house. They went upstairs in the room where grandmom was sleeping and woke her up, then they went into the basement and was looking around." My heart fell to the floor. I knew that if they had a chance on finding Rafeek for the murder of Paul then they would damn sure get my fat ass.

"Well, did they say what the warrant was for?" I asked while getting the toothpaste out of the medicine cabinet.

# Smoking Cigarettes

"They said that it was from a warrant that he had a few years ago."

"Well, what do you need to speak with my mother for? He's a grown man. She don't have time to be dealing with his shit."

"I don't like all this happening while my daughter is here. He should take that shit to where he lives."

"Well, Shay I have to get myself ready for work. I don't have time for Rafeek and his stupidities. I'll call you later."

Work was getting stressful. The girls in the office were starting to dislike me for what reasons I didn't know. As I did one of my bankruptcy reports I came across a check that was written to our establishment for more than $6,000. I slipped it into my pocket to see if I could use it for later. I hated this job, but at the moment it was the only thing I had to pay my bills. It seemed that my relationship with Calvin was starting to fade, and I couldn't let that happen.

I went to work every day and barely called out. Calvin started a tutoring session after school and was always co-starring in a play at his school. I tried my very best to be there while he went through the trials of coping with the death of his son. Camisha made a few phone calls to him from prison saying that she still loved him, and hopefully that if she didn't get the death penalty that they could be together again.

Calvin is just like all men. They think with their dicks and not their brains. He should have known after the incident with the hot water that Camisha was not to be fucked with. Now a lot of things had happened since then. The only bond that they had together was now gone. Camisha had it in her mind that as a minor she couldn't be tried as an adult. It's funny the way the law works. Sometimes in a fishy sort of way they're on your side, then in another, they can fuck you.

# Reginald L. Hall

I hated to know that in one way or another Camisha was going down and the baby had to suffer because of her anger and guilt toward Calvin. But could I blame Camisha for how she was acting? Calvin once loved her and now he's fucking with dudes. I mean, she has a heart too that was broken by a man that she might have truly loved. I love Calvin even through all of his mistakes that he made in the past, through all this bullshit that has been going on; shit, that gotta tell you something.

## How Come You Don't Call Me?

I lay in my bed holding my pillow tight as I stared at the floor hoping that this nauseating feeling would go away. These Xenadrine pills were getting to me and making me feel sick. The room was spinning as I grabbed my pillow tighter. It was nice that my supervisor understood that I felt sick after taking those diet pills; she said I could go home. I tried to sleep but couldn't because the diet pills were a stimulant, like a speed pill. I was restless.

I paid $40.00 for those pills and I knew they were gonna make me lose weight like crazy, but I couldn't deal with the after effects. I just didn't like the way they made me feel. My pants were slowly falling off my ass, which was a good thing. I fumbled around for a pen to take down the phone number to the plastic surgeon that Wendy Williams always talked about on the radio. I wrote the number down, then saved it to my computer's desktop. I called the number and spoke to the nice secretary who told me that they were booked until July.

Damn, I had to wait that long just for a damn consultation? I set an appointment anyway. I don't know why I was so fucking impatient. I mean, it's not like I had the money for a tummy tuck today if I had wanted one. If I did have money, I wouldn't spend it on that. I was pinching every penny I had to pay my bills; there was no way I had a mere $8,000.00 for a tummy tuck.

There was nothing left to do but lie in my bed and feel sorry for myself. I tried taking some sleeping pills to help me sleep but even that was like fighting a losing battle. This weight was getting ridiculous. And, to top it off, I would wake up at six in the morning just to run around the track. I had to drink lots and lots of water, which I hated doing because the shit didn't have any taste. I'd drink water and eat fruit all day long. I even had to cut out fried chicken, the shit that I loved the most. Someone asked me one day do I like to hang around a lot of big people to make myself look thin. Who the fuck were they talking to? Do these niggas know who I am? I am Rashad fuckin' Smith and those new faggots that started hanging down 13th Street think that they are taking my face trophy away from me, think again.

Yes, oh yes I did walk a ball or two in my day and I won. I might be overweight but I won. I won over a lot of those pretty boys that think they could give me a run for my money. If those pretty-faced boys that are living in Atlanta think that they could steal a trophy from this big body pretty boy, they better think again. I got this and there aren't too many big boys that can take me.

I knew that there was a petite person trapped inside me that was trying to get out. I would be more than happy to let that bitch out if I had the chance. My mother even started taking some of the pills to help her out with her weight. My cousin Tamika didn't like the pills any longer because they made her sick to her stomach and oh, the drama queen. Shay had to be taken to the hospital because she swore that the pills made her catch an asthma attack. They were too much for me too, but the only thing I needed to do was slow down and stop taking them. It took me a whole week to regain my normal eating habits and get my life back to normal.

* * *

"What the fuck are you bringing me all this stuff for?" I asked Rafeek as he was unloading the sandwich bags containing white powder onto my couch.

"I need you to hold this for me. Put it with the rest of the stuff," he said, huffing as if he was out of breath.

"No, Shay said that the cops were looking for you. What if they come here?"

"Man, ain't no cops gonna come here. They don't know where you are, and besides they are only looking for me because of some shit that happened like two years ago. Do you still want me to open that account?" he asked, changing the subject.

"Yeah, where are you gonna open it up at?" I asked as I cleaned off my couch and took the stuff into the back room.

"What bank do you think I should open it up at?" he asked, following me. "Aren't they gonna need two forms of I.D.?"

"Yeah, make sure you have a Pennsylvania photo I.D. and your birth certificate or social security card. And, Rafeek, don't fuck this up," I said before seeing him to the door. I walked back into my room to prepare for bed. I thought I'd sleep in the living room tonight because I was a little shaken from the dreams that I'd been having about Dwayne lately. For some strange reason I felt his presence somewhere in the apartment with me. It was either that or the cool breeze that came through the window. Yeah, right, how could I fool myself to think that my place was haunted when I only saw his sexy ass when I was asleep.

As I drove to work early in the morning Calvin called to sing happy birthday to me. I sat and listened to his horrible voice until I pulled into the parking lot of my job. After hanging up the phone with him, Mia called to do the same. For this to be my 24th birthday, it didn't feel like it. It seemed like the year wasn't going according to plan at all. For my birthday I wore a red Dickie set and a pair of black timbs. I thought the outfit went well with my new look. I was wearing my hair curly. I'd get a shape-up and leave the rest curly. I got tired of the same old hairstyle so I figured I'd try something different. Besides, if Calvin wasn't paying any attention to me with my hair the other way then I had to change it.

After work I went past my grandmother's house because Shay had gotten me a birthday cake. I played with Kaniyah for a while, trying to get her to walk but she was just beginning her crawling stages. I love this little baby girl so much. I'm really not too fond of little babies, baby girls at that, but it was something about Kaniyah that I loved. I played with her all day on my birthday while it rained.

Shay came though the door carrying my birthday cake. She also gave me a card. I thanked her, and then we cut the cake and distributed pieces before I left and went back to being secluded inside the four walls of my apartment.

Before heading home I bought some food from Burger King. I couldn't even be upset that Calvin didn't give me a card. My mother stopped by to bring me an ice-cream cake, which has been a tradition since I was nine years old. I sat on the living room floor as I scarfed down my Whopper with cheese. I felt sad and lonely, and only God at this point could help me.

"Hello?" Kevin said as he answered the phone.

"What are you doing?" I asked, trying to find some sense for why I was calling.

"Nutten, what's wrong wit' ya?"

"I'm feeling lonely and I don't feel a reason why I should live any longer. Let's face it, I am not doing anything with my life and it seems like I can't find the proper person to love me."

"Well…"

"And this is my birthday and I shouldn't be feeling this way. Right now I should be laughing and having fun and being around people I love. Instead I'm lonely and in the house eating fast food and watching old TV shows. I'm tired of living like this." The tears began to roll down my face. "And to top it off, I have this big-ass belly that makes me look five months pregnant. I don't know what to do."

"Is cool runnings, mon. Pull yo'self up," Kevin said, while listening to me sob. "You gwan waste yo' time wit dat bumba clot? You get bun by de youth, ya no see it?"

I listened to Kevin while I went into the bathroom to get some tissues. My food was starting to get cold.

"So, wh'appening? What I-man have to do?" Kevin asked.

"What do you mean?"

"If you tryin' to mash yourself, you wasting plenty time," he said sarcastically.

"What do you think I should do?"

"Tek dem pills and gwan to bed," he said as if he was sparing me some of his time on the phone. "Well, I have to make dinna, I call you back."

"Yeah, that's if I'm still living," I said, before the line went dead.

It was the night of my birthday and there was nothing for me to do. I sat and looked out of the window to see day turn into night. My misty tears flowed down my face as the tap on the door scared me.

As I opened the door for Rafeek I wiped the tears from my face so he wouldn't ask any questions.

He shoved his hands into his pockets as he rushed into the living room.

"Here is the account information. I opened a checking and a savings account. I put $25.00 in each of the accounts to open them up." I took the checkbook and register from him and looked them over. "They said that a box of checks and an ATM card should be coming in the mail. I used grandmom's address." He pulled all the information out of his pocket and laid it on the love seat. "Do you still have all the stuff I gave you to hold?"

"Yeah, I put it away," I said, still looking over the checkbook.

"Well, go get it, because I need it."

I retrieved all the items that he had given me to hold, and then I stood back to look at him shuffle everything into a duffel bag.

I shook my head left to right, then sat down on the couch and waited for him to leave.

"So, when can we start with the account?"

"I'll have to give it some time; you know, play with it first," I told him. I always like to give the bank accounts some time to mature so the bank employees will no longer look at the account as new. Then, I could start my craft and be on easy street.

"All right, well just hold onto the information and I'll get back with you. How long do you think it will take?"

"About thirty days," I said, crossing my arms and leaning back on the couch.

"All right, I'll talk to you later," he said as he walked out the door and closed it behind him.

After locking the door I walked back to my room and continued feeling sorry for myself.

Calvin's cell phone had been turned off for some time now and he wasn't home so there was no way I could get in contact with him.

The next morning I was halfway along my travels to work when my cell phone rang.

"Why didn't you call me last night?" I asked Calvin.

"Because me and my friend went to the arcade."

"You went out with your friend? Your friend who?"

"My friend, Denim."

"Denim, who the hell is that?" I asked, trying to calm myself down. Not because he went out with his friend, but because he went out with his friend on my birthday.

# Smoking Cigarettes

"Denim, I met him last week." I couldn't believe what I was hearing. Who the fuck is Denim? I thought to myself as I pulled into a parking space.

"All right, am I gonna see you tonight?" I asked.

"I have to go to church with my grandmother tonight." I couldn't believe this shit. As fine as I am why would he want to cheat on me? OK, I thought to myself. I'm jumping to conclusions. But at least he would have consideration to call me last night and tell me good night as he always does.

"All right, Calvin, I'm heading into work now so I'll call you later," I said as I walked in the front door of the building. "I love you," I said as I waited for a response. The phone got silent. "You're not gonna say it back?"

"I'll talk to you later, OK."

I looked at the phone as if it failed to send me Calvin's reply that he loved me, too. I hit the end button and thought to call him later.

The loads of paperwork that sat on my desk did not catch my attention, as it should have. My mind clearly wasn't focused on work. I needed to know if Calvin was lying, and if he was, then why? I always thought that older people had an answer for what it seemed I was going through. Was it me or was it that I gave up my goodies too soon? I needed to know. Was he tripping off of what he was going through with Camisha?

By the time I got home, I went straight to bed. I was awakened by a phone call from my aunt who needed me to jump-start her car on City Avenue in the pouring rain. Before leaving the house I called Calvin four times, and he didn't answer. As a matter of fact no one answered. Is he out with that Denim boy? I wondered.

I jumped in my car and slipped a tape into the cassette player to hear Phyllis Hyman's, *The Answer is You* play like smooth sounds as the rain tapped the window of my car and tears rolled down my face. I dialed Calvin

again from my cell phone just to get the same response. By
the time I reached my aunt Denise, I was all cried out. I sat
in the car the whole time while two workmen handled their
business under the hood, trying to get my aunt's car started.
Her car needed a new battery so I had to take her to my
grandmother's house. She'd be back to get her car later.

I pulled up in front of my grandmom's house to see
Shay-Shay and Pookie on the covered porch arguing as
always. Shay was not having it. She was yelling trying to
get him away from her. Dealing with my own troubles I
walked past her as she followed me into the house and left
Pookie outside. He eventually got the picture that she
didn't want to be bothered before he left. Shay and I sat at
the dining room table looking back and forth at one another
wondering where we went wrong in selecting men. My
grandmother stood in the kitchen washing dishes before she
came in the dining room to join us.

"I don't know why y'all deal with street trash," she
said as she walked over to a chair that was against the wall.
She sat down.

"What did your friend do?" she asked as she drunk
a glass of Kool-Aid filled with ice.

"I don't know, grandma; he acting crazy. I don't
know what's wrong with him," I said, holding my head and
playing with my keys. Without even giving some type of
advice she got up and walked into the living room to look
at TV.

It was getting late and the rain was hitting the
streets. As I was leaving, Pookie was walking up the steps
onto the porch. Not knowing why he came back I just got
in the car and pulled off. My cell phone rang. It was
Calvin.

"Where were you?" I asked.

"Didn't I tell you that I had to go to church with my
grandmom!?" he yelled in disgust. I sat quietly on the
phone. I needed to know why my boo was acting like this.

"Yo, I'ma call you later," he said, before hanging up in my ear. I pressed the gas pedal and sped the rest of the way home. I walked into my apartment and threw my keys down on the floor then grabbed the cordless and dialed Calvin's number without even waiting to see if the phone had a dial tone.

"Hello," he answered.

"Calvin, we need to talk," I said, without even saying hello.

"All right, I'ma call you back in five minutes 'cause I'm talking to Denim. He was telling me something."

"OK," I said as I clicked the phone off and took my shirt off to wait for his phone call.

After fifteen minutes the cordless phone rang, but somehow the base didn't. I grabbed the phone anyway.

"What you wanna talk about, shawty?" Calvin asked.

"Calvin, this is not funny," I said, holding the phone close to my ear as I stood in the center of my bedroom.

"What's up?"

"Calvin, I really need to know if you want to be with me or not. I can't keep going on like this. I need to know." Calvin didn't say a word. He let me speak from start to finish. "If you want to date other people you can. I'm not gonna stop you, I just need to know where I stand because one minute you're loving me up and down and then the next minute you're saying you don't want to be with me." Calvin had been silent until I heard him sniffing trying to hold back his tears.

"What's wrong with you, Calvin?" He continued to cry as I consoled him and tried to figure out what was going on.

"That's not what I want, Rashad. I want to be with you," he blurted out.

"Well, then why do you keep saying that you don't want to be in a relationship with me?" I tried to get some sense out of all this.

"I don't want to be with anyone else. I don't want to date anyone else and I do love you. I'm sorry if I caused you some pain through all this," he said, trying to hold back his tears.

"So, Calvin, are you saying that you do want to be with me?" I asked for reassurance.

"Yes."

"I love you, Calvin," I said as closure to the argument.

"Rashad, I'll call you back tomorrow," he said, still sniffling.

"I love you, Calvin," I said, feeling happy about what he said.

"I love you too, Rashad."

I climbed into bed feeling wonderful. I finally got the answer that I had wanted from Calvin so we could finally be happy with one another and leave all that devilish shit in the past. The both of us needed guidance from the man upstairs at this time but it seemed like it was so hard for us to find an answer from him. I knew that Calvin was dealing with some personal issues just like me, but nonetheless, I said my prayers and went to sleep.

* * *

"So I asked him if he wanted to be with me or not. He said he does, so that means from now on he should start acting like he has sense and I don't want to hear no more of that *I don't want to be in a relationship* crap no more," I said as Mia and I sat at a table at Perkin's restaurant for breakfast.

"Yeah, because saying that meant he just signed a permission slip for you to kick his ass," she said while adding sugar into her cup of hot tea.

"I know that's right." We began to laugh while

eating our pancakes. Mia just moved into a one-bedroom apartment with her boyfriend. It seemed as if she was having trouble in paradise herself. These men just didn't have any decency as humans. It seemed as if they didn't care how the other person felt as long as they were getting the satisfaction that they wanted. For me just starting in this struggle, I didn't realize that this was just the beginning of a long, drawn-out process for Calvin and me. I looked out the window and saw the sun shining and heard the birds chirping as Mia sat across from me in a pair of dark shades, sipping on her hot tea with lemon.

Mia seemed to act like she was in love with her boyfriend even if she knew it wouldn't last. She knew that he was cheating on her but she just didn't have the right evidence to prove it. She knew that when her man wasn't coming home at night that he was with another woman although he would tell her that he was with one of his boys and he fell asleep. Come on now what type of shit is that? You fell asleep? That's bullshit. Don't fall asleep, *come home*.

I always said that men are the dumbest creatures that ever walked the earth and unfortunately God made me one of them. They'll tell a lie and expect you to believe it. I realized they had three famous sayings: "I fell asleep," "I forgot," and "What?"

I mean, what the fuck!

You fell asleep, what? When you walked through the door you fell straight to the floor? How could you forget if my fucking picture should be right there staring at you in your face? I'm the one that you're supposed to love so much. How the fuck did you forget? And what? What the fuck do you mean what? Nigga, you heard what I said.

I snapped out of my trance and commenced to finishing up my pancakes because Mia had to be back at work.

The Pennsylvania County Fair was in town and I

wanted so badly to go. Of course I called and asked Calvin but he was preoccupied with something he said he had to do for his grandmother, so I ended up going with Shay-Shay and the baby. I saw Eric and Tyree there as well. I had fun but it would have been better if Calvin could have accompanied me. I would love to have someone love me so much that he would take me to different events and care for me the same way I cared for him.

I hadn't seen Calvin all week, what was going on? He hadn't even called to say good night like he normally did.

"Hello," he answered.

"Where have you been all day? I wanted to spend some time with you today." I was in my room listening to the radio.

"I went to Dorney Park with Denim."

"Damn, why didn't you ask me if I wanted to go? Calvin, you know I love amusement parks."

"I didn't think of it."

"Calvin, are you dating Denim?"

"No, Rashad I am not dating Denim, we are just friends."

"So, how did y'all meet?"

"I met him off the party line when I was on the three-way with Dontae. We were bored so he called the party line. We were all playing around. I wasn't looking for no one to date. Why would I look for someone to date when I have you?"

It sounded good. I smiled and believed that what he was saying was true.

The next day while picking up a few items from Kmart I came across a talking Scooby-Doo. I knew that Calvin would love to have one, so I bought it and took it over to his house.

As I pulled up in front of his grandmother's house, there was Calvin standing out front talking to a male who I believed to be Denim. It was.

I hopped out the car and walked over to them as Calvin smiled at me like he knew I was coming.

"Denim, this is Rashad, and Rashad this is Denim," Calvin said, as I extended my hand to give Denim a handshake. He wasn't at all what I had pictured him to be. Since I thought Calvin was going behind my back, I pictured him to be a little more attractive than what he was, or at least a person who looked better than me.

Instead, I was introduced to a very skinny dark-skinned guy and there was nothing at all attractive about him. My racing heart was at ease because I knew Calvin would not stray away from me with a piece of trash like this. I continued to smile and hold a conversation with them until I remembered that I had a surprise for Calvin in the car. I walked back to the car and pulled out the talking Scooby-Doo and gave it to him. He smiled and kissed me on my cheek as I stood there and admired the way he held on to the toy.

An hour later, I was back in my apartment. I was relieved that I had finally met Denim. I could always say about Calvin that no matter what he did, or wanted to do, he was always up front with me and would never lie.

* * *

It was four o'clock on the dot when I barged out of the front door of my job. It was a nice breeze and spring was finally making its debut. I thought about Calvin all day and couldn't wait until I knew it was time when I thought he would be home so I could call him. I jumped in my car as I heard my cell phone ring. My face lit up like a child on Christmas morning, it was Calvin.

Wassup, Rashad?"

"Nothing, just got into my car, I'm leaving work. What are you doing?"

"I just came in the house to call you to see if you were coming over because the people are out here having a water fight, and I was gonna say don't come."

"Shit, they better not throw any water on me if I come because it's gonna be hell to pay," I said, jokingly. "So, what do you want to do today?" I asked him, hoping that his schedule would be free. He sighed. "What's wrong? Calvin, what's wrong?"

"Rashad, you know what I'm gonna say," he said in between sighs.

"No, I don't Calvin, I don't know anything unless you tell me." There was a long pause before he finally began to speak again.

"Rashad, I just want to be friends. I don't want to be in a relationship right now." I held the phone and the steering wheel as I sat at a red light and prayed a silent prayer that this wasn't happening again.

"Calvin, what do you mean? We just had a talk about this the other night and you said that you wanted to be with me and everything was fine. What changed since then?"

"Because it's like I won't have any type of freedom. If someone asks me to go to the movies or something with them I can't say yes because I'm in a relationship with you," he said, trying to make excuses.

"So, Calvin, what's wrong with that? If you want to go to the movies you can go with me. You don't need to search outside for someone or something when you have me right here," I tried to explain to him as I made a detour from going home to taking a drive to my grandmother's house. I continued to go back and forth with Calvin on the phone. By the time I got to my grandmother's house I was dripping with sweat. If my heart rate could have been tested at that moment it would probably have shot through the roof.

I walked past Shay who was sitting on my

grandmother's porch, and I went straight to the phone that hung on the wall in the dining room. I called Calvin.

"You making me mad," I said to him as soon as he picked up the phone.

"How am I making you mad, Rashad, because I don't want to be in a relationship wit' you?" he said, raising his voice.

"No, because you seem like you're trying to play a game. I'm gonna fuck you up when I see you," I said, and then slammed the phone down. I called back.

"As a matter of fact, I'm gonna fuck you up now, pussy," I said, before slamming the phone down and walking back to the porch without a word to any one.

"What's wrong with you?" Shay asked, as she gathered her things to give the baby a bath.

"I'm about to go fuck him up," I spat.

"Who?" She stopped to look at me.

"Calvin, are you coming?" I asked her, slowing down so that I could hear her response.

"Wait, I have to give my daughter a bath—then I'll go with you," she said, walking up the steps.

"I can't wait, I'll tell you about it later." I sped off down Race Street and cut the corner when I got to 55th and Vine. I picked up my phone and called Drew as an incoming call came through on my phone.

"Hello," I answered abruptly.

"Are you going to fight my cousin?" Ron asked, without even saying hello.

"Yeah," I said without hesitation.

"Well, I'll see you there," he said, before hanging up the phone.

"Oh, these niggas think they're gonna jump me?" I said to myself as I tried to redial Drew's phone number.

"Hello?" he answered.

"Drew, what are you doing?"

"Nothing, just sitting here. Why, wassup?"

"Because I'm about to go to Calvin's house and fuck him up because he keeps playing games with me, and his cousin just called me talking about he's gonna meet me there," I quickly explained.

"Well, where are you now?" Drew asked frantically.

"I'm on my way to your house."

"All right, I'll be outside."

I pulled up in front of where Drew was sitting on the steps at 17th Stenton. He jumped in the car and noticed that I had on sandals.

"Bitch, where you think you're going in a pair of leather sandals? I'ma be right back. Let me go get you a pair of sneakers," he said before making a dash back into his house. Drew came back with a pair of old Air Force Ones. I slipped my feet into each sneaker then made a quick get away to the expressway.

I took the quick way back to southwest Philly, getting off at the Gray's Ferry exit instead of taking 30th Street so I could avoid the afternoon traffic. I pulled up in front of Calvin's grandmother's house where I saw Ron standing in the middle of the street talking to someone that was double parked in a black Acura Legend.

I pulled up behind the car and put my car in park without even braking all the way. I jumped out of the car to see five people sitting on the steps of Calvin's grandmother's house.

This motherfucker called all these homeless faggots out here to fight me? I thought as I noticed some familiar faces from the chat room. Among his friends were Denim, Tyree, Eric, and a guy I assumed to be Joseph. I walked up to Calvin who was standing there with his arms crossed. He handed me a bag with my belongings in it—a few of my CDs and computer games.

"So, what the fuck, you showing off in front of your friends?" I asked him in a rage.

# Smoking Cigarettes

"Rashad, the cops are out here!" Drew yelled from inside the car.

"Take that shit somewhere else!" one officer yelled from across the street. The mayor had put officers on every street corner in Philadelphia to stop drug trafficking. It was called Operation Safe Streets, but it wasn't working.

I balled my fist up as Calvin stood there ready to take anything that came his way. Drew jumped out the car and grabbed me from behind and lured me back inside the car.

*"I can sing about love lost, but what if there's no love to lose if every day I saw sunshine and it never rained the blues? If my fears were tears I wonder could they fall? If a smile could stretch a mile even if I had no money at all, but I'm willing to take whatever life brings 'cause you're the only one that seems to know me. Even if the bad times come, if I had you back—I wouldn't complain at all.*

*I can dream about tomorrow even if it's still today. I wear down my knees every night even if I had no hands to pray. If my friends were dead and gone leaving me here alone, could I depend on some spirit to ease me when my souls on its own? If my eyes were blind and I couldn't feel at all to see, nothing in this world but you complete me. And even when the bad times call, if I had you back I wouldn't complain at all."*

*-Tweet-*

# Reginald L. Hall

## Complain

My body felt numb. Other than my foot pressing down on the pedal to take Drew back home I could not move. What have I just done?

"Wait till we see those bitches down 13<sup>th</sup> Street, ooh I can't wait!" Drew screamed as we entered the expressway. "And, Calvin acted like he wanted to be bad in front of his friends," he continued. "Are you OK?" Before waiting for my response, he continued. "And, you better not drop a tear."

I could not see anything but the sunlight gleaming down on my face. Drew just kept talking but I didn't hear a word he was saying. I glanced to the backseat of the car and noticed videotapes hanging out of the bag that Calvin had given me. I wished he still had those tapes. He wasn't supposed to give anything back to me. We were a couple since the beginning of the year, and a couple we were gonna stay. I knew about the old saying, whoever you bring the New Year in with is supposed to be the one you'll be with that entire year. I was sticking to the rules. I wanted to be with him.

We pulled in front of Drew's house and he stepped out the car.

"Are you gonna be all right?" he asked, checking in the back to see if he forgot anything.

"I'll be fine," I said, just to get him along his way. If I never lied before about anything, I was lying now.

As soon as the door slammed I pressed my foot on the gas and the tears began to fall. The sunlight still continued to shine in my face, making my tears look golden brown as they slid down my cheek. I couldn't stop crying.

By the time I got to my apartment I pulled off all my clothes and went into the bathroom to run a hot shower.

# Smoking Cigarettes

My heart was weak. Through all the steam in the bathroom my aching heart made me feel as though I couldn't breathe. With the hot water running against my face, my tears continued to fall. The harder the water ran, the louder my cries got, but no one was near to hear me. I needed help. I needed help from one person, and the one person that could help me, didn't want to speak with me at all.

After showering I slipped into a pair of basketball shorts and a blue T-shirt, then grabbed my Tweet CD and my car keys to share some of my tears with my mother. While riding in the car I continued to let my tears flow. I pulled up in front of my mother's house as I noticed her standing in the doorway. She leaned back to let me pass by her.

"What is wrong with you?" she said, looking at me while I went to sit on the couch. I grabbed one of the throw pillows and held it tight while my mother still stood in the doorway. "What the hell is wrong with you?" she asked again. I didn't give her an answer. I just sat there and rocked back and forth while sobbing before I finally began to speak.

"Calvin and I broke up," I said in a muffled voice that she couldn't understand.

"What?" she spat.

"Me and Calvin broke up," I said again, still sounding muffled.

"I can't understand you with all that crying, shut up!" I buried my face in the pillow letting the soft cotton fabric soak up all my pain and emotion. I spoke once again and this time she heard everything I said.

"So what are you crying for?" she asked as if she'd never been hurt before.

"Mom, my heart hurts," I whined as she turned her head and closed her door to walk back toward the kitchen.

I finally got the strength to get up and walk into the kitchen with her. I was glad to know that she was home alone. No stepfather and no twin girls. She had the house to herself so I could pour my heart out to the only woman in my life, except this woman didn't understand all the pain I was going through.

"Fix your face," she said as she opened up the newspaper and began reading. I just sat there looking at the back portion of the newspaper as she held it in front of my face. I stopped to think about Calvin and what it was he was doing at this moment. I thought to call him but I knew that it would be of no use. I didn't listen to my instinct. Instead I picked up the phone and dialed.

"Hello," I said, happy to reach his grandmother. "Is Calvin there?"

"Who is this?" she asked in a sweet old lady tone.

"This is Rashad."

"Rashad, you can't speak to him," she said, letting her sweet tone become vicious.

"Why not?"

"Rashad, did you come over here to fight my grandson?"

"Yes, ma'am, but I was upset at the time and I said something that I didn't mean."

"Well, Rashad, you can't be going around thinking that you can fight people especially in my family because we're gonna have to get together and come after you.

*Yeah, just like y'all had to get together to go after Camisha after she killed Little Jon,* I thought to myself.

"I know, I know, but can I please speak to him?" I said in a quiet voice so that my mother wouldn't know that I was calling.

"No, sweetie. Calvin doesn't want to speak with you. Just give him some time to cool off and maybe he'll talk to you later, OK?" she said as her voice returned to normal.

"OK," I said, disappointed. I hung up the phone. I didn't understand. What the fuck did she mean, OK? I was there with Calvin when he was going through all that shit with Camisha. I stood by him just like I was supposed to do and now he wanted to throw me away like I didn't even matter to him. I began to cry once more as I walked into my mother's room and sat on the side of the bed.

"If you don't shut up, I'm gonna knock the shit out of you," she spat. "What are you crying for? I don't see anyone crying over you. He was too young for you anyway," she added.

"But, mom, I loved him," I said in between cries. She turned away and continued to read her newspaper as I made my way to the front door. Out of all the people in the world I thought at least she would understand what I was going through. I wasn't born back in the day, but I knew she wished she would have had someone to go to when my father was beating and cheating on her. I'm sure she cried many times in her day and now she was looking at me like I was crazy because I was crying over a man who I thought loved me. How could she? My mother was supposed to be the one true person I could go to for support but now I must cry alone.

I kept Kevin up all night crying on the phone with him. He just sat there and listened to me cry. He knew how much I loved Calvin.

After hanging up the phone with Kevin I cried myself to sleep. Waking up the next day was torture. I woke up with a painful hangover, a love hangover that is. I felt like something was blocking me from breathing. I couldn't get any air to circulate from my nose to my mouth. I felt a huge burning sensation in my chest. It was burning from not feeling the presence of Calvin.

I reached over to the phone on the nightstand to call my job. There was no way I was going in to work like this. I was sick. I couldn't move let alone get in the shower. I could barely see the numbers to dial on the phone.

Once that business was done, I walked into the

kitchen and made a cup of tea, then sat on the couch to figure out any thoughts that I had left. I could feel my heart beating inside my chest. But it wasn't a normal beat; it was a beat for Calvin, the love that I had for him and the baby. Some of the pain that was leftover from seeing the death of the baby still shocked me. First, I lost the only thing to me that was close to having a son then I lost the only thing to me that was close to having a husband.

I thought about all the good times we had shared and my heart began to drop once more. It had been on this same couch that Calvin and I had sex about a month ago. I didn't understand how he could let me lick him up and down, and swallow his babies, then turn around and do some shit like this to me. Did his mother know what was going on? I needed to know. Did she know that Calvin gave me her ATM card to do craft? I shook my head in disbelief as I got up and went into my bedroom.

I tried to make some good out of my day by starting a new daily planner. From this day forward I would put myself on a strict diet and stick to it this time. By using those pills I already went from a size 40 to a size 38. I knew it wouldn't be long till I reached my goal. *But what's the use? Calvin's not here anymore. You will have no one to love you. No one to talk to. No one to call you boo, and most of all, you will have no one to make you smile anymore.*

I couldn't take this. I ran over to my pillow and grabbed it and held it tight as the tears began to flow once again. *Live and let live---God is the answer.*

That was the only thing left to do, God was the only way. I kneeled down at the foot of my bed and asked God for help.

*Dear Lord, I weep and I weep hard, Lord. I really don't know what to do. My heart is broken and Calvin is gone. I ask that you help me please. Lord, can you please bring my baby back to me? I can't live without him. I need him in my life. He was the only one who knew how to make me laugh; he was the only one who knew how to make me smile. I ask you, Jesus, can you please bring Calvin back to me?*

*Amen*

I continued to cry as the phone rang.

"Hello," Kevin said. "Wh'appen? Why you still home? You not wukking?"

"I didn't feel well. Can you come over when you get off?"

"Cha, you better gwan to work. Why I should come for?"

"Because I need some company," I said in between cries.

"No, you shouldn't lose a day's pay cus ah sum boy. He not cry ova you. Him nah love you. Why you wastin' time an' energy ova this? Ya no see it?"

"But..."

"But nutten, if I come ova there, I go punch yuh in yo face."

"Why?"

"Cos, bredda, you actin' stupid. This is stupid."

I palmed my forehead and looked straight at the floor.

"Well, call me when you get off work," I said before the line went blank. The tears started to fall again. My life felt like it was without meaning. I was hopeless living in this dangerous gay world, a world where people are filled with lies and deceit. If I could be straight, I would be. I would not have picked this lifestyle.

I picked up the phone to call Troy because I felt empty. My soul was not at rest and I needed a clear head to talk to, but of course with my luck he wasn't home.

I took three Xanaxes, which made my head hit the pillow harder than a rock. When I awoke it was already the next day. I ironed my clothes and got myself ready for the day that lay ahead. I slipped into a tan Dickie outfit and textured my curly hair.

I casually walked into the office with a smile turned upside down. I was getting stares all over. The job that I set out to do today could not be done. I needed a sense of happiness in my life.

"It seems like you lost your best friend," someone said as I entered the cafeteria.

"I did," I responded. I sat in the café and watched Koz and wished that it were him that granted me such joy. He had a smile that I knew would light up my life. He sat at a table across from me eating a slice of pizza. His braids were neatly plaited past his shoulders. I watched him as he took one bite at a time of his pepperoni pizza. Then my mind focused back on the situation at hand and what I was going through.

I visualized the events of the horrible day in my mind. The few people who were on Calvin's steps were people I had chatted with on the Internet, but it was my first time seeing some of them in person. I had seen pictures of Tyree but not actually met him before. I could tell that the pictures I had seen on the computer did him justice because he didn't look as cute in person as he did on his pictures. When I jumped out of the car he continued to sit there on the steps looking at me like he was surprised to see me or surprised to see how cute I was.

Joseph sat quietly as well, and I could definitely tell that he wanted a piece of my dick by the way he stared. It was the first time I had ever seen a white boy with braids. You could tell he was about 21 years old and I guess he was there since he was dating Ron. Eric had seen me on plenty occasions and from what I had heard he couldn't fight at all. I thought he and Calvin were not speaking. I didn't understand what the fuck he was doing there. I guess like they say, maybe they weren't speaking, but when

Calvin needed him the most, he was there, cool.

I didn't have a choice but to finish out my day. I sat at my desk in a dark corner and thought about Calvin. Out of all that went on, I was going to miss him. Shit, I can't go through this. I need to think and I need to think fast. I remember I still had Denim's phone number saved on my caller ID at home.

There had to be some way that I could make it up to Calvin and make him feel at ease at the same time.

As soon as I got in the house I checked the caller ID for Denim's telephone number; it was still there. I dialed the number and got the voice mail. I left a sweet but short message, asking him to give me a call when he was available. At this point there was nothing to do but wait. I watched reruns of *Good Times* until I was sure the phone would ring.

At one o' clock in the morning it finally rang.

"Hello?" I answered.

"Hey, Rashad, wassup it's Denim."

"Hey, Denim, wassup with you?" I asked before getting into the reason for my call. There was a moment of silence. I had to make my point known before he started to talk about something else.

"Denim, I need you to help me get Calvin back. I really miss him," I said, leaving him room to speak.

"Well..."

I cut him off. "Well, let me ask you this first, do you think I have a chance getting him back?"

"Yes," he said, without giving it a thought. I smiled.

"Well, tell me what I should do? I want to go shopping and I want you to go with me."

"When?"

"Tomorrow, what are you doing tomorrow?"

"Well, I have graduation practice in the morning, but that's over at twelve. Do you want to meet me on

Broad Street? Then we can go from there?"

I smiled as I felt progress was being made.

"All right, Denim. I'll meet you tomorrow at twelve."

That time would be cool because I could get off early tomorrow in time to meet him. I only had $100.00, which I was supposed to use to pay my phone bill, but tragedy called and I needed to do everything in my power to get Calvin back and have everything like it was.

Waking up the next morning I felt excited. Not my usual excitement because I was going shopping, but because I was going shopping for Calvin. I knew that Drew had some things lined up and places for us to go. I was happy to know that I was getting my baby back. I had high hopes for this one. I prayed to God and this was His answer so I needed to take everything and use it to the best of my ability.

I drove through the rain while listening to the sweet, soothing sounds of Tweet's new CD, *Southern Hummingbird*. I sang along to track 11, *Complain*. I thought of all the times that I would complain about Calvin and the things he would do or the things that he didn't do. I would give anything to have my man back. I wouldn't complain at all.

I approached Denim who was waiting patiently on the steps of the Apollo Temple on Broad Street. He wore a pink shirt and a pair of khaki shorts and a fresh pair of Adidas. He hopped into the passenger seat while removing his headphones from his ears then placing them into his book bag.

"Hey, Rashad," he said, getting himself settled in the front seat.

"Wassup?" I asked as I drove off. "So where are we going?" I was excited to be with one of my man's close friends to shop for the man I loved and adored the most.

"We can go to South Street to see if we find

something down there," he suggested.

Once we got to South Street we went into the Gap where I bought Calvin a pair of jeans and a shirt to match. Then, we went to the flower shop and I bought a dozen long-stemmed red roses. I decided to take a trip to the toy store where I bought all Scooby-Doo paraphernalia. I mean, we went Scooby-Doo crazy: eating Scooby, walking Scooby, talking Scooby, etc. I even bought Scooby-Doo wrapping paper to wrap his clothes in. Now the only thing was how was I going to get these items to Calvin? I needed a way where I could give him the gifts and let it be a surprise.

Denim thought quickly.

"I know, I could call my godmother," he shouted. I continued to drive as he directed me to his godmother's house in North Philly as he called her from his cell phone.

Once we reached her house she awaited us at the door. We got out of the car and walked up to the brownstone row home as she fingered her ponytail.

"Rashad, this is Carla," Denim said, as Carla and I shook hands before she invited us in. I walked into the living room where she had a huge stereo system and no furniture.

"Denim, he is cute," Carla said from behind.

"I know he is. This is Calvin's friend. Remember Calvin, the dude I had with me last week when I came over here?"

"Yeah."

"Yeah, they're going through problems and I'm trying to get them back together."

"Aww," Carla said as she walked toward me with her arms out to grace me with a hug. I extended my arms to hug her back.

Carla was in her early thirties. She was dark-skinned with a petite frame and she had a pierced lip. Her outgoing personality was what I really needed at a time like this.

"I know what!" she snapped.

"What?" Denim asked.

"Let's have a party," she said excitedly. "Denim, you call Calvin and ask him if he would like to go to a party with you tonight. That is a way that you can get him to my house. Then, Rashad can come from upstairs with the gifts while I play his favorite song."

"That sounds like a good idea," I said. I looked at Denim and smiled and I knew there was a reason for me calling him and him calling Carla. With both of their minds working how could I lose?

"And once you bring him here then I'll talk to him for a while and tell him how much you love him and how much he means the world to you," said Carla, looking into the sadness of my eyes.

"Well, I have to go home and change. Denim, don't forget to call Calvin," I said.

"OK, I'll do it right now," he said as he dialed Calvin's number from his cell phone. I waited while he spoke to Calvin. Hearing Calvin's voice sent chills through my spine. What I wouldn't do to hear his voice again telling me that he loves me.

"He's gonna meet me at 7 o'clock," Denim said, hanging up his cell phone. "Now, Rashad, I need you to already be here and ready when I get here with Calvin. If we're meeting at seven on Chester Avenue it will take about an hour to get here. Be here no later than 8 o'clock," Denim said, giving orders.

I knew I had the right man for the job.

"OK," I told him before giving them hugs and heading to my car. Full of excitement, I jumped into my car. After what seemed like a lifetime, I was going to see Calvin again.

Once I got home, I wrapped Calvin's gifts individually before I got myself dressed. I had to stop by

# Smoking Cigarettes

the barbershop to get my hair shaped up so I could look extra good for my dude. I had each curl lying in its proper place. I wore a white T-shirt and a pair of blue Girbaud jeans that Calvin had bought me during our happier times.

I knocked on the door three times before Carla finally opened it. I had three big boxes and the flowers for Calvin in my hands. She helped me into the house, and then proceeded to take everything into the kitchen.

"I just talked to Denim and he says that him and Calvin is on the bus so they should be here any minute," said Carla, as she fixed her hair in the mirror. "Do you have the CD with his song on it?"

"Yes, I have the CD with our song on it." I pulled out Phyllis Hyman's CD from my bag and put it in the CD player, tuning it to number 3, *The Answer is You.* My heart pounded each minute. Carla gave me a hug to calm me down.

"Listen, don't worry. I do this sort of thing all the time. Like a year ago, one of my girlfriends and her boyfriend separated and she called me to help her get back together with him and now they're married," she explained. "Boy, I know what I'm doing."

I smiled as I thought about the prayer I said before I left home. I knew that God would stick by me and if Calvin and I weren't meant to be, then all this stuff wouldn't be taking place. I would not have been able to get in contact with Denim nor would I have met Carla, and she was right on time.

Tap, tap, tap.

Someone was knocking on the front door. I knew it wasn't Denim and Calvin because he said that he would call when he got closer. Carla went over to answer the door as I stood in the doorway of the kitchen singing along with Phyllis Hyman.

"Hey, Robbie," Carla said to a young man as he entered her house.

"Denim told me to meet him over here," he said as he began to walk toward the kitchen. Robbie then came to me and shook my hand.

"You're Rashad aren't you?"

"Yeah," I said, shaking his hand.

"Yeah, don't you mess with Calvin? Well, used to."

"Yeah," I responded.

"Oh, OK, because he called me the other day when y'all were outside about to fight."

"Well, how do you know him?"

"I'm Denim's boyfriend."

"Oh OK," I said, looking at him up and down. He wasn't the greatest catch but he didn't look half bad. He had short braids, and his gear was all right; nothing to write home to mom about.

"Yeah, he told me all about what happened. He says that he's not mad at you. He just thinks that you are going to hurt him," Robbie said.

"Man, I love him too much to hurt him."

"Well, that's what you need to tell him when he gets here."

"I know," I said, moving my head up and down. Then the phone rang.

"He's coming around the corner now!" Carla yelled, grabbing me to run upstairs with Robbie following. The gift boxes were still sitting on the kitchen table. I could feel the sweat pouring from the back of my head and also down my face. Once upstairs I grabbed the fan and turned it on high and focused it right in my direction.

"Are you nervous?" Robbie asked, as the doorbell rang.

"Yeah, kind of."

"I can tell," he said, putting his hands into his pockets. I heard the door open and I could see that the lights had been turned off and the strobe light was lit. I heard footsteps coming toward Carla's bedroom. Denim appeared through the door, giving me the thumbs up. I grabbed the dozen of roses that sat next to me on the bed and waited for my cue as Denim approached Robbie, planting a soft kiss upon his lips.

"I'll let you know when it's time to come down," Denim said as he left the room, taking Robbie with him.

I felt strange. Like this was my wedding day and I was waiting to walk down the aisle in front of thousands of people. But I needed to realize that this was a moment where I needed to get back with my man, and no matter what it took, I was gonna get this night over with. I took a piece of paper and dabbed the sweat from my forehead as I heard the sweet sounds of the piano playing the beginning to *The Answer is You*. I stood up and walked toward the door as Robbie met me in the hallway and took me by the hand and guided me down the steps like he was giving me away at my wedding.

I walked down the dark steps until I was able to see the back of Calvin's head. He sat there in a chair and held a conversation with Carla just like he didn't know I was there. I walked over to him and without him seeing me I grabbed his hand. He did a double take to see if it was really me or not. I gave him the flowers, leaning over to him and whispering in his ear.

"I will never do anything to hurt you." He reached up to me and gave me the biggest hug. The others left the room as I took his hand and we danced to the sweet sounds of Phyllis Hyman. I grabbed him and inhaled his scent as we spun around the living room floor like we had been married for years. I held him tight and vowed to never let him go. We danced in the middle of the floor for about ten minutes while the song repeated.

"I miss you," I said to him.

"I miss you too," he whispered back. I held him tighter once again before the lights came on and the gang was back in the room clapping like they had just seen a good show.

"Look what you have," Carla said, bringing the boxes into the living room and sitting them in front of Calvin.

I sat in a chair directly across from him as I watched him open all his gifts. He smiled at the clothes from the Gap as well as the Scooby-Doo items. After opening them all, he leaned over and gave me a big hug as the gang clapped again. I was so happy.

The night was coming to an end and I couldn't stop kissing Calvin and touching on his hair and arms. The more I touched him the hornier I got.

"Calvin, I need some tonight, bad," I said to him as I kissed over his face while he leaned on the kitchen wall.

"Do you?" he asked, teasing me with his hard rod.

"Yes, Calvin, I missed you so much. These past couple of days have been the hardest days of my life; I couldn't go to work. Calvin, I need you in my life. I told you that I couldn't live without you, now do you believe me?" I said, placing a few more soft kisses upon his lips. I laid my head on his chest and inhaled him some more. I couldn't wait to take this boy home to my apartment and try something new with him; something that neither of us had ever done. While Denim and I were down South Street earlier I picked up a tube of Anal Ease. Just a little something to add new flavor to our sex life.

I twiddled the tiny hairs on his neck as I thought about all the good and bad times that we shared together. This was now May, and Calvin and I had come a long way together since watching *Vanilla Sky*. I think I found the man of my dreams and with him there wasn't a need for me to look any further. Calvin and I would be inseparable and there would be nothing that those faggots down on 13th Street could say about me now because I had a good man.

\* \* \*

"Who could be calling me so late at night now?" I said as I reached over Calvin to answer the phone.

"Hello," I quickly answered.

"You have a collect call from Rafeek at the Clinton Frazier Correctional Facility. If you accept the charges, dial 1 now," an automatic voice instructed. I firmly pressed the #1 button on my phone.

"Hello," I said.

"Yeah, wassup."

"What the fuck are you doing in jail, Rafeek?"

"Man, they got me in here for some nut-ass shit. But I need you to get in touch with mom for me. I can't call her because she has the block on her phone."

"Well, can I use the three-way?"

"Naw, because it will disconnect. Tell mom where I am, and tell her to get in touch with Sheila for me."

"Who the fuck is Sheila?" I got out of the bed and turned on the light.

"Some bitch that I got pregnant. Tell mom to call her because she got some money for me and I need to be bailed out."

"Well, what are you in there for?"

"I can't talk now just take down this number and have mom call her," he said as he rushed to give me the digits.

"OK, what is it?"

"It's 215-555-8442. You got it?"

"Yeah, I got it," I said, after I quickly wrote the number down on a piece of paper I found on my computer desk.

"The phone is about to hang up so I'll talk to you later."

"All right," I replied, and the line went dead.

I sat down at my desk and started up my computer. Since I was already up I might as well surf the Net, I thought to myself as Calvin squirmed in the bed. I figured there was no need to wake my mother up with the nonsense about my brother so I decided to let her know in the morning.

*Bling...*

I received an instant message on my screen. I had never received an instant message from this person before. The screen name read *only12nv*.

*Hi*, I typed.

*Hi.*

*Who is this?*

*This is Tyree.*

*Hey, Tyree, how are you?*

*I'm fine, what are you doing?*

*I'm about to go to sleep.*

*Are you and Calvin still together?*

*Yes, why?*

*Because I wanted to know if I could holla.*

*I thought you had a boyfriend?*

*I do, but I don't think it's gonna work. He's getting on my nerves.*

*Well, I'll talk to you later, Tyree.*

*Bye.*

I signed off and went to lie next to Calvin. I couldn't understand for the life of me why he wanted to get at me. I knew that he and Calvin were friends, and if he already has a boyfriend why does he want me? I hope he didn't think he would get me that way. I didn't like cheaters and I was always taught that cheaters never win.

I would never tell Calvin what just happened because all that would do is put a strain on what I just fixed and I couldn't have that type of negativity going on in my relationship. I did more than enough to get my baby back, and I was sure glad that I had him home right next to me. I know it's hard to fight temptations when seeing attractive people out there, but surely being in this lifestyle you have

# Smoking Cigarettes

to find a mate you can trust who will not go astray.

> *Dear God,*
> *Thank you for all the blessings that you've given me. I also want to thank you for bringing Calvin back to me. You know as well as I do that this is the love of my life and in no way shape or form that I would let him go. Once again, thank you.*
>
> *Amen*

# Reginald L. Hall

## Call Me

"I don't give a shit where he is, I don't have any money to bail his ass out of jail," my mother said to my grandmother while we sat on the front steps of my grandmother's house. The one place I felt like I could get a peace of mind was sitting on my grandmother's steps. I know it can be dangerous sitting here in the heart of West Philly, but this was a place I could call home.

My mother rushed to go home to check on my sick stepfather who was now in the late stages of congestive heart failure. She tried for many years to contain herself and live with the fact that her husband wouldn't be around much longer. No matter what happened between them two, she always kept him around. She could be struggling with the mortgage or having trouble paying the gas or electric bill, and there was nothing he could do because he was out of work and on disability.

The whole situation was crazy. That's why I had no choice but to move out and get my own place because the place that I once called home, had turned into a madhouse. There was no way she had the time or the money to help bail my brother out of jail. That girl, Sheila, said she didn't have any money either, and from what I heard from the conversation that my mother had with her on the phone, she already had an abortion. I guess Rafeek would have to sit there for awhile until the judge let his ass out.

\* \* \*

By the time I got to work it was already past 8:15 and I knew I was gonna be late. Things have been so crazy lately. Calvin and I aren't talking again, so you know I'm training myself not to call him. I figured I have to start from somewhere and the first thing I was gonna do was not call his ass. I had never been so embarrassed in my life as when Calvin humiliated me to the utmost last week when we were at Carla's house.

She was so nice to have a dinner for me where she made my favorite: fried chicken and baked macaroni and cheese. She invited us all—me, Calvin, Denim, and Robbie. I was beginning to have fun until Calvin started to look me up and down and said that he didn't want to be with me. My heart fell for the third time in a week. I couldn't let Calvin continue to get the best of me. It took Carla hours of talking to him before he started crying and said that he wanted to be with me. All day, every day it's the same shit. He wants to be with me then he doesn't. That was the fastest turnaround time of love that I had in history. I would rather jerk my dick until I kiss his ass again. I'm sick of his bullshit and if he wants to be with other people then so be it.

I went to work and came home every day like I should. I knew that Calvin and Dontae would be going to Busch Gardens for the weekend but I wasn't gonna be the one to call him and tell him to have a good time. Who the fuck does he think I am?

The phone rang twice as I laid on the living room floor watching *Training Day*.

"Hello?" I answered.

"Wassup," Calvin said in a low voice.

"How are you?"

"I'm fine, we just got back from Busch Gardens."

Just got back? Today is Wednesday, I thought to myself. "I know, Denim told me," I said.

"Oh, OK, I'll call you right back."

"OK."

I wasn't gonna wait for his call even though I did. I was so disgusted with him after he told Denim that he would be giving me back the clothes I'd bought because he didn't want to be with me any longer. If I'm gonna be depressed, I'm gonna be depressed on my own and he will not contribute to it. I took the clothes back to the store and got my money back with pride. You live and you learn so I'm just gonna take this escapade I had with Calvin and use it as a lesson learned. I loved a man with all my heart and what happened, he wanted to see other people because he felt he couldn't get from me what he could get somewhere else.

Friday had come and I still hadn't heard from Calvin. I wanted us to have a clean break and I didn't plan on looking back. I removed his name from my cell phone and erased his numbers from my caller ID and my memory. Denim was now trying to fill his shoes. He would come see me almost every day. He would call and ask if I was OK whether it was day or night. Even though my heart felt heavy I would damn sure not show it to anyone. The only shoulder that was left to cry on was Carla's. She made it her business to make me her first priority. I needed to break all the ties that I had with him. Only thinking of myself, I told Denim that the only way we could be friends was if he got rid of Calvin—meaning, talking on the phone and going out with him.

Before leaving out with Denim to go down 13th Street my tears made an appearance. As I stood in the bathroom mirror I cried over Calvin; Denim appeared in the doorway rubbing my shoulders. I turned around and gave his frail frame a hug.

On our way downtown we made a stop down South Street where I bought a brand new pair of Adidas sneakers with a shirt to match. I liked having Denim around, he would actually listen to each word that I had to say and let me know that it meant something to him.

"So, what do you want to do this weekend?" he asked while we sat on the front steps of Carla's house. We waited for Carla to get ready because she wanted to take a trip down to the gayborhood with us.

"I don't know, what do you have plans to do?"

"I don't have plans to do anything. I want to take you out." He looked into my eyes to see my reaction.

"You mean as a date?"

"Yeah."

"Denim, how could we date when I used to go with your friend?"

"Come on now, you know just as well as I do that he's not worried about us seeing each other," he said, smirking at me.

"What do you mean?"

"Because I asked him would it be OK if I asked you out and he said that he doesn't mind."

"What?" I was astonished.

"Yeah, he said it was cool, and he also told me that you liked the little M&M characters, and that you love going to amusement parks."

I tried to compose myself as I stood up in disbelief. But in actuality, since I never told Denim my likes, I figured Calvin must've told him something.

"I can't believe this shit," I spat while covering my face and looking down at the steps. Denim grabbed my hands and put them against his heart.

"Rashad, I really like you and I see that Calvin acts like he doesn't want to be with you. As a matter of fact, I'm gonna be honest with you," he said looking into my eyes.

"Be honest about what?" I was begging to know more.

"The reason why you haven't been hearing from him lately is because he has been in Jersey seeing someone else."

"Stop lying man," I said as I held my heart with my right hand so it wouldn't jump out.

"I'm not lying, and I feel as though you needed to know that so you will let him go."

"He told me that he was visiting his mother in Jersey." Denim looked up at me with raised eyebrows. "How could he!?" I said with teary eyes as I jumped up from the steps. "I have to go!" I jumped into my car and left Denim on the steps.

"Where are you going!" he yelled.

"I gotta go!" My heart was in my feet. My mouth was dry and I couldn't breathe. I wanted so bad to call Calvin but what would be the use? I quickly dialed Kevin's number.

"Hello?" he answered.

"Oh, my God, Calvin has been cheating on me!" I yelled into the phone as I floored onto the expressway.

"Bredda, ketch youself. He ain't cheating when yuh not dealing. Him nah want you."

"Well, you know what I mean," I said, trying not to sound dumb.

"Yeah, mon, and I know de frustration but..."

"Do you think I should call him?"

"Fa' what?"

"I don't know, I want to ask him."

"Jah know, you could. I don't think you get anything out of it," Kevin said as he munched in my ear.

"Kevin, I don't know what to do."

"Go to your yard, get some rest, and ah'll call later afta I eat."

"OK."

Deep in the back of my mind I knew something was funny about the way Calvin had been acting. I tried to keep myself calm as my cell phone rang and I saw that it was Denim. I didn't answer. I didn't know if he was telling the truth or not. He likes me, so he probably would say anything to get me to stop liking Calvin and start liking him. I'm not falling for that. I love Calvin and although he made it clear that he didn't want to be with me I never had a reason to believe that he cheated nor lied to me about anything.

When I got home I grabbed two Xanaxes off my dresser and gulped them down with a tall glass of orange juice. I lay in my bed and watched the *Flintstones* until I was out like a light. I missed Calvin. I missed him lying in my bed right beside me. Would I ever get the chance to touch him again? I needed to know. I wondered if the guy in Jersey that he supposedly is dating looks better than me. What does he have that I don't?

* * *

Carla made a nice breakfast for me the following day, and boy could she throw down in the kitchen. There were scrambled eggs, sausage, bacon, toast, and some down-home grits. We sat at the table and joked about this and that as she tried her best to mend my broken heart and let me know that I was a cutie and everything would be all right. She invited me into her life and let me know that things could be a lot worse. She also informed me that Denim really likes me and if I wanted to take a chance with him she would approve.

"Well, he did ask to take me to Dorney Park," I said.

"Well, go, and have a good time. You need to get Calvin off your mind and move on. Trust me if it was meant to be, he'll be back."

"Right."

"This life is crazy, especially when you think you found that special someone and y'all keep going and keep growing and then he wants to bail out. And having a broken heart isn't easy. It's gonna be tough but you need to know that our Father will pull you through this and you will come out on top," she said as she finished up her cup of coffee.

Even though Carla was still young, she was as wise

as an 85-year-old woman. I knew that we were gonna get along great, things happen for a reason. God brought us together in an unfortunate situation where Calvin and I had to part. Right now it seemed Carla's only problem at this time was money, and I sure knew of a way to help her with that.

"Do you have a bank account?" I asked her, while munching on toast.

"No, why?"

"Because if you did, I could find a way to get you some money."

"No, I don't have a bank account but my girlfriend does, and she needs money too. Let me call her. What is it you would need her to do?" she asked as she dialed the phone.

"Well, see if she has an ATM card."

"OK."

\* \* \*

June was coming to an end, and the more time went on, the hotter it would get, and the more my heart would hurt. I returned to work with my sad face, hoping that someday I could change my life around. Kya invited me to go with her to New York for Gay Pride for the weekend. We would be staying at her cousin's house in the Bronx. I was so excited to go.

First, I needed to see if my craft was going to work with Carla's friend. She met me at a spot in North Philly and gave me her ATM card. I was definitely gonna get me some money from this. She didn't know me and I definitely didn't know her. What the fuck, I needed money like yesterday. I deposited the check like I was supposed to. Since it was a credit union account I couldn't really get as much out of it as I wanted. I took out the $100.00 that became immediately available without letting her know anything. Then, as each day went by, another $100.00 would become available.

I collected $400.00 from the account, which I was supposed to give half to her. But like I said, she didn't know me and I didn't know her, so I didn't have to give her shit. I packed my bags and left for NYC with Kya, leaving Carla and her dumb-ass friend penniless.

With Calvin still on my mind, I walked through the crowd of cute boys in the Village. I was wearing a jacket in 90-degree weather. I wasn't gonna show off my stomach today. I made the jacket look like it was part of the outfit. Even though my underarms were sweating, I never removed the jacket.

Once we returned home that Sunday I had to get myself together for work the next day. I had purchased a porno tape from NYC to keep me busy while Calvin wasn't around. Denim waited for my return, and my phone was ringing as soon as I hit the door.

"Hello?" I answered.

"Wassup," said Denim who was happy to hear my voice.

"I'm chillin'. What's going on with you?"

"I'm all right. I'm glad that you're home. I talked to Calvin today," he said, as my heart dropped to my feet.

"Yeah?"

"Yeah, he called me asking me why I don't call him anymore. I told him that I'm trying to get at you now and I don't want him to call me no more."

"And what did he say?"

"What could he say? I banged on his ass," he said, laughing.

I laughed. "No, you didn't."

"I did."

Denim and I sat on the phone and talked for hours until I noticed it was late and I had to get myself ready for bed so that I could get up in the morning. We made a date to go to Dorney Park on Saturday. Kya had asked me if I wanted to go with her and her girlfriend, so I figured we might as well make it a double date. I took two Xanaxes and placed myself underneath my soft sheets and fell asleep.

The next day was a drag as always. I had been dodging the phone calls from Carla and her girlfriend who wanted to know what was going on with the bank account. I was two hours late for work because I needed to get a little more sleep after being up on the phone with Denim half the night. I walked into the office and found a note on my computer stating that Ellen needed to see me right away. After putting my belongings down in my chair I walked around to her office. I didn't get a chance to wave at the girls who were waving to me. I was on a mission. I could hear them talking about me acting shady toward them as I walked into my supervisor's office.

"Have a seat, Rashad," she said as she stared into the computer screen, not even looking at me as I walked in.

I sat down in the lovely chair draped in lace.

"I received a complaint about you yesterday from a fellow employee of yours. The person states that you were on the phone arguing with someone and using foul language. Also, I have been watching over your computer and notice that you have been using the Internet for your own personal use," she said, as she finally turned to look at me.

"Are you aware of the company's policy, Rashad?" she asked sternly.

"Yes."

"Well…" her ringing phone interrupted her. I sat there listening to every word that she said on the phone.

"Yeah, I have him in my office now…OK. Thanks, bye." I hated being in the hot seat, and for some reason, I had a strange feeling about what was about to go down.

"So, are you aware of our company's policy?" she

asked again as she called another supervisor into the office.

"Hey, Lisa, can you watch Rashad for a minute? I have to go handle something," she said, letting the other woman into the office as she left.

Watch me? Why do I need to be watched? I sat for about five minutes, looking at the white on white walls that graced Ellen's office.

Ellen returned and took a seat behind her desk.

"Thanks, Lisa," she said, signaling her to step out of the room.

"Well, Rashad, at this time I will have to terminate your position here for not following company policies. Do you have your I.D. badge on you?"

"Yes," I said, unclipping the badge from my belt loop. I couldn't think straight at this point. My life seemed like it was slowly deteriorating. I was now being fired from my job, the only source of legit income I had. What was I gonna do about my rent, my bills? I looked deep into her eyes. She could have given me a warning. I made a mistake and I guess this damn company doesn't forgive people who make mistakes. I needed my damn job!

I gave her my I.D. badge as two security officers entered the office to escort me to the door. By the time I turned around, Lisa had already packed all my items into a box and had it sitting in front of the office.

"Do you have any questions?" Ellen asked as if she cared.

"No, not at this time."

"Well, your benefits will resume until the end of the month, then at that time you will have an option to file for COBRA or you can choose your own benefit plan independently."

I rolled my eyes into the back of my head. It's like I knew what lay ahead of me. I knew that without a job the road would be tough. It was hell finding this job so I knew it was gonna be rough to find another one. I didn't even have Calvin to tell me that everything would be all right. Of course, I would lose my man, now my job.

"Good luck, Rashad," Ellen said as I got up from the chair and grabbed the brown box that contained my radio, magazines, pencils, ink pens, and all of my pictures of J-Boog from B2K. Fortunately, to my surprise, there wasn't anyone in my path on my way out to ask me any questions or wonder why I was getting fired. Like I always said, when it rains it pours and I damn sure was in the middle of a thunderstorm.

I jumped into my car after throwing the entire box into the trunk and sped off, leaving the entire office complex in the dust. I went straight to my grandmother's house where everyone was gearing up for tomorrow's Fourth of July cookout that was taking place at Tamika's.

"You got fired?" Shay asked, whispering so her mother couldn't hear her.

"Yeah, chile, they packed my shit for me and told me to hit the road," I said. We started giggling.

"So, what are you gonna do for money now?"

"I don't know, I'll have to think of something." I began playing with the baby who was now teething and getting bigger by the day.

"Man, I am good for this month though. I paid my rent for this month but I don't know what I'm gonna do about the next month," I said, still playing on the floor with the baby as Shay sat on the couch looking down at us.

"Well, don't forget about tomorrow, you are supposed to bring sodas," she said as she scratched the tip of her nose.

Damn, I just got fired. Now where am I gonna get the money for that? I said to myself. I continued to play with the baby, not letting the problems from the rest of the world get to me.

I made it my business not to tell everybody about my sudden unemployment. Once I told my mother, Kevin, and Shay, my lips were sealed. I went to my apartment to try and figure out what my next step would be. I needed to wait until Sunday to at least browse the Job Section, but for now I was gonna put my feet up and rest.

I watched my phone ring off the hook as Carla and her friend called to see what I did with the money from the bank account. I thought about that saying, *what goes around, comes around,* and it touched my heart when I heard the girl on my voice mail crying her eyes out telling me that the bank took $400.00 out of her account because of the bounced checks, which made them take the direct deposits from her job. She went on and on telling me that she didn't have any food in her house for her and her kids, and for this to be a holiday, she didn't have any money to take her kids anywhere.

"Blah, blah, blah," I said as I listened to every message she left. But think about it, she didn't know me from Adam, so why would she trust a total stranger with her ATM card? I didn't force her to give it to me. So what if I took all the money. I'm a thief. I don't just steal from banks, if the price is right I'll steal from anybody.

I finally got up enough heart to pick up the phone after the thirtieth time they called.

"Hello?" I answered. I could tell they were on the three-way.

"Hello, Rashad? Where were you, I have been calling you for two days?" Carla asked in a calm voice.

"I was in New York."

"But you was supposed...."

"Rashad!" the girl yelled, cutting Carla off.

"Yes."

"Where's my money!?"

"I didn't get any money. It didn't work," I lied.

"The credit union called me this morning and said that there was two counterfeit checks that were deposited into my account. Then, there was $400.00 withdrawn out of the account, and they are going to take my direct deposit out of my paycheck.  Now, where's the $400.00?" she demanded to know through her tears.

"I didn't take any money out, I don't know what you are talking about."

"Rashad, you might as well tell the truth.  I called Calvin looking for you and he told me that you did the same thing to him when y'all did this with his mother's account," Carla said.

First of all, why the fuck would she call Calvin, knowing that we weren't messing with each other anymore?  Ain't this some shit, I thought.

"Man, Calvin is lying."

"All that I know is that I don't have any money to pay the bank $400.00.  You will have to give me something because I'm not gonna take this loss," the girl cried.

"Well, I have to call you back," I said before pressing the end button so they couldn't say anything else.

I stood there for about three minutes before I was over the whole situation.  I lost a friend, but oh well, she had no business calling Calvin and telling him anything about me.  I resent her for that.  She is supposed to be a personal friend of mine so what business does she have calling Calvin like he is my father or something, shit.

I woke up early the next day thinking that I had to be at work.  I didn't have any money, it was hot as shit, and I didn't have a job.  It was nice that Denim said that he could get a case of sodas for me to take to Tamika's house so I didn't need to spend any money. The heat index was more than 95 degrees and it was going up.  The humidity must have been higher than that because every movement I made, I broke a sweat.  Even though God woke me up this morning in some strange way I knew that it would have been better if He hadn't.

But I couldn't think about negative stuff now because I had to get ready for the holiday. I had to go to

# Smoking Cigarettes

Denim's job to get the case of sodas and be at Tamika's by four. I gave Denim a call.

"What time do you want me to come to your job to get the sodas?"

"Come around two," he said.

By the time I got dressed and was ready to head out to Denim's job, my mother was already at the door. Since we were going to the same place, she drove and took me past Denim's job to pick up the sodas. My stepfather's sister also accompanied my mother to the barbecue today. I really wasn't to keen on having her around. I didn't get along with my stepfather so I didn't see a reason to have her in my company either. But I couldn't decide who my mother could be around or who she could have in her car. She didn't listen to me anyway because she went and married a man that I despised, and now she had to help him raise his two bad-ass lesbian girls so that was her problem.

\* \* \*

"This is my nephew… Rashad," my drunk Uncle Gary said to someone as we sat inside Tamika's house.

I couldn't take it any longer, the heat plus my broken heart were not mixing together right. I needed space, some air to release the pain and hurt I was feeling.

Tap, tap, tap.

Denim looked through the bars on the door then walked in.

"Everyone, this is Denim," I said to all the guests sitting in the living room trying to get some of the air that circulated from the rotating fan. Denim wore a pair of blue jeans and a white shirt with an all-white Kangol cap and a pair of dark shades. We had plans to visit 13th Street before the night ended because I needed some loving bad and now was the right time for me to find a nice piece of meat to chew on while I went through my vulnerable stage.

Everyone ate and seemed to be having a good time. The food and the drinks were being served, and Shay, Tamika, and I took advantage of all the festivities. After popping a Xanax and drinking a shot of tequila that Shay had made for me, I was done. I fell asleep on the couch until the sun went down. By the time I awakened, I glanced up to notice Tamika's gray and white cat running up the steps. I remembered two years ago, I had given my cat away to Tamika along with the cat's cage. I remembered telling her that she could keep the cat but she had to return the cage.

"Tamika!" I yelled into the kitchen where she was probably on her fourth round of Heineken.

"What?" she said, turning to face me with red eyes.

"Where's my cat cage?"

"It's on the porch. Why?" She took a few more sips of her beer. Shay walked through the door and sat the baby down in the swing.

"Because, since I'm here I might as well take it," I said, getting up and walking toward the porch.

"You gave me the cage when you gave me the cat," she explained without sitting her beer can down.

"No, I remember telling you that you could have the cat but you needed to give the cage back." I was still walking toward the door.

"Well, you can't take the cage because I need it for my cat." I totally ignored her as I walked onto the porch to retrieve the cage.

"Don't you touch that cage!" she yelled as she followed behind me. I turned around as she swiftly walked past me to get the cage. She walked back into the house holding the cage in her hand as I stormed after her.

"What the fuck are you following me for?" she asked as she turned around and walked from the living room to the kitchen, still holding the gray and green cage in her hand. I followed her into the kitchen where she sat the cage down on the floor.

"Give me my cage, Tamika." I was getting annoyed with the situation and sweat started to form on my forehead. She ran toward me as my aunt Denise jumped between us.

"You want some of me, pussy?" Tamika blurted while trying to turn herself loose from Aunt Denise's arms. I began walking toward the front door as I turned around and noticed Tamika charging toward me.

"What the fuck..." I said as I started swinging. Tamika and I went for broke. She swung her fist as I swung mine. The crowd formed as the both of us fell through the front screen door. I felt hits coming from all directions as I handled myself. I threw punches as fast as I received them. It was dark and I felt faint, but the heat couldn't and wouldn't stop me now. I needed to win this war at all cost. My mother grabbed me.

"Get the fuck off me!" I swung my arms back and forth not caring who took a lick.

"Stop it!" my mother yelled as she tried to keep her balance and grab a hold of me at the same time. She couldn't get a hold on me and I couldn't get a hold of myself. I stumbled down the steps while pulling my shirt from over my head. My face was covered with sweat.

Shay and another girl from up the street had started their own fight on the side while I waited for Tamika to come down the steps.

Aunt Denise grabbed Shay and tackled her against the car.

"Mom! Where she at... I'ma fuck her up!" Shay yelled as Aunt Denise pinned her against the car.

Tamika finally came down the steps as I ran over to her trying to get a couple of more hits in before the fight was officially over.

"Bitch!" I said as I swung on her again and she swung back. Immediately my cousin Eryk grabbed me from behind. Eryk was no older than fourteen. He held me tight in his arms as I struggled to get loose.

"Eryk, get off me! Eryk, get the fuck off me!" He was not letting his grip loose. He had a hold tighter than a bug in an airtight jar. I tried everything from swinging him around to forcing my fist through his muscular arms, it wasn't working. I couldn't focus on the fight at this moment through all the noise, the yelling, and the banging on car windows.

"Stop! Stop!" was all I could hear from the hyped crowd—from my mother to my grandmother, aunts, cousins and friends.

"I'ma fuck you up!" I yelled to the crowd that stood on the side as Eryk finally let me go and I grabbed a green porch chair and flung it into the crowd.

"Pussy!" I yelled to the crowd as my aunt Denise rushed up the street to grab me and force me into the car. I waited in the car trying to catch my breath as my mother jumped in on the driver's side then fled down the street. I huffed and puffed as the sweat continued to run down the sides of my face. I could still feel the heat from the earth rubbing up against my skin as I sat there and watched my mother and her sister-in-law shake their heads in disgust.

By the time I got home, I seemed to have calmed down a bit. Still focusing on my heartbreak I wondered how my family could just change on me. Why would they want to fight me? It seemed as if I was jumped, but the only one that seemed to stay in my corner was Shay. What was that all about? Why was she fighting that girl? I didn't know what was going on.

Denim took my torn shirt from me as we entered my apartment. He left the cookout right after we did. A strong force of air blew on me as I opened the door. I was glad to be home. I didn't have any energy to do anything but walk to my bedroom and flop down on the bed with Denim following behind me. He sat in front of me on the floor.

"Bitch, you are crazy," he said, getting up and rubbing my back. His soft, cool hands felt so good on my body. All the anger I had built up inside for Calvin was let out today by fighting with my family, but I guess all the sexual tension was still inside. I looked into Denim's eyes with a fierce erection in my shorts that had to be tamed.

"What's wrong with you?" he asked as I continued to smile at his black ass. I stood up in front of him, pulling my zipper down on my Guess jeans shorts when he got the clue.

I smiled at the thought of what was about to go down as I grabbed his head and forced him closer to my groin as I pulled out my throbbing man stick.

He licked the head thoroughly before deep throating me so I could touch his tonsils. He started to unzip his pants and I searched around on the dresser for a condom. When I spotted one I tore the package open like a wolf grabbing at a steak. I gracefully slipped the condom onto my dick as I pulled his pants off from his dark, thin body.

He turned in a doggy-style position so I could slide my dick right between his love tunnel. I was finally getting the piece of ass that I deserved as I plunged deeper and deeper into his hole. He yelled as I pumped faster.

"You want this dick, don't you?" I asked as I pounded harder. "Take that shit," I said, going deeper as he flinched his face and grabbed the pillow in front of him. I kissed the back of his neck, letting my tongue explore freely as I licked around his earlobe while I stroked my dick deeper into his ass.

"Yeah, whose ass is this?"

"It's yours!" he yelled.

"Who?"

"It's yours!"

"What's my name?!" I yelled while grabbing his waist and pulling his body back on my dick so he could get all of me.

"Rashad."

"What?!"

"Rashad," he said with the agony of passion.

"Say it louder, pussy!" I shouted while feeling my muscle tense up. I felt my nut about to be released.

"Ahh, Rashad!" he said even louder while trying to catch his breath.

"Yeah!" I yelled, shooting everything that I had in me directly into him through the busted condom. I fell on top of him, letting my stomach hit his back.

This had to be the night of all nights. I was full, I was drunk, and I had just fucked the shit out of Denim. What could I say? The day wasn't so shitty after all.

# Smoking Cigarettes

## Make Your Move

*Ring, Ring,*
I reached over to grab the cordless off the base.

"Hello?" I answered, trying to wipe the cold from my eyes.

"Are you sleep?" Shay asked in her energetic voice.

"Yeah, why?"

"Wake up, the sun is shining."

"So, who said that's a good thing?" I said in a crackling voice.

"It is, and guess what?"

"What?"

"Kaniyah took her first steps."

"Whooptie do," I said, being sarcastic.

"You know grandmom is mad at you."

"Mad at me for what? I didn't start the fight, she should be mad at Tamika if anything. And who was that girl you were fighting?"

"I don't even know her, she lives down the street from Tamika. She ran over to you and started hitting you so I started hitting her. Uncle Gary said that we need to have a family meeting," Shay said, laughing.

"A family meeting? For what?" I laughed back.

"Because he said that we are family and we shouldn't be fighting. You know he was drunk. Did you hear that new song by Isyss?" she asked, changing the subject.

"What song?"

"I think it's called 'Day and Night.' *You gotta house on the hill...*" she started singing as my hangover began to kick in. I laid back on my pillow and continued to listen to her sing. "Shay, hold on while I answer the other line."

"OK."

Hello?" I answered.

"Yes, Rashad Smith please," a gentlemen said on the phone. I could tell he was white.

"Speaking."

"Mr. Smith, this is Mr. Townes calling from the repossession station about your 2000 Plymouth Neon."

"Yes," I said, as I got out of the bed.

"The address that your car is registered to is different from the address where you actually live, is that correct, Mr. Smith?"

"Yes."

"I have reason to believe that you are using your mother's address. Is that correct?"

"Hold on, sir." I clicked back to Shay. "Shay, I'll call you right back," I said before clicking over to Mr. Townes. "Yes, sir," I said, letting him know that I was back on the line.

"Is it true that the car is registered at your mother's address, Mr. Smith?"

"Yes."

"Well, my men were at your mother's house this morning to get the car and it wasn't there. Sir, what I will need you to do is bring the car to that address and leave the keys with your mother if you could."

"Why, what's wrong?" I walked over to the window to see if my car was still there.

"Sir, your car payment is four months past due. For more information you will need to call your finance company, but for now I will need you to take your car to the address and park it and someone will be there to get it."

"OK, sir," I said, and hung up the phone. I immediately called my mother because I remembered that I had the doctor's appointment for my consultation with the plastic surgeon today.

# Smoking Cigarettes

* * *

I'm not leaving shit no where, I said to myself as I backed my car out of the driveway and drove it around Mia's house and hid it in her garage. My mother sat there and waited for me while I shut the door and locked my car inside of the garage.

After calling around for the actual balance that I owed the car company, I knew that I needed to come up with a plan to get the money. I wasn't that smart about what happens when your car gets repossessed, but I did know that I needed to do something fast before they reported my car stolen, then I would be up shit's creek.

"Do you think that grandma will loan me the money?" I asked my mother as we drove to Center City for my consultation.

"I don't know, nothing beats a failure but a try."

"You know it would be better if you would ask her," I said, smiling in her direction.

"I'm not asking her for money," she spat.

"Mom, I can't let them take my car and she would give you money faster than she'd give it to me and besides, Shay said that she was mad about yesterday."

"All right, pass me the phone."

Of course my plan worked. I knew that it would be easier for my mom to ask and not me. She gave into my mother just as easy. All I needed to do was Western Union the money to the car company by three. I had it made.

* * *

I was happy to at least be sitting in the waiting area with all these rich, white people who are spending their money on plastic surgery because they didn't have anything else to do with the funds. I needed every nickel, dime, and penny I could use. Even though I didn't have any money to waste on plastic surgery, I knew it wouldn't hurt to at least go for the consultation. It was free, so what the hell. My mother sat on one side of the all-white room as I sat on the examining table with my shirt off and a hospital robe on with the front open. I turned and looked out the window to see all the cars that drove on the street below and thought about Calvin and how deeply I am in love with him and how badly I miss him.

The doctor came in, smiled and then introduced himself. He was young, cute, and rich. A white man who had to be about in his mid- or late-thirties, he was wearing a gray shirt and blue necktie under a long white lab coat.

"You look much younger in person," I said to him as he and my mother began to laugh.

"So, how are you, Mr. Smith?" he asked while starting the examination process.

"I'm fine. I hear Wendy Williams talk about you on the radio all the time," I said, making conversation as my mother sat back and watched.

He started massaging my stomach, his hands felt so warm and soft as they maneuvered over my belly. I looked over at my mom and smiled.

"So, Doc, what do you think?" I asked.

"Well, you could lose all this fat by just working out and eating right, you know."

"No, that doesn't work for me. I tried everything from exercising to taking diet pills and nothing seems to work. I think it's a tumor in my stomach," I said as he and my mother began to laugh.

"Well, if I was to do anything, I would do liposuction around your waistline," he said, looking over at my mom. "But as I said before, you don't need it. All you need to do is eat right and get plenty of exercise and you'll be fine."

I really wasn't trying to hear it.

"Well, I'm done here. Just go to my receptionist

and she'll give you the price of what everything would cost, OK?" he said, before walking out the door. I began to put my shirt on and talked to my mom before going out into the receptionist area.

We had to wait about 15 minutes to receive a quote for a procedure that I was never going to get. While waiting, I began to look through the different pamphlets to see what else the doctor had to offer. Then, the receptionist called me over to the desk and wrote a number down on a yellow sticky note. The number was $5,000.00. I looked at it then slid the paper over to my mother.

"Well, now you see, do you have the money for that?"

"No."

"All right then, let's go." We walked out of the doctor's office as I put the yellow piece of paper deep into my back pocket. We proceeded to my grandmother's house to get the money to pay my car note.

* * *

After the activity I had with Denim, my mind was in a total frenzy. It was nice, but it seemed so empty. I was getting deeper into my depression as the days got longer. There was nothing left for me to do but sit in the house and listen to the sounds of Phyllis Hyman and Tweet; the songs that would put me in the mood to do the unthinkable. There was nothing for me to live for and for damn sure there was nothing for me to look forward to.

The computer seemed to be my only escape to find new friends. For about a week Tyree and I chatted on the computer back and forth, from him trying to get in my pants to him telling me his problems with his current boyfriend. It was like he used me as the support system for what he was going through, and I used him for the same. Calvin was starting to wear on my soul. Tyree and I would spend countless hours chatting on the computer about nothing. We even exchanged numbers one night so that we could carry our conversation on the phone. I sat on the edge of the bed at six in the morning listening to Tweet and talking with Tyree.

"So, how long were you and Calvin seeing each other?" he asked with femininity in his voice.

"Well, it's been like eight months."

"Were y'all together for eight months or just talking off and on?" I tried to rethink and answer his questions to the best of my ability.

"Where are all these questions coming from?" I asked, confused.

"Because you know he was…" he paused.

"He what?"

"Never mind, I think I should keep my mouth shut."

"No, what are you talking about, Tyree?" I asked as my heart dropped, but I wasn't gonna stop there because I wanted to know.

"Well, I shouldn't be telling you this because Calvin is my friend, but you know him and Joseph messed around, right?"

"Yeah, he did tell me that they messed around before we started going together."

"No, this was recently," he said, as my mouth dropped to the floor.

"Stop lying," I said in disbelief.

"Yeah," he continued. "Ron and Calvin aren't speaking right now because you know that they are cousins, and Joseph cheated on Ron with Calvin. That shit is foul."

I had to stop and think about this for a minute. Calvin and Joseph were always together, but Calvin didn't give off any clues that they were seeing each other. I continued to listen.

"Are you there?" he asked.

"Yeah, I'm here."

"I know that we just met and I shouldn't be telling you all this but I just want you to keep this between you and me, OK?"

How does he expect me to keep this information between us when I was getting played the whole time. No, I won't let it happen. I know within myself that Calvin never lied to me and I know that Tyree is probably telling me all this because he wants to get with me himself. I won't fall for it.

"So, how did you know all this was happening?" I asked.

"Trust me, Rashad, I know," he said with assurance. I just looked straight ahead at the wall with the dumbest feeling ever.

"So, is that all you know?" I asked, digging for more information.

"No."

"What do you mean, *no*."

"Did you know that Calvin messed around with some boy named Tyrone, too?" Now I know he was going too far.

"No, I didn't know about that," I said in amazement.

"Yeah, he messed with some boy named Tyrone that lives in Darby."

"What the fuck…"

How could I not ask Calvin about this? First, Denim lies about Calvin, saying that he was seeing someone in Jersey then Tyree starts lying. I still stick by what I said. Even though Calvin and I are not together, I'm going to stick by him no matter what.

The following Friday Tyree and I met up on 13th Street to hang out, and yes, Calvin was there as well. With all the broken pieces of my heart, I embraced him with a hug. It'd almost been a month since I had seen him and he was fagged the fuck out.  He switched up and down the strip wearing tight clothes and had his hair in twists.

"Calvin, I need to speak with you for a minute," I said, grabbing his hand and pulling him to the side of the parking lot.  I missed Calvin so much.  I was grateful to be standing in front of him, holding a conversation, even if it wasn't what I really wanted to talk about.

"I have to ask you a few questions," I said as I watched the sweat run down his face as he wiped it off with his shirt.

"Did you ever cheat on me?" I asked with a straight face.  His entire group of friends sat on the side and watched.

"No."

"Well, why is it that all of your friends are basically telling me different stories about you that are not true?"

"Rashad, I don't know.  You know I would never have done anything to hurt you when we were together.  I wouldn't lie.  I have never lied to you," he said, staring me in my face.

I had a good mind to bring all his friends in on our conversation, but I didn't.

"Calvin, I know that you have never lied to me.  That's why I don't believe all the things that they are telling me."  We both looked at one another and began walking back toward the crowd that Calvin had separated from.

Tyree and Denim stood by the car talking to a tall, brown-skinned boy named Cliff.  He was about two or more inches taller than me.  He wore glasses, sported a net baseball cap, and had a chipped tooth.  His eyes followed me all the way around until I stood behind Tyree.

"Hey, Rashad," he said.  Now how does he know my name?

"Hey," I said, while still looking over at Calvin.

"I asked Calvin was it OK for me to ask for your

number and he said it was fine," Cliff continued.

I looked him up and down. No, this nigga didn't just ask me for my number when my ex is standing right here. These niggas are crazy.

"I'll talk to you later," I said to him as I began to walk toward 13$^{th}$ and Locust. I bumped into Ron who was talking to a boy named Reem. I did take notice that Calvin walked past Ron and didn't say anything, which meant that I needed to start my investigation process immediately.

"I'm ready to go home," I said to Tyree as we began walking toward my car.

Tyree and I talked until the sun came up. We discussed different issues about our lives and relationships and how he had a crush on me for the longest time. We also talked about crafting, and he told me that he knew how to make his own checks and how he had been to jail numerous times during his teenage years. He was now twenty.

I wasn't attracted to him at all. Although he was cute, he didn't get a rise out of me. I knew that he would work well as a friend, and even if I started to craft again, he'd be one hell of a business partner.

\* \* \*

It has been a while since I have been on a date with anyone. I needed a date in the worst way. It even resulted in going out with one of Troy's longtime friends. His name was Chad. He was mixed with black and white and had long curly hair that he kept in braids. His skin was smooth and light, and I was in love with his sense of humor. Still, nothing could top Calvin's personality. Chad was shorter than me and smoked weed just like he washed his ass, every day. After seeing him on 13$^{th}$ Street all the time, we exchanged numbers one night and started talking regularly on the phone. He took me to the movies and we went out to dinner, which I had to pay for because he stated either he'd pay for the movies or for dinner, he wasn't paying for both.

After playing with him for about a week we decided to keep it as friends, which was a good thing because I couldn't stand the smell of weed, and I couldn't and wouldn't dare let Troy find out that I was dating Chad without him knowing.

I received a phone call early in the morning from a familiar number that hadn't appeared on my caller ID in a long time. It was Calvin.

"Hey, Rashad."

"Wassup, Calvin?" I asked, wanting him to get straight to the point that he wanted me back. I was all ready to say yes.

"I just wanted to say thank you for the other night. You know, pulling me to the side, speaking with me and not causing a big scene downtown."

"It's cool, it wasn't about causing a big scene. I just needed to know what was going on."

"So, can we be friends?"

"Sure we can," I lied.

"Well, you can call me sometimes you know." I could tell he was smiling from the sound of his voice.

"Calvin, the phone works both ways," I said.

My line beeped.

"Calvin, hold on," I said before clicking over. "Hello?"

"What you doing?" asked Ron.

"Talking to your cousin," I said, knowing that he'd be surprised.

"Who, Calvin?"

"Yeah."

"What does he want?"

"He just called to say thanks for not making a big scene downtown the other night."

"Oh, OK. He still didn't tell you the whole truth about everything?" He wanted to see what I was going to say.

"What do you mean about everything?"

"Chile, he didn't come clean about Joseph and Tyrone?"

"No, he didn't say anything, and besides, I don't believe that shit."

"Well, you should because weren't y'all together when he came home with the sores on his dick?"

"What do you know about that?"

"Everyone knows how he got the sores on his dick. That boy Tyrone from Darby was sucking on his dick and he bit it."

"Wha…?"

"Yeah, chile, it's a long story."

"Well, hold on because I still have him on the other line," I said before clicking over. "Hello?"

"Yeah, I'm here."

"Calvin?"

"Yeah."

"How come Ron is on the other line telling me that some boy named Tyrone bit your dick and that's where those marks came from?" I asked sternly, but my heart was still in pain.

"I don't know what the fuck he's talking about! I don't even talk to him."

"Yeah, he said that y'all are not talking because you had sex with his Joseph!"

"Look, Rashad, I never cheated on you, and like I told you, I got the scars from washing up too hard. I don't know what those raggedy faggots are trying to prove by telling you a bunch of lies."

"Well, I'll call you back later," I said before clicking back to a dead line where Ron had already hung up. I clicked the end button and then walked into the living room to watch *Sponge Bob*.

I laid my head back on the couch for a second for some peace. The sound of the phone startled me. I pressed the phone's talk button and before I could say anything, I heard the sound of Calvin's voice.

"I feel the same way as I felt back in May…"

"Hello?" I answered.

"Hello?" Dontae said.

"Hey, Dontae."

"Wassup, Rashad?"

"What's going on?" I asked because I knew that he and Calvin were together on the three-way.

"Well, Rashad, Calvin has something that he wants to tell you."

"OK, what is it?" I was ready to take back my man at any cost.

"Rashad, I need to say something," Calvin said, taking over the conversation.

"OK."

"I know Tyree told you that I was messing around with Joseph while we were together and that's true."

"Wha…?" I gasped.

"Let him finish," Dontae said.

"And yes, I did have sex with Tyrone, and he did suck my dick."

My eyes began to fill with tears as I held the phone tighter.

"Are you there, Rashad?" Calvin asked.

"Yeah, I'm here."

"Can you please forgive me?" he asked as Dontae sat on the phone in silence.

"Well, Calvin, did you pray and ask God for His forgiveness?" I asked him, breaking the silence.

"Yes."

"Well, then if God can forgive, so can I."

"I never meant to hurt you, Rashad."

"Calvin, I know," I responded with tears falling down my face.

"So, can we still be cool?"

"I don't see why not," I said, still trying to hold back the tears.

"We'll call you later, OK?" Dontae said.

"OK."

I sat in the living room on the couch and cried until my heart was content. I didn't want to live in this life any longer, I couldn't live this life any longer. I just sat on the couch and let the tears fall. There was nothing that could be done to pick up the pieces of my broken heart. I wondered why he lied. Why didn't I just ask him? I dared not to call him back, but I did.

"Hello?" he answered.

"Yeah, Calvin, it's me."

"Yes."

"Why did you feel like you had to lie to me?" I asked with my eyes still filled with tears.

"I never meant to hurt you, it was just something that happened. I really feel bad about the whole thing and I know it's hard for you to forgive me but I really need you to understand."

"Understand what, Calvin?"

"I need you to understand that I have been under a lot of pressure lately. You know, with my school and I might have to repeat the eleventh grade over again, the death of my son, and then there's my mom and her bullshit. I been going through a lot lately." I could tell by the sound of his voice that he hated to tell me all that was going on. I continued to flip through the channels as I sat back to hear his sob story as to how everything went down.

"But I don't understand, Calvin, if you had a problem you knew you could come to me and talk. You didn't have to go sleep with other people to get through it." I was talking normal to him, but deep inside, my heart burned. I was burning from the strong feelings that lay within me. My fire burned hot for Calvin.

I wiped my tears as I continued to listen before he told me that he would call me back a little later on. He also told me that Denim told him that I had a crush on him. He said Denim talked to him every day about me.

See, I had to realize that Denim was playing double standards. He would go to Calvin and give him a bunch of information on what I was doing, and on the flip side, he would then give me the low down on Calvin. Either way, with him, I wasn't losing; he was just a person that got what he wanted. He wanted me to fuck his brains out and that's just what I did. But, on the other hand, I had confided in him as a friend thinking he was on my side and knew that the things that Calvin was doing were indeed wrong.

"Hello," I answered the ringing phone. It was Ron.

"Yeah, what did Calvin say?"

"He came clean about everything."

"Everything?" he asked, feeling that I was missing something.

"Yes, everything." I could hear Tyree in the background, laughing at the situation.

"Bitch, you can't hold water with a bucket," Tyree chuckled in the background.

"What is he talking about?" I asked Ron.

"What did Calvin come clean to you about?" Ron asked.

"He told me that he had sex with Joseph and he told me about that boy Tyrone."

"And, that was it?"

"Yeah, that was it."

"So, he didn't tell you about the threesome that he had with the boys Kareem and Mike?"

"What!" Damn, will these faggots ever stop? I wondered. "When did all this happen?"

"I don't know, Rashad, you should have asked him," he said sarcastically.

Ron knew everything else so how come he didn't know this?

"Well chile, I don't know what you gonna do. I know that Joseph keeps calling my cell phone apologizing and saying that he wants to get back with me."

"Are you still talking to him?"

"Yeah, I talk to him but we're not getting back together because what he did was nasty. How you gonna cheat on me with my own cousin? And besides, just because I'm talking to him doesn't mean anything, I'm not anything to Calvin. He doesn't have shit to say to me."

I continued to listen to the antics that were playing out on this dreary Saturday afternoon. I couldn't take any more of this mess.

"Well, I'll call y'all back later," I said before the line went dead. I ran into the bathroom and covered my entire face with a cool washcloth. I needed a way out. I wanted a way out and calling Calvin seemed to be my way.

"Hello?"

"Yeah, Calvin, it's me again."

"Hey," he said, and then the phone went silent.

"Calvin, I keep hearing different shit every day about the things that you have been doing while we were together," I said, getting straight to the point.

"What now?"

"I just heard that you had a threesome, is that true?"

"Oh, I forgot about that," he said as I sighed into the phone taking the back of my hand and wiping my teary eyes.

"What do you mean you forgot about that?"

"Well, Rashad, that happened a long time ago, when we first started messing around."

"Calvin, that doesn't mean anything."

"Well, I asked you for your forgiveness. It's either

you're gonna forgive me or you don't."

"I forgive you, Calvin," I said, still sniffing to hold back more tears.

"Now, I'll call you back, all right?" he said before getting off the phone. I laid my head down on my pillow and thought about old times. I really missed being around Calvin. I couldn't make any sense out of this whole situation. I mean, do you know how many guys out there would want to be with a person like me, and then, I have this young boy actually cheating on me?

What type of shit is that? I asked myself over and over again. I picked up the phone to call Chad because I needed someone to talk to and fast. He told me that he'd be more than happy to come over when he got off of work. Even though Chad still lived at home with his mother, he was the HNIC—head nigga in charge—in his living quarters and in the workplace.

To get my mind off things, I decided to get together a little group and we'd all go on double dates. It would be so much fun. Tyree was dating someone named Doug. I always thought Tyree was so sexy. He had commentated all the mini balls in Philly, and he'd even commentated some in New York. He was a shorty, though, but little did anyone know that I had the hots for that boy. He used to wear glasses but they were replaced with clear contacts. He had his own name for me. Since my skin is so smooth, he always thought I wore makeup, so he called me the *Maybelline Queen*. And, since it was coming from him, he could say whatever he wanted. So Tyree and Doug were together; then there was Chad and myself; Ron and his new date Jeff; and Shay and Drew. Poor Cliff came to the set solo.

Well, of course Cliff would go because we needed two cars and Cliff had his own. Tyree bribed him into going and being the driver even if he didn't have a date. We all went to the movies to see the new Lil' Bow Wow film *Like Mike*. I had a fun time even though my heart still wasn't at amends. It was nice to be around a different crowd for a change. After the movies, of course we all went down to 13th Street, where I saw Calvin and Denim. I had already told Denim to stop calling my house because of all the lies and games that he had tried to play.

Downtown was semi-full for a Friday night and the clubs were just letting out. I had seen Calvin but I did not speak. As a matter of fact, I didn't speak to him or Denim. All the anger and frustration that I had built up was ready to come out. On top of being confused, I realized that this nigga had played me for a fool for the past eight months. How could I sit up here and let him think that it was cool to play with my feelings after all that we'd been through? Hell no, I wasn't the one.

From my sense of direction, I could tell that Calvin noticed the fire in my eyes as he began to walk toward the parking lot where he had driven one of his friend's cars. After making a scene by removing my shirt and walking at a fast pace, all the faggots started to follow behind me.

"See, I told you," Denim said, yelling at Calvin to hurry up and walk the other way. I ran around to the parking lot where Calvin had already jumped into the car and sped off. I noticed the car approaching a red light so I immediately began to approach it when it stopped at the intersection. Luckily for me, Calvin had the driver's side window rolled down as I slowly caught up to the car.

"Yo, let me talk to you for a minute," I said to Calvin, just before the light turned green.

"I'll call you later," he said as I balled up my fist and threw a jab across his face while he sped off through the light. The crowd continued to look on as Cliff walked over to me to hand me my shirt. I didn't care about anyone seeing my stomach because I was in one of my massive rages.

# Reginald L. Hall

* * *

I needed to have all of my things in order to attend this job fair at some credit card company out there in Horsham, PA, again. It seemed as if all the jobs were all the way the fuck out there. I mean, I should at least be able to get a job in Center City or at least in West Philly but hell no, they want a bitch to travel far as hell just to make a couple ducats. I already revamped my résumé; it would be full of lies. I would always lie and say I worked for numerous companies just to make the piece of paper look good. I have never done any bookkeeping a day in my life and I damn sure don't know shit about accounting.

But, that was the catch though. I needed to have that type of stuff visible on my résumé so the employers would be impressed. I was always grateful that no one had ever asked me any questions about my previous jobs except the customer service one, and I could answer all of those questions in my sleep. I also had to take a vow to God and myself. If I get a good job, then I wasn't gonna try any slick shit to get over on them. I was going to work honestly. I wasn't gonna take anyone's information and open up an account with it nor was I gonna steal any checks from my place of business. I needed to do right this time and stop trying to cheat the system.

I pressed my green slacks once again and attached my clip-on tie and I was out the door. I arrived early for the interview because I wanted to avoid the afternoon rush. I waited patiently for a rep to call my name. I had a good feeling about this anyway. My name was called by a tall, dark-skinned, slim man. Off the back I caught an attitude. I could sense that his day wasn't going so well, and I knew that it would take a toll on the interview and me. Nonchalantly, I sat through the entire interview answering his questions with one-word answers. After about 5-10 minutes the interview was over and he said that someone would be getting in touch with me soon.

I grabbed my bag and stormed out of the interview because I knew that he was just talking shit. I knew he wasn't gonna call me. I jumped into my car and floored my way down Route 611. I popped in Tweet's CD and let the tears fall. I hated not having tinted windows. I felt sorry for myself. My mother couldn't help me any longer because she was getting behind in her rent, and on top of that, she had to take care of my sick stepfather. I didn't have any money, not even to buy food. I had some change in the cup holder left over from the movies the other night. My electric bill was due and the phone bill was due. I didn't have any where to turn.

My grandmother was starting to hawk my back for the six hundred dollars that my mother borrowed from her for me. I cried all the way home while watching the sun set through my rearview mirror. By the time I reached my apartment, my eyes were bloody red. I needed to think of something quick, fast, and in a hurry. The thought that came to mind was the bank account information that Rafeek left, and the $6,000.00 check that I had stolen from my old job.

I sat at my kitchen table and contemplated my ideas before I went to retrieve the items from my dresser drawer. I had already given the account more than enough time to sit so the account wouldn't seem new any longer. I had made a date with myself that after I finished eating my peanut butter and jelly sandwich, I would ride to the bank and do an ATM deposit and wait for the check to clear within a couple of days.

For the next couple of days, Tyree and I continued to hang out and get to know one another. He told me all about his escapades as a juvenile and how he used to run away from home just to get put in a boys' home and then he would run away from there. He told me all the mishaps I didn't know about crafting. Tyree started crafting at fifteen. At first I was impressed that he learned a lot of devious things before me, but when I thought about it, it wasn't too impressive because if he was that good, then how come he didn't have anything to show for it? At least I had a car and had maintained my apartment. He didn't have anything—no car, no house, he barely had clothes. I knew that from being around me, he would come together and start to dress to impress, and not look like an old man. He also used to dress up in drag and that too was a turnoff for me.

Cliff, on the other hand, tried his hardest to be a part of my world. I could tell that Tyree was using him for his car, and Cliff's dumb ass would take him and Ron everywhere they needed to go, and they didn't even offer him gas money. Cliff tried his hardest to fit in even though his best wasn't good enough. I would still give him an E for effort.

Without a job, and no money, I had no choice but to turn to Tyree as a resource. He'd tell me the ins and outs on how to craft officially. I always had my own scheme going but Tyree and I made a perfect combination because the things that I knew about crafting, he didn't and vice versa. I never told him about Rafeek's account that I was dealing with on the side.

I woke up early on Tuesday to check the account and see if the check cleared, to my surprise it did. I swung around to the ATM and noticed that all $6,231.05 was there. My eyes had never been so happy. Before I made another move, I withdrew $400.00 as I proceeded to go inside the bank to retrieve the rest.

With this money, I could make my dreams come true in a heartbeat. I could pay to have my surgery and still have some leftover to pay my bills until I found a job. I went into the bank with Rafeek's identification, posing as him. I filled out the withdrawal ticket and placed it on the counter along with my I.D.

# Smoking Cigarettes

"Yes, I'd like to make a withdrawal," I told the gray-haired African-American lady sitting behind the counter. She carefully inspected the piece of paper and then the I.D. She kept studying my movements as I stood there trying not to break out in a sweat.

After waiting in line for an hour and a half thinking how good I am going to look after the surgery, the teller came to me and told me that she was unable to give me the funds. Rafeek had put the wrong damn information on the paper. Furious, I had to drive all the way to the northeast where the account was opened and speak with the branch manager. That was a wasted trip, and no help to me because all she did was freeze the account and tell me she would be getting back to me within a few days.

I couldn't believe how Rafeek could be stupid enough to open the account in his middle name and not his first. I hated him for that. I hated Calvin for what he did.

Watching the sunset through my mini blinds and recollecting my feelings toward life, I tapped the edge of an unopened pack of Newport's and sat there contemplating on lighting up a cigarette. I had never put a cigarette to my mouth before but there was no better time to start than now. I placed a lit cigarette in the middle of an ashtray and watched it burn down to ashes as my tears fell. I began writing a letter to the people who mattered most in my life.

As scared as I am of dying and coming face to face with my maker, I know that it has to be done soon. I've come to grips that there is no way out of this mess I had gotten myself in. I know that my heavenly Father will understand my wanting to join Him on his throne, even though He didn't take me away from this cold place called earth. I've decided to join Him on my own, He wouldn't deface me.

Look, Phyllis Hyman did it, and a slew of other people had done it as well. Phyllis Hyman had all that a person could dream of—she was pretty, wealthy, and she had the voice of a bird—and now look at her, she's dead. She didn't just die of natural causes. She couldn't stand the smell of earth any longer and neither can I. Who could blame her? When children are born, they are raised by their parents, who feed and clothe them and send them to school. They teach their kids right from wrong and even their manners. But no one ever tells their children the truth about life. I can only speak for myself when I say that my mother never told me the downsides of life. She never told me that I would meet the grimiest people and one day I would get my heart broken. She never said that.

All I knew was that once I graduated high school I would go to college, and get a good job. My mother never told me that I had to worry about the conniving people who I would work with one day. She never told me that I would get evicted from my apartment. She didn't tell me any of those things. So how could anyone blame Phyllis Hyman for taking her own life? The least I can say is that she tried. She made great songs and she will always be known for her beautiful voice but she wasn't happy living here on earth. Who are we to judge whether or not she should have taken her life? She was living alone, and the one thing I will always hate, is living alone.

Her weight was also a factor for killing herself. She felt she was bigger than average, and diet pills and drinking lots of water weren't helping. I feel the same way. I need out and my mother who loves me so dearly, can't help me. I had a trick for them, yes them. Everyone who crossed my path throughout my entire life. Through all the heart breaks and the beatings, I wouldn't be happier than to let them see me lying plush in my beautiful casket with my head propped up on my fluffy pillows while everyone would sit there in the church crying because of their guilt.

If I am gonna go, I'm gonna go in style. I know that Shay wouldn't let them just dress me in any old thing, so I know that she will pick something nice for me, and to top it off, my shoes were going to match too. No one would know where I was, I could be in heaven or I could be in hell, but at least I would be away from these horrible people. I hated life, I hated Calvin. I've tried my hardest to live my life to the fullest but shit just keeps happening. I know what to do. My life would come to an end Friday at 7 p.m. sharp. God bless, I've got my plan.

I'm not the one to take a few pills and lie out on the floor next to some kind of death letter, then have someone rescue my body and take me to the hospital and have my stomach pumped. My theory is there's no such thing as trying to commit suicide. It's either you do it or you don't. It's funny how you hear people talking about how they had taken a whole bottle of pills because they tried to kill themselves but it didn't work. I knew the deal. For me it wouldn't happen that way. I made sure that I would put the $400.00 that I took out of the ATM to good use.

I went to CVS pharmacy and racked up on my daily drugs: 5 bottles of Tylenol PM, 7 bottles of Excedrin PM, 3 bottles of Nyquil, 10 packs of Nytol, 9 diabetic testing insulin needles with the sugar medications, and I already had about 20 Xanaxes left over from my stash before Rafeek went to jail. My total bill came to $263.51. I was set, so there would be no way that anyone could wake me up from the permanent dream I would be having.

I let my mother's phone ring four times before she answered.

"Yes," she sounded like she was asleep.

"Hey, mom, were you asleep?"

"No, just lying here in the bed reading my newspaper. What are you doing?"

"Mom, can I tell you something?" I asked, hoping she'd take time to listen.

"What is it, Rashad?"

"Mom, I'm tired."

"Tired of what?"

"Tired of living."

"Listen, Rashad, don't call me talking this craziness," she spat as the phone got silent and my tears started to fall.

I started thinking of Calvin and how he didn't care enough for me that he could go out there and sleep with other people while I sat at home and waited for him every night. My tears fell as I thought about my precious goddaughter and the day she was born. I contemplated that day and I made sure that I would be one of the first people she saw when she came into the world. It would be a shame that she would have to grow up not knowing who her godfather was.

All the guilt that was stuck in the back of my mind from Paul's death was beginning to eat away at my soul. Even if I wanted to live, I couldn't because Paul didn't. Who gave me and my brother the right to do what we did?

"I don't know what to say, Rashad," my mother said with a sigh.

"Goodbye, mom," I said before hanging up the phone.

I walked into my bedroom and turned off all the lights. I unplugged the phones, the refrigerator and the stove. I went back into the kitchen and spread all my sleep aids on the table. I filled the syringes with fluid as I sat them down on the glass so that they were visible.

I poured myself a bowl of cereal and milk. That would be my last meal for this lifetime. I slowly opened each package containing the pills and poured them all into one big pile so that it would be easier for me to scoop them at once. I turned off the lights.

*"Meet me on the moon. Soon as you can in the middle of the sky, you and I. Riding on clouds soft as you please, we can sail upon the breeze to the everlasting moment of love. I feel your symphony so strong and so*

# Smoking Cigarettes

*pure it echoes on through me. I am so sure that we were meant to be here sharing this love we share.*

*Meet me on the moon, please don't be late, you know how I hate to wait 'cause you're so great. Fly into my love that's what I need so my spirit can be free in the everlasting moment of love. I feel your symphony so strong and so pure it echoes on through me.*

*You be my love and I'll be yours too. As long as the sun warms heaven. Tell me you be my love and here's what we'll do; we can sky write our love to the heavens. We'll sing through our lives forever..."*

*-Phyllis Hyman-*

## Meet Me On The Moon

I heard them banging on the door. I didn't move out my bed until I heard them banging on the door again. I finally got up to see who the hell was at my door so damn early in the morning. Well, it wasn't that early because I looked up at the clock, and it was already 2 p.m.

"Who is it!?" I yelled before unlatching the chain from the door.

"It's the police," I heard someone say. Then, I heard a familiar voice.

"Rashad, it's your mother, open up!" I didn't understand what was going on. I hoped nothing had happened. I opened the door.

"Hallelujah, thank you, Jesus!" my mother yelled from behind the two officers who accompanied her up the steps.

"What's going on?" I asked as they entered my apartment.

"You're still alive!" my mother yelled.

"Thank God," said one of the officers as my mother cut in front of them bringing in a box of Popeye's chicken and sitting it on the table.

"Are you all right now, ma'am?" asked one of the officers.

"Yes, I'm fine and he's fine. Thank you!" she shouted as I closed the door behind the officers. My mother proceeded to retrieve two plates from the cabinet.

"Mom, what's going on?" I asked as she sat down and started placing the chicken on her plate. It smelled good.

"I needed someone to escort me here. I didn't want to find you in here dead from what you told me last night. I woke up this morning and your voice was replaying in my head over and over again. I felt like you were in danger," she said, taking a bite of her drumstick. I sat across from her and grabbed a breast and a wing out of the box.

"Yeah, I was too scared to do it. I started to take the pills, but then Drew called and started talking to me. I had forgotten to turn off my cell phone. He told me that I was his best friend and how he didn't think that he would have been able to go on without me. Then, he started saying how Kaniyah and Shay would feel if I were to kill myself," I continued to talk as Mom listened and sipped her Sprite.

"Well, you know when people bump themselves off, their families don't get to collect the life insurance."

"Well, how would my funeral have gotten paid for?"

"I don't know. I'm sure I would have gotten the money somehow."

We sat at the table and continued to eat our meal. I was so glad that she came over with my favorite food in her hand. If this didn't make me feel better, I don't know what would have.

"I don't know what to do, mom. I don't have no job, no money. And, my heart is broken into a million pieces. What should I do?"

"Rashad, when things happen in your life you just have to be prepared for them. That boy was too young for you and you know that. What possibly could y'all have done together? He's just coming out and finding out what life is all about. You, on the other hand, have been out for awhile. Just look at it this way. He's the one that lost a good thing, you didn't," she said, lighting up a cigarette.

"But I didn't mean to fall in love with him. It just happened."

"Rashad, I understand that you can't help who you fall in love with, but the boy was eighteen. You should have known that it wasn't gonna work," she said, taking a puff of her cigarette.

"So, what do I do now?    It's like everything I worked so hard for is falling apart.   It's like a snowball effect.  First, one thing happens, then there's another."

"Well, I'm gonna tell you what my mother told me—what doesn't kill you makes you stronger.  So you're just gonna have to take the bitter with the sweet and keep going."

"But what am I going to do about this broken heart? I mean, I know I can find another job but my heart is broken and it hurts really bad, I don't know what to do," I said with my eyes tearing.

"Just put your faith and trust in the man upstairs and know that He's gonna take care of it," she said, clearing the plates off the table.  I continued to sit there and stare into space.  My mother was telling the truth.  What doesn't kill us only makes us stronger, but putting all my trust and faith into the Lord was something that I lacked.

* * *

"Yeah, we can go check writing tomorrow if you want," Tyree said as we sat on the couch in his sister's house in South Philly.  He was beginning to teach me different aspects about  crafting, and I would start my first lesson tomorrow.   I had never been out check writing before, and from what I heard, it was a lot of fun, especially if you have never gotten caught.  See writing checks was more than just stealing; it was an art, a skill, a craft.  And, you needed to know what you were doing because if you didn't, you were sure to jam yourself up.

The first thing Tyree and I set out to do was the basics.  We would visit Kmart stores where I would get toilet paper, deodorant, washcloths, bath towels and so forth.  Then once we got to the register, I would whip out my professional looking checkbook and write out a check for the order, totally aware that I didn't have any money in my checking account. As a matter of fact, the account had been closed a long time ago. I was learning and it worked. After that we headed to the mall where I bought shoes, jackets, pants, a new stereo system; just put it like this, if it was on sale, I bought it.

I knew that my checks were going to be bouncing from left to right and I didn't care. In my eyes everything in the store was free. All I needed was a pen and my checks, and I could get anything I wanted. I was burying my feelings for Calvin in the midst of crafting. Tyree and I would get up early in the morning as if we had jobs and would go to work faithfully. I made sure that I was at my j-o-b every day and I would work hard till quitting time. We piled bags galore in the trunk and in the backseat of my car. Up and down Baltimore Pike, North Philly, South Philly, wherever there was a store that wasn't using the Certegy system, we were there.

You see, Certegy is a secure system for writing checks. They used extra precautions for check fraud, which made it harder for us to do our craft, but if a particular store is using Equifax, or Telecheck, oh yes, we were on it. I'd buy things for my mother, my goddaughter, and redecorate my apartment. Then, at night Tyree and I would sit back and drink wine and toast to a hard day's work. In fact, Doug would refer to us as the devil's advocates—we certainly were doing the devil's work.

In between the crafting I still felt a need to get to the bottom of all the craziness that surrounded Calvin. I wanted to know who, what, where, when, and why. My first subject would be Joseph. I would split his wig the first chance I got. He knew that Calvin and I were seeing each other and he still commenced on making a move with my man. I really wasn't worried too much about him cheating on Ron, but when you start to fuck with what's mine, I'm coming after your ass.

I had gotten all the information from Tyree because actually Joseph rented a room in Tyree's sister's home. He had the basement. I finally paid a visit to Joseph one late summer evening, and to my surprise it seemed like he knew I would be coming. He was not shocked when we made eye contact in his doorway. I couldn't wait to throw my fist across his face, but before I could be a monster I had to start out as a gentleman. I asked him if he wanted to come out onto the street or did he want me to come after him.

After Joseph carefully explained that Calvin had told him that we weren't in a relationship, I started to reevaluate the situation. This boy didn't have anything to lose. He doesn't have any parents, he is dirty, and on top of that, he is living in the basement of someone else's home. All those things in itself could drive a person insane. I know what it's like to have the world crashing down on you. Who am I to have a hand in all of his drama?

I could see the pain in his eyes that said do what you came here to do so we can get this over with. I was not gonna have that on my conscience.

My next subject was the threesome. I ran into the dude, Kareem, sporting a baseball cap while standing on 13$^{th}$ Street in front of the pizza shop. Ron pointed him out to me. I pulled him aside.

"Are you Kareem?" I asked with sweat beads forming on my forehead from the heat.

"Yeah," he answered, dazed and confused, wondering why I was asking him his name.

"Do you know Calvin?"

"Yeah."

"Well, Kareem, I'm just gonna get to the point. Did you have sex with Calvin, and if so, did y'all have a threesome?" I was covered in sweat because I was nervous and damn sure trembling.

"Well, actually it was a foursome."

"A foursome?" I repeated to make sure I heard him

correctly.

"Yeah, it was four of us," he assured me.

"And, when did all this happen?"

"It had to be like two months ago."

"And, did Calvin tell you that he had a boyfriend?" I asked, looking dead into his eyes.

"No, I asked him and he said that he was single," he said, now acting nervous.

"So, how did you meet him?"

"Well, it was early in the morning. We were on the PL (party line) and I asked him and a few of my friends to come over to my house and they all agreed. Once they came over we all had sex and one of my friends shitted on his dick and Calvin wanted to stop."

I was outraged, but again, before I could let the monster come out I needed to be a gentleman first. I hated Calvin at this moment. The man I loved so much treated me so dirty.

"Is that all you wanna know?" Kareem asked, looking over at his group of friends hoping that they would wait for him.

"Yeah, that's all," I said, letting him walk away and catch up with one of his friends. I stopped and turned around to look Ron in his eyes.

"I told you," Ron said, as he walked beside me up the street.

* * *

The third day on the job and my apartment was filled with merchandise from all the check writing I had been doing. I didn't have a particular love interest so I had to take my sexual frustrations out on my love for crafting. I met a guy named Art down on 13th Street who attracted me with his muscular figure. He reminded me so much of Calvin that it was scary. Drew introduced us late one night when I stayed downtown till the sun came up. Art and I talked on the phone for hours before I invited him over.

He didn't know what was going on in my personal life and I wasn't going to tell him either. The only thing he knew was that I was depressed over what my ex had put me through. He didn't know that I craft and couldn't pay my rent. He didn't know that my car note was due. The only thing that was shared between us was the company. He would lie in my bed and I'd cuddle underneath his arms while we watched TV. And, when it was time for lust making, not love making, it was on. Art was short and his dick was long and fat, and I loved every minute of it.

Fortunately, that escapade didn't last very long because he wasn't what I was looking for. Besides, like I said, he reminded me too much of Calvin and I couldn't have the burden on me that every time I saw him, Calvin would come into my mind.

Things weren't working out as I wanted them to. I was getting all the material things that I wanted and needed, but my bills weren't getting paid. I came up with a plan that I was sure Tyree wouldn't mind. He made checks on his computer using a VersaCheck program that could be purchased from Office Max or Staples. My idea was to take one of the checks that he made and go into the check-cashing place with it. The idea was carefully thought out, and to my surprise it worked. I had my rent money and money to pay my electric bill.

Not only did I do it once, but I did it twice, which made my mind start to work even more. I decided to use my skills and techniques to move onto bigger and better things—the banks. All I needed was to get hooked back up with my connects down at the bank, and I would be a shoo-in. And, I did.

After a long day of crafting, Tyree and I decided to call it quits so we went in for the night. Back in South Philly, we stopped at Tyree's sister's house where Ron and his new friend were lounging. Now, I know my hormones were raging and all, but I don't think I ever laid my eyes on anything cuter than this sexy boy named Cory. I didn't understand, for a boy to be that cute, how come he was dating Ron and not me? That was a boy that I had to have. He was eighteen and although I vowed never to date anyone as young as Calvin again, I knew that sometimes vows were made to be broken.

I wasn't even dressed for the occasion but I made myself available to him as I walked back and forth in front of him. Cory was a little on the short side with brown skin, a pretty smile, and braids neatly cornrowed to the back. Ron had just finished braiding his hair, which made me jealous because I wanted somehow to be close to this individual. Nevertheless, it was time for me to go home.

"I don't care, Rashad, we are not staying in tonight because if Calvin and his friends are down on 13th Street, we are going to beat them," Drew said to me on the phone.

"I'm gonna fuck him up when I see him," I said as I put my pants on and started to look for my boots.

"All right, I'll call you on your cell phone when I get down there," he said before hanging up the phone.

I called my mother because for some reason I couldn't find a hammer and I wanted to be totally prepared for what was about to happen.

"Mom, is the hammer over there?"

"Yeah, what do you need the hammer for?"

"Because I want to take it with me tonight just in case something happens."

"Why don't you just keep your ass in the house?"

"Because I really need to let him know how I feel, and after I handle this, I bet you he will think the next time before cheating on someone," I said before the line went dead.

I dressed myself in a pair of black jeans, a gray and black jersey, and a pair of dogged timbs. I rushed because

I didn't want Drew to beat me down there. I also had to wait for Cliff to pick me up because I was not driving my own car.

"What you doing?" I asked Shay as soon as she picked up the phone.

"Nothing, I just put Kaniyah to sleep, why?"

"Because we are about to go down 13$^{th}$ Street to get Calvin, are you going?"

"When?"

"Now."

"All right, are you coming to get me?"

"Yeah," I said, trying to rush her off the phone so I could continue to get ready.

"All right, I'll just have to put the baby in the bed with Grandmom. How long are you going to be?"

"Cliff is outside beeping the horn now so we'll be there in about 15 minutes."

"All right, let me get dressed," she said and hung up.

I rapidly walked outside and met Cliff in the parking lot. I wanted Tyree to come get me, but after we both worked all day, he had a headache so he took some sleeping pills and went to bed.

"Wassup, Cliff? Take me to my mother's house real quick so I can get a hammer," I said to him as we sped off into the darkness.

I walked up the driveway to my mother's house as she stood in the doorway holding the hammer.

"Don't go down there acting like a park ape," she said, holding the hammer in her hand before I took it.

"I'm not, I'm taking it, just in case," I said, walking back toward the car. I jumped in the passenger side as we began to pull off.

My heart was racing because I didn't know what was about to go down. I might not even see Calvin down here, I said to myself. I figured that after last week's event he knew that I had it out for him, and basically wanted his head on a stick.

By the time I reached my grandmother's house Shay was waiting on the porch. She was dressed in all black as she ran down the steps and hopped in the backseat before we proceeded on our mission.

We drove around for five minutes looking for a parking space. The scene was crowded this particular night. Everyone was out, Chad, Troy, Art, Kyle, and of course Keith and Jeff. I stepped out the car holding the hammer in my pocket before deciding there was no reason to carry it around with me. I would only reach for it in an extreme emergency so I left it in the car.

We walked around for about a half hour when I saw Drew dressed in his fighting gear, willing and ready for anything. The lights were bright on 13th Street and as always everyone huddled in front of the pizza shop. After giving and receiving hugs from different people I decided to call it a night and go home until I saw Calvin walk past me switching, carrying a black book bag on his back. Turning my attention off Drew and noticing that Calvin was making sure that I saw him, made my mind go crazy. I watched him as he walked past me a second time, this time with Denim following directly behind him.

"There he is, so what are you gonna do?" asked Shay who stood close to my side in the event that something jumped off. "You didn't come down here for nothing, so do what you came here to do." Calvin walked back a third time and spoke to her. Of course, she waved a shady hello just to keep him on his toes.

I stood back by the gate as Calvin walked past me for a fourth and final time.

"Ayo, Calvin," I said, walking up to him as he stopped to face me.

"What?" he said, looking deep into my eyes.

"So what's your problem?" I asked as I felt my

right hand trembling.

"Rashad, I don't have a problem with you," he said, holding onto the straps of his backpack.

I stood there in front of him thinking about all the good times that we shared together. I gazed into his eyes thinking how there would never be another session of lovemaking for us. I loved Calvin deeply and there wasn't anything that I wouldn't do for him.

How could I bring back the love that Calvin and I once shared? I missed the days of lying in his arms. I felt my eyes tearing, thinking of the times when we would sneak in his house late from our date and have hot and steamy sex until the next day. Oh, what I wouldn't give to have those days back.

I looked to the left of me and saw Shay backing up away from where Calvin and I stood. I glanced over to the right to see Denim standing on the side waiting for a move. I balled up my fist and swung around hitting Calvin in the eye with all my might.

I couldn't see through all the drama and the commotion. I felt hits from Calvin and I tried to get my hands free so I could hit him back. We both fell in the street and I continued to swing my arms more. Calvin reached and swung his fist, jabbing me directly into my nose causing blood to gush out nonstop. I didn't let up as I continued to swing on Calvin as I tried to regain my composure when I heard Drew yelling.

"The cops are coming, Rashad, come on, the cops are coming!" Drew yelled over the noise from the crowd.

I staggered over to him holding my nose, which was still leaking blood as Art ran into the pizza shop for tissues and bottled water. Drew carried me over to the side of the building and sat me down on the steps. I couldn't see Calvin anywhere. It was like he had disappeared into thin air.

"No, hell no, it's not over!" yelled Denim as he

snapped his fingers in the air and walked toward me.

I didn't want to fight anymore, I was hot and tired. I couldn't breathe through all the heat and the antics on 13<sup>th</sup> Street.

"Let's go," said Denim, still snapping his fingers.

"I'ma get that bitch," snapped Drew as he dabbed my nose with the wet tissue, trying to stop the bleeding.

"Let's go, Calvin wants to fight you next," Denim said to Art because without me noticing, Art had jumped in on the fight.

"Hold up, he wants to fight me?" Art said, removing his shirt, showing off his erotic muscles as he started to walk over to Denim.

With Drew right by my side, I held my head back, keeping the blood from rushing down my nose. It seemed that the crowd on 13<sup>th</sup> Street had multiplied. It was always like that once a fight broke out downtown.

I wished I had kept my ass home tonight. I thought about my bed and how it would be so nice if I could lay there right now. I didn't need all this drama because I had to be at work early in the morning. I always had a mind to mind my mother and she had told me to stay in. After what just happened, I wished I had listened.

\* \* \*

My body ached from head to toe. I couldn't lift my left arm and I dared to lift my right. I needed to take a shower but was too weak to stand under the water so I just sat in the tub, letting the water run over my face. I cried from all the pain that had caused this whole thing to go down. I wondered how would life be if Calvin and I were still a happy couple. I didn't have the energy to climb in bed so I spent the night on the living room floor.

*Ring, Ring, Ring.*

"Hello," I answered the phone, sounding half dead.

"Bitch, get up!" Tyree yelled.

"I can't," I responded in a sluggish tone.

"What do you mean, you can't? Bitch, get up."

"I was downtown fighting Calvin last night and my body is hurting."

"What, you mean to tell me that I went to sleep and missed a good fight?" he said with excitement. "Who won?"

"What?" I was surprised that he would ask that.

"Bitch, you heard me. Who won the fucking fight?"

"He bloodied my nose," I said, still lying on the floor with my face pressed against the carpet.

"Oh, no, Rashad, are you OK?"

"No, my body feels weird."

"Well, you have to get up from there 'cause we got checks to write, dammit." I continued to lie down until I realized that I needed to get all I could get while this check writing process was still good.

While riding in my car to Tyree's house, I began to think about Calvin. I really needed to think long and hard about the situation that had just occurred between us. I knew that something had to give because I couldn't keep living my life walking around miserable and being sad because of him.

"Bitch, you look a mess," Tyree said as he jumped into my car, smiling as he always does. I put the car in gear and sped away in the direction of the King of Prussia Mall.

"Can you give me a massage please?" I asked before he got comfortable in the passenger seat. "Don't look at me like that, you know you want to do it." He grabbed my hand and slowly started massaging my fingers. It felt so good but what I really needed was a body massage.

The sun was shining extremely bright today for

some reason. Maybe because I knew that the relationship between Calvin and I was definitely over and there was no going back.

As we reached the mall we prepared ourselves for our adventure. We walked into Modell's Sporting Goods store on the upper level, and before we could get in the door good there was a sign that read Certegy so we left.

Throughout the rest of the day, we crafted more than $3,000 in merchandise and I was beat from the whole ordeal. So after dropping Tyree off at his mother's I went home to rest. I called Art over to help me relax my mind, body, and soul.

\* \* \*

He laid me down on my stomach after he turned off all the lights in my bedroom. He lit three candles and placed them on the nightstand. I grabbed my pillow tightly as he started from my neck and worked his way down to my feet. I had never received a massage that was so stimulating and relaxing in my life.

He used his muscles to work his magic as he made me feel like I was the only one on earth that existed to him. He kissed the back of my neck as he massaged it even more. He lit an incense stick that had my mind in a daze. I could smell the aroma spreading around the room as I fell into a deep sleep with him holding me in his strong arms.

\* \* \*

I sat on the couch at Tyree's sister's house watching TV while waiting for Tyree to come back from crafting with his cousin. I saw Ron's cell phone laying on the dining room table and I figured that this was my only chance to get Cory's number. I knew Ron wasn't going to give it to me even though he acted as if he didn't like Cory anyway.

I quickly searched the phone book of his cell and found just what I was looking for. I didn't say a word to anyone. I would just call him and see what happened.

All day Saturday, it rained. Tyree and I took our crafting spree on tour as we went over to New Jersey to the Cherry Hill Mall and the Deptford Mall. We bought CDs and baseball caps and I bought a new pair of Dolce & Gabbana jeans. By the time we made it back to Philly the rain had stopped and I made plans to give Cory a call. After I dropped Tyree and his bags off, I rushed over to my grandmother's house so I could use Shay for the venture. Of course, she was more than willing to do what I asked.

"Hello, can I speak to Cory?" Shay asked.

"This is him, who is this?"

"This is Shay-Shay."

"Who is Shay-Shay?"

"I'm Rashad's cousin."

"Who is Rashad?"

"You know, Rashad, the one who hangs around with Tyree and Ron," she explained as I sat there watching her every move.

"Oh, OK, what does he want with me?"

"Hold on," she said before handing me the phone.

"Hello," I said once I got the phone from Shay. My palms were sweaty and I was nervous. This boy was so cute and I couldn't believe that I was actually talking to him.

"Wassup?" he asked in a sexy voice. My skin broke out in goose pimples all over. Shay watched me as I blushed on the phone.

"Hey, Cory, what are you doing?" I tried to make conversation.

"I'm watching videos. How did you get my number?" I knew that was coming.

"Well, you want to know the truth?" I asked, knowing he did.

"Yeah."

All right, I'm gonna be real with you. I got the number out of Ron's cell phone."

"For what?"

"Because, since the first time I saw you, I thought you were so cute and I needed to talk to you. Is that cool?"

"Naw, that's not cool," he said, sounding angry.

"Why isn't it? Are you still dating Ron?"

"No."

"So how come we can't talk?" I asked with disappointment.

"Because it would feel weird."

"No, it wouldn't."

"Aren't you and Ron real close?" he asked.

"Naw, we are cool, but I wouldn't say close."

"Oh, but it still would feel weird."

"Man just let that go. I liked you so I made a move. First, let me ask you this, are you attracted to me?" I asked, knowing I would break him down that way.

"Yeah, you are cute," he said, laughing.

"So what's the problem?"

I sat and talked to Cory for about another thirty minutes. The conversation carried over once I got home and we were on the phone until the early morning. We talked about everything imaginable. From his schooling, to his family life, and what made him attracted to guys. I felt a great deal of excitement in my heart. This was a guy I needed in my life. I would love to have him every day, all day. Although he was young, he showed a level of maturity I was sure I could deal with.

We made plans to hook up later that day and I couldn't wait. I tossed and turned early that morning trying to get some sleep before I would see my caramel cutie. I couldn't do it. I primped myself to get ready for my date.

I went to Broad and Diamond to pick him up and we returned to my apartment where we had a night of love, lust, and passion. He kissed me all over my face and down the shaft of my groin as I cringed with emotion. I needed this, and to have my dick become erect from him was right up my alley.

I learned that good things took time and everything happens for a reason. I felt like it was a waste of my time to be running around Philadelphia with Calvin when he really didn't love me at all. I should have known something when he lied to his mother about us crafting on her account. Now if he would lie to his own mother, what makes me think that he wouldn't lie to me?

He wasn't even all that cute, and his legs were messed up, but I still loved him for him, and this is what I got—a broken heart and a bloody nose. But all my love and tenderness I would now give to Cory because he is the one that I should have been with in the first place.

## Drunk

"Get your ass up!" my mother yelled as she used her keys to get into my apartment. I could barely open my eyes from the good night of sleep that I had.

"What?" I asked as my eyes tried to adjust to the light.

"Get your ass up, them motherfuckers turned off my electric."

I removed myself from the carpet and wrapped my robe around me.

"What are you taking about? Did you pay the bill?"

"I gave them what I had and that wasn't enough," she said, lighting up a cigarette.

"Well, what do you want me to do?" She looked at me one time, then proceeded out the door.

I went into my room to call Cory who was still at home asleep. Then, I called Tyree and requested an emergency meeting ASAP.

I jumped in my car and headed to South Philly. Tyree was already dressed and waited for my arrival. I already had a few account numbers on me that I could use for checks. Tyree and I went into the basement where Joseph was to begin our craft.

I studied him thoroughly as he made each check using the program along with a laser printer. I was amazed at all the information he knew about the system. The check looked perfect, and although I had never done this before, I was about to have my skills put to the ultimate test.

The check was written for $4,526.50. Since Rafeek was still incarcerated I felt as though I would have a better chance at using his I.D. I stopped by my house for a minute to change. I suited up in a shirt and tie where my goal was to look prestigious for the bank tellers. I was then on my way.

I parked on the other side of the parking lot just in case the bank employees wanted to be shady and call the cops and get a bitch in a jam. I walked into the bank and to my surprise they weren't crowded for a Friday afternoon. I walked up to the Asian teller.

"How are you today?" she asked with a smile.

"I'm great, and yourself?"

"I'm fine, thanks," she said, holding her hand out to retrieve the check.

I handed her the check and my I.D. She looked it over as I waited for her response.

"I'll be right back," she said as she locked her drawer, then walked through the wooden door as it closed behind her.

I waited for about 2 ½ minutes. I glanced down at my watch to see how much time I had left. The sweat underneath my arms started to form. I looked around the bank to see the other employees continuing with their day as if they didn't know I was standing there as a complete fraud.

"I will count to fifteen, and if she's not back I'm walking out," I said under my breath.

By the time I got to number eight, the Asian girl came out from the back and sat back in her chair. I carefully studied her movements as she proceeded with the transaction.

"How would you like this?" she asked nicely.

"All large bills please," I responded with excitement.

I watched her count out all the funds down to the last penny. Although I needed to help my mom with her electric, I made it my top priority to put a down payment on my surgery. Fuck Calvin, I had Cory in my life now and on top of that I had more than enough money to survive.

I slowly exited the bank then drove away smiling at

the world. I called Cory who was now awake and excited that I called.

"Hey boy," I said passionately into the phone. I loved the gritty sound of his morning voice.

"What's up?"

"Driving, what are you doing?"

"I just woke up actually, where are you?"

"I'm on my way to the doctor's office to pay for my surgery."

"So, you're gonna go through with it?" he asked in between yawns.

"Yes, do you know how much this means to me?"

"Well, good luck. Am I going to see you later?"

"Definitely," I told him before hanging up.

I drove past my mother's house and dropped off $500.00 to pay her electric bill, and then I headed straight to the doctor's office in Center City. I put down $2,000.00 and told the receptionist that I would be back with the rest.

I immediately went to Tyree's house and requested that he make me four more checks in the amount of the high four thousands, and I made it my intention to visit all the banks in the surrounding areas to do my craft.

Late that evening, after seven o'clock, I grossed a mere $20,000 to play with, without anyone knowing. I worked from sun up to sun down by myself. I put $10,000 away in a shoebox and placed it under my bed for a rainy day.

I had made all the money that could cover my bills for the next 5 ½ months, plus I locked in my date to have my plastic surgery done. Not only did I pay to have a tummy tuck, but I also paid to have liposuction on my waistline and I paid to have the fat removed from my chest and my back area. I figured if I was gonna do it, I would do it right. I was so excited. My date was set for September 20, and I couldn't wait. Still being greedy, I made a deal with the people that were close to me, such as

Damien and Kevin, agreeing that we'd all go in on this craft and split the profit.

Throughout the week, I had Damien work the other banks in Philadelphia that I hadn't done yet. Within the middle of the week, Damien grossed more than $15,000 himself, leaving me with a profit of $10,000. Kevin, on the other hand, was a little leery of taking on more than one bank so he only grossed $5,000 in one shot leaving me with a profit of $2,000, which I went shopping with.

Tyree and I decided that after my surgery we would go into business together with him making the checks for Damien and I, and we would split the profits with him. He really didn't have an idea as to how I was making the money, all he knew was that I was depositing the checks into an account and taking the money through the ATM.

Cory and I had a very festive evening. After a little wining and dining, we cuddled on the couch to watch a movie. I felt so at peace with him around. Especially now that I didn't have to worry about how I would get my bills paid. I kept everything a secret from him until I felt it was the right time to let him know my hustle.

"You did what!?" Tyree yelled when I told him about my rendezvous with Cory.

"Yes, I got the number from Ron's cell phone and I called him."

"Does Ron know what you did?"

"No, and judging by the way he acts, he really doesn't like Cory like that," I said, as we drove to the mall to do some check writing.

"Rashad, you're shady as boots," he said, laughing.

"No, I'm not. I just find Cory attractive, that's all. And he seems to be a really nice person," I said, sipping my soda.

"Well, do you plan on telling Ron?"

"I guess. I mean, what do you think?"

"I think you should tell him. He's gonna find out

one way or another and I don't want no part of this."

"All right, I'll tell him tonight when I see him. I'll let him know in an easy way."

"How the hell are you gonna tell him in a easy way that you are fucking his man?" he said, laughing.

"He's not his man."

"Well, ex, talk to person, I don't know, whatever," we both laughed as we approached the Springfield Mall.

"Don't forget to remind me to get a television stand for my room," Tyree said, exiting the car and walking toward the mall entrance.

"We all should go on a double date. You, Cory, Doug and me. That would be fun," I said.

"No, Rashad I told you that I don't want no part of this. You know, Ron is like a daughter to me and I can't betray my own child," he said in a motherly tone, smiling. "And what do I look like agreeing with you and Cory dating anyway when I still have a crush on you," he added.

"Come on now Tyree, you're dating Doug," I said, trying to hide my blushing.

"Yeah, now I am, but even before we started dating, I told you that I liked you."

"Well, right now don't you think we are better off as friends, and I guess you can say, business partners?"

"Yeah, but just don't forget that I still like you." I felt flattered.

"OK Tyree, I won't forget," I said as we both entered the Radio Shack where I bought a cordless phone and a cable jack.

We walked through the entire mall. Tyree bought clothes galore and finally got his television stand. I bought Cory a pair of pajamas for when he spends his time at my apartment and I also bought him some sweet smelling cologne.

Another day, another dollar. I was forced to give my mother some extra money so she could finally bail my brother out of jail. We rode all the way to Doylestown where he would be put into a work-release program; he started working at the Old Country Buffet restaurant. My mother and I sat and ate while discussing the past summer's events, such as my broken heart and the fight with Tamika on July 4. Somehow I knew the need for me fighting was irrelevant, but I wasn't going to take the rap on my own. At times, that's what families go through.

Now, a new life has begun for me. I didn't have to fantasize about being with a true thug any longer because Cory was just what I needed. I thought about him every chance I got. I kept my mind focused on finally having my stomach done, and knowing that Cory was by my side, which was enough for me.

His body was just right for me to handle, a six-pack that was out of this world with a cute face to go with it. Intelligence was a plus especially when it came to Cory. He got straight As and was about to graduate at the top of his class. Tyree was happy for Cory and I, but the hardest part was having to tell Ron. It wasn't so bad because Ron approved. That just made things easier and just so there would be no hard feelings between us, I treated everyone to Dorney Park.

We never made it to the park because I was pulled over by the cops while on my way to get Ron and Tyree. Although my life had changed, some things remained the same.

"Officer, my license is suspended and I don't have insurance. Can you please cut me a break?" I knew that the mayor had passed the new Operation Live Stop program in Philadelphia where if you don't have the correct paperwork for your car, it can be impounded at any moment.

"No, sir, the mayor gave us specific orders and we have to obey them. I'm gonna have to ask you to step out of the car."

# Smoking Cigarettes

I began to dial my mother's number on my cell phone. It was after four so I knew she was already off work. I needed her to come and get me. All this is some bullshit. What I wouldn't give to be alone with Cory right now sipping on a glass of cherry Kool-Aid. After my car was impounded, my mother and I went to my grandmother's because we had to pay the money back that we had borrowed.

It rained all day Sunday and I didn't have a car. I waited in the house for Cory because he needed to take public transportation to my house. We lounged that whole evening, ate pizza, and watched movies. I was very relaxed in his arms as we lay in my bed under the covers. He fell asleep while I played in his hair and listened to the sweet sounds of Tweet. Outside, the rain hit the window pane. I recalled everything I had been through in the past year and was grateful to have accomplished some things even if it was through crafting.

I went from being broke to having money; I went from a broken heart to having the man of my dreams lying right across my chest. This was the perfect moment. Yes, the perfect man and the perfect setting. I will try everything in my power to make Cory happy and keep him satisfied at all times. God has shown me a sign that there is life after Calvin and I would rather be with Cory any day.

It was after midnight when Cory woke up from his short nap.

"Oh, shit, I have to get home," he said as he jumped up off my lap and put on his shirt.

"Do you want me to call you a cab?" I asked, reaching for the phone.

"Please," he said, trying to put his foot in his Air Forces.

I dialed the number to the cab company and luckily they had a car in the area. I gave Cory the biggest goodbye kiss like this would be our last time. He walked toward the door then turned around to kiss me again.

"Call me when you get home," I said.

"All right, I will. Just wait up for me, all right?" he said, trying to leave but not before kissing me one last time.

"OK," I said, closing the door behind him and getting myself ready to get in the shower.

About forty minutes later, my phone rang. It was Cory.

"Hello," I answered.

"Yeah, wassup, Rashad. I'm home now."

"OK, good."

"No, not good."

"Why, what's wrong?"

"My mom is bitchin'."

"About what?"

"Because I came in the house late. I have to call you back," he said as he quickly got off the phone.

It seemed weird for him to hang up the phone the way that he did. I wasn't the one to start blowing things out of proportion, but I thought it was rather weird.

After saturating myself down with my new fragrance bottles from Victoria's Secret, I slipped into my pajamas then laid across the bed and waited for Cory to call back. The next thing I realized, I was fast asleep.

The next day I awoke early because I needed to get down to traffic court to get my car back. I took public transportation, something that I hated doing, while I tried to get in contact with Cory. I needed to know if everything was OK with him and how he made out with his mother. From my understanding, his mother didn't know about his down low lifestyle and was questioning why I called the house so much.

By the time I got to 8th and Spring Garden, the courthouse was packed. I had to go to different windows to take care of my business. Everything that I had was crafted—from my registration to my insurance. Tyree had crafted me an insurance card the night before. After I saw the judge and paid a total of more than $600.00 I was able to get a release form to go to Lot 4 and get my car. Luckily I had the money for all this because if I didn't, I would have been shit out of luck.

My mother met me at 8th and Spring Garden then we headed over to Lot 4 in South Philly. We stood in the line at four o'clock, and we didn't actually leave the lot till 8:30 p.m. I couldn't believe all the shit that had to be done in order to get my car back.

Once I got home, the first thing I did was call Cory because I hadn't spoken with him all day. After what I'd been through alone today, I needed peace of mind.

"Hello," I said, happy to be talking to him.

"Hey," he said in a low tone.

"What's up, how was your day?"

"It was cool," he said, still with a low tone.

"What's wrong, Cory? You sound like something is wrong." He sighed.

"I don't think you should call here any more."

"Why, what's wrong?"

"Because I explained the whole situation to my mother and she said that she doesn't want you to call here anymore."

"Well, did she say why?"

"She says that you are too old for me."

"Well, Cory, how do you feel about this?"

"Well, technically she is my mother. I'm not grown yet."

"But Cory, I'm confused," I said, wanting to know if he even argued his point to her and at least let her know that he really liked me.

"Rashad, it's nothing to be confused about. Just don't call here no more."

"So, what's gonna happen to us?"

"We can still be friends but let me call you, just

don't call here anymore, OK?" he asked as I felt my dreams were about to be crushed.

"OK," I said before he rudely hung up. I was left standing there with my mouth hanging open.

I didn't understand. What was going on? Was he telling me the truth or did he just not want to talk to me anymore?

* * *

"Well, if he ain't want you to call him house, then you have to respeck dat," said Kevin. I sat on the phone with him for hours trying to make some sense out of the situation.

"Man, where did I go wrong?"

"I ain't know, nah, mon, but dat is a question you better ask yourself."

"I thought the time we spent the other night was perfect. How could he say that he liked me, then up and leave? Did he ever like me at all?"

"I ain't know, mon."

After hanging up the phone, I realized I was going through the same thing with Cory that I had gone through with Calvin. I wasn't gonna be the one. What I was gonna do now was hold my head high and chuck this up as a loss. If he really liked me the way he said, he'd be back. Besides, we had only been together for a week so there was no way I could have been fallin' in love within that short period. Now, don't get me wrong, there are some people who fall in love in less time. Look at J-Lo and Ben Affleck. But I'm not a superstar, even though I wish I was, and if that was the case, I would have someone to call my own by now and not waste my time on these bullshit niggas.

But I'm not complaining because all my troubles are about to come to an end once I get my tummy tuck. I will have a new attitude and I'll become a totally different person.

\* \* \*

Drew, Tyree, Cliff, and I were out and about. It was so hot, and we had been invited to a party that the House of Karon was having in Mt. Airy. At first, I started not to go because I didn't want my fun to be interrupted if I ran into Calvin.

We walked in, and the room was filled with all kinds of house kids. I mean so many people from different houses were there. You had people from the House of Karon, Prestige, Cartier, Revlon and the Prodigy's. For my mom's sake I wasn't in any of the houses because she felt that they represented a gang. My first year at Cheyney, my mother had told me not to join any of them, so I didn't. There often was a lot of drug use, promiscuous sex, and fighting in the houses. About three years ago, I walked in the face category at a ball and won, but my mother threw my trophy down the basement stairs and I haven't walked a ball since.

I sipped on my drink and stood in the corner by the stairs when a tall, slender-built guy with his hat tilted to the side approached me. I had never seen him before, but I knew whoever he was, he was fine as hell. He sported a white tank top, a pair of gray sweat pants in which I could see his man stick bulging through the seams, and he sported a pair of gray and white Air Jordans. He smiled at me as he looked me up and down, then whispered in my ear.

"Wassup, sexy?" he asked.

I really couldn't make out what he was saying because my mixed drink and the two Ecstasy pills I took had me a second away from being half baked.

"So, what's your name?" he asked, as I could feel his hot breath on my earlobe. It sent trembles through my entire body.

"I'm Rashad," I said, still sipping on my drink. He got closer to me as I saw Drew walk up to me and look me dead in the eyes.

"Are you OK?" Drew asked me.

"Yeah, I'm OK."

"Bitch, he is sexy. Let me leave you alone," he said, walking away and bobbing his head to the sound of Mario's *Just a Friend.*

"So, wassup with me and you tonight?" said the guy, now finding his way up and down my earlobe with his tongue. I took another sip of my drink and before I could swallow it, he had his tongue in my mouth.

I kissed him passionately in the corner of the semi-dark and crowded room as I felt him forcefully grab my ass. I grabbed his back then put my fingers beneath the front of his tank top and slid my hands inside his pants. This guy was long and fat and in about 1-½ seconds he was standing at attention.

"I have to go," I said, making my way to the door so I could find Tyree and Drew so we could leave.

"Naw, don't leave yet. We was just getting to know each other," he said, licking his top lips. I was getting hot but I knew that I needed to leave soon. The DJ then played Brandy's *Full Moon.* The guy took my hand and walked me toward the stairs where everyone was sitting, but the majority of the people were now getting up to dance in the middle of the floor.

He kissed me again as I paused to take another sip of my 151. I could see Drew from a distance standing across from me as I leaned back and fell into the stranger's arms.

\* \* \*

Next thing I recall was feeling the insides of my

body tearing as the stranger stuck his pole into me. I felt a lot of pain and I tried to resist him as I began to hit him in his head. In the midst of my Ecstasy high he had gotten me upstairs to one of the bedrooms in the house.

"Yeah, baby, I like it rough," he said as I started to scream. I heard voices outside the door in the hallway laughing and joking as the music from down below played louder and louder. I tried to scream as he filled my mouth with his tongue. The pain was unbearable as I began hitting him again.

"Get off me!" I yelled at the top of my lungs, but no one could hear me because of the loud music down below. I looked around the room and saw roaches on the walls and dirty condoms lying around on the floor. As I laid there I cried with every plow he made into my rectum.

I tried to squirm, but the more I moved the harder and deeper he went inside of me. It seemed like the more I tried to yell the louder the music got. Tears started to fall from my eyes. I wanted to be home where I knew I would be safe.

"This dick is good, ain't it?" he said in my ear, still plowing into my anus. "I'ma 'bout to come." He bust everything he had inside of me as I laid back on the blood-covered sheets.

He then got up and pulled up his pants. He looked deep into my eyes as he turned off the light and walked out the room. I couldn't move. All I could think about was why? How? And where is Calvin? This is the time when I really needed his help. I laid there and stared straight up at the ceiling into darkness as I could feel blood leaking from my anus onto the bed. I was exposed from my waist down. I couldn't understand why I couldn't move. It was like I was glued to the bed. The only thing that wasn't moving was the tears that ran down my face.

What was I to do? Who was I to tell? Who just had unprotected sex with me against my will?

# Reginald L. Hall

What the fuck? I said to myself as I began to get up and pull my underwear to my waist without even cleaning the blood or semen off. I walked out the room with a slight limp from the pain in my ass. I limped down the steps where the party was still going on. I limped past everyone; they seemed not to notice me as I walked outside past Drew who was fighting Ron in the middle of the street. One side of Drew's face was cut while the back of Ron's head was bleeding. Tyree was in the middle trying to break it up. I didn't know what that was about. It wasn't any of my business. I just jumped in my car and drove as I tried to find my way home. The tears fell long and hard.

Although I couldn't see what was ahead of me I still continued to drive. Finally, I ended up in Upper Darby where I hurried into the house to soak my bloody rectum in the tub. After soaking for about 2 ½ hours, I dried myself off and lotioned my body. I walked into my room and laid down on the bed, pressing my aching head against the pillow. I couldn't go to the police because I didn't want to be perceived as another statistic or just another faggot who claimed he was raped by a man, but actually liked it.

I started to feel the effect of the five Tylenols I had taken to ease the pain of my burning anus. I began to have flashbacks of tonight's episode as it replayed in my mind, over and over again. The tears formed in my eyes as they started to fall down my face. How could a person be so cruel?

Was there someone I could confide in? I felt as though I'd been raped way before that guy even touched me tonight. Calvin and Camisha raped me. They were two lonely demons who scorned me and didn't feel any guilt of it. Everything happens for a reason and I felt that Calvin and Paul had to get to me somehow and me showing up at tonight's party was just their way of saying payback is a bitch!

\* \* \*

## A Friend In Deed

The alarm clock went off at the same time the phone began to ring. I reached over and hit the snooze button as I quickly answered the phone.

"Hello," I said.

"Yeah, are you up?" asked my mother.

"Yeah, I just got up, I'm about to get in the shower."

"Well let's get a move on. I'll be there in a half hour," she said before the line went dead.

I jumped out of the bed. I couldn't believe the day had finally come when I would be getting plastic surgery. I turned my radio to Power 99 and hopped in the shower.

After putting on some lotion, I figured I would wear my Tasmanian devil pajamas and slippers that I bought from Target one day when Tyree and I were out crafting. My mother was already outside beeping the horn and I knew I couldn't keep her waiting.

"You didn't eat anything, did you?" she asked as soon as I got in the car. I was instructed not to eat after midnight.

"No, the last time I ate was early last night. I went to Big George's restaurant and pigged out on some ribs, mac and cheese, chicken wings, mashed potatoes, rice and gravy, and cornbread," I said as she started to drive off.

"What made you eat all that?"

"Because if yesterday was my last day being fat, I wanted to live it up."

We pulled in front of the hospital in Roxborough, Pennsylvania. It took awhile for my mother to find parking so she just let me out in front of the building so I could check in.

"Hi, how may I help you?" an old lady at the front

desk asked with a smile that was so perfect, I could tell she wore dentures.

"Yes, I'm here for a tummy tuck," I said, smiling ear to ear at her.

"Oh, are you?" She smiled.

"You have to go through those double doors over there and someone will be out for you," she said, pointing over to the metal double doors as my mother walked in.

"She says I have to walk through the double doors," I said to my mother as she followed me.

I walked over to another desk where another old white lady was sitting.

"Your name please?" she asked without lifting her head up.

"Rashad Smith."

"OK, sir, you can go over there to have a seat until your name is called." My mother and I walked over to the plush gray chairs and sat down.

"So, what will you be doing while I'm in there?" I asked my mother.

"When you go to sleep, I'm going to sleep," she responded as I heard my name over the loud speaker.

I walked over to the counter and sat down as my mother stood behind me. The old white lady asked me a few questions while filling out a form and then she asked for my arm to take my blood pressure.

She led my mother and me into another small room.

"Could you please remove all of your garments and put these robes on?" she asked me as she left two sleeveless hospital gowns on the table. My mother stood outside as I removed everything except my underwear and my socks.

I lay in the comfortable chair and began to read my magazine when the doctor came in.

"So, you really are gonna go through with this?" he said as he sat himself down on a black leather stool. His assistant and my mother accompanied him as well. I stood up as he sat in front of me, massaging my stomach. He pulled out a black magic marker and began drawing lines and circles around my stomach, back, and waistline.

My mother continued to look on at whatever the doctor started to do.

"I'll see you upstairs," he said as he walked out the room. The little old white lady returned.

"I need you to remove all your clothing," she said once again.

"Even my socks?"

"Everything," she said.

I proceeded to remove my socks and underwear. I began to feel extremely uncomfortable as I began to shake.

"Is there a bathroom around here?" I asked, trying to get away.

"Yes, it's over there," the old lady said, pointing to the wooden door in the hallway.

I walked over to the bathroom, leaving my mother in the room with the old lady. After taking a piss I continued to stay in there a little while longer to gather my thoughts.

Am I doing the right thing? I asked myself, over and over again, still trying to bide my time while waiting inside the restroom. Then, my mother knocked on the door.

"Rashad, come on, let's go. You're holding up the process!" she yelled through the door as she continued to bang.

I finally opened the door and slowly walked out across the cold floor in my bare feet.

"I don't think I want to go through with this," I said to my mother as she took my hand and led me to the bed to lie down where the lady waited for me.

"Well, it's too late to turn back now. You're the one that wanted this crazy shit," she said, holding on to her newspaper while helping me to the bed.

I hopped up on the bed and laid all the way back.

"Just sit tight and someone will be down to get you," the lady said.

I started to shake as my mother stood and watched, smiling at my reaction to the moment.

"What is your problem?"

"I just don't think this is the right thing to do. I should have just listened to Grandmom." She had always told me to join the gym and workout more often and stop eating fatty foods. I could have given her some of my money and she could have taken it to Atlantic City, but that wouldn't have been any use because she would have just gambled it all away.

A short, fat, black guy stepped off the elevator and came over behind the bed and began rolling me onto the open elevator.

"Where am I going?" I asked the gentleman.

"You're going upstairs to visit with the anesthesiologist." My mother and I rode the elevator together to the 10th floor.

"Ma'am you're gonna have to wait in there," he said to my mother while pointing over to the waiting room with chairs, a TV, and a few vending machines.

"Well, if she can't go in the room, then I can't either," I said, lifting up off the gurney.

"Boy, lie down," my mother said, still standing there and not going over to the waiting room.

I laid back on the bed until an old white man came over to me and asked my name.

"Rashad Smith," I said, looking around the hallway, still watching my mother while she watched me.

"Rashad Smith," he said.

"Yes."

"Well, Rashad, how are you feeling today? I am the anesthesiologist."

He began to roll me into another room as I began

waving to my mother, and she cracked a smile and waved back.

Once inside the room, I looked around at all of the bright lights and operating equipment, and to my surprise, it was extremely cold. I began to shiver.

"You cold, huh? Well let me tell the nurse to get you some warm blankets," he said, walking out the room.

I couldn't believe this was actually happening. I heard about the stars getting plastic surgery all the time, but I never thought it would be me who would get it one day. I began to think of Calvin, Cory, Chad, and Troy, and how I would miss them all today, but all and all I would miss Calvin the most.

I began to think crazy thoughts as well like what if I don't wake up, or what if they cut my heart, then what? I had to get a grip and fast because like my mother pointed out, there's no turning back, now.

The old man and a female nurse came in and placed two warm blankets across my chest and legs. I felt so comfortable compared to the coldness I'd felt just a minute ago. He began to hook me up to all types of machines and what not. He had tubes going in one arm and another tube coming out of the other arm. My right arm started to feel numb then my left arm started to get cold all by itself.

"So, what kind of music to you listen to?" asked the old white man.

"I listen to rap and R&B."

"OK. What radio stations to you like to listen to?"

"Oh, I listen to Power 99, 103.9…"

\* \* \*

**Seven hours later…**

"You're waking up," the old white lady said.

I tried opening my eyes to focus on the subject that stood in front of me. I could barely talk, although I knew what I was trying to say.

"Pain..." I said to the nurse. "Pain..." I said again, trying to get her attention.

She walked over to me.

"I'm giving you some medicine through the I.V.," she said, while fidgeting with the cords that led to the machine.

"Where's... my... mo-ther?" I asked slowly.

"She'll be back." I immediately knew something wasn't right. I know my mother. I know her too well and she would not leave me to go anywhere. The nurse rolled my bed out into the hallway.

I saw my mother through my blurry vision.

"M...ommmm," I said softly as the nurse rolled my bed down the hall.

My entire body felt numb. My stomach down to my crotch was wrapped tightly in bandages. I couldn't feel my legs or my feet and all I wanted to do was sleep.

"Wake up, Rashad," my mother said as she began touching my arm. I still couldn't see clearly but I tried my best to recognize her.

"I wanna ... go... to sleep," I said, feeling very drowsy and wanting to turn over, but I couldn't.

The nurse came over to me handing my mother my pajamas and underwear.

"Here, Rashad, put on your clothes," my mother said as she handed me all the garments.

I just looked at her and dropped them on the floor. I wasn't in any position to do anything. I laid back on the bed.

"Before you leave, you will have to use the bathroom just once," the nurse said as she opened the door to the restroom. My mother helped me out of the bed and into a wheelchair to roll me over to the bathroom. I held onto the walls as I walked into the bathroom. I couldn't feel my penis, and on top of that I wasn't urinating correctly.

I finally had the chance to urinate when a painful sensation shot through my body. I felt like the worst thing walking. Was it all a dream?

My mother helped me up the steps and into my apartment where I went straight into my room and went directly to sleep. I had taken two painkillers, they weren't helping. My body felt as if it was torn into a million pieces.

I had my tummy tuck on Tuesday, which meant I could show my new body at the club on Wednesday. However, I didn't know that I had to wait for all the swelling and shit to go away, and the pain. It was the worst pain I'd ever felt. I mean, what the fuck. I needed someone to feed me, take me to the bathroom, put me to bed. If I would have known about all of this, I think I would have had second thoughts. I thanked God for my mother, Shay-Shay, Kevin, Damien, and Drew because if it wasn't for them who knows where I would be. I couldn't do anything but lay in the bed all day and take painkillers. Listen, this shit was not worth it. I should sue. Even though my surgery was crafted. But you know what? I need to calm down and just wait for the after effects. *I am going to look F-A-B-U-L-O-U-S.*

**A month later...**

I found myself in the living room playing a video game when Shay knocked on the door. She brought the baby by to see me, and also to pick up the money for her first birthday party that was coming up.

My room was filled with cards and balloons from people who thought of me while I was on bed rest. Dontae called to check on me a few times, which I thought was nice but it just didn't seem right because he still had ties with Calvin.

I needed to stop saying his name every day, that

was my first step in my plan to get over Calvin, and then eventually I would stop thinking about him. It was in my best interest to tell Dontae not to call me anymore. Well, of course I didn't tell him that, I had Ron do it for me.

Being around Tyree made me feel different too. He looked at me as a brother, and at some point I looked at him in that light as well. In the future I knew that we would knock 'em dead with our powerful crafting.

Tyree was still going strong with Doug, although he did find a new love interest. I needed to tell him to slow down and wait for me because even with these stitches I knew it would only be a matter of time before I was on the dating scene again.

With all the money that I made from the last crafting event, I set out to go apartment shopping where I found the right one in Camden, New Jersey. The Victor Apartments would be my new home. I needed to represent. I began to move up like the Jeffersons. I would have wall-to-wall shiny hardwood floors and two bathrooms. Paying $2,000 a month, I knew I would be in for a treat.

Man, was my new place hot or what? I was the envy of all the faggots. The apartment had a window overlooking the river, three walk-in closets, and two fireplaces—one in the living room and one in my bedroom. After Kevin and Damien helped me move my things in, and I became settled, I would throw a big party and invite my close friends and relatives.

I was now living the new life and leaving all that bullshit behind me. I had a new body, new apartment, and new friends.

Damien felt we needed to make some money so we had to hit the banks a few more times before our money could get right. Tyree would make the checks and Damien would cash them at the banks. I would get the account numbers from the girl I knew at the bank and it would be smooth sailing.

# Smoking Cigarettes

From the three jobs that were positioned, it was hard to tell who got what and why. I came to the conclusion that to simplify things, I would lie to Tyree about the whole ordeal. He never knew that Damien actually went inside the bank to cash the checks at the teller window. To his knowledge, he only knew that he supplied me with the checks and I would then give them to Damien to deposit and then he would take the cash out of the ATM, which we would split three ways. Now, come on, if we were crafting that way, none of us would have made any money because you can only take $400.00 out per day through the ATM.

Damien and I would travel all across Philadelphia in rented cars to different banks and cash the checks. Checks totaling $20,000 I would break down three ways— Damien would get $10,000, I would get $8,000, and Tyree would get $2,000. In a way, we weren't stealing from Tyree because all he did was sit in the house and make the checks. Damien and I could have done that on our own. Besides, with crafting, it's stolen money, so by right no one is stealing from anyone.

My bank account was stacked and I would still feed Tyree money even when he didn't deserve it. I took it upon myself to learn how to make my own checks using the computer program. Somehow, Tyree figured it all out. He found out that Damien and I were getting more money than him, and he flipped.

I wasn't ready for this to happen the way that it did. I needed to keep my friendship with Tyree, and besides, he and Damien weren't friends anyway. I was indeed money hungry and I didn't want to share my wealth with anyone. I needed to think of a plan and fast.

My plan was to tell Tyree that Damien took the money from both of us and kept it for himself. Since Damien made all the transactions using his own information, I just said that I didn't know that he withdrew all the money from the account.  In turn I would tell Damien to play along, as I would get mad at him and act as if I was on Tyree's side the whole time.  That made it look like Tyree and I got the same amount and Damien turned out to be the shiesty one.

After days of trying to talk with Tyree, my plan worked.  I would act as if I wasn't friends with Damien any longer just to gain points with Tyree.  I just needed to make sure that it didn't blow up in my face because Tyree wanted to harm Damien and I couldn't let that happen due to my greed.

I kept the two distanced.  Tyree didn't know that I still talked to Damien nor did he know that we were still working together.  Although Tyree was out of the picture, Damien and I still had our side hustle going on.  I continued to stack my cash and rebuild my life that had been torn apart just three months prior.

I started going out more, I needed to flaunt my new and improved body, and even though it hadn't fully healed yet, I knew I was the bomb.

Tyree's birthday was coming and he threw a big bash for himself at his sister's house in South Philly.  I was excited about the event because this would be the night where everyone got to see my new body.  I wore a pair of blue Akademiks jeans and a thermal shirt.  I looked in the mirror one more time at my size 32 waistline and admired myself until I was ready to leave.  Mia was going to pick me up in 15 minutes so I knew I had to be ready.

We were sharp as we sang the words to Heather Headley's new song, *He Is.*  It was time to party.  Mia sported a long ponytail that flowed down her back, a pair of form-fitting jeans, and a black halter top that made her boobs stand at attention.

When we arrived at the house, Tyree was sitting in the kitchen wearing a pair of dark sunglasses.  I went over to him and kissed him on the cheek and gave him a bouquet of flowers that I had bought for him. The place was packed. Everybody who was somebody was there that night. I had seen Troy for the first time in months and he was looking tight. He wore a motorcycle jacket with no shirt on underneath. He came up to me and gave me a hug.

"So, now that you have a new body you can't speak now?" someone said from behind. I turned around and it was Art, smiling. We embraced one another as we sat down and began to talk.

"So, why did you stop calling me?"

"I don't know. I was really going through some things at that time. You know with my heartbreak and what not, I just really needed to breathe," I said, hoping that that would be a good enough excuse. We sat there and talked for awhile. Everyone was partaking in the festivities of Tyree's birthday. I ran into Kelly.

Kelly is Doug's best friend and house brother. He's tall, brown skin, sexy, and has long hair that he always keeps braided. It flows off his shoulders and down his back like butter. And, luckily for me, he was checking me out too. Kelly is a college student and one of the few people that I would consider dating despite his membership as a house kid.

"Wassup?" he said, giving me a hug and kissing me on my neck.

"I'm OK, what's up with you?" I asked, looking into his dreamy eyes. I could tell he was high off of something but I just didn't know what.

We walked outside on the porch to get some privacy while Mia and Keith talked while sitting on the couch. I stood in front of Kelly's sexy figure and told him how I always had a crush on him. We covered a lot of ground. I gave him my number and he gave me his, which I recorded in my 2-way pager. I was having the time of my life.

Back in the house I was getting looks from

everyone. I felt like a superstar because I wasn't getting this much attention when I was bigger and now I was pulling the numbers in. I was on a roll.

The night winded down and morning was arriving. I cut the cake for Tyree, distributed the pieces and then wrapped up a piece to take home myself. Mia and I had a lovely time but it was time to go.

The year was coming to an end. Tamika and I were speaking again. We started talking at Kaniyah's birthday party and we laughed about the whole situation that went down on July 4th. A lot of things had happened throughout the year—I had my heart broken, plastic surgery, I moved into my new apartment at the Victor, and now I'm dating Kelly. Everyone said that we are the perfect couple. He even came to my grandmother's house for Christmas dinner. This is what life should be about.

We had a ball; I was able to buy Christmas gifts for everyone. I bought Kevin, Shay, and Tyree 2-way pagers so that we all could keep in touch. And I bought Kelly a Temple University sweatshirt that he loved. This year had truly been a life lesson and now I could see things more clearly. I should have known that Calvin was too young for me. I could finally see what everyone was talking about.

* * *

After working out in the gym on the rooftop of my building, I rushed into the shower to get ready for my date with Kelly. This would be our last date of 2002 and I had to prepare myself for the upcoming year. After dinner with Kelly, the plan was for me to meet Shay and go to church. I had survived another year thanks to the man above.

I made sure that I put on some extra smell goods for Kelly tonight. I came this far to find a distinguished man and I wasn't gonna let him slip away. Tonight would be better than our first date anyway because that was worked out at the last minute.

I waited for him to come out of his house on 17<sup>th</sup> and Reed Street in South Philly. He jumped in the car and smiled.

"What's up?" he said, leaning over and planting a kiss on my lips. We drove off to my favorite restaurant, the Italian Bistro in Cherry Hill, New Jersey. I had already made our reservations because I knew that it would be a hassle to get a table on New Year's Eve.

The dinner was nice. We talked about a lot of different things that were happening in our lives, and we talked about our New Year's resolutions as well. He needed to meet his friends at the airport before midnight so that they all could be together, which I thought was a sweet thing.

Shay left for church without me so I ended up spending my New Year's with Tyree and Ron. We had fun, but I felt myself coming down with a cold.

The next couple of days I stayed in the house, trying to take care of my cold. Kelly came over once or twice and made me some soup. I felt very good about our relationship since it was growing, it seemed as if we were on the same page. His parents knew about him, but his father didn't approve. But he had to go on and live his life for him, and not for his family. I stood strong behind him and everything that he did because I now had someone in my life to hold on to and hopefully without the work of the devil, our friendship would turn into something very special.

# Reginald L. Hall

## A Million Dollars

After spending three hours in the gym I went for a ride to Tyree's sister's house. He didn't call me on my cell phone and give me a head's up or nothing. He didn't even stop to think about what I would do once I got there and found out that damn boy was sitting there.

I looked rough. I didn't have a haircut or nothing and I smelled sweaty. I walked in the door and he looked up at me.

I didn't know what to say. I was surprised. I felt like talking in Swedish, Spanish, or whatever. How I missed him, how I started to fall in love with him.

"Hey, Cory," I said, as he looked at me smiling.

"Wassup, Rashad?"

"How are you?" I asked nervously, but I tried not to let him notice.

"I'm fine," he said, sitting at the computer looking good enough to eat.

"How is school?" I tried not to look him in the eye.

"School is going well. I just got my report card yesterday."

"Oh, how was it?" I asked as if I was really interested.

"It was good. I got all A's."

"Oh, that's what's up," I said before Ron called him in the other room to braid his hair.

I wish I could have seen my own face when I walked into the room. Goddammit. I wish Tyree had told me that he was here. This is the first time he'd seen me since the surgery and I was in sweat pants and a raggedy undershirt.

"How come you didn't tell me that he was here?" I asked Tyree quietly as they sat in the other room.

"I forgot all about that y'all had something going on," he said, smiling. "I didn't think of it."

"Shit, he is fine," I said, still thinking about his sweet kisses.

"You still like him?" he asked, looking into my eyes.

"Yes, I think he is the sexiest nigga to ever walk the face of the earth," I said, laughing.

Tyree continued to fold his clothes up on the bed as I popped in the DVD for *Diary of a Mad Black Woman*.

"Oh, and my curse worked," snapped Tyree.

"What curse?"

"I didn't tell you?" he asked, pulling up a chair and sitting in front of me.

"No, you didn't."

"Remember I told you that Doug has been acting crazy lately, you know by not returning my phone calls and acting like he doesn't care about me?"

"Yeah."

"Well I put a curse on him," he said, while reaching under his bed and pulling out a shoebox full of candles and voodoo objects.

"What the fuck are you into, witchcraft?" I asked, looking through the box.

"It worked. Now, he is calling me nonstop and he won't leave me alone," he said, smiling.

"Where did you get this stuff?"

"I looked on the Internet and found out how to cast a circle and put a curse on people and it worked."

"Come on, Tyree, I'm sure you don't really believe in that shit, do you?"

"Yes, look it worked."

"Well, I'm not gonna fuck with it," I said, turning my attention back to the movie. My mind started to race.

"Do you think I could do it?" I asked, laughing because I couldn't believe that I was asking him a question like that.

"Sure, but you will have to know what you are doing because you can mess up the curse if it's done incorrectly."

"Well, I want to do one."

"On who?  You better not be trying to get Calvin back," he said disgusted.

"No, I want to do one on Cory."

"Damn, you like him that much, huh?"

"Yes I do," I said, blushing. "Are you gonna help me do it?"

"Sure, but you will have to get the materials."

"OK, what materials would I need?"

"You will need two image candles, six regular candles, love oil, and a couple of other items.  We can go down South Street tomorrow and get the stuff."

"So, how come you didn't tell me about all of this, Tyree?"

"I thought I did tell you about this.  Why do you want Cory if you are dating Kelly?"

"Because first of all, Kelly acts like he's always too busy for me, and besides he smokes too much weed and that shit is a turnoff."

The next day, Tyree and I went down South Street to the store to get all the items that I needed to cast my circle later that evening.  I had discussed this with a few other people and had been warned not to do the obvious.  My belief in the Lord is very strong and I didn't understand how I could believe in the witchcraft shit, but it was worth a try because honestly, my bed was lonely, and Cory was the perfect person to try this on.

Later that evening, Tyree and I sat in my living room in total darkness.  We lit a few candles and were ready to begin our séance.  I had Cory on my mind just like the directions said.  I could see him calling me or walking through my door at any minute.  We had two image candles that were named after the both of us. One was Cory's and the other was mine.

Tyree read the directions as we cast our circle and I felt the presence of the witches entering my world. The candles continued to jump as Tyree spoke the spells into reality. I closed my eyes and smiled, waiting for Cory's presence.

After the séance was over, Tyree went home, leaving the image candles burning on the table. My candle seemed to be burning faster than Cory's, which meant that the spell was working. I needed to have faith in what was happening in order for the spell to work.

The next few days I waited patiently for the phone to ring, but it didn't. I didn't receive a phone call or a visit from Cory, but unfortunately the witches were still present.

\* \* \*

Keith called and left me a message on my cell phone. He said he needed to ask me something. I wondered what he needed to ask me.

Keith is like a brother to me. In some ways we look alike, well, when I was bigger we looked alike. I consider him the Wendy Williams of the gay world because he gets the entire dirt on the gay people and knows just about everyone's business.

I answered my ringing phone.

"What's up, Rashad? How are you?" Keith asked.

"I'm fine, what's up? How are you?"

"I'm OK, I just got off work."

"Oh, OK."

"I have to ask you something."

"Go ahead."

"Are you and Kelly still dating?"

"Yeah, we are."

"OK, well do you know he's dating Rick?"

"No, I don't think he's dating anyone else."

"Yeah, him and Rick are dating," he said with assurance.

"No, I think you have him mixed up with someone else."

"No, I don't bitch, Kelly with the braids that's in the House of Prestige, is dating Rick. I know what I'm talking about."

"Well, let me ask him," I said, getting the same feeling in the pit of my stomach that I once felt when I found out about Calvin.

"Well, whatever you do, don't put my name in shit because if you do, I'm never telling you anything else ever again."

"OK, I won't."

"All right, call me back."

"OK," I said before dialing Tyree.

"Hello?" Tyree said.

"Yeah, I just heard that Kelly is dating Rick," I spat.

"I thought you two were dating?"

"I thought so too, but he has been acting funny lately," I said, getting nervous. Tyree sat quietly on the phone. "Well, I'm going to call him, I'll call you back." I called Kelly and the phone rang four times before his voice mail picked up. I immediately called back. He picked up.

"Hey, Kelly," I said, trying not to let any anger show.

"What's up, Rashad, what's wrong baby?"

"I just heard something and I need you to tell me if it's true or not."

"What?"

"I just heard that you and Rick were seeing each other, is that true?"

He sighed and sat silently on the phone before uttering no.

"What did you say? I didn't hear you?"

"I said, no."

"Well, that's what I heard."

"Yeah, well whoever told you that is lying," he said, starting to get upset.

"OK," I said, now sitting down on the bed. I heard his friends yelling in the background telling him to tell me they said hi.

"Tell everyone I said hello," I said, continuing to sit and listen to him.

"You know what, Rashad, I think we need to chill for a minute and just be cool."

I began to get confused.

"What do you mean?"

"Just what I said."

"Why? What did I do?"

"Man, I'll call you back," he said before clicking me off the line. I called Keith.

"Hello?"

"Yeah, he said that him and Rick are not dating."

"Well, I seen them two at the basketball game together the other day. And they looked like they were together to me."

I began to get even more confused.

"How long ago was it that you seen them two?"

"It was some time last week but I wanted to get my story straight before I called you. Well, did he say anything besides no? What else did he say?"

"I'll call you right back, OK?" I called Kelly back and the phone rang before going straight into voice mail. I continued to call back until he picked up his cell phone. After calling for about the tenth time he finally picked it up. "What!?" he yelled into the phone.

"Why are you treating me like this, Kelly?" I asked, getting annoyed.

"Because you are acting crazy like we are together

or something."

"So, are you and Rick seeing each other?"

"No, I am not seeing him and if I was, that's none of your business!"

"How can you say that's none of my business when we are supposed to be building something?"

"Well, I just told you that I don't want to date anymore," he said before the line went dead. I sat down on the bed and wondered where I went wrong. I thought he was at least gonna be the one for me. We made such a nice couple. I figured he'd be back.

Friday night after a dreadful day of crafting and only grossing about $900.00, Tyree, Jay, and I decided to go to the club. Jay is another friend of ours who Tyree would call his child. Now that Tyree and I call ourselves brothers, that made Jay my nephew.

The new Breakfast Club was now open on Girade Avenue so we all wanted to go see what it was like there. Once we got there, it wasn't good, but we made the best out of what we were working with as far as boys were concerned. The loud music and twirling strobe lights made the club look extra festive. I hadn't spoken to Kelly all week and I wasn't stressing it because I vowed not to let these low lives bring me down any longer.

After spending about an hour at the club, Doug started to conduct a mini ball upstairs in the corner. I sat at a table by the entrance of the club and was sipping on my soda when I saw Rick come in the club and realized that Kelly was following directly behind him puffing on a Dutch. I reached over for Tyree to get a closer look to make sure I wasn't hallucinating.

"Bitch," said Tyree. "That's some shady shit."

Rick walked straight upstairs as Kelly came over to give Tyree and me a hug. I wasn't about to let his lying ass put his hands on me. I continued to sit there and act as if I didn't see him standing next to me with his hand holding the back of my chair.

"He's right behind you," Tyree said.

"I know," but I still didn't move a bit. Kelly walked upstairs to where Doug was commentating the mini ball. Tyree began to walk upstairs as well so I followed behind him.

Tyree and Doug were no longer in a relationship because of a disagreement they had some time before Christmas, but Tyree would cheat on his current boyfriend, Donnie, to give Doug head from time to time.

Tyree was also sleeping around with other people besides Doug, but I wasn't at liberty to say. What I do know is that Donnie calls me almost every night crying and asking me if Tyree is cheating, but what could I say? Tyree is my boy so I couldn't dime him out. Tyree said that the relationship would be over after he and Donnie returned from their trip to Disney World.

The lights came on and the mini ball began. I couldn't concentrate on the show because my eyes were glued on Kelly who stood in the corner necking with Rick.

What the fuck? I said to myself. I noticed that Tyree and Jay were high because they had already smoked some weed before they got to the club so I knew I had to look out for myself.

"Hold my coat," I said to Tyree as I threw it into his arms and walked over to the corner where Kelly and Rick were.

I never knew why Kelly lied to me about Rick because Rick didn't have shit on me. He was skinny, had fucked up skin, and on top of that he was dumb as hell.

I pulled on Kelly's shoulder to break up their escapade.

"What the fuck do you want?" Kelly said with eyes red from smoking weed.

"I thought you told me that you and Rick weren't seeing each other!"

"Shut the fuck up." I turned to Rick who stood there with his face decked out with acne; fuzzy braids were on his head.

"Are you and Kelly dating?" I asked Rick, smiling.

"Yes," he said when Kelly pushed me out of the way. I grabbed one end of his braid and pulled. Doug and two other people ran over.

"What the fuck is going on?!" Doug yelled.

"This nigga lied to me!"

"No, are y'all together?" he asked Kelly candidly.

"No, but we were dating!" I yelled.

The crowd began to get bigger as Kelly threw his arms up, ready to swing on me.

I backed up as Tyree came over and gave me my coat.

"Rashad, let's go," he said as he pulled me down the steps onto the street. We walked across the street to my car when I heard the noise of a rowdy crowd following behind us. I turned around to see Kelly, Rick, and about six more people walking out of the club. Kelly ran across the street toward me. I took off my coat and waited for the unexpected.

"What the fuck did you pull my hair for?!" Kelly yelled as he ran up on me then swung and hit the side of my face.

I began swinging when Doug ran over to me and swung his arms at the back of my head. The crowd became overbearing as everyone moved closer to the fight. I was getting hits from every angle. I fell on the concrete and felt the bottom of Doug's boots pounding the back of my head. I tried to get control of my balance and get up.

I could hear Tyree trying to work his way into the crowd without any luck. I was pulled up by someone that I didn't even know.

The crowd began to scatter. I reached down on the ground and picked up my 2-way pager, which was broken in half. I turned around to walk toward the car and catch my breath at the same time.

"Fuck you, pussy!" Doug said as he tried to break away from whoever was holding him. When he did, he ran back over to me and began pounding on me once again.

I tried my best to fight back but it wasn't any use. All the energy that I had within me was lost as someone came over to us and grabbed him once again. Tyree finally managed to get me into the car, but then, Doug ran back over and started to kick the side of the car door. I sat in the backseat of my car as Tyree drove off.

The next day my body ached and I was so distraught about the night before. Again, who would ever have thought such a thing and I always looked at Kelly to be one of the nicer ones. After all that was said and done, Doug called me numerous times apologizing, which I thought was very nice of him because I knew that he had been under the influence.

\* \* \*

I said my prayers and did everything I needed to do to get my life back on track. I had no business out there in the street fighting again and getting my ass whipped at that. I am a grown man and I should've handled things better. If Kelly felt that he would have a better chance with Rick than with me, that was OK, but the problem I had was why would he lie about it? I have lied before as well but I wouldn't lie about whom I'm dating just to keep another nigga waiting for me in the wing.

Whatever happened to the old days when you like a person and the person actually liked you back and you went from there? Nowadays, you can't trust anyone and besides that, everyone wants to cheat. It's like it is a fad now or something. If you're caught with one person and actually being faithful to them, then you're considered to be corny or a nerd.  There's gotta be a better way.

I can tell you one thing, I'm tired of dealing with these sorry-ass niggas.  I decided to change my standards when it comes to men.  From this point forward I would be extra careful with the men I chose.  I don't just want a man. I want a gentleman.  Someone that's gonna pick me up and take me out on a date.  So, that means he has to have a car.

I'm not taking any shortcuts this time around.  I won't ever let their lips touch mine for one to three months during the *getting to know you* process.  I figured that the only man I should be kissing is either my boyfriend or my husband and just because we're dating doesn't mean anything.  If he's neither, then there should be no reason why his lips should touch mine.  From now on, I am going to start looking out for myself and doing me.  Fuck 'em all.

A week had passed and things were starting to look better for me.  I was just hired as an orderly at the City Avenue Hospital.  Using some of the money that I had left over from crafting, I bought a little puppy and named him Angel.  He was the cutest thing and I named him a unisex name to fit his character as a pretty dog.

One night while going to Club Paradise with Kevin, Drew, and Damien, I felt someone strange looking at me. The craziest thing happened.  Kevin needed to use the bathroom and couldn't wait until we got into the club, so he decided to piss on the wall next to someone's house.  The cops were lurking around in the neighborhood and caught him red-handed.  They handcuffed him and sat him inside the patrol car.

We waited outside the club until the officers were ready to let him go.  I continued to feel someone strange staring at me.  Looking slightly to my left, there he was, standing and smiling at me like there was no tomorrow.

"Who is this guy that keeps staring at me?"  I asked Damien.  Damien's boyfriend, Donyo, walked behind me.

"Yo, Rashad, my boy is trying to holla at you," he

said, walking from behind me to the front.

"Who?" I asked, hoping that it was someone cute and not the guy that stood there smiling, but to my luck it was.

"He's ugly," I said to Donyo when Damien started to laugh. Kevin walked out to the crowd as they were starting to exit the club.

"Damn, you made us miss everything," Donyo said to Kevin. "What did the police say?"

"De beast. Dey sending a citation to my yard, that is, if dey can find it," said Kevin who gave them the wrong address.

"You are so stupid," I blurted out. We all began to laugh.

"So, bitch, he is still looking at you," Donyo said.

"Oh, well. I'm cold," I said as I hugged my torso.

"Well, you should have put on a coat instead of trying to be cute and show off your new body," Donyo said, laughing and giving high-fives to Kevin.

"Shut up, you're just mad because your stomach is still there."

"Bitch, I love my stomach and my baby likes it too." I could still see the guy smiling at me from a distance. He stood around five feet eight inches at 180 pounds. His skin was like a dark brown color and he had poppy eyes. He sort of looked like Kermit the frog.

"What is he, some kind of pervert?" I asked Donyo.

"No, just go over there," he said, as people were coming up to us and embracing us with hugs.

"No, if he's trying to holla at me then he'll have to come to me," I said. Donyo then went over to the guy and they both began to walk toward me.

He approached me wearing a green hooded sweatshirt, a pair of blue jeans, and a pair of timbs. He continued to smile, showing off his stained teeth.

"Rashad, this is Damon and Damon, this is Rashad," said Donyo, before he disappeared, leaving Damon and I alone to talk.

"So, wassup, how old are you?" he asked.

"I'm twenty-five," I lied. "And you?"

"I'm twenty-two."

"OK. Do you have a job?" I asked, getting straight to the point.

"Yeah, I do," he said, still smiling.

"Yeah, where?" I asked, rubbing my arms up and down from the cold.

"I'm a manager at a sneaker store."

"Oh, really? Which one?"

"Foot Locker," he said, smiling and staring deep into my eyes. I started to turn around and walk away. Why do I always get the ugly, corny guys? I asked myself. The guy he's with is cute. How come it wasn't him who tried to get with me?

"So, where do you live?" he asked. I looked at him strange.

"I'm not telling you where I live, you might try to kill me," I said laughing, but I was serious.

"I don't want to hurt you. I live in South Philly."

"Oh, OK, where in South Philly?" I wasn't really interested in his answer.

"22$^{nd}$ and Wharton Street."

"OK, I live in West Philly," I lied again as he continued to smile. "Well, it was nice meeting you," I said as I turned around and started to talk to Kevin.

"Cha, you being a rude bwoy," Kevin said.

"I know you're not talking about being rude. Pissing on the side of buildings and shit."

"Bredda, him looking at you," Kevin said, nodding his head in Damon's direction.

"OK, I spoke to him," I said as Damon got the hint and walked away.

# Smoking Cigarettes

"He's ugly," I said rubbing up against Kevin for heat. "Show me where the real men are." We began to laugh. As we walked toward the car, I saw Damon once again.

"Yo!" I called out to him. He came running to the car sporting the biggest smile. "Here's my number," I said to him while passing him a torn piece of white paper.

"Thanks," he said, as he turned away and ran to catch up with his friends.

Half an hour later, I received a call on my cell phone from a long distance number; it was Damon.

"Why is he calling so soon?" I said to Kevin as I drove. Kevin laughed.

"Hello?" I said.

"Hey, it's Damon."

"What's up?"

"Nothing, are you home yet?"

"No, I'm gonna call you when I get home."

I hung up the phone still laughing with Kevin because we couldn't believe that he'd call right away. I thought you had to at least give it two or three days before you called a number that you got at a club.

After I dropped off Kevin and drove over the Benjamin Franklin Bridge to the Victor, I decided to walk Angel before I went to bed. I could use the fresh air anyway to clear my mind and think about my life and my career. My cell phone rang again; it was Damon.

We talked while I sat on a park bench, letting Angel run loose for a while. Damon told me that he had just moved to Philly from Washington State because he was in the U.S. Navy. I was intrigued with his outgoing personality despite his looks, but I already had it in my mind that after this conversation I wasn't gonna call him back.

Over the next couple of days I spent some time decorating my new apartment and shopping for things that I knew I needed for the house. I purchased knick-knacks and different specialty items to complement my style. I hung pictures and bought a brand new leather sectional for the living room. I had to take a step back and realize how my life had changed in just a couple of months and I was damn proud of it. I was living La Vida Loca and in style and was single as could be and very proud of it.

After ignoring all of Damon's phone calls for the past couple of days I decided to call him back just because of the pity that I felt for him. I was already trying to juggle the few dates that I had a week but for some reason I found that it would be necessary to have Damon in the loophole.

We spent countless hours on the phone before he got up enough courage to ask me to dinner. I was hungry and I didn't have anything else better to do so I went. He took me to Denny's only because there was no other place open at 3 o'clock in the morning. He came to Jersey to get me.

What I can say about him was that he was sweet. I was coming down with a cold, and he stopped to get me some cough drops, and he placed them inside a gift bag with a card and I thought that was the sweetest thing.

* * *

I rushed home from work to catch *America's Next Top Model* on TV. I worked overtime last night, 16 hours is no joke, especially to someone who hasn't worked in awhile. The rain was coming down rapidly as I thought about winding down to dinner and a night with the TV.

I quickly jumped into the shower then sat on the couch and waited for the opening credits to begin, when I heard a stern knock at the door. I got up, ran to the window, and noticed about twelve police cars outside my door. My heart dropped as I contemplated for a moment.

I knew that they would come, I just didn't know

when.   Tyree was in Disney World with Donnie, my
mother was home in Philly, and I was here all alone.  The
first thing that came to mind was to not open the door, but
then I thought they would force their way in.  I had all of
my crafting materials laid out on my computer desk, and I
had no way of getting rid of them at the moment.

I swallowed my spit and opened the door.  There
were six officers standing in rain gear and the one who was
nearest to me was a black man wearing eyeglasses.

"Are you Rashad Smith?" he asked.

"Yeah, that's him," said the other officer, looking at
me while glancing down at my picture that he held in his
hand.

"Yes, I am," I said, not to make things more
complicated.  Angel began to bark.

"We have a warrant for your arrest," the black
officer said who was now standing in my living room.

Angel began to bark louder.

"Shut up, Angel," I said before turning back to the
officers.

"Have a seat," the officer said.

"I don't have on shoes," I said, as the other officers
began to check the house.

"Where are your shoes?  We cannot allow you to go
get them so we'll have to get them for you," the officer said
while wiping the rain from his glasses.

"They're right there in the doorway," I said to the
officers, hoping that they wouldn't see all those
checkbooks and check paper sitting on my desk.

"May I ask why I have a warrant, officer?"

"Sure, you have a warrant for depositing and
cashing fraudulent checks at the Flower's Bank in
Philadelphia," he said reading from the paper.

I really wasn't scared because I knew the process
all so well.  Once I had seen the judge and he set bail, I
would be out in the morning.  I had the money so I was

cool. I just remained calm.

After putting on my shoes and being handcuffed, the police escorted me to the car. I could still hear Angel barking even behind the closed door.

As I walked to the car in my pajamas and sneakers, the rain was hitting my face. I shook and shivered at every wind that blew as we headed over the bridge to Philadelphia.

I was taken to central booking in downtown Delaware County where I was placed in a holding cell. The cells were cold and dark. I walked in and sat down on the cold, metal gray bench.

"Can I make a phone call?" I asked the officer from inside the cell.

"You're gonna have to wait until you're fingerprinted," he said while he prepared for the process.

He opened the gate so I could be fingerprinted. Afterward, I needed to have my picture taken. Not once, but more than twice, then I was allowed to use the phone.

"Mom, I'm locked up," I said in a whisper so the cop couldn't hear my conversation.

"What happened?"

"The cops just came to my apartment after I got off work. I need you to go to my place and make sure Angel is OK," I said, trying not to take up too much time.

"So, what are they saying?"

"Nothing, I'm fine. I have to see the judge in the morning and he's gonna set bail. Just come to court. I'm at central booking, then go to the bank and get the money."

"OK, I'm going to the apartment now. I'll see you in the morning. What time do I have to be there?"

"Nine o' clock."

"OK."

"Bye."

I didn't feel that I needed to tell her to remove the crafting items from the apartment because if the cops wanted to search the house they would have done it while they were there. I would just sit back and wait until the morning.

The night was cold and rough. I couldn't get comfortable for shit. I didn't have any blankets or pillows so I had to tough it out sleeping on a metal bunk without a mattress.

I could see the morning arriving through a slit in the wall that led to a window. I heard the jingle of keys as some officers came closer to my cell.

"Good morning, Rashad I'm Sergeant Hagwood," said the old, tall, white man in a gritty voice.

"Hello," I said as he opened the gate to the holding cell.

"Come with me please," he said. I followed him down to his office and walked in.

"Have a seat," he said as I admired the different pictures of his family and his children's baseball trophies that were posted around his office.

He noticed that I was shaking.

"Are you cold?"

"Yes," I said, trying to keep my teeth from clicking together.

He went over to the space heater, turned it on, and then went to sit back down. He began to pull out different pictures taken from the security cameras at the bank and asked if it was me in the photos. I couldn't lie because it was me on every picture.

"So, Rashad, tell me the story as to how you made these fake checks," he said, while putting on a pair of reading glasses.

"I didn't make the checks, sir," I said looking directly into his eyes.

"Well, who made them then?"

"Some guy that I know named Rich."

"Do you know where this guy lives?"

"No," I said knowing that my story didn't sound too convincing.

"Well, how do you know him?"

"I know him from being around my godmother's way in North Philly." He looked at me as if he didn't believe my story. I figured he couldn't make me tell the truth. As I talked, he took notes on his tablet.

"Can I have permission to check your apartment?"

I swallowed my spit once again. Is this a trick question? I asked myself. If I say no, then they're gonna just go in there anyway.

"Yeah, you can check my apartment. What will you be checking for?"

"Nothing, just looking for things here and there and taking a few pictures."

After I was questioned I returned to the holding cell until it was time to see the judge. In the meantime, I needed to speak with the bail bondsman.

Nine o' clock finally came and I was up for court. I walked outside in handcuffs as I was led inside the building to another holding cell.

I sat inside the cell as I could hear Sgt. Hagwood talking in the hallway.

"I just did a search at Mr. Smith's apartment at the Victor in Jersey, and man, does he have it hooked up nice. He has glass tables, a fish tank, and when I walked in his room and checked his closets, he had a basketball jersey from every team you can imagine."

I listened to his every word, and then my name was called. I walked into the courtroom where my mother was sitting in the back along with two white women. The judge was an elderly white man. He sat on the bench draped in his black robe with the lights bouncing off the gray highlights on his head. I stood in the front of him with Sgt. Hagwood standing at my side.

"State your full name," said the judge, looking

straight at me through his glasses.

"Rashad Monroe Smith," I said with my hands handcuffed to the front.

"Mr. Smith, this is an arraignment of your charges in the State of Pennsylvania, do you understand?"

"Yes, sir," I responded, taking in all the heat that was coming from the vents.

"Mr. Smith, you have the right to remain silent, anything you say or do will be held against you in the court of law. You have the right to an attorney, and if you cannot afford one, one will be appointed to you. Do you understand that, Mr. Smith?"

"Yes, I do," I said, turning from him and looking back at my mother.

"OK, you're being charged today as follows: (5 counts) receiving stolen property, (5 counts) fraud, (5 counts) working with device fraud, (5 counts) bad checks, (5 counts) theft by unlawful taking, and (5 counts) forgery," he said, looking from the paper to me, then back down at the paper.

I listened to the words that he said and acted as if I was interested. All I wanted him to do was set bail so my mother could go get the money and I could go home. I tried to watch the judge as he wrote on the paper, but I really couldn't tell what he was writing.

"OK, Mr. Smith, your bail is being set at $1,000,000.00 cash. Do you have it?"

I was breathless. Was this a fucking dream? A million dollars? Where was I gonna get that from? Even at ten percent of my bail, I still wouldn't be able to afford that. He must be joking.

"No," I said, standing there trembling, hoping not to fall.

"Well, until you can come up with the money you will be detained at the Delaware County Prison," the judge said as the sergeant began to pull me away.

Did I miss something here? What just happened? I didn't want to go there, I wanted to go home. I turned around and looked at my mom who had a confused look on her face as the white people gasped for air, feeling sorry for me.

I know my mother cried on the inside when she saw the look on my face. Her youngest child was being taken away to Delaware County Prison. Talk about déjà vu!

## From Sugar To Shit

Someone pinch me quickly because this has to be a dream, this is not happening to me. I thought my situation over and over while riding in the prison van to the county jail.

Once I arrived at the jail and endured a thorough strip search, I thought about last night and why I didn't tell my mother to remove all those items from my apartment.

I sat in a small holding cell in Intake and waited to have my picture taken. The guard began to walk through as I yelled out to one of them.

"Sir, can I please make a phone call?" To my surprise, he opened the gate and let me out. I immediately called my mother. I kind of had the feeling that she wouldn't be home so I called my apartment to see if she was there, she was.

*"Bell Atlantic has a collect call from:* Rashad Smith, inmate number 203158 *at the Delaware County Prison. To refuse this call hang up, to accept this call please do not use three-way or call waiting features or your call will be disconnected. To accept this call dial one now---thank you."*

"Hello," my mother said.

"Mom," I said as the tears began to fall down my face.

"Yes."

"What am I gonna do now?"

"I don't know, Rashad, we're trying to think of something now," she said, trying to catch her breath.

"I don't think I can stay here. I can't take this," I said, sobbing louder, trying not to be heard by the other inmates.

"Well, Rashad we're trying to contact the lawyer

now. Damien and Rafeek are here with me."

I started to cry more as she handed Damien the phone.

"Hello," Damien greeted.

"Yes."

"Calm down, we're trying to get you a lawyer. Just don't do anything stupid and stop crying."

I heard Rafeek talking in the background. "Why is his bail so high?" he asked.

My mother got back on the phone as I heard Angel bark.

"Yes, I'm here," she said. "That judge was just being a smart ass. It seemed like he was racist," she said as I held the phone close to my ear.

"Mom, can you please get me out of here. I can't take it," I moaned.

"Rashad, I'm doing the best that I can. Hold on, Damien has the lawyer on his cell phone so hold on," she said before passing Rafeek the phone.

"Wassup?" he said, with a loud tone.

"I'm in jail, that's wassup."

"Don't worry, that judge is just doing that to scare you. He can't give you a million dollars bail. That just can't be."

"Well, how come you're saying that it can't be but it happened?" I figured he'd been wrapped up in the system so much he should know.

"Because like I said, he is only doing that to scare you. Hold on, mom wanna talk to you," he said before passing the phone back to her.

"Yeah, I just got off the phone with the lawyer. He said that he would represent you but he will need $500 for a deposit."

"Well, don't you have all the bank information?"

"Yes, how much do you have in the account?"

"The last time I checked it was over $6,000 in

there," I said, still wiping my face from the tears.

"Well, sit tight. I'm going to the bank now and get the money, then I'm going to take it to the lawyer's office."

"How long do you think I'm gonna be here?" I asked as I started to sob all over again.

"Rashad, I'm trying to get you out. You just have to be patient."

"OK, if I get some time I'm gonna call you later. Where are you gonna be?" I asked so she could be near a phone.

"I'll be at your house. I have to feed Angel."

"OK."

"Bye."

The correctional officer escorted me back to the holding cell where there were now about 10 people in there. The cell was big with two benches sitting opposite one another and a small brick wall that sectioned off the toilet. I took a seat in the middle of a tall, white guy, and a short, fat, black guy. There were people lying across the floor and some people were standing up.

We all were lounging around in our county blues. I leaned my head back on the wall; I didn't deserve to be here. I had to be at work today at 8:00 a.m. and I know my mother didn't call there for me and I forgot to ask her.

After seeing the nurse and getting booked, it was time for us to head over to the cellblocks. I walked on the block holding my sheets, my cup, and my toothpaste. The inmates were staring at me as I frowned with every step that I took.

"Don't worry, young blood," said someone from the side of me as I walked up the steps. I wanted to cry but I didn't. I figured I'd save that for later when I was alone.

The first night I cried myself to sleep. Thank God, at Intake I had two other people in the cell with me who were close to my age and were handling things a little bit better than I was. It was nice to have someone to talk to that was at least on the same page I was.

I woke up to applesauce and white bread. I was hungry and all I could remember was the chicken wing platter I ate the day I was arrested. I didn't feel like eating so I slid my tray over to one of my cellmates so I could continue to get some rest.

I had a visit from my lawyer; I was surprised that he came on such short notice. I thanked God all the way to the visiting room. I got to the room where the other inmates were enjoying their visits from their family and friends and there were even some people in the visiting room who I used to go to school with. I noticed a slim, white man sitting in the corner at a small white table in the back. I looked up at the guard as he pointed his finger toward him; I knew he was my lawyer. I walked over to him and shook his hand before I sat down.

He had a briefcase and a folder sitting on the table with my name on it. The folder seemed thick as I sat there and watched him go through each piece of paper and look over every document.

"Hi, Rashad, how are you?"

"Do you have to ask? Look at me, I'm in jail," I said before putting my hands over my face.

"Yeah, I know that this is an unfortunate situation for you, but you have to realize that if you do the crime you have to do the time."

"Look, I just want to get out of here. Isn't there a way that I could get out of here and then fight the case on the street?"

"Yes, there is, but I talked to the sergeant and he told me the story that you told him, and I'm gonna tell you now, they're not buying it. They know that the story is bullshit so you're gonna have to start talking," he said, looking straight into my eyes.

"Yeah, I know."

"Listen, you're gonna have to tell me the truth and

tell me all that you know. I work for you, I don't work for those guys and they are talking about handing this case over to the feds, and you don't want them to get their hands on this case. If the feds pick this case up, you're talking at least 15 years, and from what the sergeant told me, he has at least $350,000 on you. He said that you stole over $350,000 from the bank," he said while rubbing his hand through his hair.

I sat back in the chair and every time he spoke my heart dropped. I started to drop a few tears but I was not gonna let all these motherfuckers in here see me cry.

"I didn't take $350,000 from the bank," I spat.

"He also said that he's waiting to hear from some more banks as well that he assumed you dealt with."

"If I had that kind of money, don't you think I would have moved somewhere far away instead of just moving to New Jersey?"

"Well, maybe the guy is bullshitting just to get you to talk. Listen, whatever you do, don't talk to anyone about your case, especially the police," he said, putting the folder into his briefcase and closing it. Your preliminary hearing is set for next Wednesday. Hold tight until then, I'll be in touch with you and your mother," he said as he got up and extended his arm out for a handshake.

I stood up and looked around the visiting room at the other inmates and then turned back around to him.

"Could you please get me out of here as soon as possible?" I asked him as he sat back down at the table.

"Do you have any reason why the judge set your bail so high?"

"No, I don't. I think he was prejudiced or something."

"Well did you do anything to piss him off?"

"No, I just stood there."

"I can't even ask him to honor at least fifty percent of your bail because even if he does that it still would be too high," he said in deep thought.

"So what do you think we can do?"

"Does your mother own her home?"

"No, she's renting. Why?"

"Because I could say she could put her house up as collateral but that still wouldn't be enough." I placed my head down on the table. He then got up and handed me his business card.

"I'll be in touch with you before the end of the week," he said as he put on his long cashmere coat and hat, then grabbed his briefcase and extended his hand again.

I shook his hand before he started to walk toward the door. I sat back down in my chair and waited for the guard to come over to take me to be strip searched.

Two days passed, and after talking to my mother, she informed me that the lawyer asked for $5,000 cash before he would start my case. My mother took the money to him right away leaving my bank account empty.

It was time for me to move to a new cellblock and leave the two cellmates who had kept me grounded.

Since my bail was so high, I was assigned to D block, where all the hardened criminals, murderers, rapists, child molesters, and big-time drug hustlers were housed. I was so scared. I was shackled from my hands to my feet to be escorted to the other end of the jail.

Once I got to D block I was assigned to cell D-12 where an old man named Neil would be my new cellmate. He was brown-skinned, short, and had gray hair. He had to be in his late fifties or early sixties. The guard from the bubble unlocked the door to the cell and Neil opened it and let me in.

"Hey," said Neil.

"What's up," I said, as I walked in and the door shut behind me.

"You want the bottom bunk or the top bunk?" he asked.

# Smoking Cigarettes

"I'll take the bottom."

I commenced to make my bed and look around the cell. The beds were mounted to the wall and a table and two chairs were mounted along the wall as well as a sink and toilet that were connected together. I sat down on the bed as I began to make small conversation with Neil, asking him what he was in here for. He stated that he was drunk and thought that he was getting in his car when, in fact, it was someone else's.

I laid down on the hard bed as I tried to get some rest. The lights were out and the cell was completely dark as I cried myself to sleep again. It was no fun being locked down for twenty-two hours a day and only allowed out for recreation for two hours. I needed more time to talk on the phone to my family.

Over the next couple of days I tried to calm myself by thinking about how I would be home very soon. My mother and friends came to see me on a regular. My mother cried when she saw me on her visit because she wanted me to come home and there was no way she could make things hurry a little faster.

Damien and my mother came together. When Tyree found that I was in prison he lent his support but was too afraid to come to the jail.

The next visiting day, Mia and her friend Robin came to see me. Through all my depression, I knew that she would be the only one to keep me laughing. The entire visit we laughed and joked about different issues about our lifestyle. We prayed, we cried, and we laughed more. I went back to my cell thanking Jesus that I was blessed with some good friends. I even had the pastor praying for me.

After two weeks had passed, my mother sent me a television and some money for me to order some food from the commissary. I cried every day as I sat in my cell watching *Judge Judy* and *Divorce Court*. Neil only had one visit, and that was from his brother who brought him a

$20.00 money order. I thought that was nice because he didn't have no one in his corner the way I did.

The good thing about it was that I had the support of all my family and friends. I even called Damon because he had gotten word that I was in jail and he wanted to lend a helping hand. My mother said that he had called numerous times and had left a bundle of messages on my voice mail. He wanted me to put him on my visitor's list and of course, I declined. I wasn't about to have some nigga come visit me in jail, which was definitely a no no.

As the days winded down I had to think of my plan. I couldn't tell on any of my friends, especially the girl that worked at the bank, and I damn sure wasn't telling on my brother. If any more banks came forward to say that I had forged counterfeit checks at their facility, I would be fucked.

The day before my court hearing I laid in the bed praying to God hoping that He heard every word that came out my mouth. I wanted to be forgiven for all my sins and I asked the Lord to wash them away. I heard His voice in my head telling me that everything would be all right. All I needed to do was put trust in Him and believe in His word. As Neil lay on the top bunk, I could feel a sense of warmness over my body. I could tell that God was with me and His presence was surely appreciated.

The next day, I prayed all day. I had to be at court at one o'clock so that gave me a lot of time to prepare for what lay ahead. Coincidentally, Neil had to be in court the same day, but he had to be there at nine.

After eating lunch, which was beefsteak and mashed potatoes, I freshened up the best that I could and the door to my cell popped open. Nervously, I walked down the steps into the day room. What if the judge didn't lower my bail today and I would have to stay in this awful place for another month? I couldn't think of that happening.

# Smoking Cigarettes

I prayed the whole time while I was in the van going to the courthouse. Once I got inside, I could see my entire family in the courtroom. I saw my brother in Sgt. Hagwood's face looking as if he was threatening him.

Oh, my God, I said to myself. Rafeek is all up in his face, man that's gonna keep me in here longer. I couldn't waste my time on that. I needed to stick with God and know that He had a plan for me and right now wasn't the time to break down.

I was the first one to be seen. As the sounds of my chains jingled from the shackles, I walked in the court room to see the smiling faces of Mia, Robin, my aunt Denise, Shay-Shay, and my mother. They all sat in the front row waiting for my hearing to begin. I walked over in front of the judge and stood next to my lawyer who stood next to Sgt. Hagwood.

The hearing started and the judge went through my charges again.

"Could I approach bail your honor?" my lawyer said, still holding his briefcase.

"I have to arraign him first," said the same judge who had appointed me the million-dollar bail. The lawyer took a few steps back and allowed the judge to arraign me. I stood there listening to everything that the judge had to say, answering him with either a "Yes, sir" or a "No, sir."

"Have any other banks gotten in contact with you?" the judge asked the sergeant.

"No, sir, there are no other banks that seem to be interested." The courtroom was silent.

"Now, you can approach bail," the judge said as he sat back in his seat and removed his eyeglasses. He touched his temple with his pointing finger. The lawyer slowly leaned toward the bench.

"During his first arraignment he was given a million dollars bond. Why is that?" the lawyer asked as the judge shifted his eyes back and forth from my lawyer and me. He then leaned up in his chair and started searching through the papers in his folder for the right documents as we waited. My heart was pounding a mile a minute as he came across my bail sheet.

"Yeah, I gave him a million dollars bail because I heard that he was a flight risk," said the judge, now shifting his eyes from the lawyer to the sergeant.

"Sir, my client is not a flight risk."

"He's not a flight risk," the sergeant co-signed. My mind was confused; this white prick was on my side?

"Sir, would you be able to lower his bail? Maybe an unsecured bail would do," my lawyer asked. He was now at the judge's mercy.

"OK," the judge said, sitting up in his seat and beginning to write on the forms.

"Bail set at one million dollars unsecured," he said as my heart felt relieved at the thought of going home.

I turned around to Mia who was now screaming with joy and my mother smiled as I walked back in the holding cell with the sergeant following behind me.

"Am I going home?" I asked the sergeant.

"Yes, you should be out by four o'clock," he said while taking out a photo of the girl who supplied me with the account information from the bank.

"Rashad," said the sergeant in his gritty voice.

"Yes."

"You see the lady sitting in the back of the court room?" he said, pointing at my aunt Denise.

"Yes."

"Is this her?" he asked, showing me the photo.

"No."

"Listen, Rashad, you cannot lie to me," the sergeant said while looking at me then back at the paper. "Is this the lady that is sitting in the back of the courtroom?"

"I said, no."

"OK," he said, before having my lawyer take over.

# Smoking Cigarettes

"Listen, Rashad, tomorrow morning come down to my office because we need to sort some things out," my lawyer said.

"OK." I was happy to be getting out.

I turned and walked back into the holding cell where the rest of the inmates were waiting to be seen. I sat down on the cold bench that didn't seem so cold anymore. I was going home to my warm bed, thank God.

* * *

I held my cell phone in my hand as my mother drove me back to New Jersey to the Victor. I couldn't wait to get in the shower and get out of my dirty pajamas I had worn when I was arrested. Since the sergeant had kicked in the door when he came back to search my apartment, I had to get a new set of keys from the landlord. That was a hassle in itself.

Once I entered the dark apartment I tried to flick on the light. The electric company had disconnected my services. I walked around the dark apartment and looked at the extreme mess the sergeant had made. My entire home was in disarray. The pillows on the couch were thrown around and my bedroom was a complete wreck. I couldn't think of anything else to do but lounge before I cleaned up this mess. I had to do a double take when I noticed that my entire computer system was gone. All of my crafting materials were gone. They even took both printers.

Damn, I said to myself. My first day home to see this shit. It was weird seeing all my furniture thrown around. Well, at least I was home now. I would call the electric company in the morning. I laid across my bed for the first time in three weeks. I didn't even have to put up with Angel's barking because my godmother was doing a nice job of dog sitting for me while I was away.

I sat down on the edge of my bed and started to

think of all the things that went on over the months. I couldn't complain at all about the way things turned out. God does things in His own timing and although I might be doing some serious time behind bars in the near future, I know that God will be with me every step of the way. I needed to straighten my shit up. I'd lost another job and had no money.

One thing I can say is that having my freedom is the best thing in life and I wouldn't give it up for anything. The next morning my cell phone rang. It was Damon.

"Welcome home." I looked at the phone and smiled.

"Thank you," I said, while my mother was standing in the doorway waiting for me.

"So when can I see you?" Damn, I had just gotten home and this nigga was already on my heels.

"I guess you can see me later today if you come get me," I told him, hoping that he would. I can say that while I was in jail Damon made sure I was all right even though I didn't want him to visit me.

I hurried off the phone with him and rode with my mother to pay the electric bill. After she paid it, I quickly hopped in the shower when I got back to my apartment because before I knew it, Damon would be on his way. A few thoughts popped into my mind as to how I was gonna pay my rent for the coming months, but I wouldn't dwell on something that major just yet. I had to realize that just because I was released from prison, it didn't mean I was out of the woods yet. I knew that it would be a long and drawn out trial to determine if I would go to jail for a long time. I was glad to find out that Camisha's judge tried her as an adult and gave her 25 years to life for the murder of Little Jon. May the Lord have mercy on her soul.

Damon met me at the door with two dozen roses and a bag of jellybeans. I thought that was very nice of him. He took me to dinner at the Soho restaurant on Broad and Locust where we sipped apple martinis and ate crab

# Smoking Cigarettes

cakes. It felt good to be back in the dating game once again, and with a person like Damon, I knew this was special because I was not with him for his looks. Even Stevie Wonder could see that this nigga was busted in the face, but I figured I would try it and see what type of person he was inside. After all the shit I had been through, it was time for me to find a real man like him.

We took a stroll through Center City in a carriage pulled by two white horses.

"Can I have a kiss?" he asked, smiling while showing off his stained teeth. I turned to him totally turned off.

"I really don't know you yet Damon, let's give it some time," I said, while looking around to notice if anyone saw us.

I had never had someone give me this kind of treatment and I thought it was rather special. Maybe this could work out between us if I would just give it a chance.

We rode around for about twenty minutes, and then he suggested that we go back to his place to watch a movie and cuddle. By the time we got to his apartment in South Philly, I began to feel a little drowsy. He helped me out of his black Toyota Camry and walked me up the steps to his third floor apartment that he shared with his cousin and a female roommate.

"So, what do you want to watch?" he asked, taking off his red and white Nikes and putting them by the door.

"What do you have?" I asked, rubbing my eyes from the drowsiness.

"Have you ever saw *Dolomite?*"

"What type of movie is that?"

"It's an old movie that was made back in the 70s and it's really good," he explained while popping the DVD into the player. I began to admire the many photos on his wall from the hit classic *Scarface*. He also had some old photos of Billie Holiday and Nelson Mandela.

After he put the DVD into the machine, he slid behind me on the bed and started to massage my shoulders. It felt so good and next thing I knew his tongue was in my mouth. He might have been ugly, but this boy sure could kiss. Then, he stopped.

"Rashad, I know that things are tough for you right now, but if you need a job I can hook you up at the sneaker store," he said to me while looking into my eyes. I thought about it in between kisses as I felt his hard dick throb through his jeans. He then pulled it out and began to stroke it back and forth.

"I want you so bad, Rashad," he said passionately in my ear, and after about three minutes of heavy breathing, white cream flew from his penis into the air and landed on his chest. He continued to stroke his muscle until every drop was out. I laid my head down on his chest and fell into a deep sleep.

## Two Queens Smoking (three hours later)

All I could see was darkness and the little bit of light that came in through the window from the moon. I could feel myself lying on a soft bed with soft pillows, but the bed kept moving back and forth.

"Take this dick," Damon said, seductively.

I finally came to the conclusion that love was being made but it wasn't with me. I didn't feel anyone going in and out of me. The only thing I could feel were my hands tied behind my back. I buried my face into the pillow as if I were dreaming, but for some strange reason this didn't feel like a dream.

The heavy breathing became intense as the bed started to move harder. I rolled over and bumped into the wall as the movement stopped and the bed became lighter. Someone ran over and turned on the light. I struggled at first to adjust my eyes to the light, and then I became focused. Damon was standing there naked with his dick flopping back and forth hitting his thighs. Lying next to me was Tyree, grinning.

"What the fuck is going on? And why are my hands tied behind my back?" I asked while still trying to adjust my eyes to the light.

"Shut the fuck up," Damon said as he began to get dressed. "Damn, I thought that percocet I put in your martini would've lasted longer than this." Tyree got up and walked into the bathroom.

"Damon, what's going on?" He turned to me with what seemed like fire in his eyes.

"Bitch, didn't I say shut the fuck up?" He then walked over to me and kicked me on my side, which made me flinch as I tried to lift myself up. Tyree returned to the room and shut the door behind him, still smiling.

"Bitch!" Damon said, while running over to a gym bag and pulling out a 9-millimeter handgun.

My eyes lit up with terror. Tyree looked at Damon, and then at me and he finally spoke.

"What, you think I'm stupid, Rashad?"

"Tyree, what do you mean? What is going on?" I asked with my eyes filled with fear. Damon stood next to him wearing a pair of red and black basketball shorts and a white wife beater and Tyree just wore a pair of boxers.

"Well, let me start from the beginning; I hate you," he said, staring directly into my eyes. I looked back at him.

"Tyree, what are you talking about? Damon, what

is he talking about? I thought you wanted to be with me?" Damon just stared at me with a blank look on his face.

"Just shut the fuck up and listen to what he has to say," Damon said, while lighting up a Dutch. He took one puff then passed it over to Tyree, all without ever taking his eyes off me.

"Now," Tyree said as he slowly inhaled the Dutch. "We found the tape that was in my brother's Walkman when you and Rafeek killed him. The whole time you thought it was just a Walkman, it wasn't. It was a tape recorder to record everything that went on between y'all to show as evidence that you cheated on Troy. While you and your brother murdered my only brother, the tape was still recording." I held my breath for only a split second.

"Now, the police couldn't find a lead to who committed the murder, but after hearing the tape of your voice a thousand times and having a talk with Troy, and studying your actions, I came to the conclusion that it was you. I listened to the tape very carefully over and over again and heard you tell your brother Rafeek that Paul had beat you up."

The whole time I sat there on the bed looking into Tyree's eyes, I could see that he had no remorse in his.

"Also, you thought I wouldn't find out that you and Damien were stealing money from me?" he asked, flexing his muscles. "I pulled up the account information on the Internet and could see that it was a large sum of money withdrawn from the checking account." He had asked me a question so I felt that I should answer but I had nothing to say.

"So, you and Damon planned this whole thing?" I asked, looking at Tyree and Damon at the same time. Tyree shook his head up and down while Damon just stood there blank.

"Did you ever think that I wouldn't find out, Rashad? I'm not your friend. I never was. I was just hanging around you to solve my brother's murder, and since the cops couldn't seem to find a lead, I took matters into my own hands."

Damon handed the handgun to Tyree as he blew me a kiss.

"So, you and Damon are together now?" I asked, as if it mattered. Damon walked behind Tyree and kissed him on his neck as Tyree smiled at me. The feeling that I felt in the pit of my stomach was indescribable.

"Rashad, you're smart so read between the lines," Tyree said, while gazing into my eyes. Damon walked over to the stereo where Ms. Jade's, *Big Head* was playing. He turned it up real loud. Tears began to fall from my eyes nonstop. I thought about all the wrong that I'd done as I could taste the dryness in my mouth, nervous from what was about to happen.

"Tyree, I'm so sorry. Please don't do this," I begged, while Damon stood in the back not saying a word.

"Rashad, it's too late. The damage is already done," Tyree said, as he pointed the gun at my chest.

"You didn't spare any grief for my family so why should I spare yours?" he said, looking directly into my eyes. I took my eyes off him and looked at Damon who stood there watching me like a raving bull with eyes filled with fire.

Tyree fired once and the bullet flew into the wall. I rocked back and forth while praying to God that this wouldn't be the end. He fired again and caught me in my waistline right beneath my stomach. He fired four more times hitting me in my chest, my neck, and twice in my head. God, please forgive me for my sins…

# Reginald L. Hall

The famed author of *Memoir: Delaware County Prison*, is an intelligent, confident, outspoken advocate for gay rights, who continues to soar literary heights. He resides with his family outside Philadelphia. Visit his website www.reginaldsworld.com.

## ADDITIONAL TITLES FROM WRITERSANDPOETS.COM

*Memoir: Delaware County Prison* by Reginald L. Hall

*Threesome: Where Seduction, Power and Basketball Collide* by Brenda L. Thomas

*Born to Lust* by Johnny Archer

*Drama Factor* by Wanda Toby

*She'll Learn* by Sybil Barley-Staples

*Diamond Drought* by Brandon McCalla

*Diamond Dynasty* by Brandon McCalla

Book promotion services provided by Books That Click.com